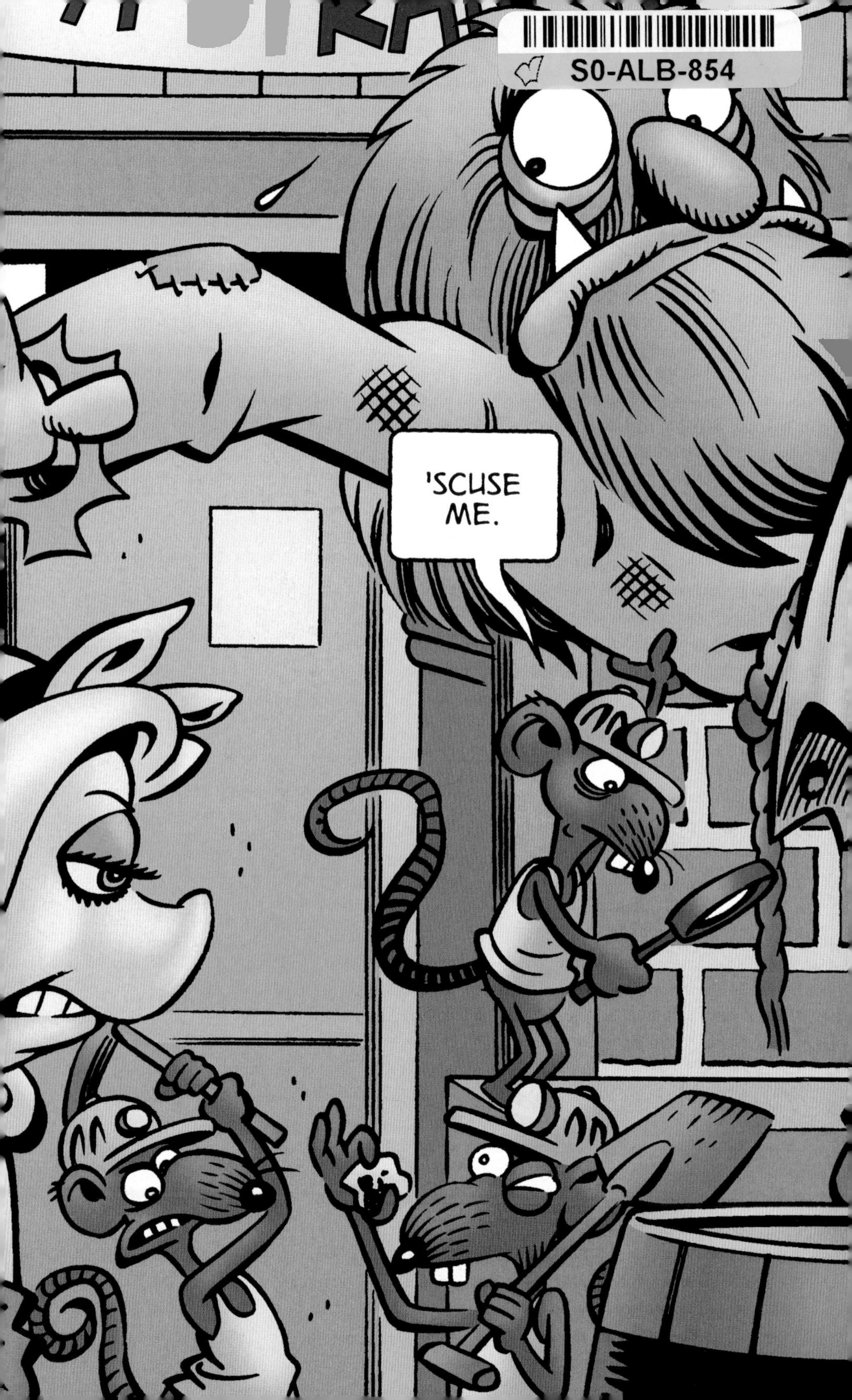
'SCUSE ME.

The MUPPET SHOW

Comic Book

ROSS RICHIE
chief executive officer

MARK WAID
editor-in-chief

ADAM FORTIER
vice president,
publishing

CHIP MOSHER
marketing director

MATT GAGNON
managing editor

JENNY CHRISTOPHER
sales director

FIRST EDITION: NOVEMBER 2009

10 9 8 7 6 5 4 3 2 1
PRINTED BY WORLD COLOR PRESS, INC.,
ST-ROMUALD, QC., CANADA, 12/09/09

Office of publication: 6310 San Vicente Blvd Ste 404, Los Angeles, CA 90048-5457.

A catalog record for this book is available from the Library of Congress and on our website at
www.boom-studios.com on the Librarian Resource Page.

The Treasure
of Peg Leg Wilson

WRITTEN AND DRAWN BY **Roger Langridge**

COLORS **Digikore Studios**

LETTERS **Deron Bennett**

EDITOR **Aaron Sparrow**

COVERS **Roger Langridge**

SPECIAL THANKS: TISHANA WILLIAMS, IVONNE FELICIANO, JESSE POST, LAUREN KRESSEL, SUSAN BUTTERWORTH, JESSICA BARDWIL, JIM LEWIS AND THE MUPPETS STUDIO

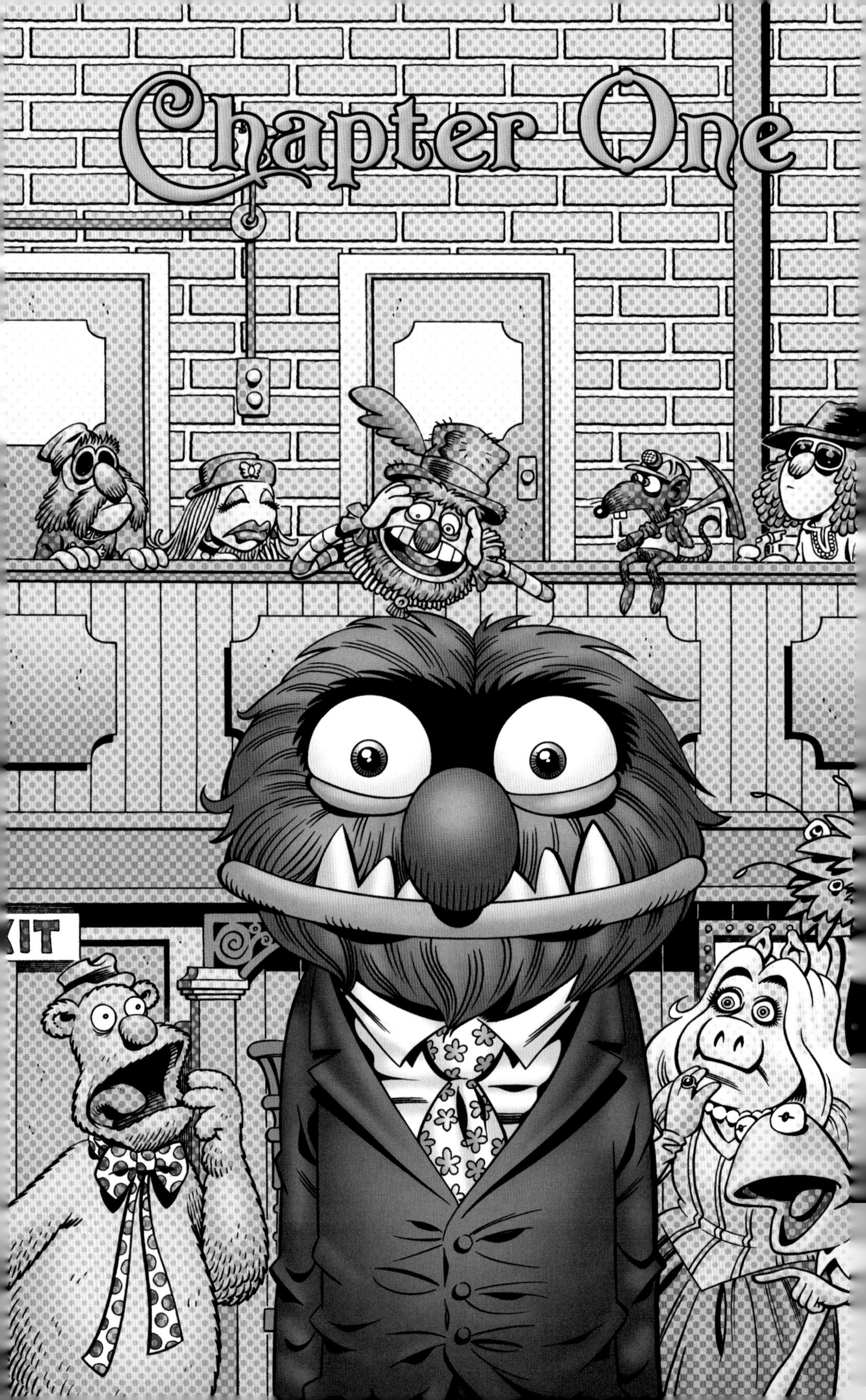
Chapter One

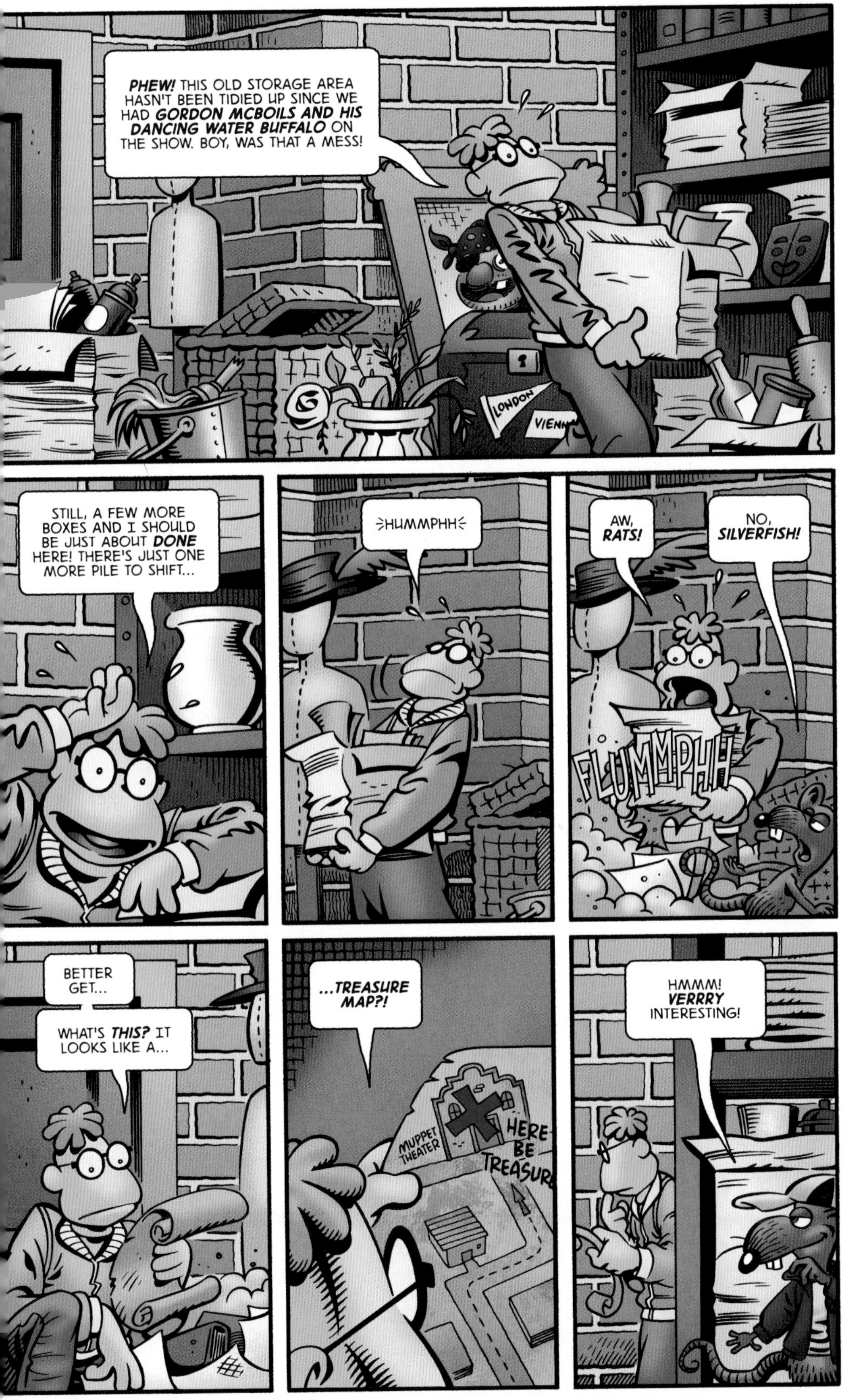
PHEW! THIS OLD STORAGE AREA HASN'T BEEN TIDIED UP SINCE WE HAD GORDON MCBOILS AND HIS DANCING WATER BUFFALO ON THE SHOW. BOY, WAS THAT A MESS!
LONDON
VIENN
STILL, A FEW MORE BOXES AND I SHOULD BE JUST ABOUT DONE HERE! THERE'S JUST ONE MORE PILE TO SHIFT...
HUMMPHH
FLUMMPHH
AW, RATS!
NO, SILVERFISH!
BETTER GET...
WHAT'S THIS? IT LOOKS LIKE A...
...TREASURE MAP?!
MUPPET THEATER
HERE BE TREASURE
HMMM! VERRRY INTERESTING!

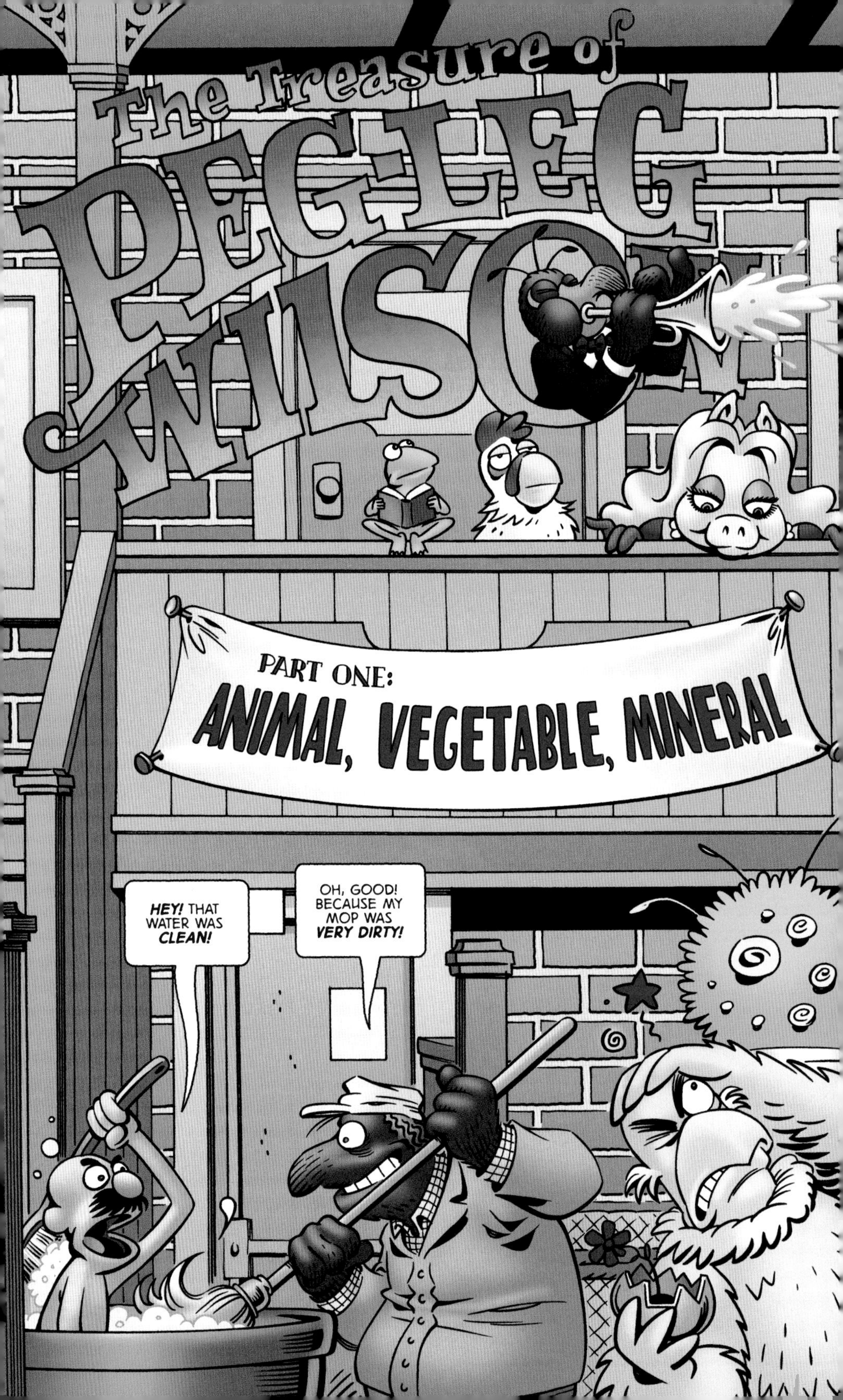

The Treasure of
PEGLEG WILSON
PART ONE:
ANIMAL, VEGETABLE, MINERAL
HEY! THAT WATER WAS CLEAN!
OH, GOOD! BECAUSE MY MOP WAS VERY DIRTY!

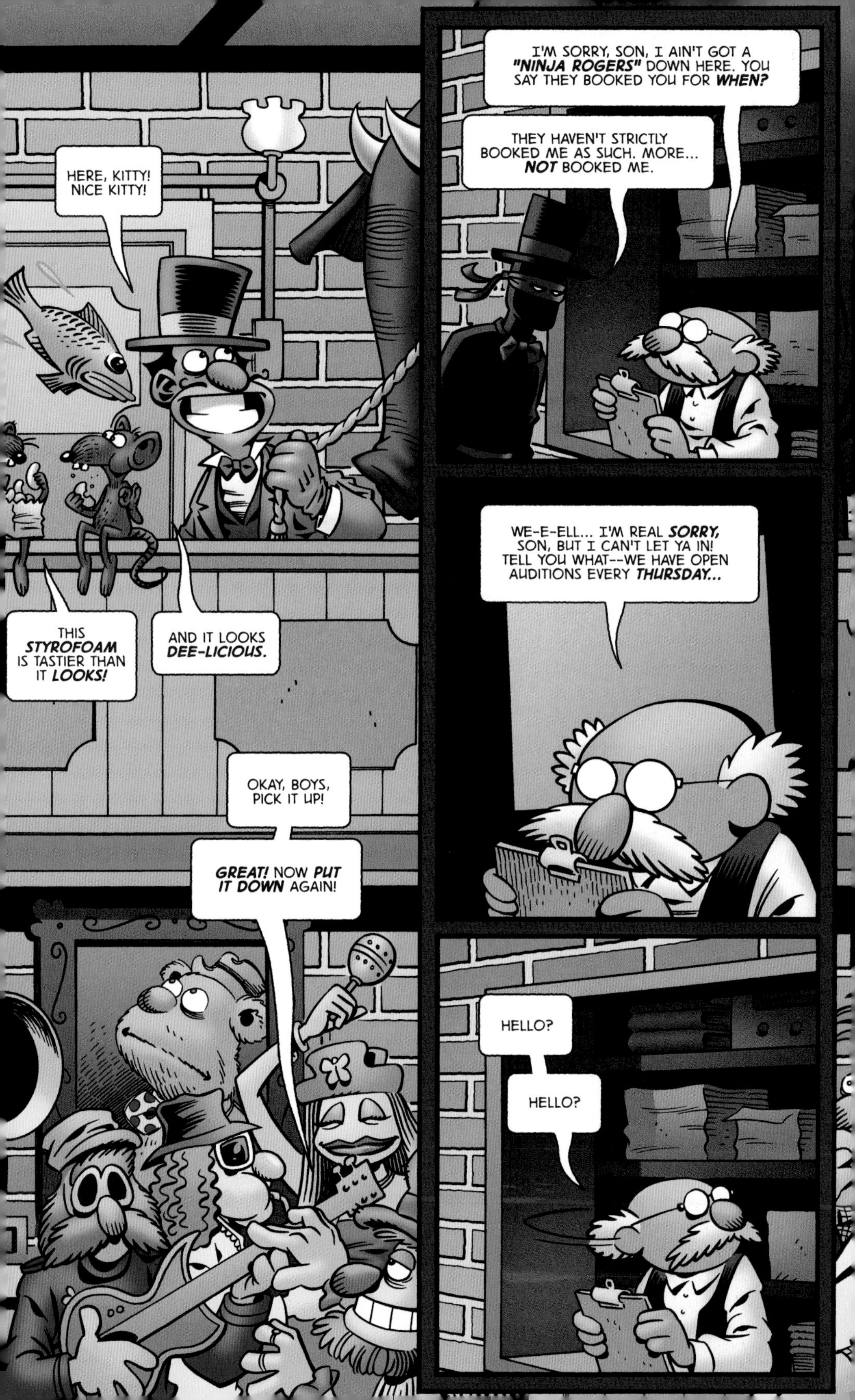
HERE, KITTY! NICE KITTY!
THIS STYROFOAM IS TASTIER THAN IT LOOKS!
AND IT LOOKS DEE-LICIOUS.
I'M SORRY, SON, I AIN'T GOT A "NINJA ROGERS" DOWN HERE. YOU SAY THEY BOOKED YOU FOR WHEN?
THEY HAVEN'T STRICTLY BOOKED ME AS SUCH. MORE... NOT BOOKED ME.
WE-E-ELL... I'M REAL SORRY, SON, BUT I CAN'T LET YA IN! TELL YOU WHAT--WE HAVE OPEN AUDITIONS EVERY THURSDAY...
OKAY, BOYS, PICK IT UP!
GREAT! NOW PUT IT DOWN AGAIN!
HELLO?
HELLO?

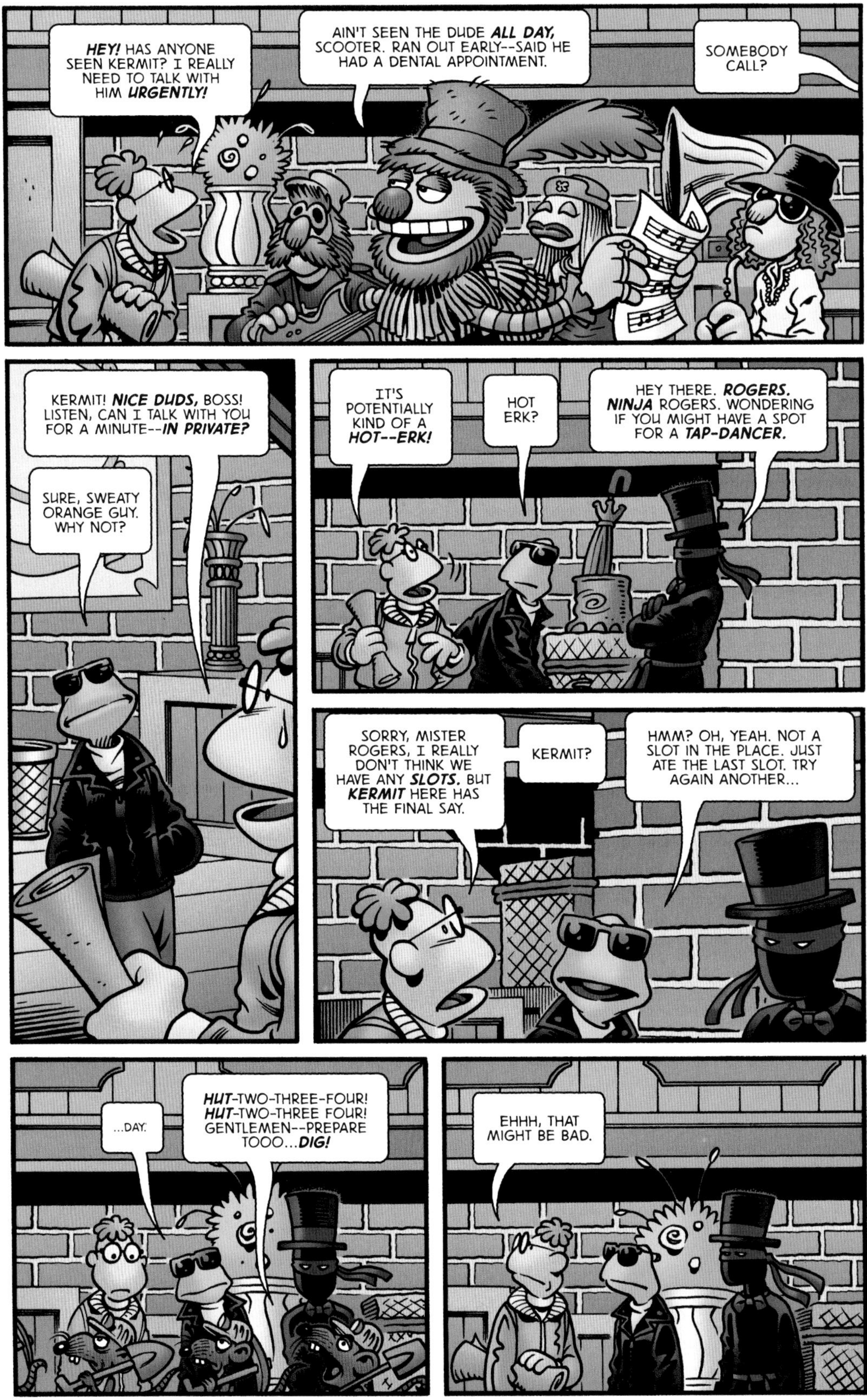

HEY! HAS ANYONE SEEN KERMIT? I REALLY NEED TO TALK WITH HIM URGENTLY!
AIN'T SEEN THE DUDE ALL DAY, SCOOTER. RAN OUT EARLY--SAID HE HAD A DENTAL APPOINTMENT.
SOMEBODY CALL?
KERMIT! NICE DUDS, BOSS! LISTEN, CAN I TALK WITH YOU FOR A MINUTE--IN PRIVATE?
SURE, SWEATY ORANGE GUY. WHY NOT?
IT'S POTENTIALLY KIND OF A HOT--ERK!
HOT ERK?
HEY THERE. ROGERS. NINJA ROGERS. WONDERING IF YOU MIGHT HAVE A SPOT FOR A TAP-DANCER.
SORRY, MISTER ROGERS, I REALLY DON'T THINK WE HAVE ANY SLOTS. BUT KERMIT HERE HAS THE FINAL SAY.
KERMIT?
HMM? OH, YEAH. NOT A SLOT IN THE PLACE. JUST ATE THE LAST SLOT. TRY AGAIN ANOTHER...
...DAY.
HUT-TWO-THREE-FOUR! HUT-TWO-THREE FOUR! GENTLEMEN--PREPARE TOOO...DIG!
EHHH, THAT MIGHT BE BAD.

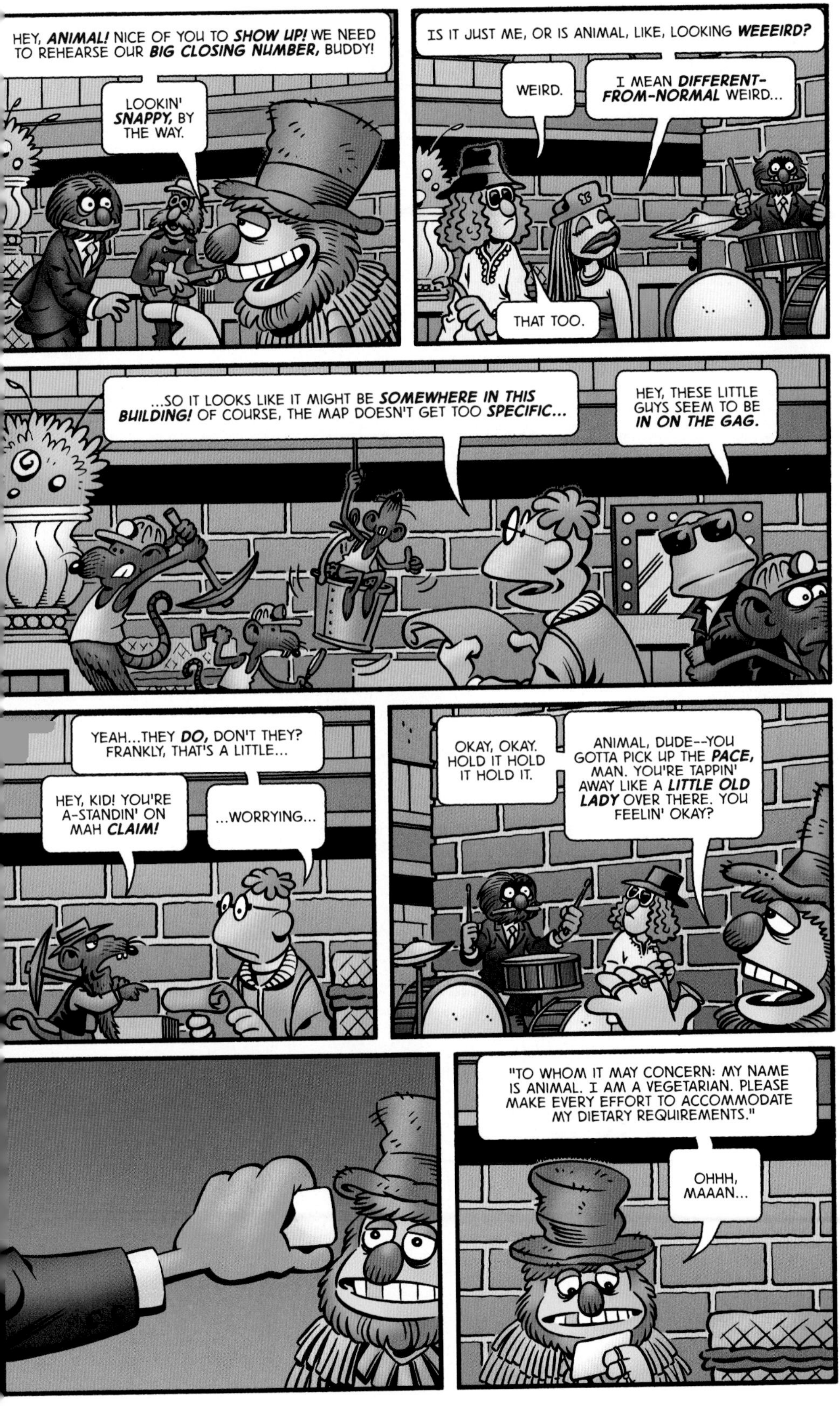
HEY, ANIMAL! NICE OF YOU TO SHOW UP! WE NEED TO REHEARSE OUR BIG CLOSING NUMBER, BUDDY!
LOOKIN' SNAPPY, BY THE WAY.
IS IT JUST ME, OR IS ANIMAL, LIKE, LOOKING WEEEIRD?
WEIRD.
I MEAN DIFFERENT-FROM-NORMAL WEIRD...
THAT TOO.
...SO IT LOOKS LIKE IT MIGHT BE SOMEWHERE IN THIS BUILDING! OF COURSE, THE MAP DOESN'T GET TOO SPECIFIC...
HEY, THESE LITTLE GUYS SEEM TO BE IN ON THE GAG.
YEAH...THEY DO, DON'T THEY? FRANKLY, THAT'S A LITTLE...
HEY, KID! YOU'RE A-STANDIN' ON MAH CLAIM!
...WORRYING...
OKAY, OKAY. HOLD IT HOLD IT HOLD IT.
ANIMAL, DUDE--YOU GOTTA PICK UP THE PACE, MAN. YOU'RE TAPPIN' AWAY LIKE A LITTLE OLD LADY OVER THERE. YOU FEELIN' OKAY?
"TO WHOM IT MAY CONCERN: MY NAME IS ANIMAL. I AM A VEGETARIAN. PLEASE MAKE EVERY EFFORT TO ACCOMMODATE MY DIETARY REQUIREMENTS."
OHHH, MAAAN...

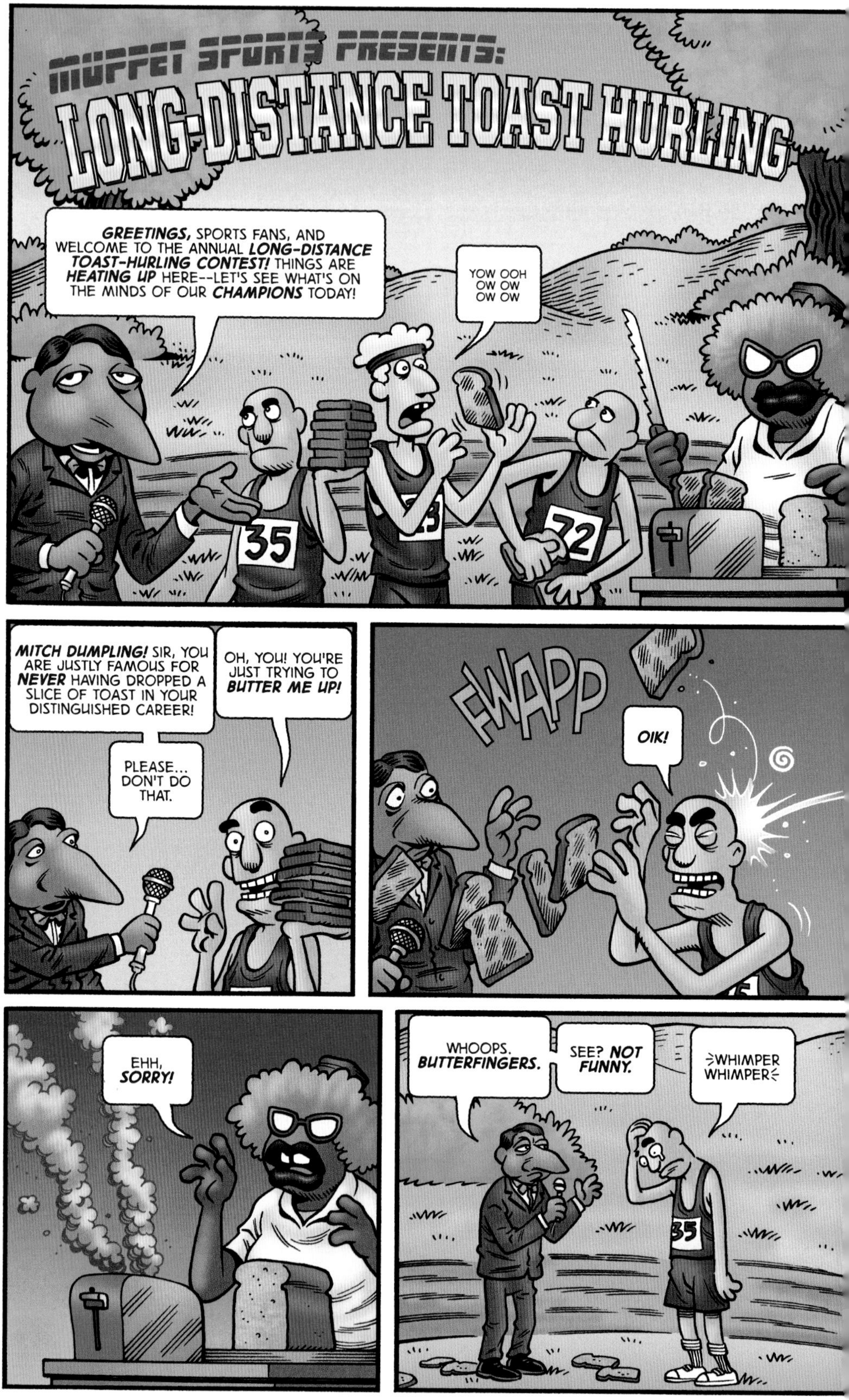
MUPPET SPORTS PRESENTS:
LONG-DISTANCE TOAST HURLING
GREETINGS, SPORTS FANS, AND WELCOME TO THE ANNUAL LONG-DISTANCE TOAST-HURLING CONTEST! THINGS ARE HEATING UP HERE--LET'S SEE WHAT'S ON THE MINDS OF OUR CHAMPIONS TODAY!
YOW OOH OW OW OW OW
35
72
MITCH DUMPLING! SIR, YOU ARE JUSTLY FAMOUS FOR NEVER HAVING DROPPED A SLICE OF TOAST IN YOUR DISTINGUISHED CAREER!
OH, YOU! YOU'RE JUST TRYING TO BUTTER ME UP!
PLEASE... DON'T DO THAT.
FWAPP
OIK!
EHH, SORRY!
WHOOPS. BUTTERFINGERS.
SEE? NOT FUNNY.
WHIMPER WHIMPER
35

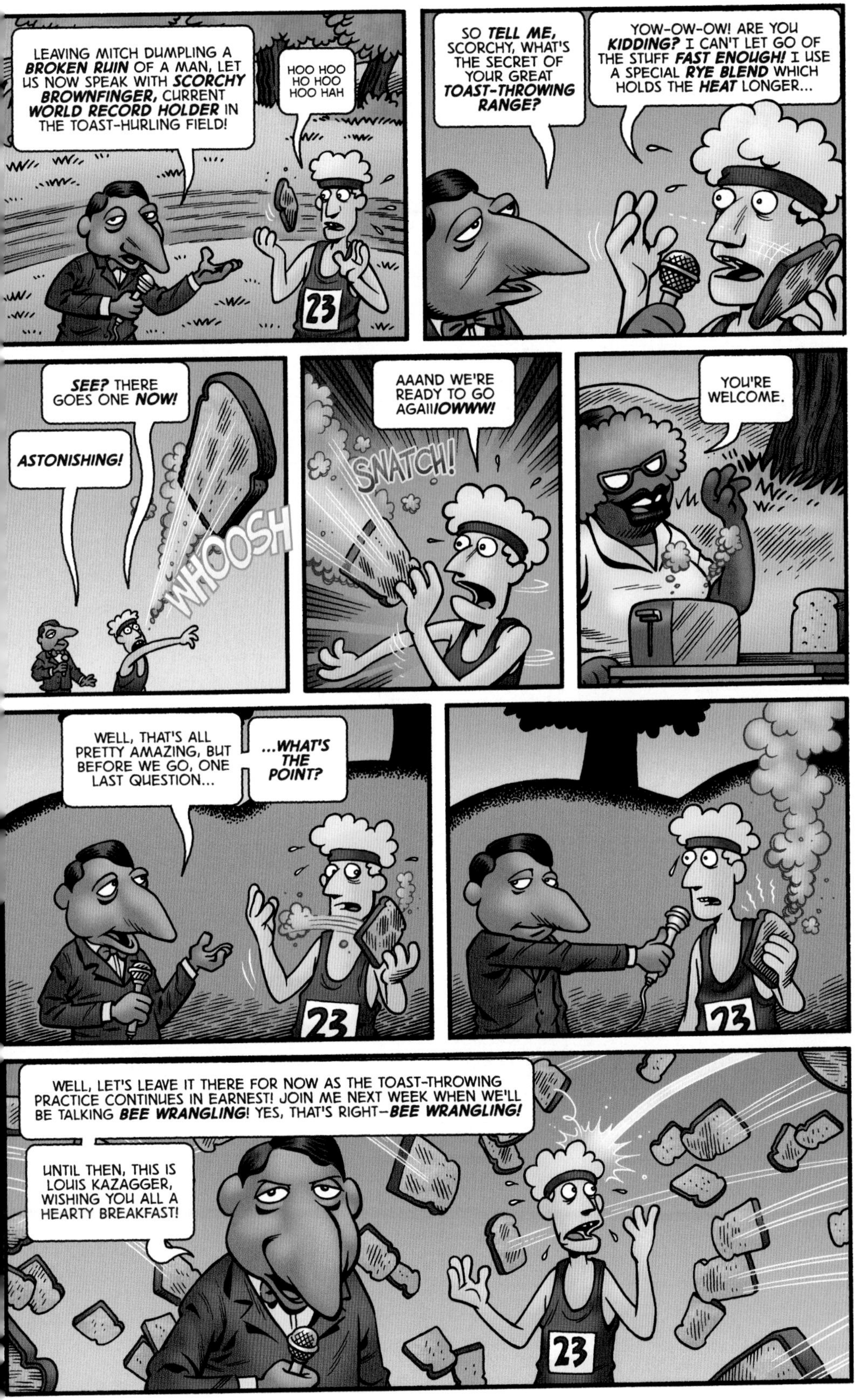
LEAVING MITCH DUMPLING A **BROKEN RUIN** OF A MAN, LET US NOW SPEAK WITH **SCORCHY BROWNFINGER,** CURRENT **WORLD RECORD HOLDER** IN THE TOAST-HURLING FIELD!
HOO HOO HO HOO HOO HAH
23
SO **TELL ME,** SCORCHY, WHAT'S THE SECRET OF YOUR GREAT **TOAST-THROWING RANGE?**
YOW-OW-OW! ARE YOU **KIDDING?** I CAN'T LET GO OF THE STUFF **FAST ENOUGH!** I USE A SPECIAL **RYE BLEND** WHICH HOLDS THE **HEAT** LONGER...
SEE? THERE GOES ONE **NOW!**
ASTONISHING!
WHOOSH
AAAND WE'RE READY TO GO AGAII***IOWWW!***
SNATCH!
YOU'RE WELCOME.
WELL, THAT'S ALL PRETTY AMAZING, BUT BEFORE WE GO, ONE LAST QUESTION...
...WHAT'S THE POINT?
23
23
WELL, LET'S LEAVE IT THERE FOR NOW AS THE TOAST-THROWING PRACTICE CONTINUES IN EARNEST! JOIN ME NEXT WEEK WHEN WE'LL BE TALKING **BEE WRANGLING**! YES, THAT'S RIGHT—**BEE WRANGLING!**
UNTIL THEN, THIS IS LOUIS KAZAGGER, WISHING YOU ALL A HEARTY BREAKFAST!
23

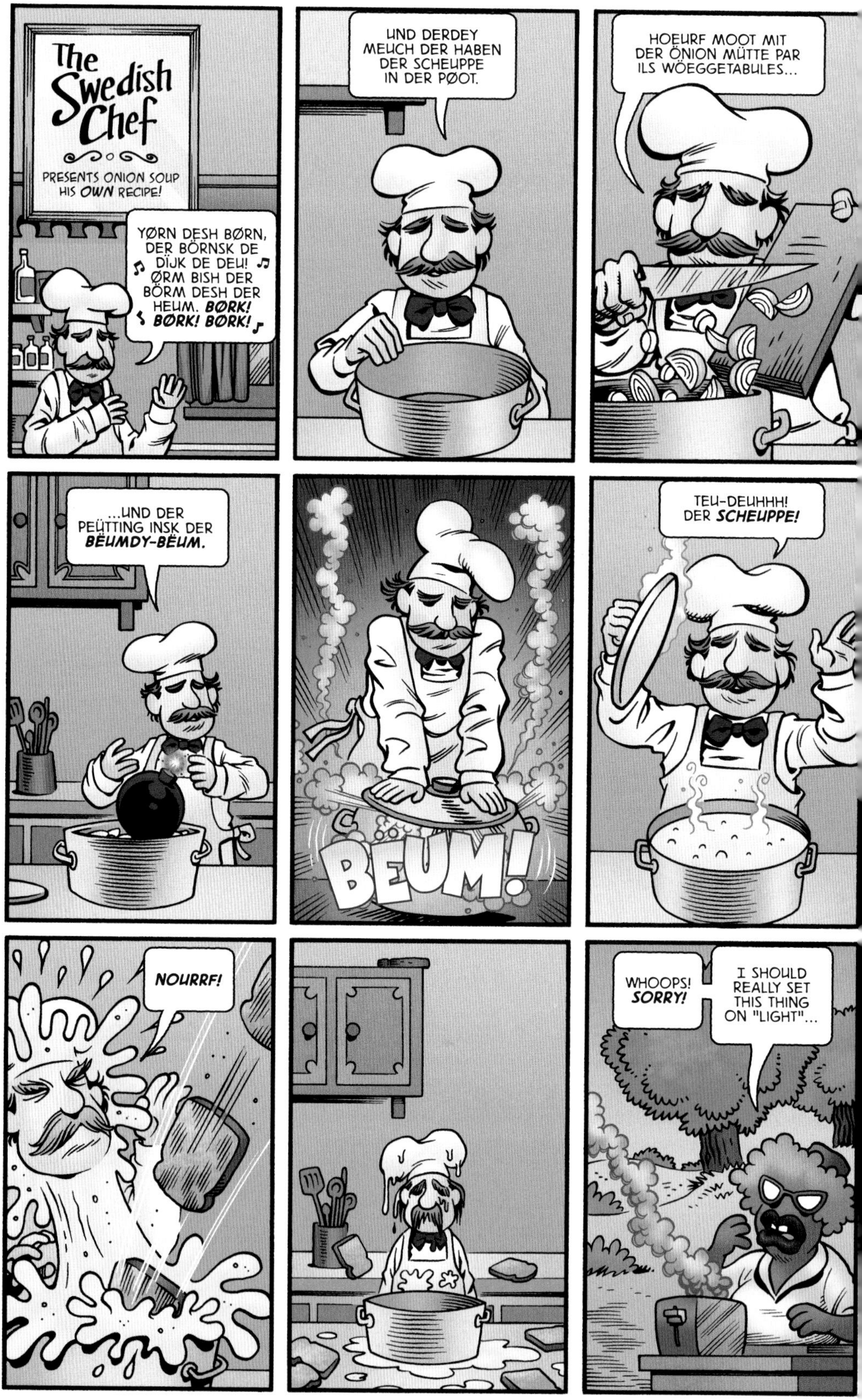
The Swedish Chef
PRESENTS ONION SOUP HIS OWN RECIPE!
YØRN DESH BØRN, DER BÖRNSK DE DÏJK DE DEU! ØRM BISH DER BÖRM DESH DER HEUM. BØRK! BØRK! BØRK!
UND DERDEY MEUCH DER HABEN DER SCHEUPPE IN DER PØOT.
HOEURF MOOT MIT DER ÖNION MÜTTE PAR ILS WÖEGGETABULES...
...UND DER PEÜTTING INSK DER BËUMDY-BËUM.
BEUM!
TEU-DEUHHH! DER SCHEUPPE!
NOURRF!
WHOOPS! SORRY!
I SHOULD REALLY SET THIS THING ON "LIGHT"...

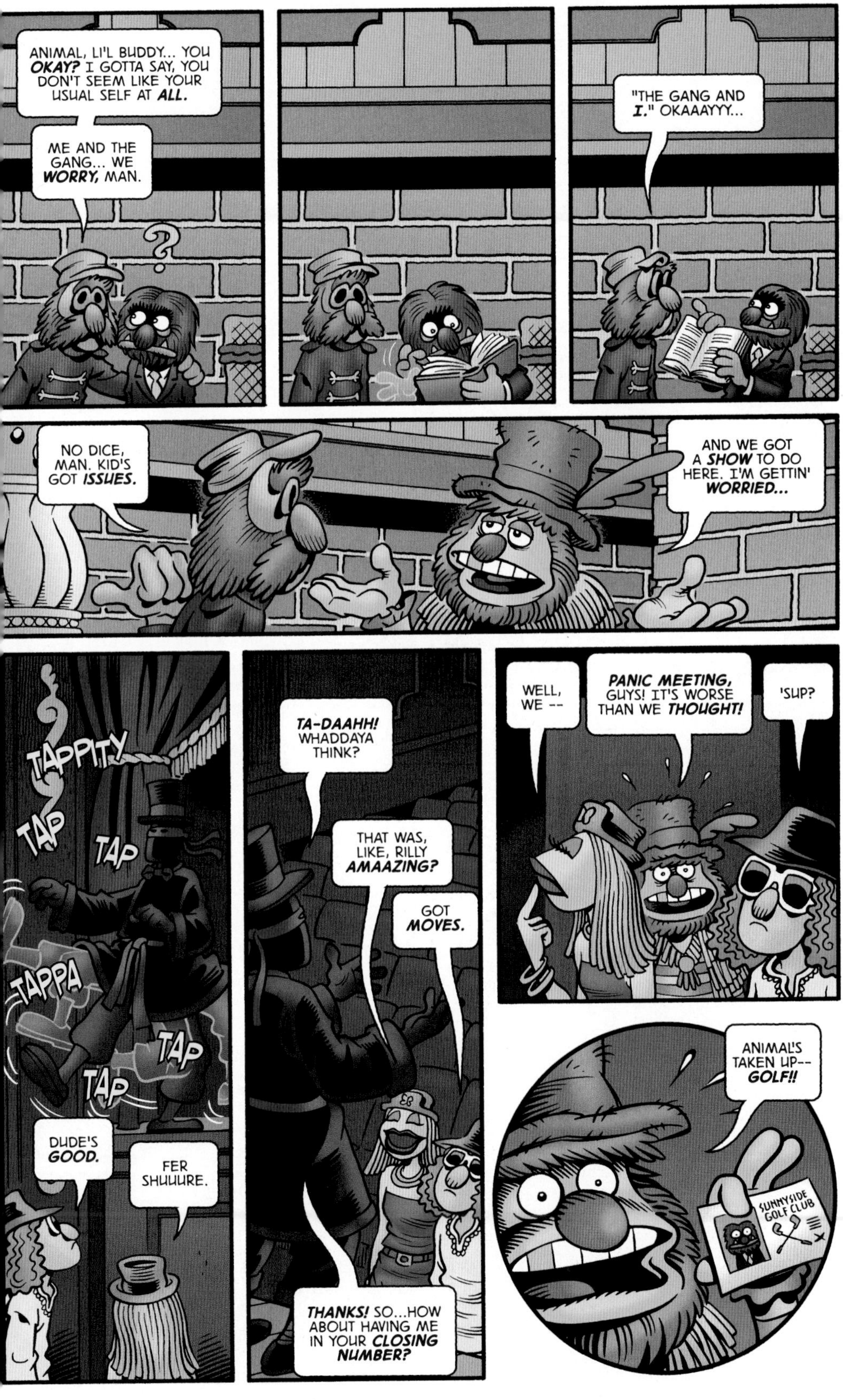
ANIMAL, LI'L BUDDY... YOU OKAY? I GOTTA SAY, YOU DON'T SEEM LIKE YOUR USUAL SELF AT ALL.
ME AND THE GANG... WE WORRY, MAN.
"THE GANG AND I." OKAAAYYY...
NO DICE, MAN. KID'S GOT ISSUES.
AND WE GOT A SHOW TO DO HERE. I'M GETTIN' WORRIED...
TAPPITY
TAP
TAP
TAPPA
TAP
TAP
DUDE'S GOOD.
FER SHUUURE.
TA-DAAHH! WHADDAYA THINK?
THAT WAS, LIKE, RILLY AMAAZING?
GOT MOVES.
THANKS! SO...HOW ABOUT HAVING ME IN YOUR CLOSING NUMBER?
WELL, WE --
PANIC MEETING, GUYS! IT'S WORSE THAN WE THOUGHT!
'SUP?
ANIMAL'S TAKEN UP-- GOLF!!
SUNNYSIDE GOLF CLUB

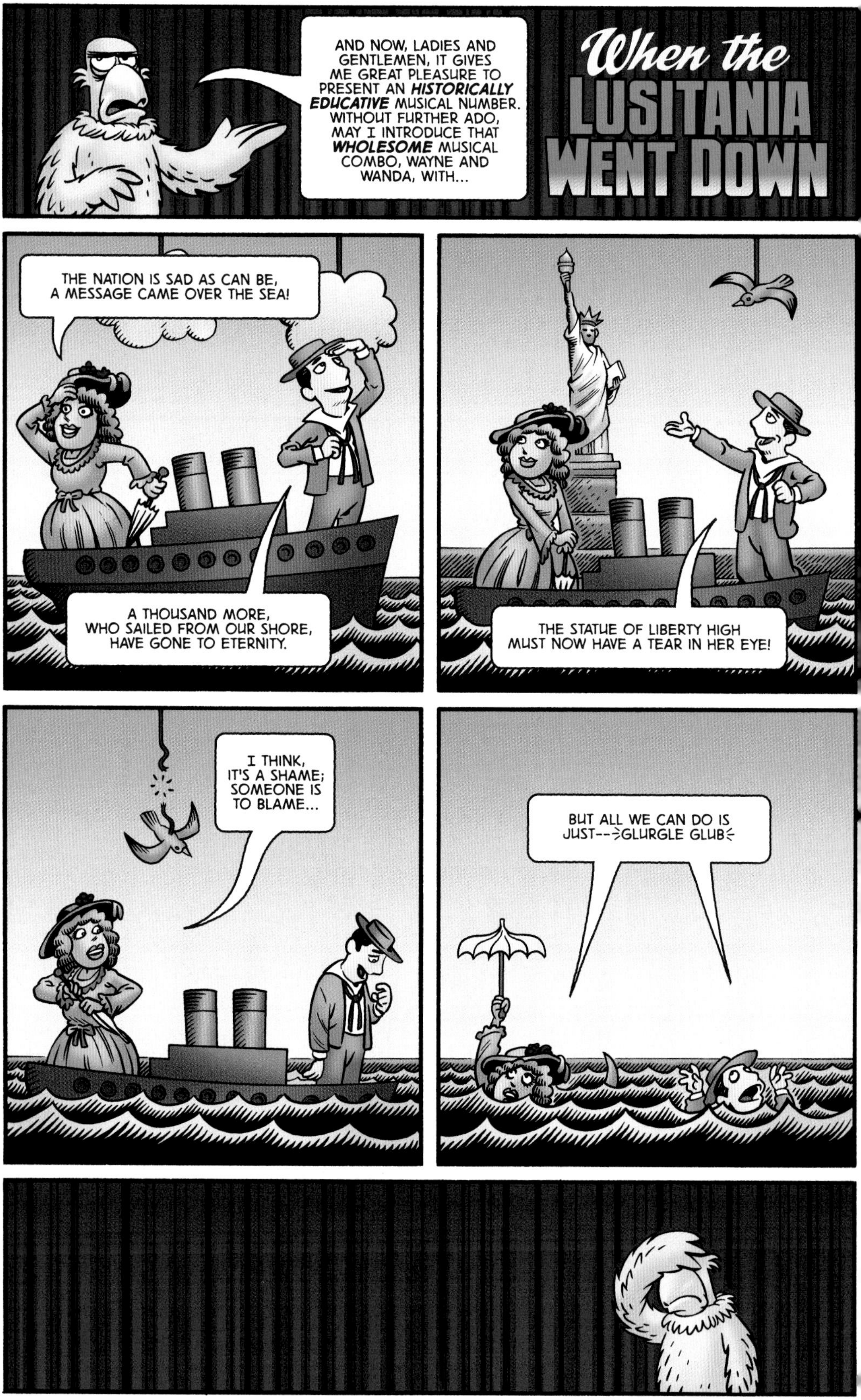
AND NOW, LADIES AND GENTLEMEN, IT GIVES ME GREAT PLEASURE TO PRESENT AN HISTORICALLY EDUCATIVE MUSICAL NUMBER. WITHOUT FURTHER ADO, MAY I INTRODUCE THAT WHOLESOME MUSICAL COMBO, WAYNE AND WANDA, WITH...
When the LUSITANIA WENT DOWN
THE NATION IS SAD AS CAN BE, A MESSAGE CAME OVER THE SEA!
A THOUSAND MORE, WHO SAILED FROM OUR SHORE, HAVE GONE TO ETERNITY.
THE STATUE OF LIBERTY HIGH MUST NOW HAVE A TEAR IN HER EYE!
I THINK, IT'S A SHAME; SOMEONE IS TO BLAME...
BUT ALL WE CAN DO IS JUST-- GLURGLE GLUB

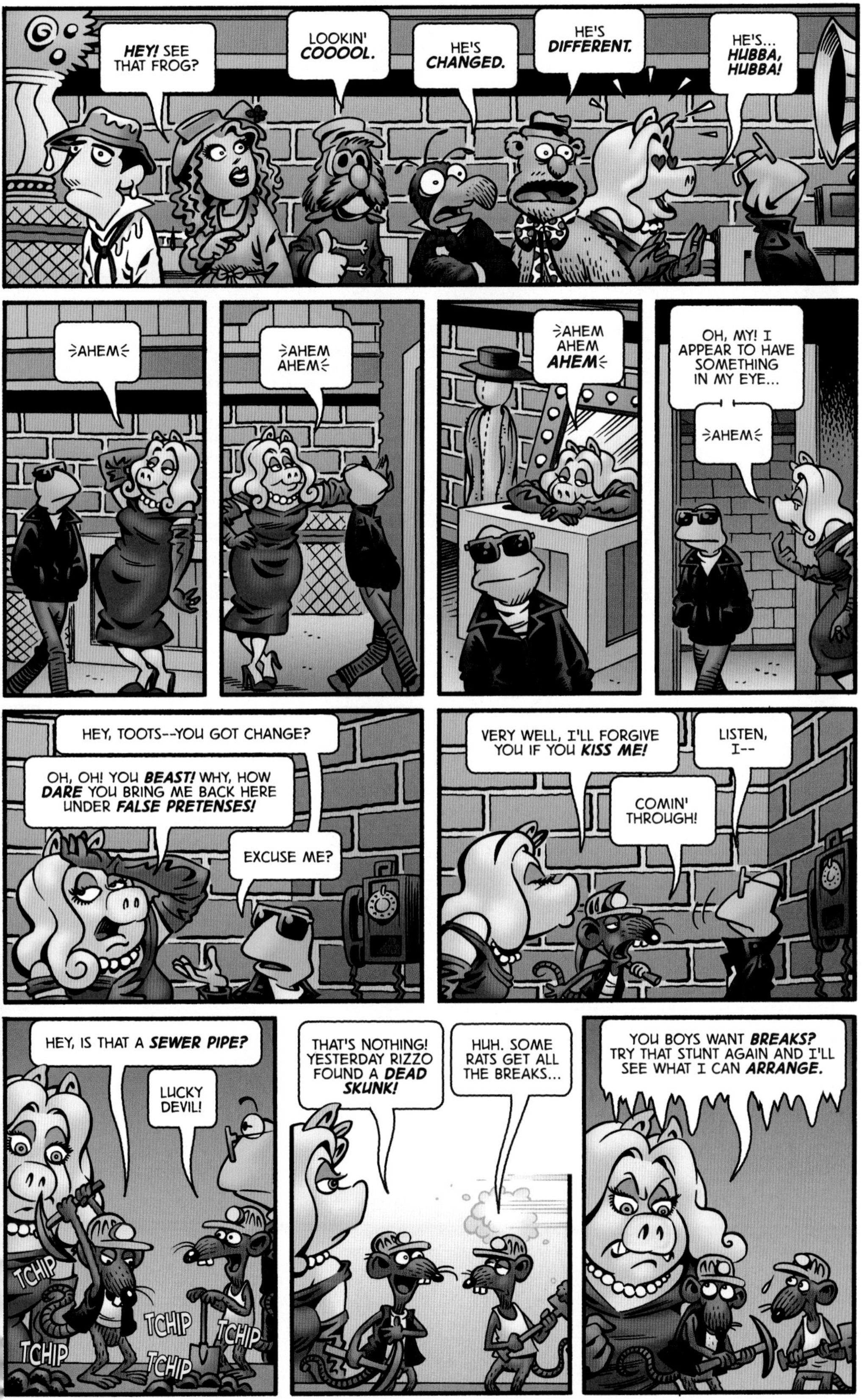
HEY! SEE THAT FROG?
LOOKIN' COOOOL.
HE'S CHANGED.
HE'S DIFFERENT.
HE'S... HUBBA, HUBBA!
AHEM
AHEM AHEM
AHEM AHEM AHEM
OH, MY! I APPEAR TO HAVE SOMETHING IN MY EYE...
AHEM
HEY, TOOTS--YOU GOT CHANGE?
OH, OH! YOU BEAST! WHY, HOW DARE YOU BRING ME BACK HERE UNDER FALSE PRETENSES!
EXCUSE ME?
VERY WELL, I'LL FORGIVE YOU IF YOU KISS ME!
LISTEN, I--
COMIN' THROUGH!
HEY, IS THAT A SEWER PIPE?
LUCKY DEVIL!
TCHIP
TCHIP
TCHIP
TCHIP
TCHIP
THAT'S NOTHING! YESTERDAY RIZZO FOUND A DEAD SKUNK!
HUH. SOME RATS GET ALL THE BREAKS...
YOU BOYS WANT BREAKS? TRY THAT STUNT AGAIN AND I'LL SEE WHAT I CAN ARRANGE.

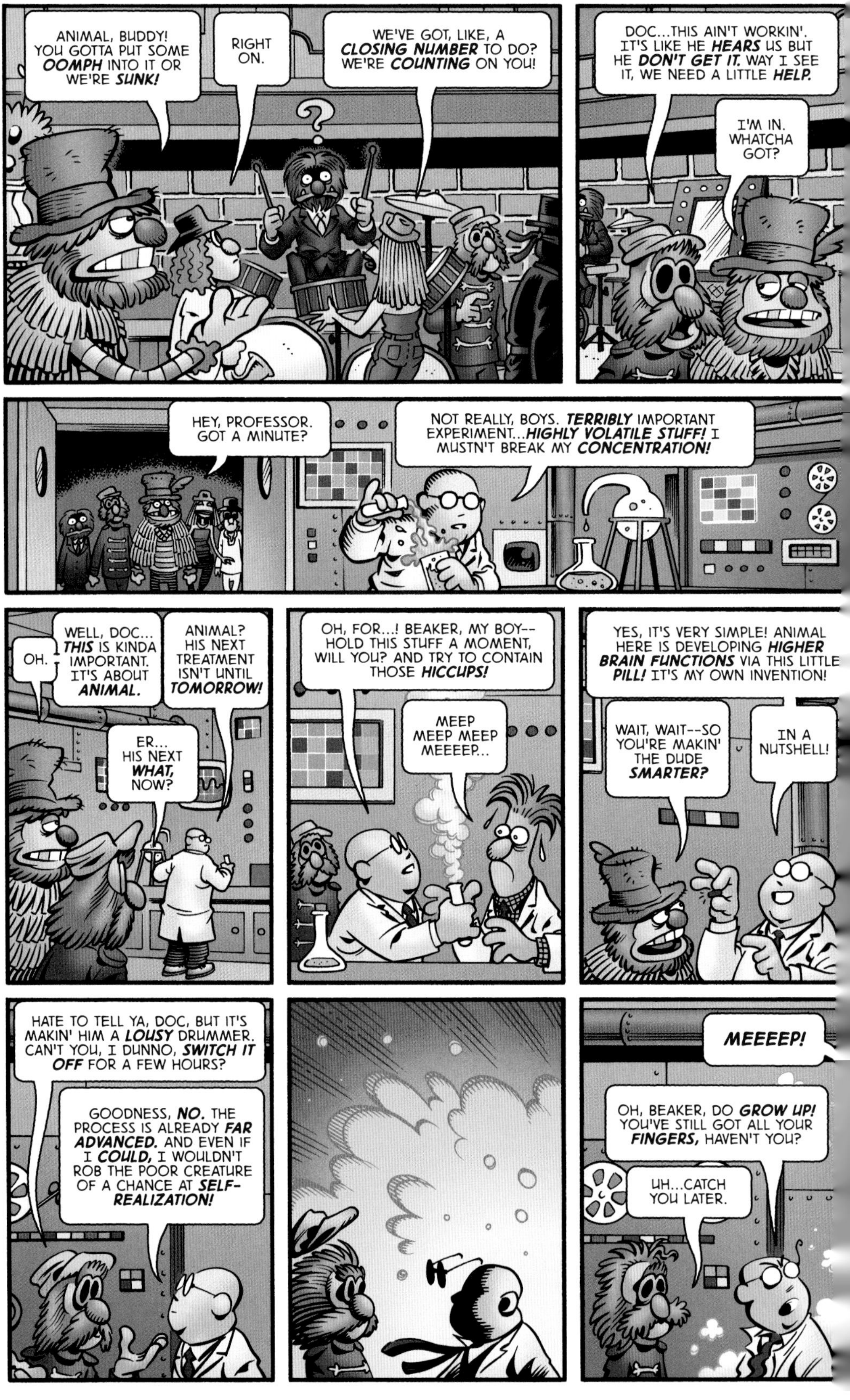
ANIMAL, BUDDY! YOU GOTTA PUT SOME OOMPH INTO IT OR WE'RE SUNK!
RIGHT ON.
WE'VE GOT, LIKE, A CLOSING NUMBER TO DO? WE'RE COUNTING ON YOU!
?
DOC...THIS AIN'T WORKIN'. IT'S LIKE HE HEARS US BUT HE DON'T GET IT. WAY I SEE IT, WE NEED A LITTLE HELP.
I'M IN. WHATCHA GOT?
HEY, PROFESSOR. GOT A MINUTE?
NOT REALLY, BOYS. TERRIBLY IMPORTANT EXPERIMENT...HIGHLY VOLATILE STUFF! I MUSTN'T BREAK MY CONCENTRATION!
OH.
WELL, DOC... THIS IS KINDA IMPORTANT. IT'S ABOUT ANIMAL.
ANIMAL? HIS NEXT TREATMENT ISN'T UNTIL TOMORROW!
ER... HIS NEXT WHAT, NOW?
OH, FOR...! BEAKER, MY BOY-- HOLD THIS STUFF A MOMENT, WILL YOU? AND TRY TO CONTAIN THOSE HICCUPS!
MEEP MEEP MEEP MEEEEP...
YES, IT'S VERY SIMPLE! ANIMAL HERE IS DEVELOPING HIGHER BRAIN FUNCTIONS VIA THIS LITTLE PILL! IT'S MY OWN INVENTION!
WAIT, WAIT--SO YOU'RE MAKIN' THE DUDE SMARTER?
IN A NUTSHELL!
HATE TO TELL YA, DOC, BUT IT'S MAKIN' HIM A LOUSY DRUMMER. CAN'T YOU, I DUNNO, SWITCH IT OFF FOR A FEW HOURS?
GOODNESS, NO. THE PROCESS IS ALREADY FAR ADVANCED. AND EVEN IF I COULD, I WOULDN'T ROB THE POOR CREATURE OF A CHANCE AT SELF-REALIZATION!
MEEEEP!
OH, BEAKER, DO GROW UP! YOU'VE STILL GOT ALL YOUR FINGERS, HAVEN'T YOU?
UH...CATCH YOU LATER.

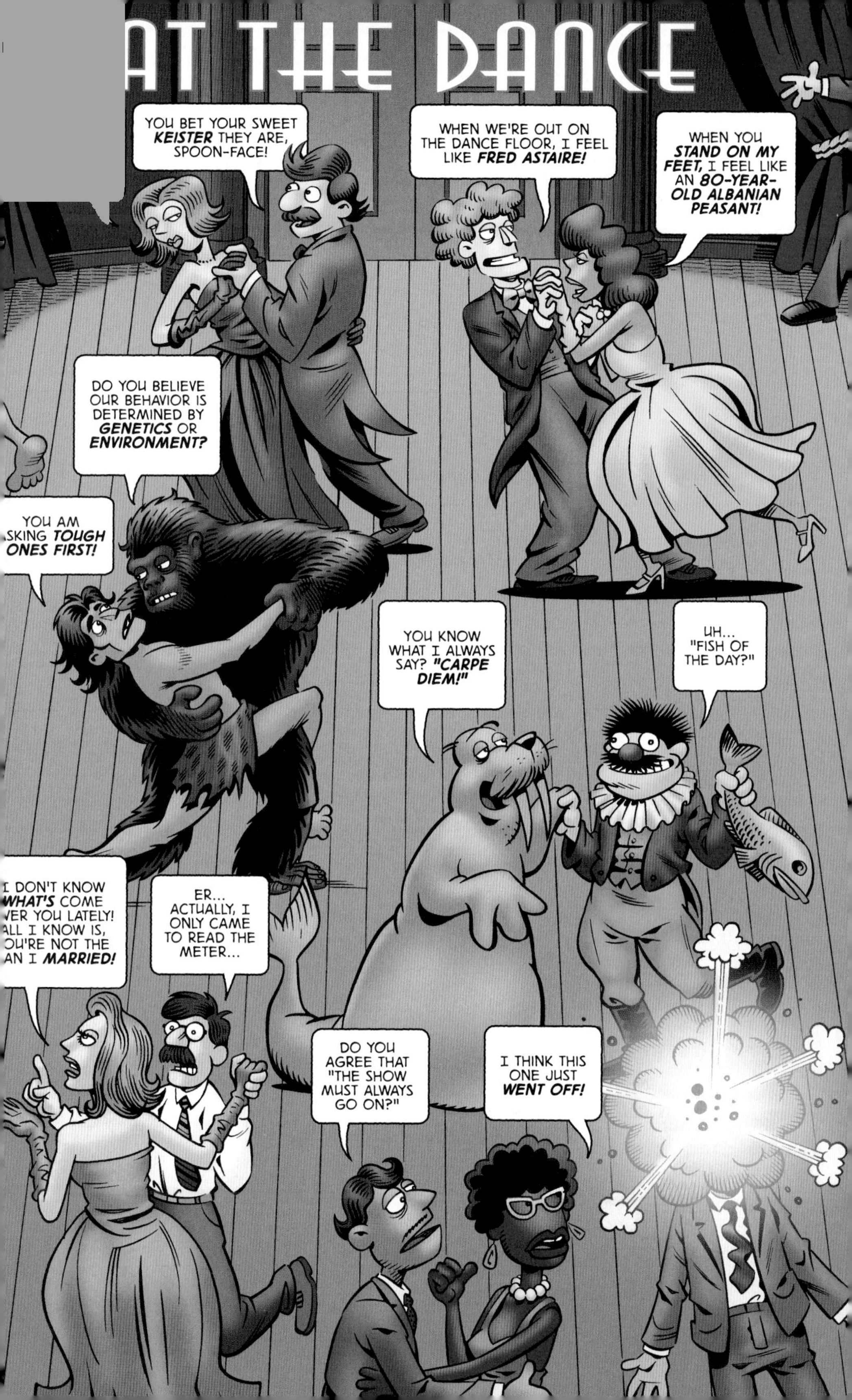
AT THE DANCE
YOU BET YOUR SWEET KEISTER THEY ARE, SPOON-FACE!
WHEN WE'RE OUT ON THE DANCE FLOOR, I FEEL LIKE FRED ASTAIRE!
WHEN YOU STAND ON MY FEET, I FEEL LIKE AN 80-YEAR-OLD ALBANIAN PEASANT!
DO YOU BELIEVE OUR BEHAVIOR IS DETERMINED BY GENETICS OR ENVIRONMENT?
YOU AM SKING TOUGH ONES FIRST!
YOU KNOW WHAT I ALWAYS SAY? "CARPE DIEM!"
UH... "FISH OF THE DAY?"
I DON'T KNOW WHAT'S COME VER YOU LATELY! ALL I KNOW IS, OU'RE NOT THE AN I MARRIED!
ER... ACTUALLY, I ONLY CAME TO READ THE METER...
DO YOU AGREE THAT "THE SHOW MUST ALWAYS GO ON?"
I THINK THIS ONE JUST WENT OFF!

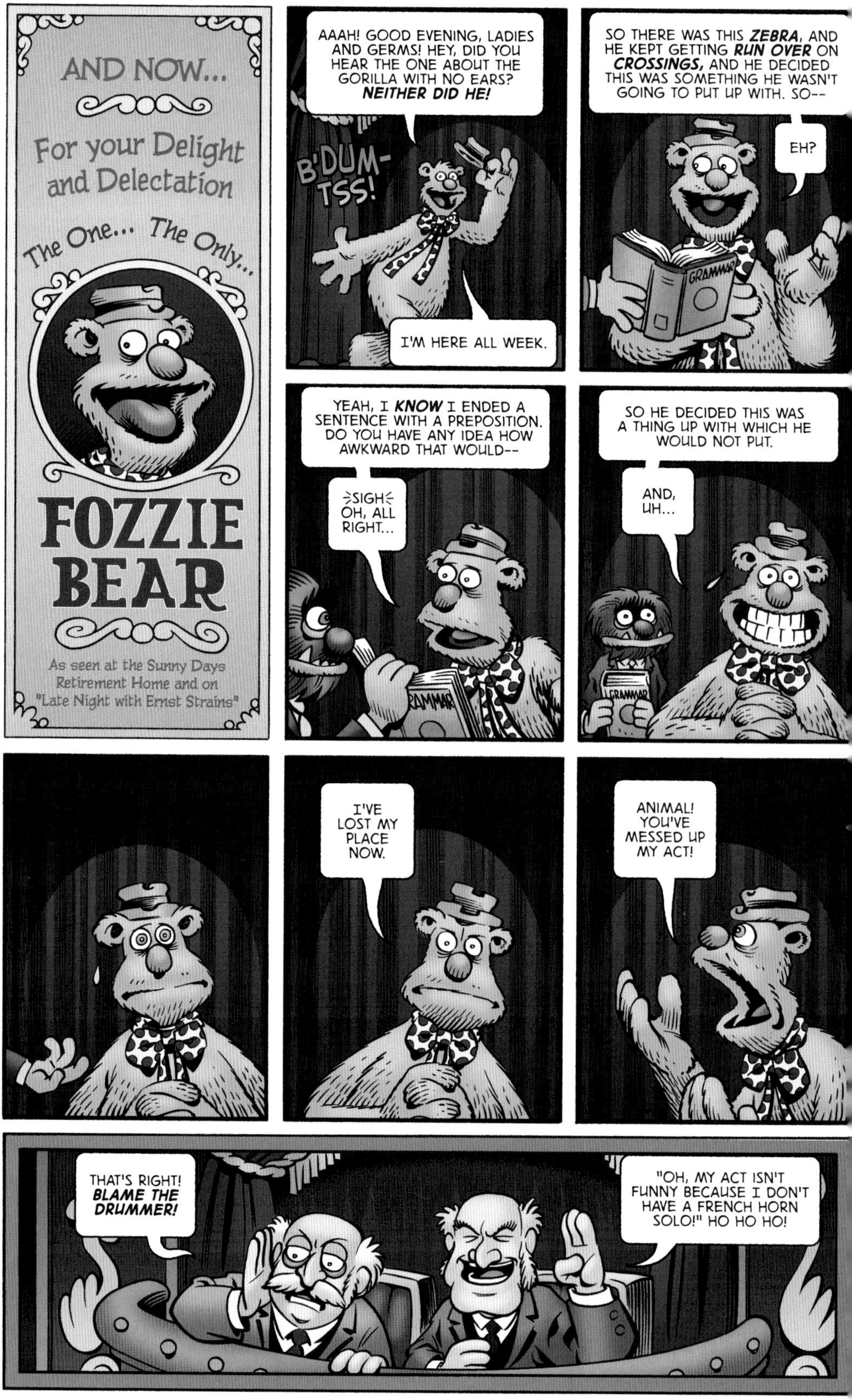
AND NOW...
For your Delight and Delectation
The One... The Only...
FOZZIE BEAR
As seen at the Sunny Days Retirement Home and on "Late Night with Ernst Strains"
AAAH! GOOD EVENING, LADIES AND GERMS! HEY, DID YOU HEAR THE ONE ABOUT THE GORILLA WITH NO EARS? NEITHER DID HE!
B'DUM-TSS!
I'M HERE ALL WEEK.
SO THERE WAS THIS ZEBRA, AND HE KEPT GETTING RUN OVER ON CROSSINGS, AND HE DECIDED THIS WAS SOMETHING HE WASN'T GOING TO PUT UP WITH. SO--
EH?
GRAMMAR
YEAH, I KNOW I ENDED A SENTENCE WITH A PREPOSITION. DO YOU HAVE ANY IDEA HOW AWKWARD THAT WOULD--
>SIGH< OH, ALL RIGHT...
GRAMMAR
SO HE DECIDED THIS WAS A THING UP WITH WHICH HE WOULD NOT PUT.
AND, UH...
GRAMMAR
I'VE LOST MY PLACE NOW.
ANIMAL! YOU'VE MESSED UP MY ACT!
THAT'S RIGHT! BLAME THE DRUMMER!
"OH, MY ACT ISN'T FUNNY BECAUSE I DON'T HAVE A FRENCH HORN SOLO!" HO HO HO!

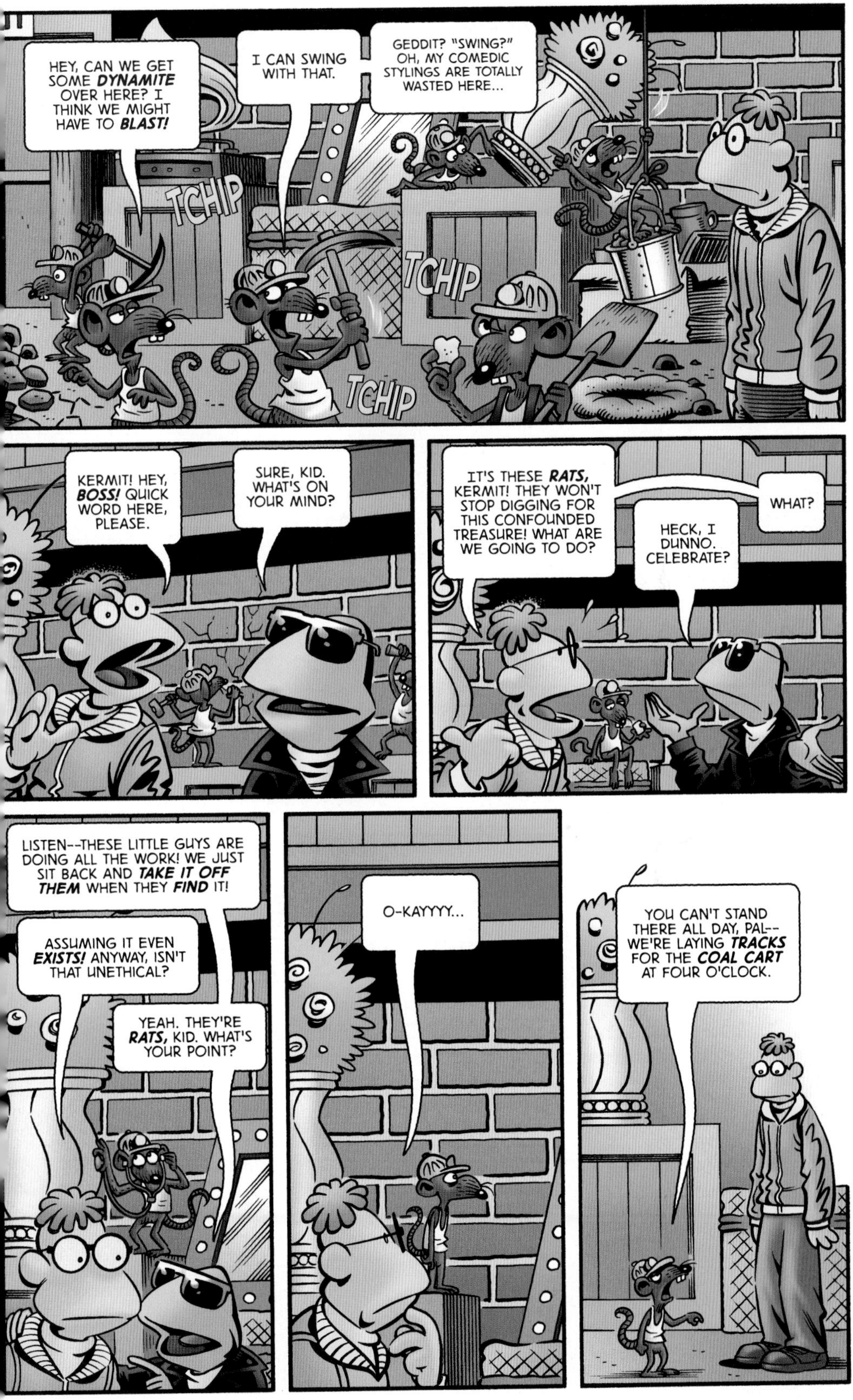
HEY, CAN WE GET SOME DYNAMITE OVER HERE? I THINK WE MIGHT HAVE TO BLAST!
I CAN SWING WITH THAT.
GEDDIT? "SWING?" OH, MY COMEDIC STYLINGS ARE TOTALLY WASTED HERE...
TCHIP
TCHIP
TCHIP
KERMIT! HEY, BOSS! QUICK WORD HERE, PLEASE.
SURE, KID. WHAT'S ON YOUR MIND?
IT'S THESE RATS, KERMIT! THEY WON'T STOP DIGGING FOR THIS CONFOUNDED TREASURE! WHAT ARE WE GOING TO DO?
WHAT?
HECK, I DUNNO. CELEBRATE?
LISTEN--THESE LITTLE GUYS ARE DOING ALL THE WORK! WE JUST SIT BACK AND TAKE IT OFF THEM WHEN THEY FIND IT!
ASSUMING IT EVEN EXISTS! ANYWAY, ISN'T THAT UNETHICAL?
YEAH. THEY'RE RATS, KID. WHAT'S YOUR POINT?
O-KAYYYY...
YOU CAN'T STAND THERE ALL DAY, PAL--WE'RE LAYING TRACKS FOR THE COAL CART AT FOUR O'CLOCK.

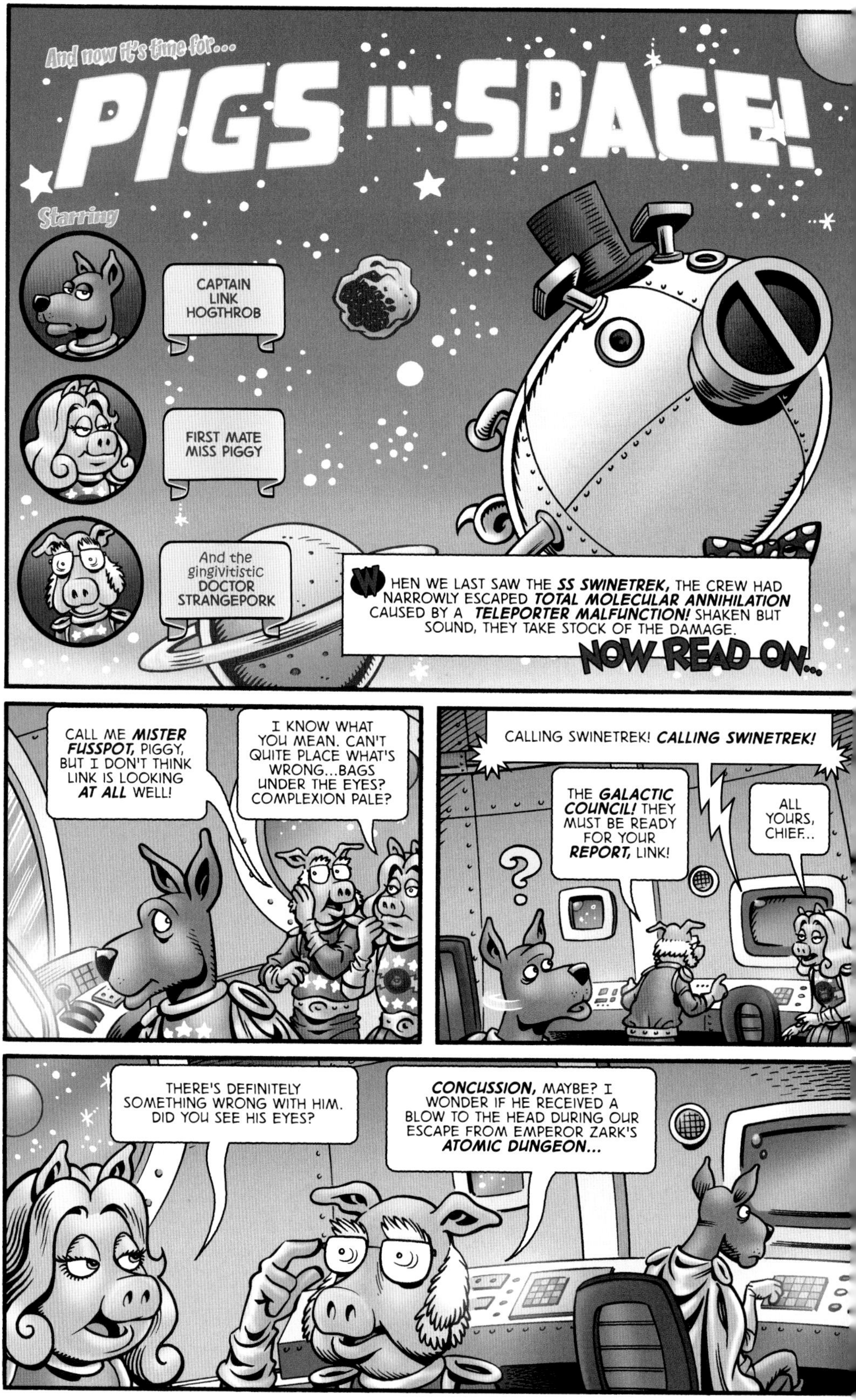

And now it's time for...
PIGS IN SPACE!
Starring
CAPTAIN LINK HOGTHROB
FIRST MATE MISS PIGGY
And the gingivitistic DOCTOR STRANGEPORK
WHEN WE LAST SAW THE SS SWINETREK, THE CREW HAD NARROWLY ESCAPED TOTAL MOLECULAR ANNIHILATION CAUSED BY A TELEPORTER MALFUNCTION! SHAKEN BUT SOUND, THEY TAKE STOCK OF THE DAMAGE.
NOW READ ON...
CALL ME MISTER FUSSPOT, PIGGY, BUT I DON'T THINK LINK IS LOOKING AT ALL WELL!
I KNOW WHAT YOU MEAN. CAN'T QUITE PLACE WHAT'S WRONG...BAGS UNDER THE EYES? COMPLEXION PALE?
CALLING SWINETREK! CALLING SWINETREK!
?
THE GALACTIC COUNCIL! THEY MUST BE READY FOR YOUR REPORT, LINK!
ALL YOURS, CHIEF...
THERE'S DEFINITELY SOMETHING WRONG WITH HIM. DID YOU SEE HIS EYES?
CONCUSSION, MAYBE? I WONDER IF HE RECEIVED A BLOW TO THE HEAD DURING OUR ESCAPE FROM EMPEROR ZARK'S ATOMIC DUNGEON...

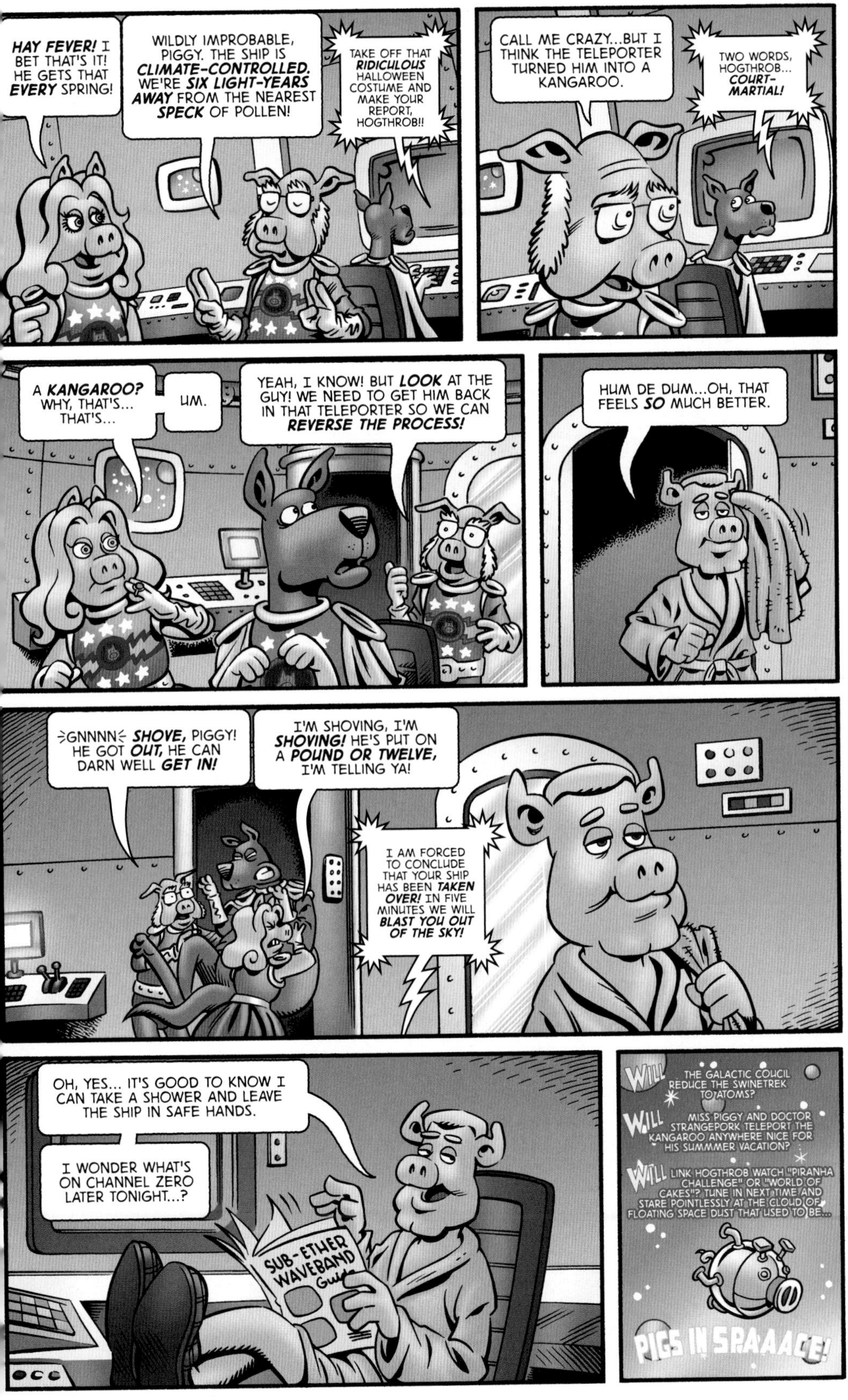
HAY FEVER! I BET THAT'S IT! HE GETS THAT EVERY SPRING!
WILDLY IMPROBABLE, PIGGY. THE SHIP IS CLIMATE-CONTROLLED. WE'RE SIX LIGHT-YEARS AWAY FROM THE NEAREST SPECK OF POLLEN!
TAKE OFF THAT RIDICULOUS HALLOWEEN COSTUME AND MAKE YOUR REPORT, HOGTHROB!!
CALL ME CRAZY...BUT I THINK THE TELEPORTER TURNED HIM INTO A KANGAROO.
TWO WORDS, HOGTHROB... COURT-MARTIAL!
A KANGAROO? WHY, THAT'S... THAT'S...
UM.
YEAH, I KNOW! BUT LOOK AT THE GUY! WE NEED TO GET HIM BACK IN THAT TELEPORTER SO WE CAN REVERSE THE PROCESS!
HUM DE DUM...OH, THAT FEELS SO MUCH BETTER.
GNNNN SHOVE, PIGGY! HE GOT OUT, HE CAN DARN WELL GET IN!
I'M SHOVING, I'M SHOVING! HE'S PUT ON A POUND OR TWELVE, I'M TELLING YA!
I AM FORCED TO CONCLUDE THAT YOUR SHIP HAS BEEN TAKEN OVER! IN FIVE MINUTES WE WILL BLAST YOU OUT OF THE SKY!
OH, YES... IT'S GOOD TO KNOW I CAN TAKE A SHOWER AND LEAVE THE SHIP IN SAFE HANDS.
I WONDER WHAT'S ON CHANNEL ZERO LATER TONIGHT...?
SUB-ETHER WAVEBAND Guide
WILL THE GALACTIC COUCIL REDUCE THE SWINETREK TO ATOMS?
WILL MISS PIGGY AND DOCTOR STRANGEPORK TELEPORT THE KANGAROO ANYWHERE NICE FOR HIS SUMMMER VACATION?
WILL LINK HOGTHROB WATCH "PIRANHA CHALLENGE" OR "WORLD OF CAKES"? TUNE IN NEXT TIME AND STARE POINTLESSLY AT THE CLOUD OF FLOATING SPACE DUST THAT USED TO BE...
PIGS IN SPAAACE!

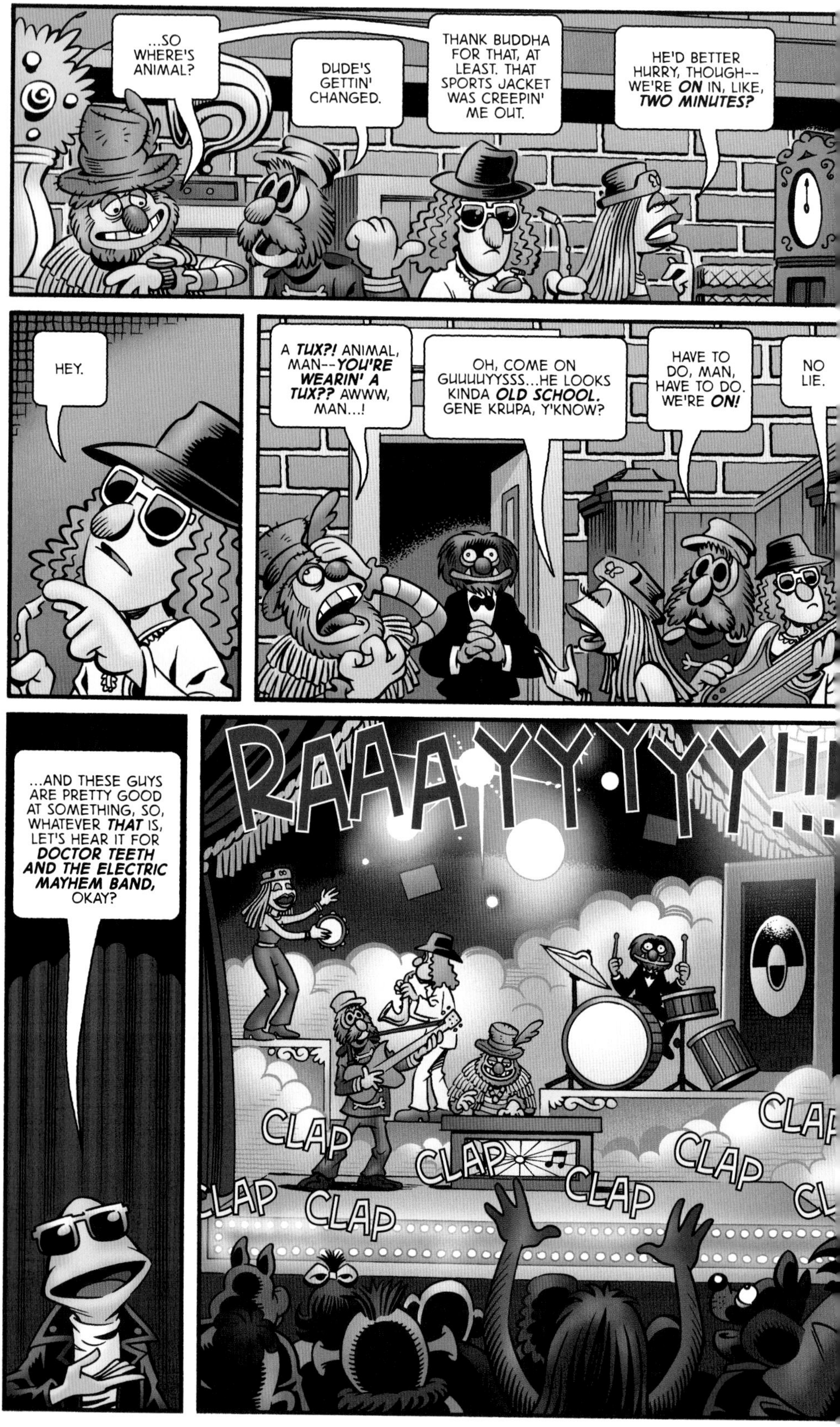
...SO WHERE'S ANIMAL?
DUDE'S GETTIN' CHANGED.
THANK BUDDHA FOR THAT, AT LEAST. THAT SPORTS JACKET WAS CREEPIN' ME OUT.
HE'D BETTER HURRY, THOUGH-- WE'RE ON IN, LIKE, TWO MINUTES?
HEY.
A TUX?! ANIMAL, MAN--YOU'RE WEARIN' A TUX?? AWWW, MAN...!
OH, COME ON GUUUUYYSSS...HE LOOKS KINDA OLD SCHOOL. GENE KRUPA, Y'KNOW?
HAVE TO DO, MAN, HAVE TO DO. WE'RE ON!
NO LIE.
...AND THESE GUYS ARE PRETTY GOOD AT SOMETHING, SO, WHATEVER THAT IS, LET'S HEAR IT FOR DOCTOR TEETH AND THE ELECTRIC MAYHEM BAND, OKAY?
RAAAYYYY!!!
CLAP
CLAP
CLAP
CLAP
CLAP
CLAP
CLAP
CLAP

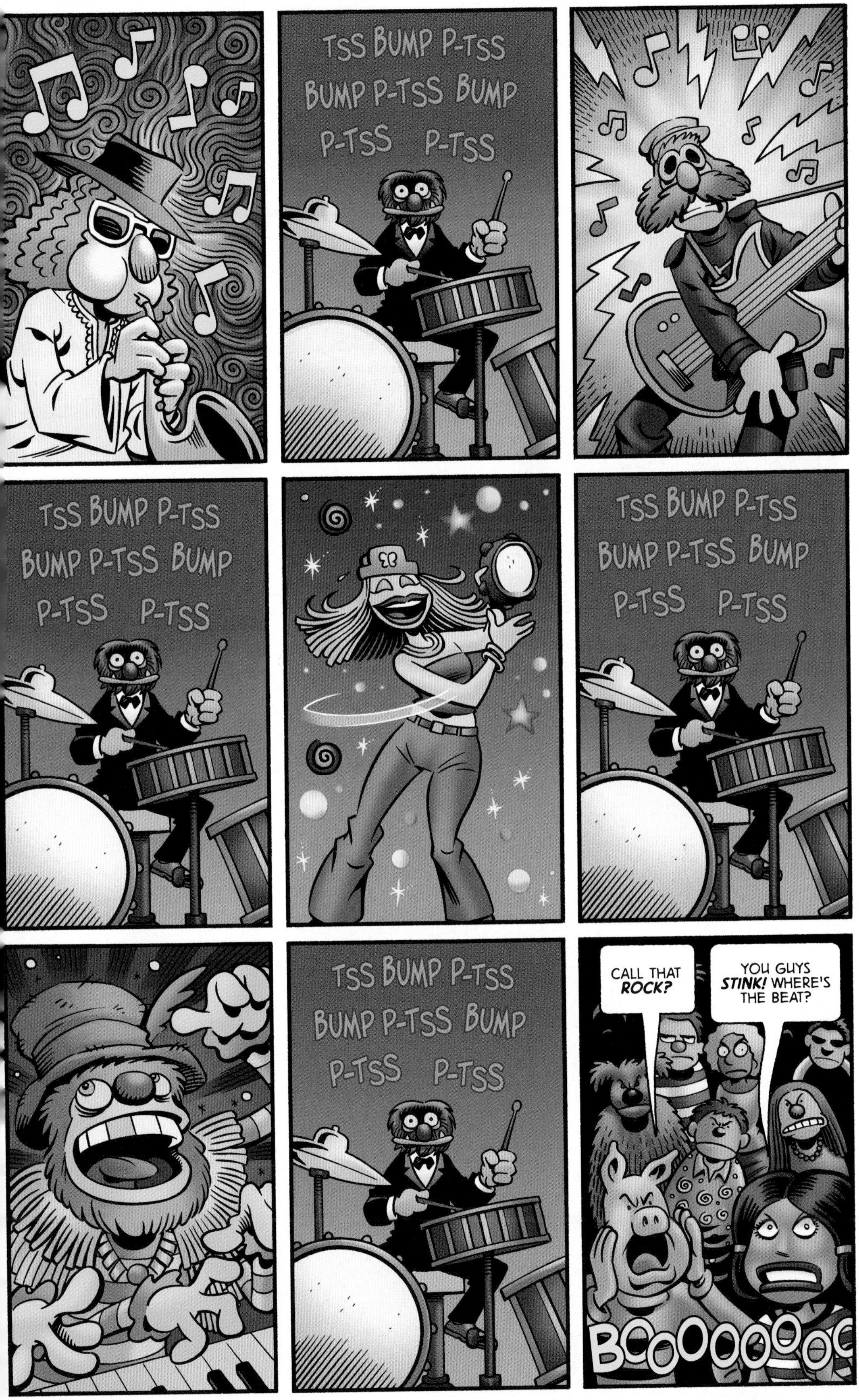
TSS BUMP P-TSS
BUMP P-TSS BUMP
P-TSS P-TSS
TSS BUMP P-TSS
BUMP P-TSS BUMP
P-TSS P-TSS
TSS BUMP P-TSS
BUMP P-TSS BUMP
P-TSS P-TSS
TSS BUMP P-TSS
BUMP P-TSS BUMP
P-TSS P-TSS
CALL THAT ROCK?
YOU GUYS STINK! WHERE'S THE BEAT?
BOOOOOOOO

WE'RE IN *TROUBLE*, DOC--ANIMAL NEEDS TO *PICK UP THAT BEAT* IN SOME KINDA *HURRY*.

TELL ME ABOUT IT! OH, OH--MY MOTHER *WARNED* ME ABOUT PEOPLE LIKE HIM...

SHH--*WAIT!* WHAT'S THAT SOUND?

BUM BUDDA BUM
PTSHHHH BUMPA
BUDDA BUDDA BOO
FA-DUMP-DUMP
DUMP 'ARRASHHH

IT'S THE *NINJA DUDE!* WHERE'S *ANIMAL?*

LATER! RIGHT NOW, WE *PLAY*--BEFORE WE GET *EATEN ALIVE!*

BUMPAB UMBUDDA
BOO DUMP-DU
DUMP BUDDA
BOO F-TSHHH

WAHEEEEYYYY!! 'RAA

WHOO

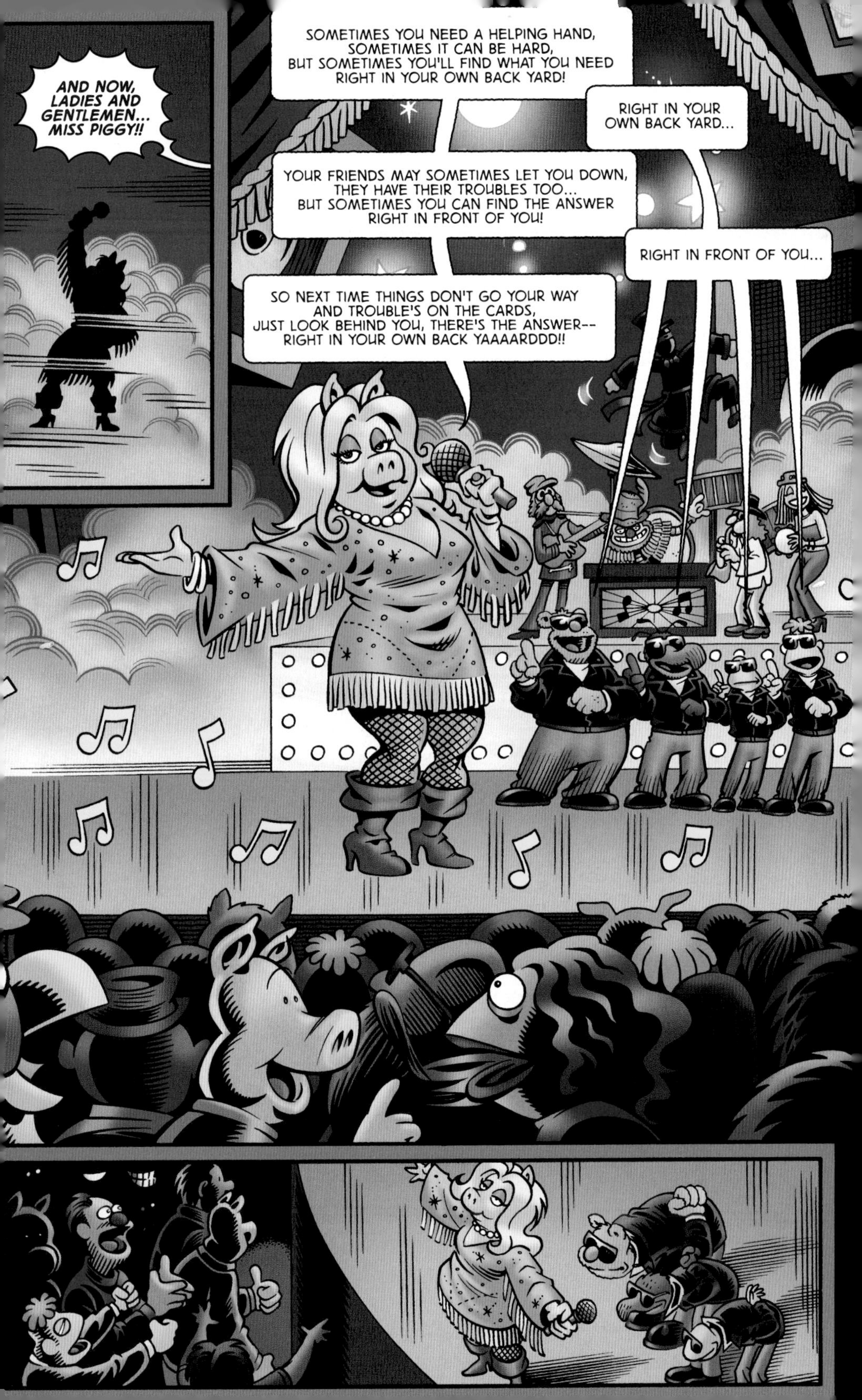
AND NOW, LADIES AND GENTLEMEN... MISS PIGGY!!
SOMETIMES YOU NEED A HELPING HAND,
SOMETIMES IT CAN BE HARD,
BUT SOMETIMES YOU'LL FIND WHAT YOU NEED
RIGHT IN YOUR OWN BACK YARD!
RIGHT IN YOUR OWN BACK YARD...
YOUR FRIENDS MAY SOMETIMES LET YOU DOWN,
THEY HAVE THEIR TROUBLES TOO...
BUT SOMETIMES YOU CAN FIND THE ANSWER
RIGHT IN FRONT OF YOU!
RIGHT IN FRONT OF YOU...
SO NEXT TIME THINGS DON'T GO YOUR WAY
AND TROUBLE'S ON THE CARDS,
JUST LOOK BEHIND YOU, THERE'S THE ANSWER--
RIGHT IN YOUR OWN BACK YAAAARDDD!!

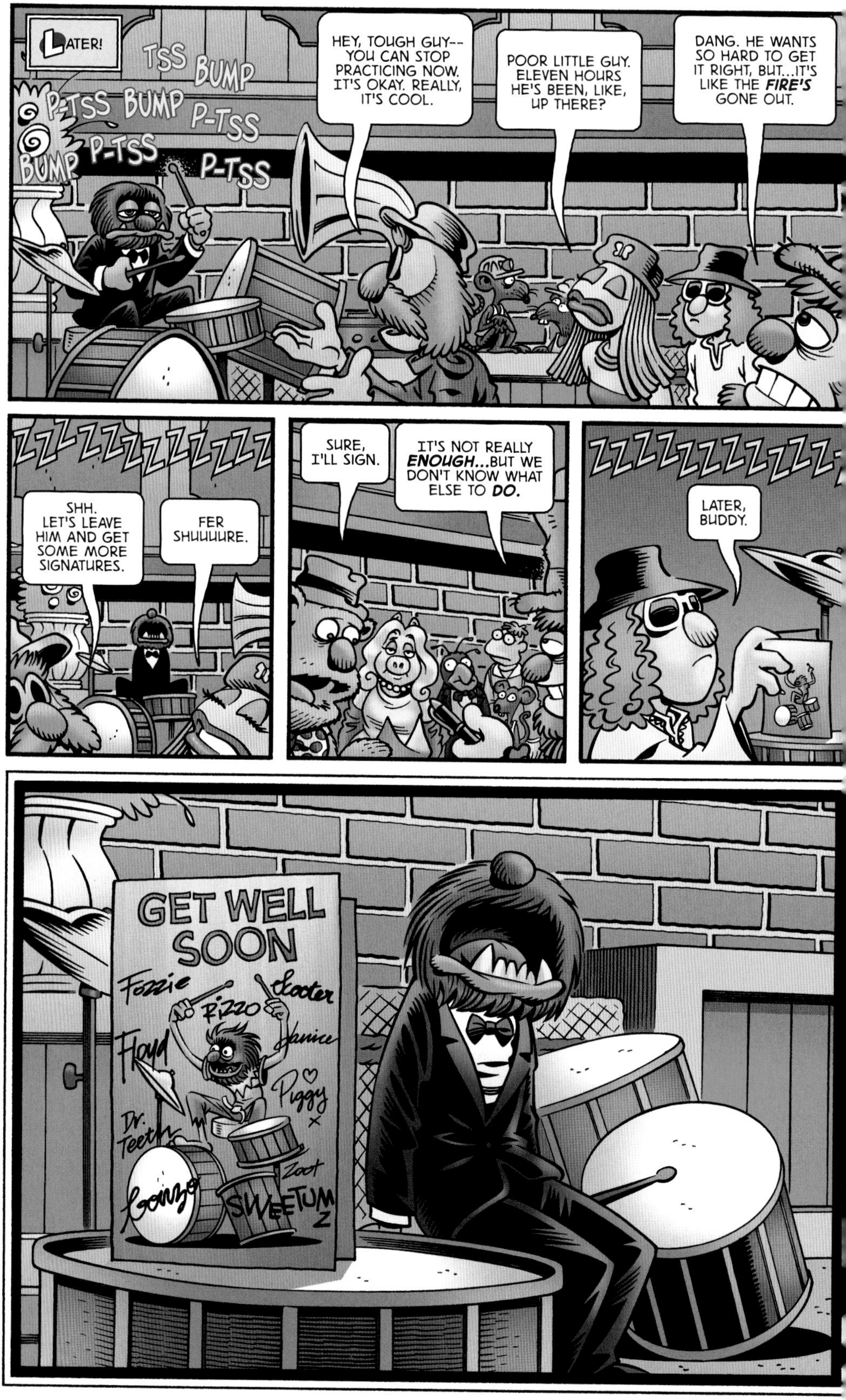
LATER!
TSS BUMP
P-TSS BUMP P-TSS
BUMP P-TSS P-TSS
HEY, TOUGH GUY-- YOU CAN STOP PRACTICING NOW. IT'S OKAY. REALLY, IT'S COOL.
POOR LITTLE GUY. ELEVEN HOURS HE'S BEEN, LIKE, UP THERE?
DANG. HE WANTS SO HARD TO GET IT RIGHT, BUT...IT'S LIKE THE ***FIRE'S*** GONE OUT.
ZZZZZZZZZZZZZ
SHH. LET'S LEAVE HIM AND GET SOME MORE SIGNATURES.
FER SHUUUURE.
SURE, I'LL SIGN.
IT'S NOT REALLY ***ENOUGH...*** BUT WE DON'T KNOW WHAT ELSE TO ***DO.***
ZZZZZZZZZZZZ
LATER, BUDDY.
GET WELL SOON
Fozzie
Scooter
Rizzo
Floyd
Janice
Piggy
Dr. Teeth
Gonzo
Zoot
SWEETUMS

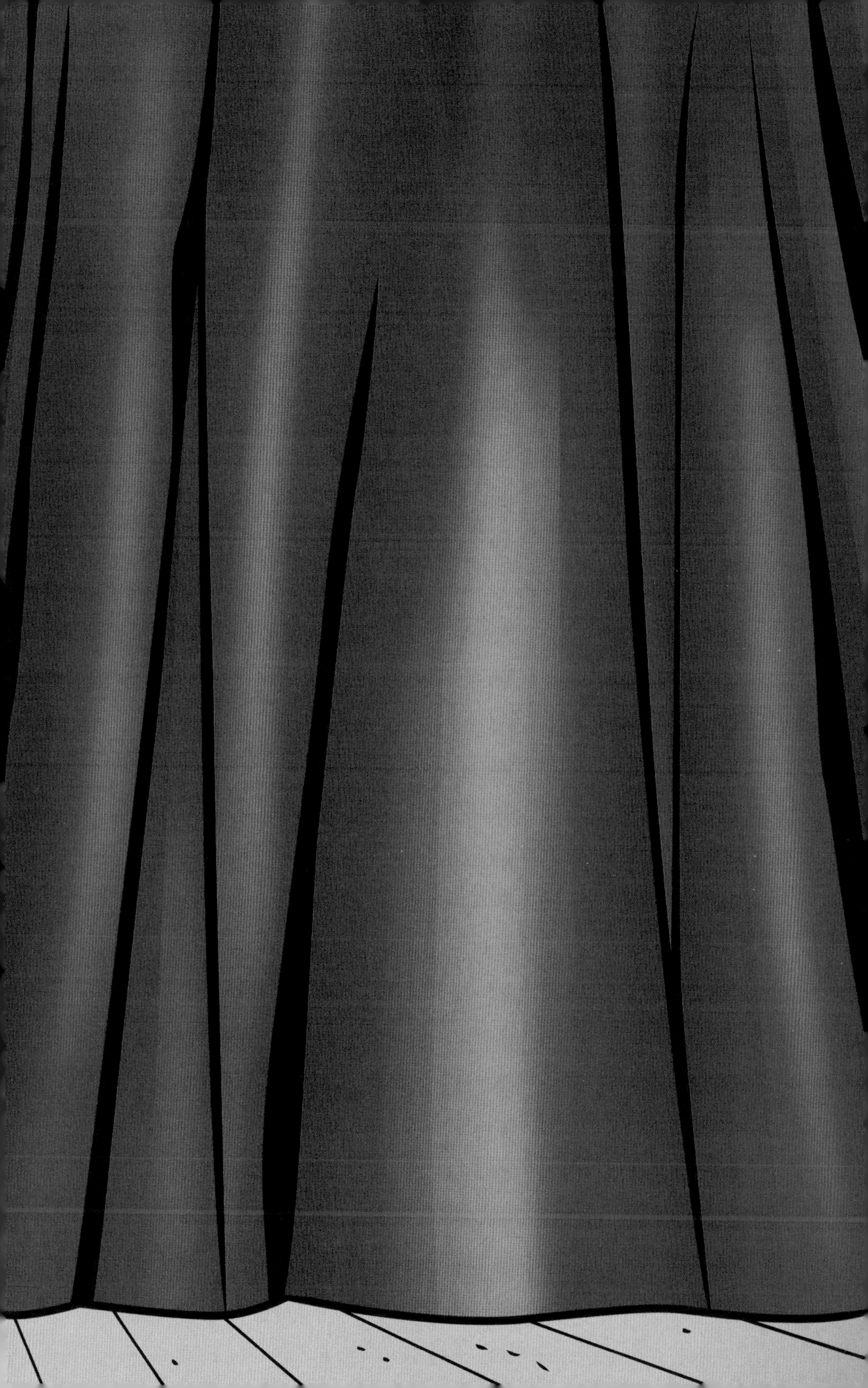

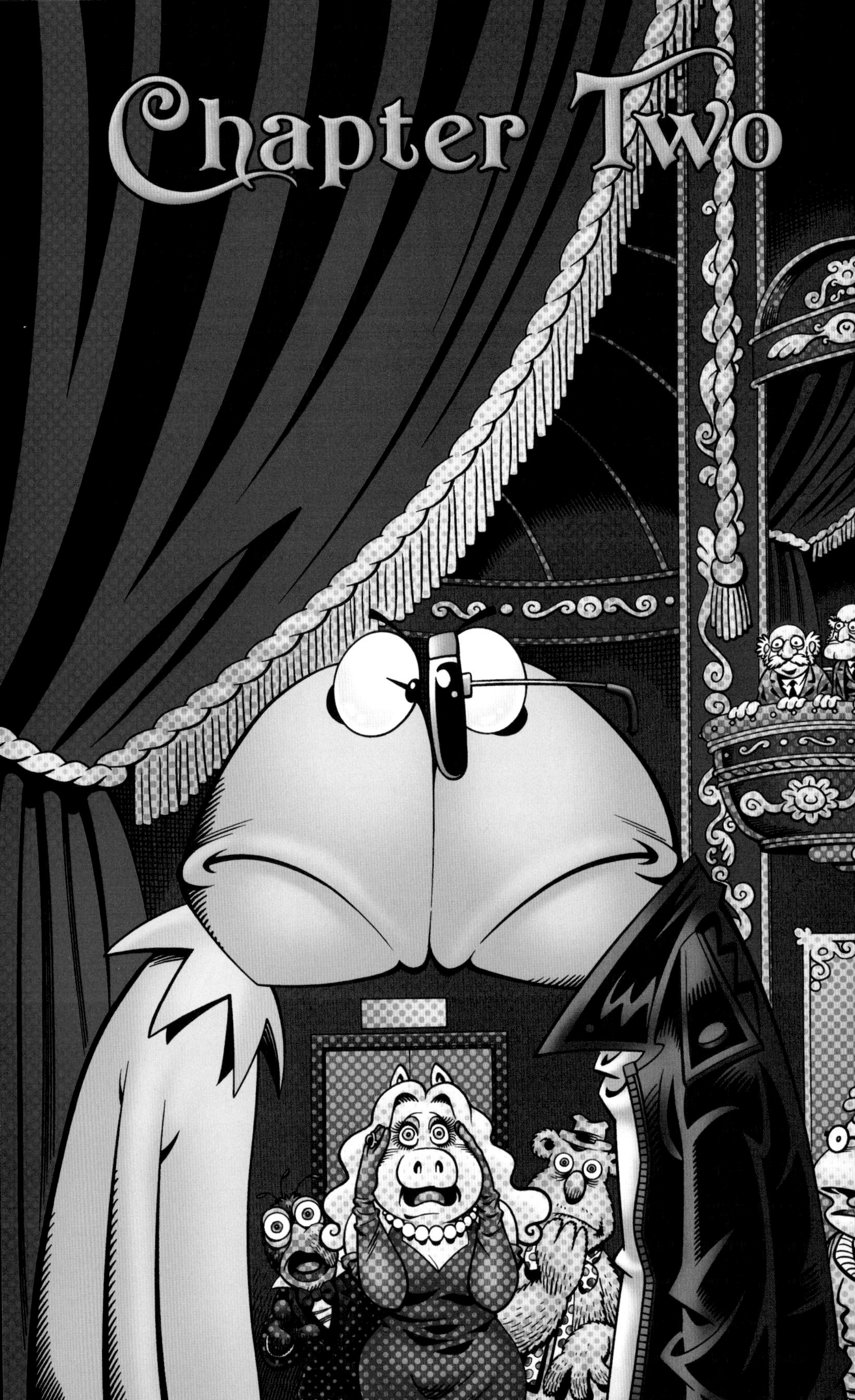
Chapter Two

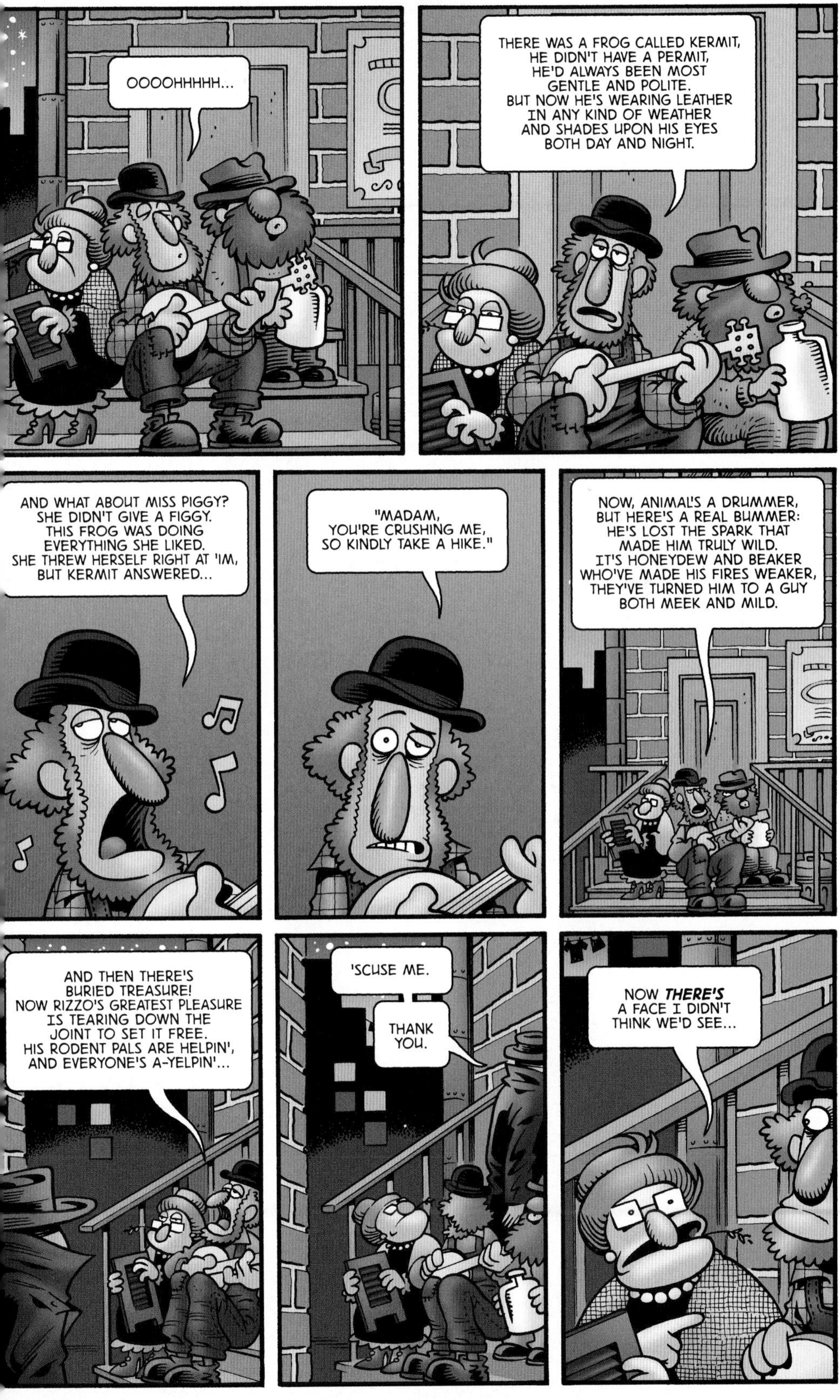
OOOOHHHHH...
THERE WAS A FROG CALLED KERMIT, HE DIDN'T HAVE A PERMIT, HE'D ALWAYS BEEN MOST GENTLE AND POLITE. BUT NOW HE'S WEARING LEATHER IN ANY KIND OF WEATHER AND SHADES UPON HIS EYES BOTH DAY AND NIGHT.
AND WHAT ABOUT MISS PIGGY? SHE DIDN'T GIVE A FIGGY. THIS FROG WAS DOING EVERYTHING SHE LIKED. SHE THREW HERSELF RIGHT AT 'IM, BUT KERMIT ANSWERED...
"MADAM, YOU'RE CRUSHING ME, SO KINDLY TAKE A HIKE."
NOW, ANIMAL'S A DRUMMER, BUT HERE'S A REAL BUMMER: HE'S LOST THE SPARK THAT MADE HIM TRULY WILD. IT'S HONEYDEW AND BEAKER WHO'VE MADE HIS FIRES WEAKER, THEY'VE TURNED HIM TO A GUY BOTH MEEK AND MILD.
AND THEN THERE'S BURIED TREASURE! NOW RIZZO'S GREATEST PLEASURE IS TEARING DOWN THE JOINT TO SET IT FREE. HIS RODENT PALS ARE HELPIN', AND EVERYONE'S A-YELPIN'...
'SCUSE ME.
THANK YOU.
NOW THERE'S A FACE I DIDN'T THINK WE'D SEE...

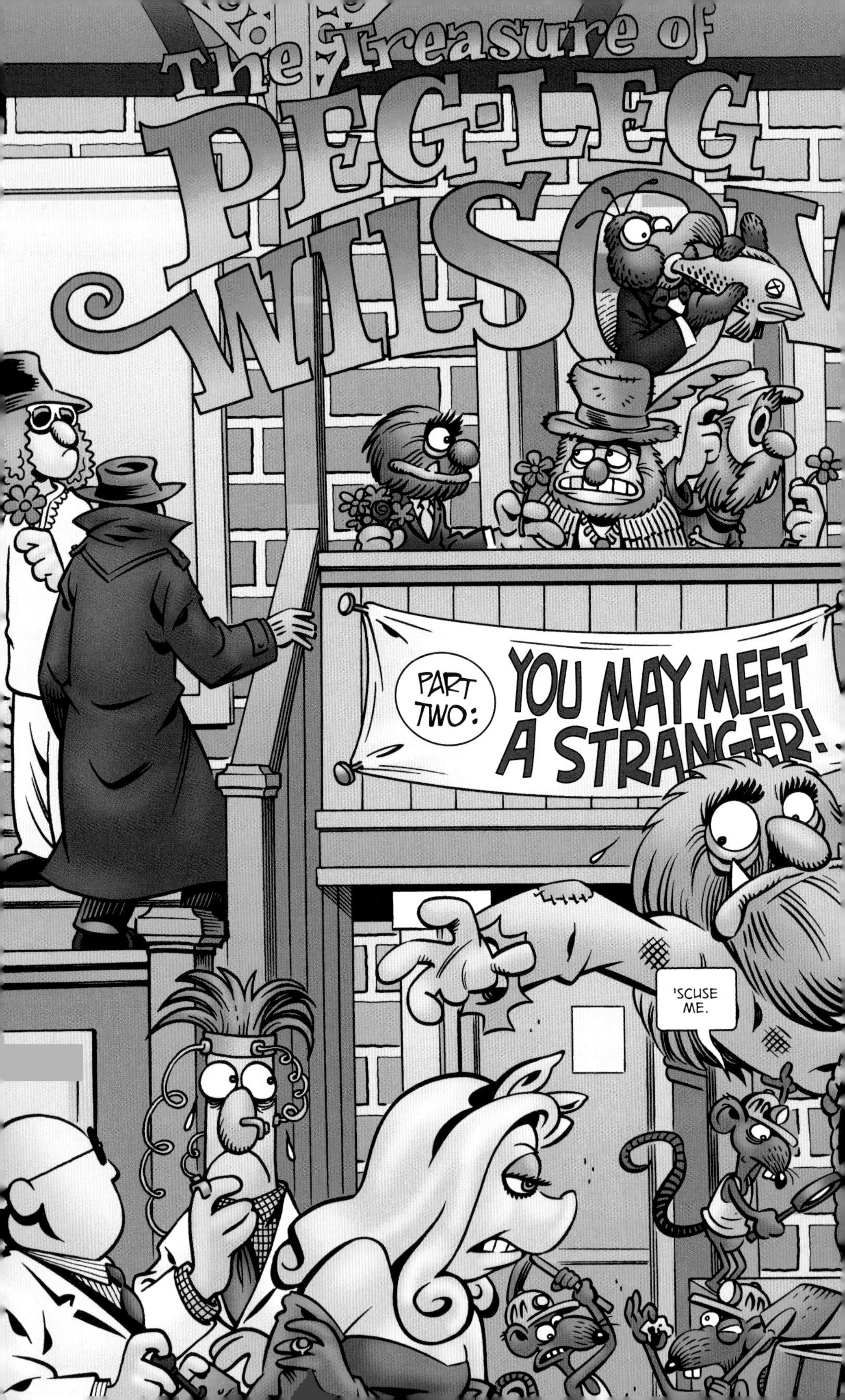
The Treasure of
PEG-LEG WILSON
PART TWO: YOU MAY MEET A STRANGER!
'SCUSE ME.

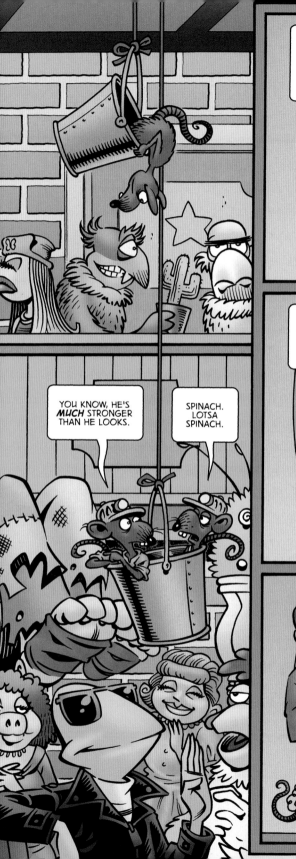

THIS JUST IN: A **MAP** HAS BEEN DISCOVERED IN THE MUPPET THEATER PURPORTING TO REVEAL THE EXISTENCE OF A SUPPOSED **"HIDDEN TREASURE"**. MRS QUATTS OF 32 PRONK STREET DENIES ALL KNOWLEDGE OF SAME.

YOU KNOW, HE'S **MUCH** STRONGER THAN HE LOOKS.

SPINACH. LOTSA SPINACH.

SEVERAL OTHER PEOPLE WE ASKED AT RANDOM ALSO DENY KNOWLEDGE OF THE MAP, SAYING, IN THE WORDS OF ONE, "IF YOU DON'T GET OFF MY PORCH I'LL SET **WUFFLES** ON YOU."

THE MAP WAS UNAVAILABLE FOR COMMENT.

COMING UP NEXT: WEATHER.

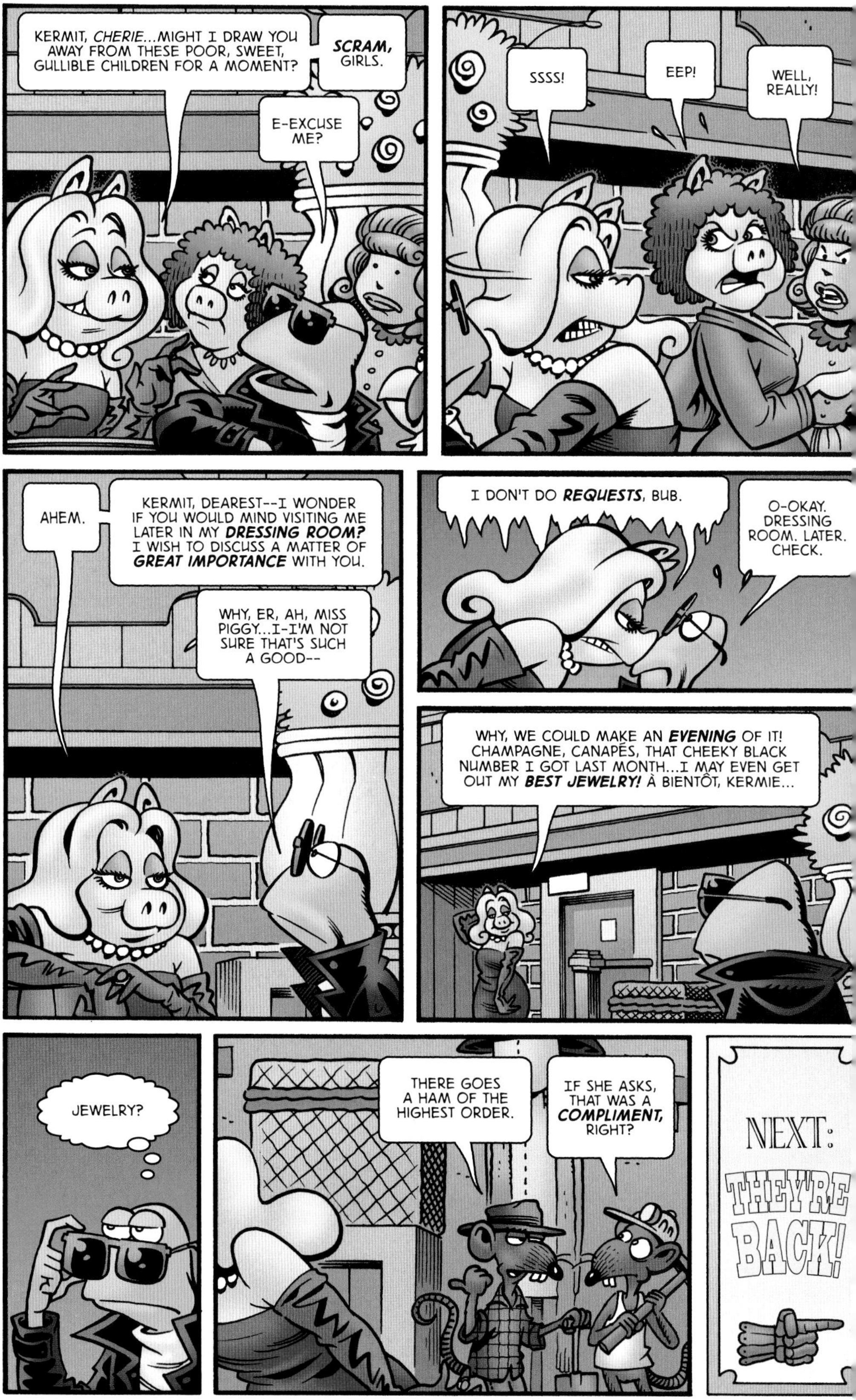
KERMIT, CHERIE...MIGHT I DRAW YOU AWAY FROM THESE POOR, SWEET, GULLIBLE CHILDREN FOR A MOMENT?
SCRAM, GIRLS.
E-EXCUSE ME?
SSSS!
EEP!
WELL, REALLY!
AHEM.
KERMIT, DEAREST--I WONDER IF YOU WOULD MIND VISITING ME LATER IN MY DRESSING ROOM? I WISH TO DISCUSS A MATTER OF GREAT IMPORTANCE WITH YOU.
WHY, ER, AH, MISS PIGGY...I-I'M NOT SURE THAT'S SUCH A GOOD--
I DON'T DO REQUESTS, BUB.
O-OKAY. DRESSING ROOM. LATER. CHECK.
WHY, WE COULD MAKE AN EVENING OF IT! CHAMPAGNE, CANAPÉS, THAT CHEEKY BLACK NUMBER I GOT LAST MONTH...I MAY EVEN GET OUT MY BEST JEWELRY! À BIENTÔT, KERMIE...
JEWELRY?
THERE GOES A HAM OF THE HIGHEST ORDER.
IF SHE ASKS, THAT WAS A COMPLIMENT, RIGHT?
NEXT:
THEY'RE BACK!

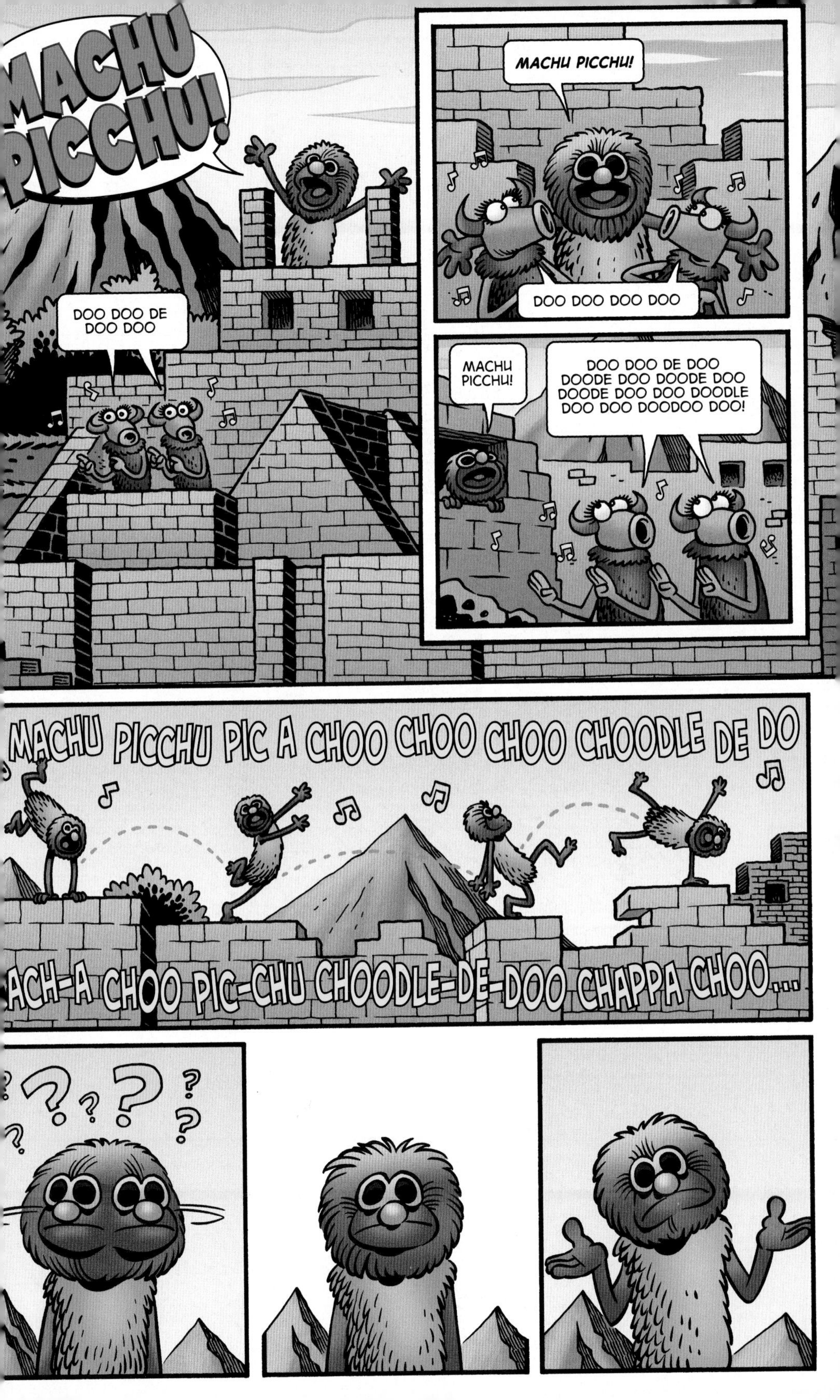
MACHU PICCHU!
DOO DOO DE DOO DOO
MACHU PICCHU!
DOO DOO DOO DOO
MACHU PICCHU!
DOO DOO DE DOO DOODE DOO DOODE DOO DOODE DOO DOO DOODLE DOO DOO DOODOO DOO!
MACHU PICCHU PIC A CHOO CHOO CHOO CHOODLE DE DO
ACH-A CHOO PIC-CHU CHOODLE-DE-DOO CHAPPA CHOO...

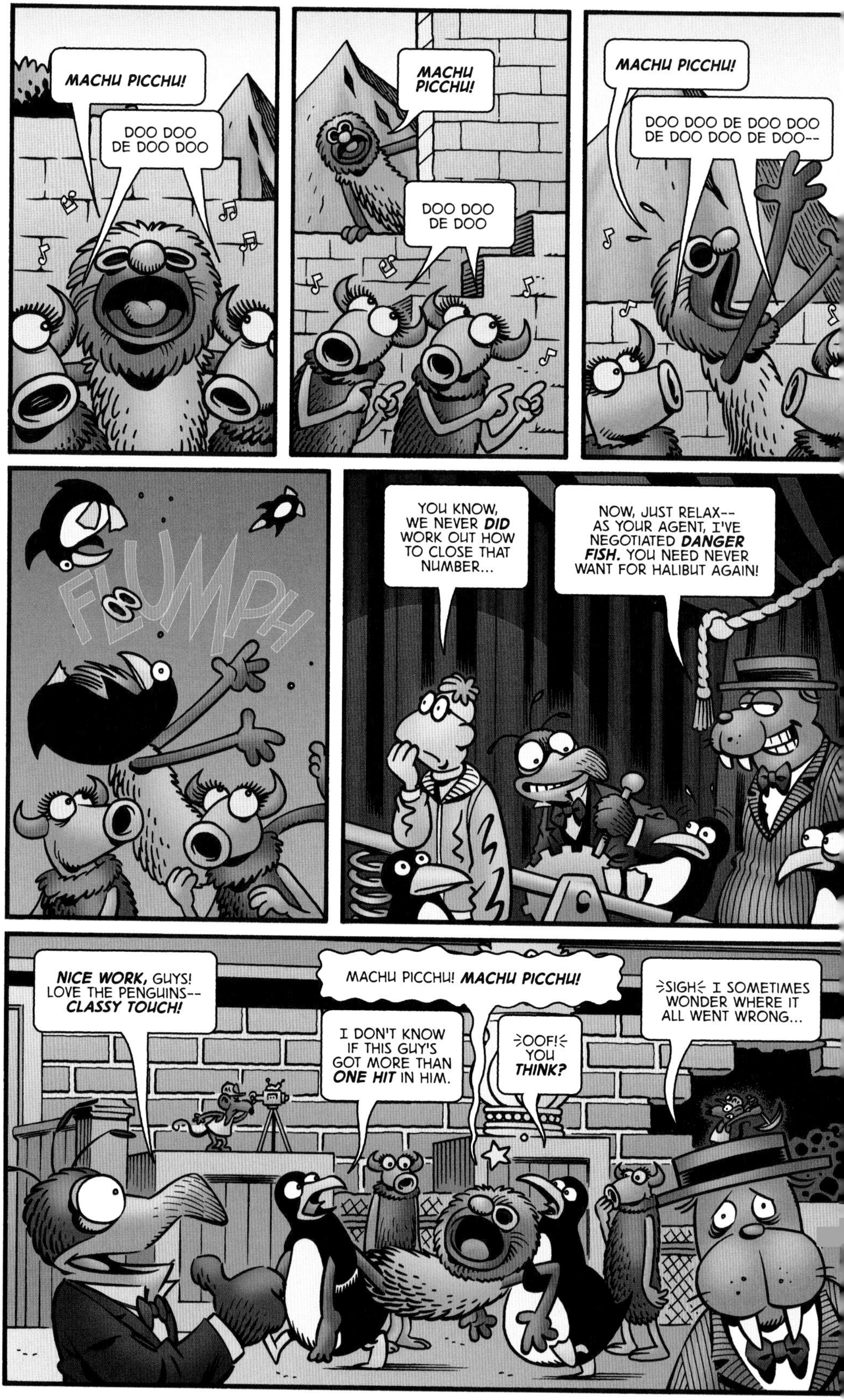

MACHU PICCHU!
DOO DOO DE DOO DOO
MACHU PICCHU!
DOO DOO DE DOO
MACHU PICCHU!
DOO DOO DE DOO DOO DE DOO DOO DE DOO--
FLUMPH
YOU KNOW, WE NEVER DID WORK OUT HOW TO CLOSE THAT NUMBER...
NOW, JUST RELAX-- AS YOUR AGENT, I'VE NEGOTIATED DANGER FISH. YOU NEED NEVER WANT FOR HALIBUT AGAIN!
NICE WORK, GUYS! LOVE THE PENGUINS-- CLASSY TOUCH!
MACHU PICCHU! MACHU PICCHU!
I DON'T KNOW IF THIS GUY'S GOT MORE THAN ONE HIT IN HIM.
OOF! YOU THINK?
SIGH I SOMETIMES WONDER WHERE IT ALL WENT WRONG...

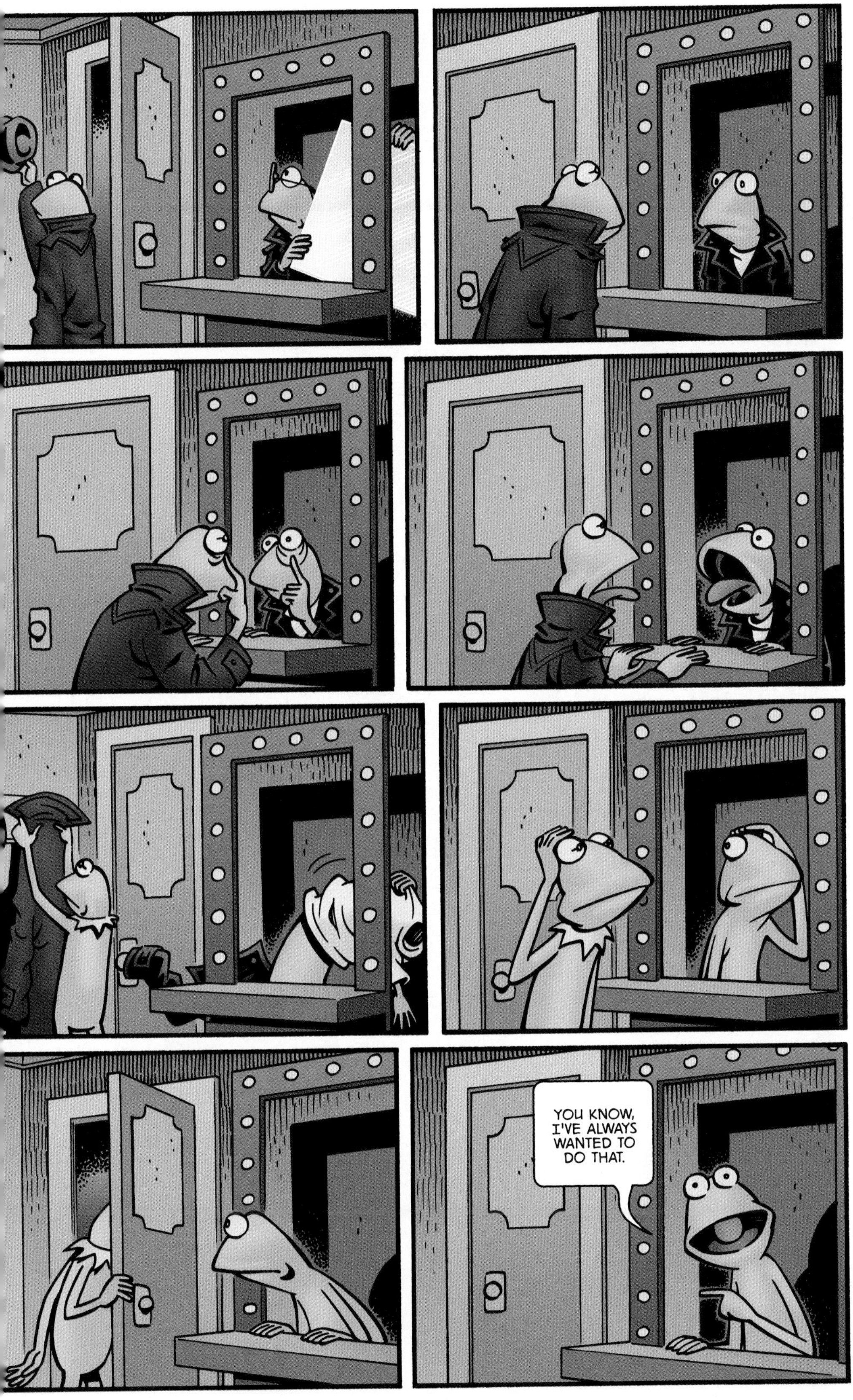
YOU KNOW, I'VE ALWAYS WANTED TO DO THAT.

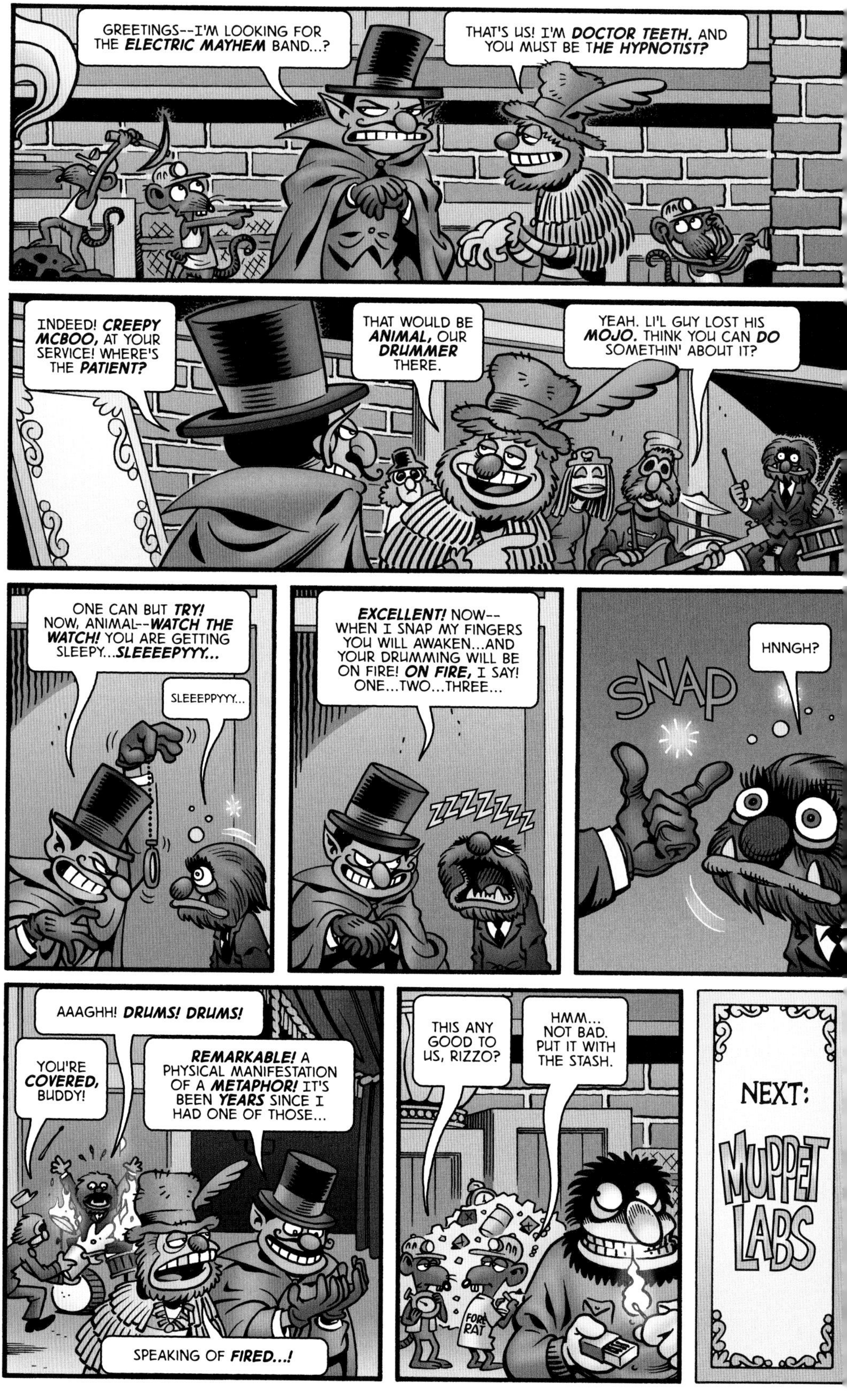

GREETINGS--I'M LOOKING FOR THE ELECTRIC MAYHEM BAND...?
THAT'S US! I'M DOCTOR TEETH. AND YOU MUST BE THE HYPNOTIST?
INDEED! CREEPY MCBOO, AT YOUR SERVICE! WHERE'S THE PATIENT?
THAT WOULD BE ANIMAL, OUR DRUMMER THERE.
YEAH. LI'L GUY LOST HIS MOJO. THINK YOU CAN DO SOMETHIN' ABOUT IT?
ONE CAN BUT TRY! NOW, ANIMAL--WATCH THE WATCH! YOU ARE GETTING SLEEPY...SLEEEEPYYY...
SLEEEPPYYY...
EXCELLENT! NOW--WHEN I SNAP MY FINGERS YOU WILL AWAKEN...AND YOUR DRUMMING WILL BE ON FIRE! ON FIRE, I SAY! ONE...TWO...THREE...
ZZZZZZZ
SNAP
HNNGH?
AAAGHH! DRUMS! DRUMS!
YOU'RE COVERED, BUDDY!
REMARKABLE! A PHYSICAL MANIFESTATION OF A METAPHOR! IT'S BEEN YEARS SINCE I HAD ONE OF THOSE...
SPEAKING OF FIRED...!
THIS ANY GOOD TO US, RIZZO?
HMM... NOT BAD. PUT IT WITH THE STASH.
NEXT:
MUPPET LABS

AND NOW OVER TO... MUPPET LABS

WHERE THE FUTURE IS BEING MADE TODAY!

GREETINGS, SCIENCE LOVERS! I AM DOCTOR BUNSEN HONEYDEW, AND BEHIND ME, MAKING SOME MINOR ADJUSTMENTS TO OUR EQUIPMENT, IS MY ASSISTANT, BEAKER.

MEEP.

TODAY WE SHALL BE DEMONSTRATING A REVOLUTIONARY NEW TECHNIQUE FOR ENHANCING SOCIAL APTITUDE!

WE HAVE ALREADY TRIED IT WITH GREAT SUCCESS ON THE ESTEEMED DRUMMER FOR THE ELECTRIC MAYHEM BAND, ANIMAL!

SAY HELLO, ANIMAL.

HALL-LO A-NI-MAL.

THE PROCEDURE MUST BE REPEATED DAILY IN ORDER FOR ITS EFFECTS FULLY TO TAKE HOLD! SIMPLY PUT, THIS DEVICE SIPHONS AWAY A PORTION OF BEAKER'S HIGHER BRAIN ACTIVITY...

M-MEEP!

...WHICH IS THEN TRANSFERRED THROUGH THESE TUBES...

...AND DISTILLED INTO A SMALL PILL, WHICH THE SUBJECT--IN OUR CASE, MISTER ANIMAL-- MUST THEN SWALLOW, ONCE DAILY, AFTER MEALS!

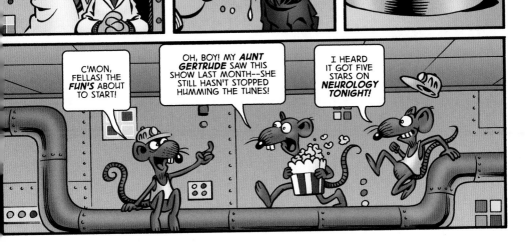

C'MON, FELLAS! THE FUN'S ABOUT TO START!

OH, BOY! MY AUNT GERTRUDE SAW THIS SHOW LAST MONTH--SHE STILL HASN'T STOPPED HUMMING THE TUNES!

I HEARD IT GOT FIVE STARS ON NEUROLOGY TONIGHT!

VERY WELL--TIME WE GOT **STARTED! READY,** BEAKER?

EXCELLENT.

M-MEEEEP...

LET SCIENCE COMMENCE!

FZZAPP

MEEP! MEEP! MEEP! MEEP! MUH-MEEEEEP!

ATTABOY, BEAKER! **GIVE IT SOME MEEP!**

FIVE BUCKS SAYS HE **FAINTS** THIS TIME.

DEAL!

OH, YES! BEAKER, MY BOY, YOU'VE **DONE IT AGAIN!** FIVE MILLIGRAMS OF PURE DISTILLED **CIVILIZATION** COMING DOWN THE PIPE!

AAAAND... THERE'S YOUR **DOSE FOR TODAY,** MISTER ANIMAL.

NIIIICE.

MEEP MEEP MEEP

CHEER UP, OLD CHUM! WHY, **YESTERDAY** YOUR REMARKABLE BRAIN EFFECTED A COMPLETE RECOVERY IN A MERE **SEVEN HOURS.**

AND YOU KNOW THE BEST PART OF ALL...?

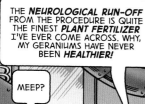

THE **NEUROLOGICAL RUN-OFF** FROM THE PROCEDURE IS QUITE THE FINEST **PLANT FERTILIZER** I'VE EVER COME ACROSS. WHY, MY GERANIUMS HAVE NEVER BEEN **HEALTHIER!**

MEEP?

SLUUURPP

THERE WE GO, MY LITTLE BEAUTIES!

PSSHT PSSHT

MMM! YOU KNOW, ME AM FEELING SMARTER ALREADY.

WHAT AM "FISH"?

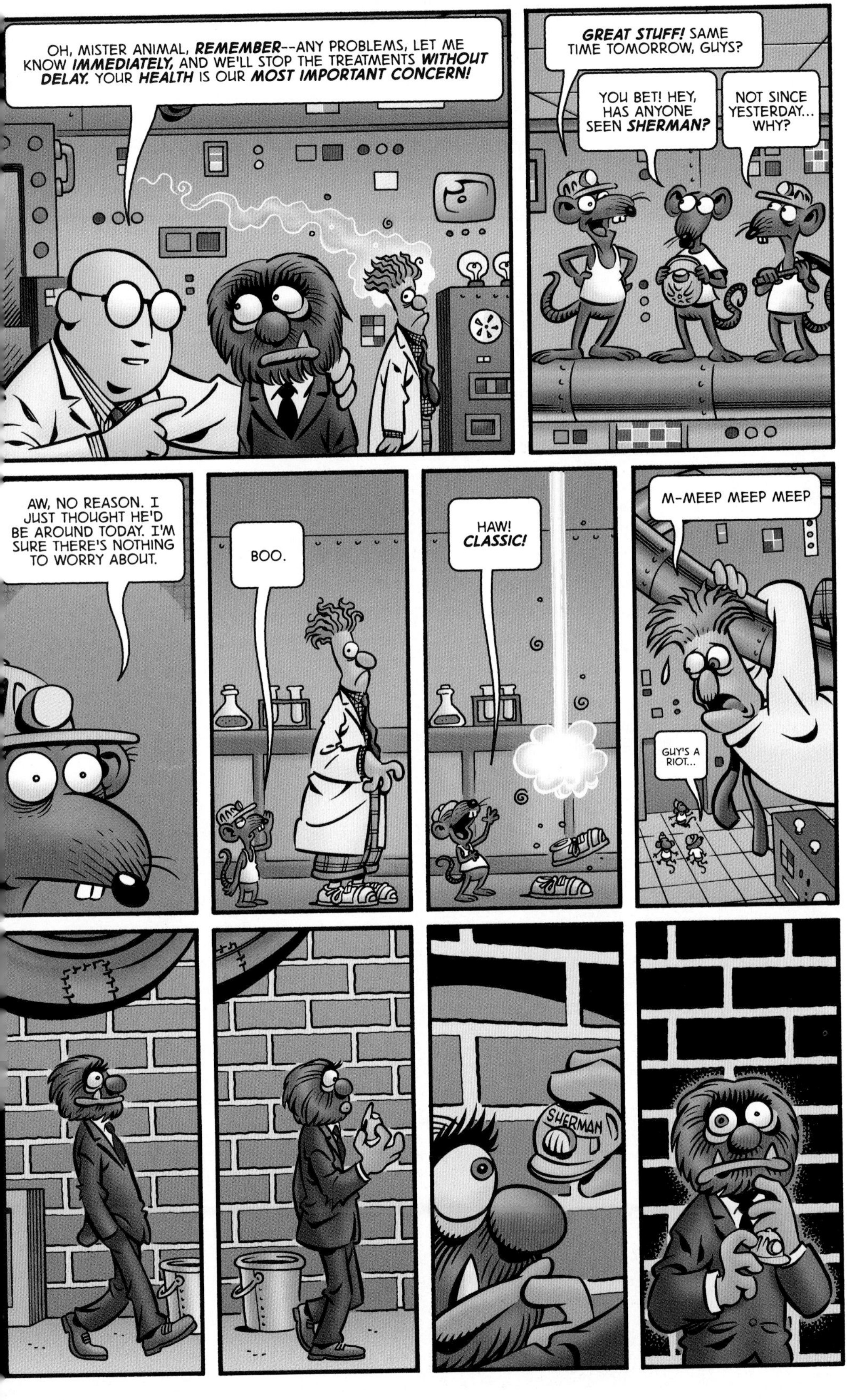
OH, MISTER ANIMAL, **REMEMBER**--ANY PROBLEMS, LET ME KNOW **IMMEDIATELY,** AND WE'LL STOP THE TREATMENTS **WITHOUT DELAY.** YOUR **HEALTH** IS OUR **MOST IMPORTANT CONCERN!**
GREAT STUFF! SAME TIME TOMORROW, GUYS?
YOU BET! HEY, HAS ANYONE SEEN **SHERMAN?**
NOT SINCE YESTERDAY... WHY?
AW, NO REASON. I JUST THOUGHT HE'D BE AROUND TODAY. I'M SURE THERE'S NOTHING TO WORRY ABOUT.
BOO.
HAW! **CLASSIC!**
M-MEEP MEEP MEEP
GUY'S A RIOT...
SHERMAN

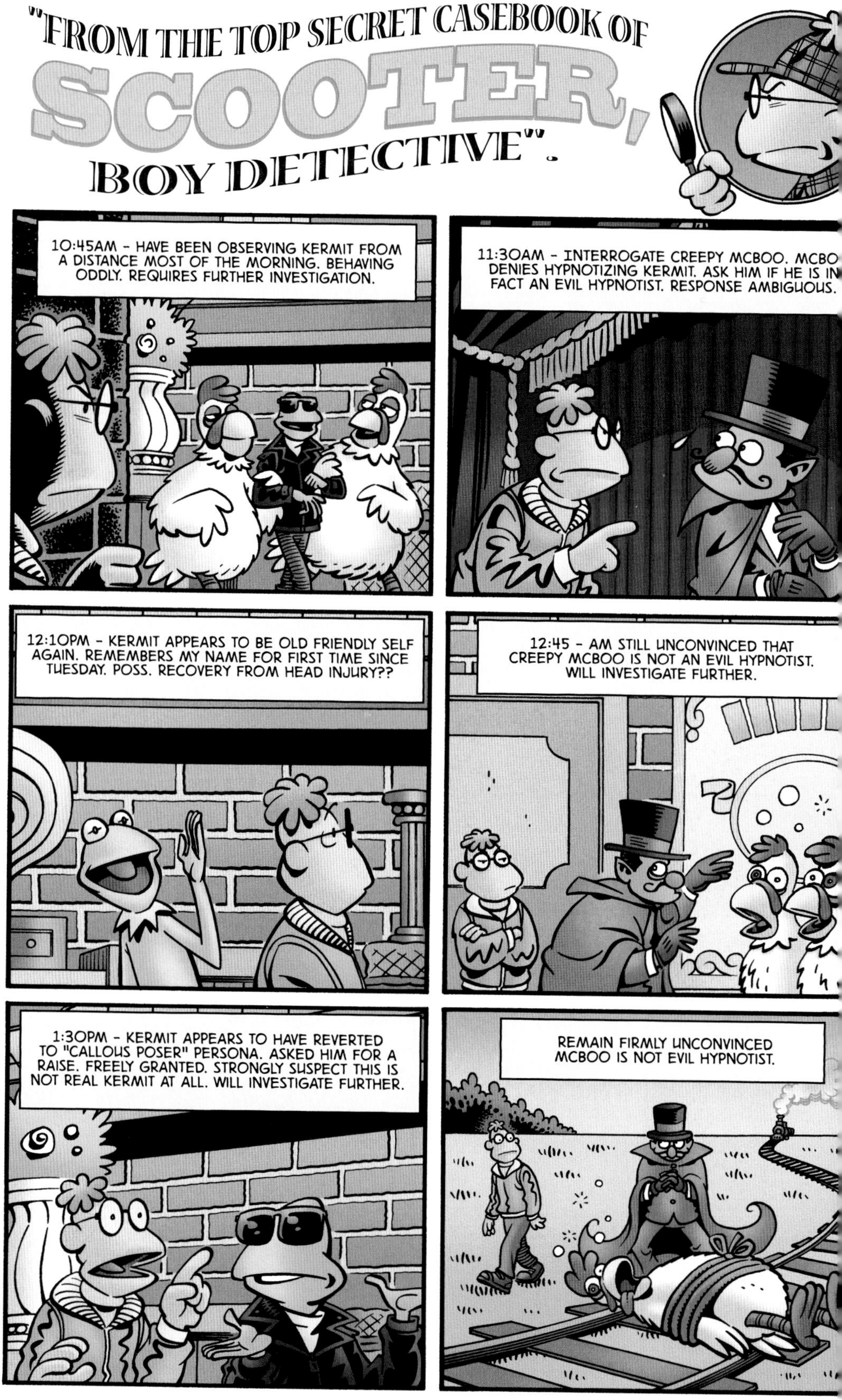
"FROM THE TOP SECRET CASEBOOK OF
SCOOTER,
BOY DETECTIVE".
10:45AM - HAVE BEEN OBSERVING KERMIT FROM A DISTANCE MOST OF THE MORNING. BEHAVING ODDLY. REQUIRES FURTHER INVESTIGATION.
11:30AM - INTERROGATE CREEPY MCBOO. MCBO DENIES HYPNOTIZING KERMIT. ASK HIM IF HE IS IN FACT AN EVIL HYPNOTIST. RESPONSE AMBIGUOUS.
12:10PM - KERMIT APPEARS TO BE OLD FRIENDLY SELF AGAIN. REMEMBERS MY NAME FOR FIRST TIME SINCE TUESDAY. POSS. RECOVERY FROM HEAD INJURY??
12:45 - AM STILL UNCONVINCED THAT CREEPY MCBOO IS NOT AN EVIL HYPNOTIST. WILL INVESTIGATE FURTHER.
1:30PM - KERMIT APPEARS TO HAVE REVERTED TO "CALLOUS POSER" PERSONA. ASKED HIM FOR A RAISE. FREELY GRANTED. STRONGLY SUSPECT THIS IS NOT REAL KERMIT AT ALL. WILL INVESTIGATE FURTHER.
REMAIN FIRMLY UNCONVINCED MCBOO IS NOT EVIL HYPNOTIST.

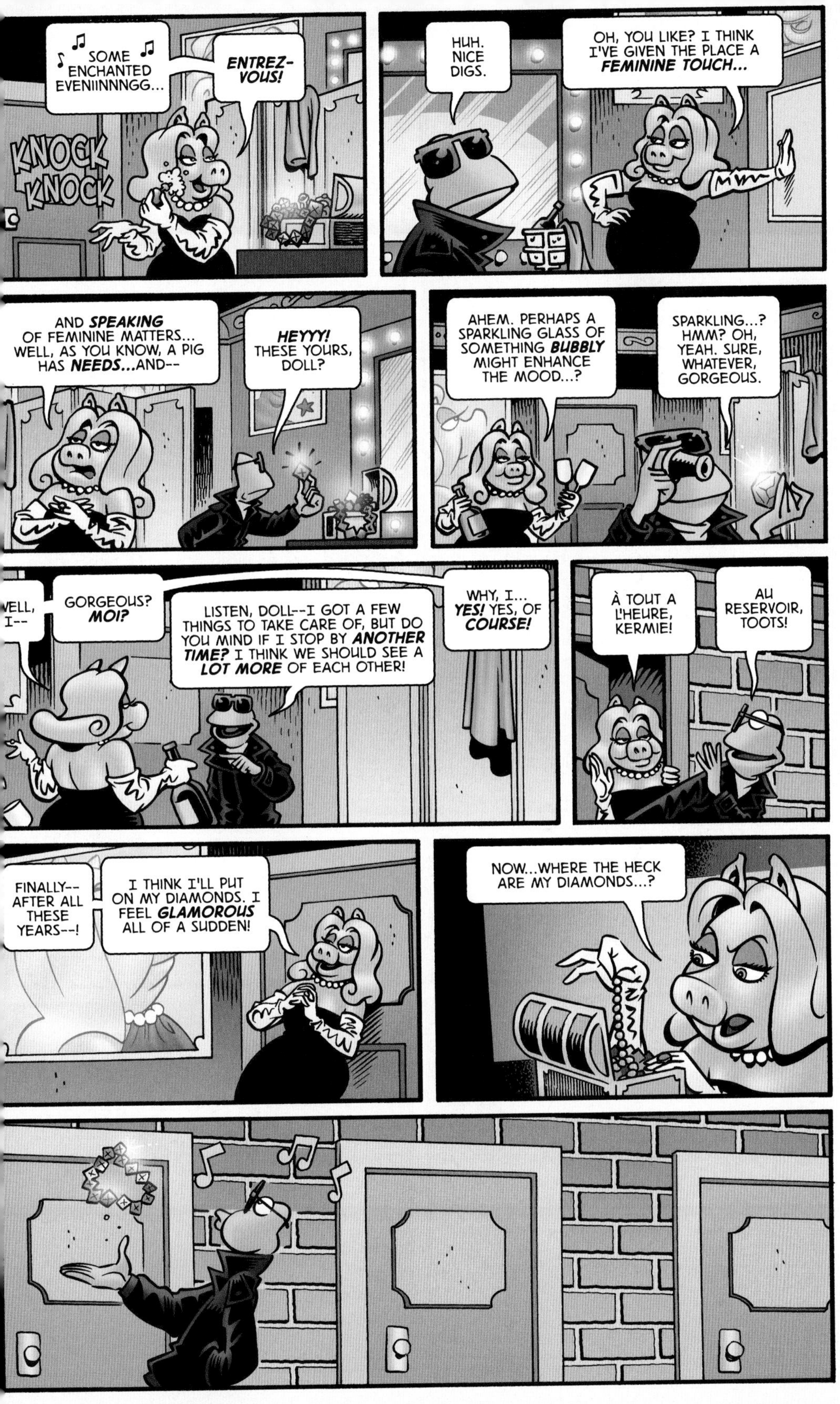
♪ SOME ENCHANTED EVENIINNNGG... ♫
KNOCK KNOCK
ENTREZ-VOUS!
HUH. NICE DIGS.
OH, YOU LIKE? I THINK I'VE GIVEN THE PLACE A FEMININE TOUCH...
AND SPEAKING OF FEMININE MATTERS... WELL, AS YOU KNOW, A PIG HAS NEEDS...AND--
HEYYY! THESE YOURS, DOLL?
AHEM. PERHAPS A SPARKLING GLASS OF SOMETHING BUBBLY MIGHT ENHANCE THE MOOD...?
SPARKLING...? HMM? OH, YEAH. SURE, WHATEVER, GORGEOUS.
WELL, I--
GORGEOUS? MOI?
LISTEN, DOLL--I GOT A FEW THINGS TO TAKE CARE OF, BUT DO YOU MIND IF I STOP BY ANOTHER TIME? I THINK WE SHOULD SEE A LOT MORE OF EACH OTHER!
WHY, I... YES! YES, OF COURSE!
À TOUT A L'HEURE, KERMIE!
AU RESERVOIR, TOOTS!
FINALLY--AFTER ALL THESE YEARS--!
I THINK I'LL PUT ON MY DIAMONDS. I FEEL GLAMOROUS ALL OF A SUDDEN!
NOW...WHERE THE HECK ARE MY DIAMONDS...?

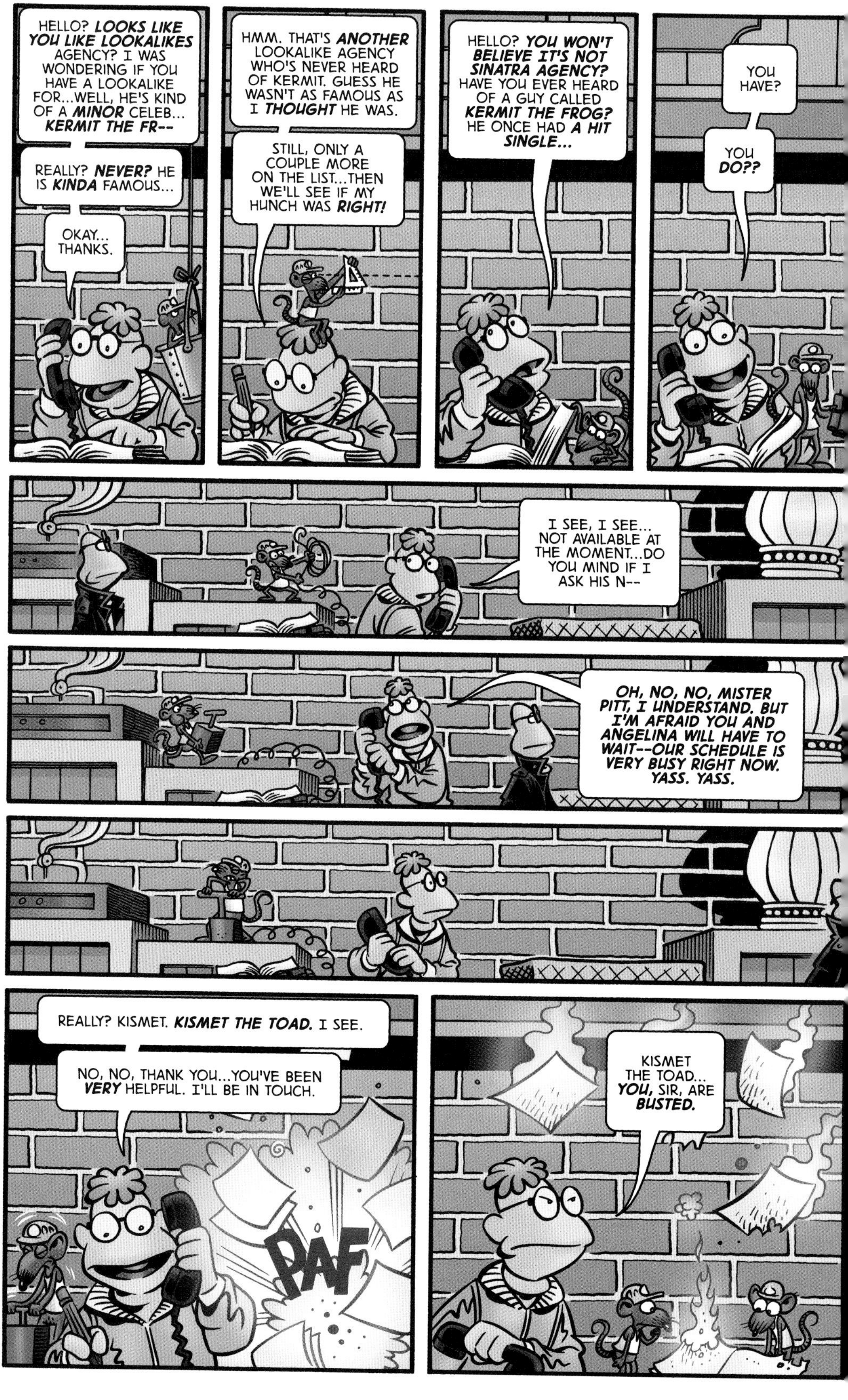
HELLO? LOOKS LIKE YOU LIKE LOOKALIKES AGENCY? I WAS WONDERING IF YOU HAVE A LOOKALIKE FOR...WELL, HE'S KIND OF A MINOR CELEB... KERMIT THE FR--
REALLY? NEVER? HE IS KINDA FAMOUS...
OKAY... THANKS.
HMM. THAT'S ANOTHER LOOKALIKE AGENCY WHO'S NEVER HEARD OF KERMIT. GUESS HE WASN'T AS FAMOUS AS I THOUGHT HE WAS.
STILL, ONLY A COUPLE MORE ON THE LIST...THEN WE'LL SEE IF MY HUNCH WAS RIGHT!
HELLO? YOU WON'T BELIEVE IT'S NOT SINATRA AGENCY? HAVE YOU EVER HEARD OF A GUY CALLED KERMIT THE FROG? HE ONCE HAD A HIT SINGLE...
YOU HAVE?
YOU DO??
I SEE, I SEE... NOT AVAILABLE AT THE MOMENT...DO YOU MIND IF I ASK HIS N--
OH, NO, NO, MISTER PITT, I UNDERSTAND. BUT I'M AFRAID YOU AND ANGELINA WILL HAVE TO WAIT--OUR SCHEDULE IS VERY BUSY RIGHT NOW. YASS. YASS.
REALLY? KISMET. KISMET THE TOAD. I SEE.
NO, NO, THANK YOU...YOU'VE BEEN VERY HELPFUL. I'LL BE IN TOUCH.
PAF
KISMET THE TOAD... YOU, SIR, ARE BUSTED.

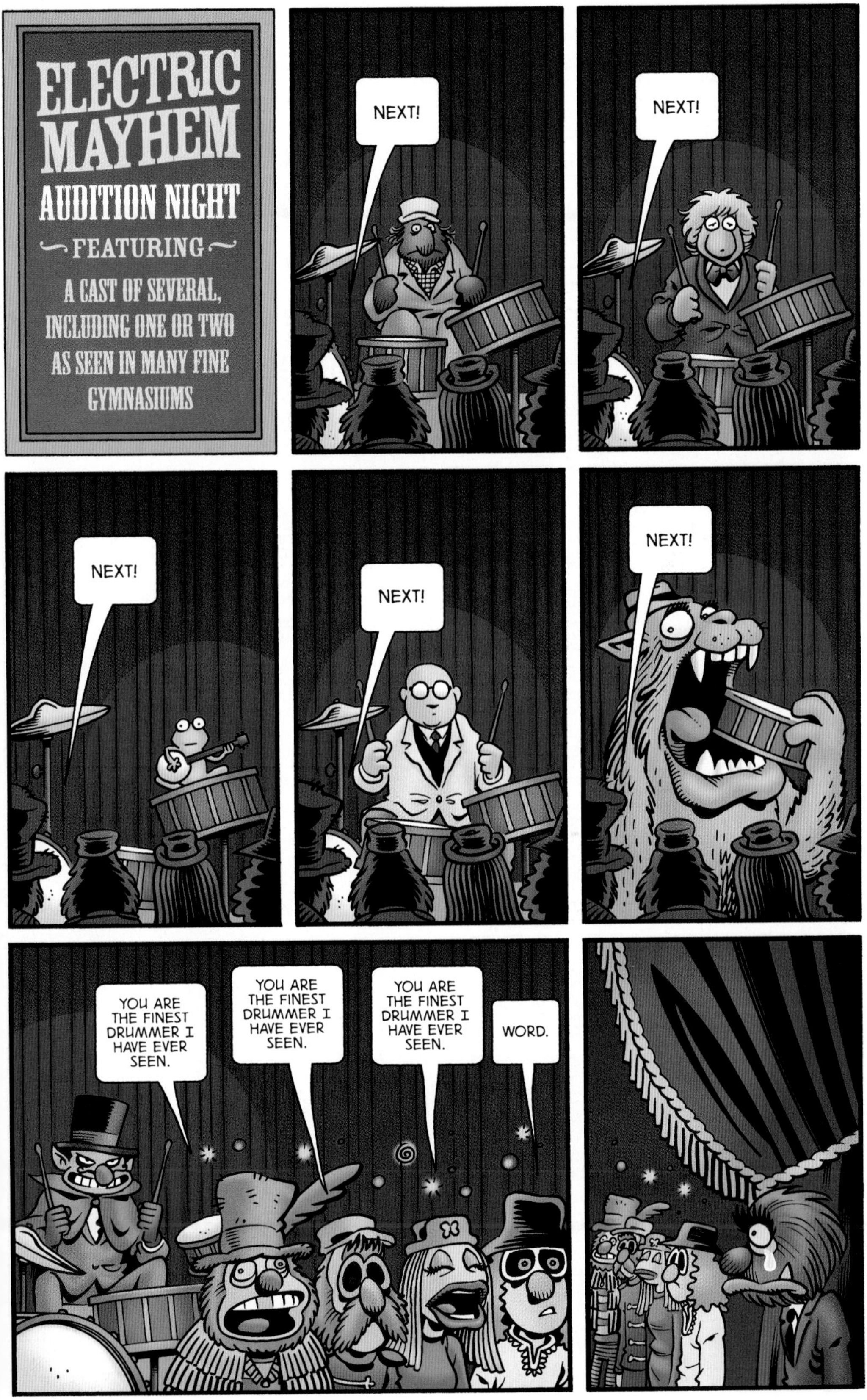
ELECTRIC MAYHEM
AUDITION NIGHT
FEATURING
A CAST OF SEVERAL, INCLUDING ONE OR TWO AS SEEN IN MANY FINE GYMNASIUMS
NEXT!
NEXT!
NEXT!
NEXT!
NEXT!
YOU ARE THE FINEST DRUMMER I HAVE EVER SEEN.
YOU ARE THE FINEST DRUMMER I HAVE EVER SEEN.
YOU ARE THE FINEST DRUMMER I HAVE EVER SEEN.
WORD.

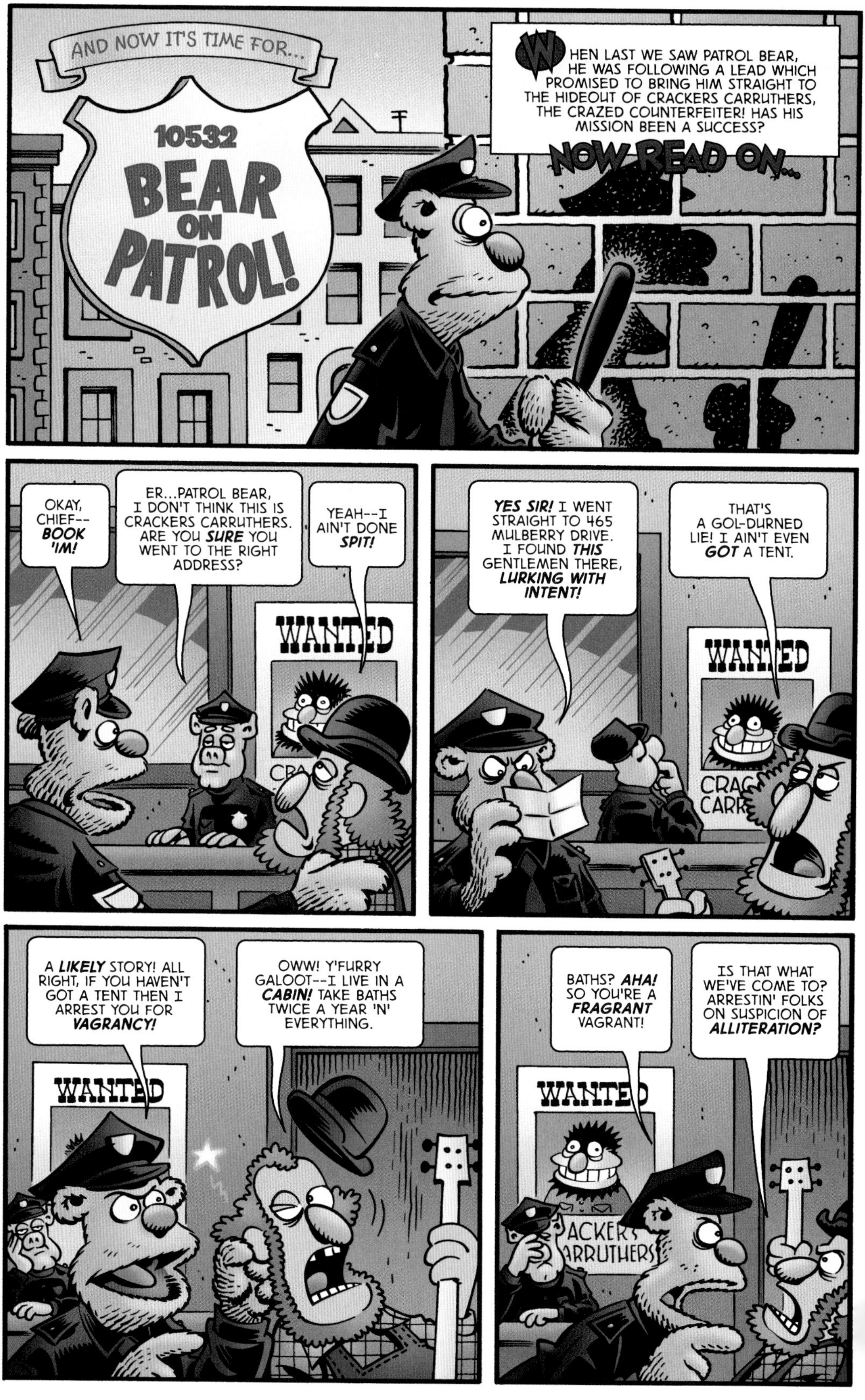
AND NOW IT'S TIME FOR...
10532
BEAR ON PATROL!
WHEN LAST WE SAW PATROL BEAR, HE WAS FOLLOWING A LEAD WHICH PROMISED TO BRING HIM STRAIGHT TO THE HIDEOUT OF CRACKERS CARRUTHERS, THE CRAZED COUNTERFEITER! HAS HIS MISSION BEEN A SUCCESS?
NOW READ ON...
OKAY, CHIEF-- BOOK 'IM!
ER...PATROL BEAR, I DON'T THINK THIS IS CRACKERS CARRUTHERS. ARE YOU SURE YOU WENT TO THE RIGHT ADDRESS?
YEAH--I AIN'T DONE SPIT!
WANTED
YES SIR! I WENT STRAIGHT TO 465 MULBERRY DRIVE. I FOUND THIS GENTLEMEN THERE, LURKING WITH INTENT!
THAT'S A GOL-DURNED LIE! I AIN'T EVEN GOT A TENT.
WANTED
A LIKELY STORY! ALL RIGHT, IF YOU HAVEN'T GOT A TENT THEN I ARREST YOU FOR VAGRANCY!
OWW! Y'FURRY GALOOT--I LIVE IN A CABIN! TAKE BATHS TWICE A YEAR 'N' EVERYTHING.
WANTED
BATHS? AHA! SO YOU'RE A FRAGRANT VAGRANT!
IS THAT WHAT WE'VE COME TO? ARRESTIN' FOLKS ON SUSPICION OF ALLITERATION?
WANTED

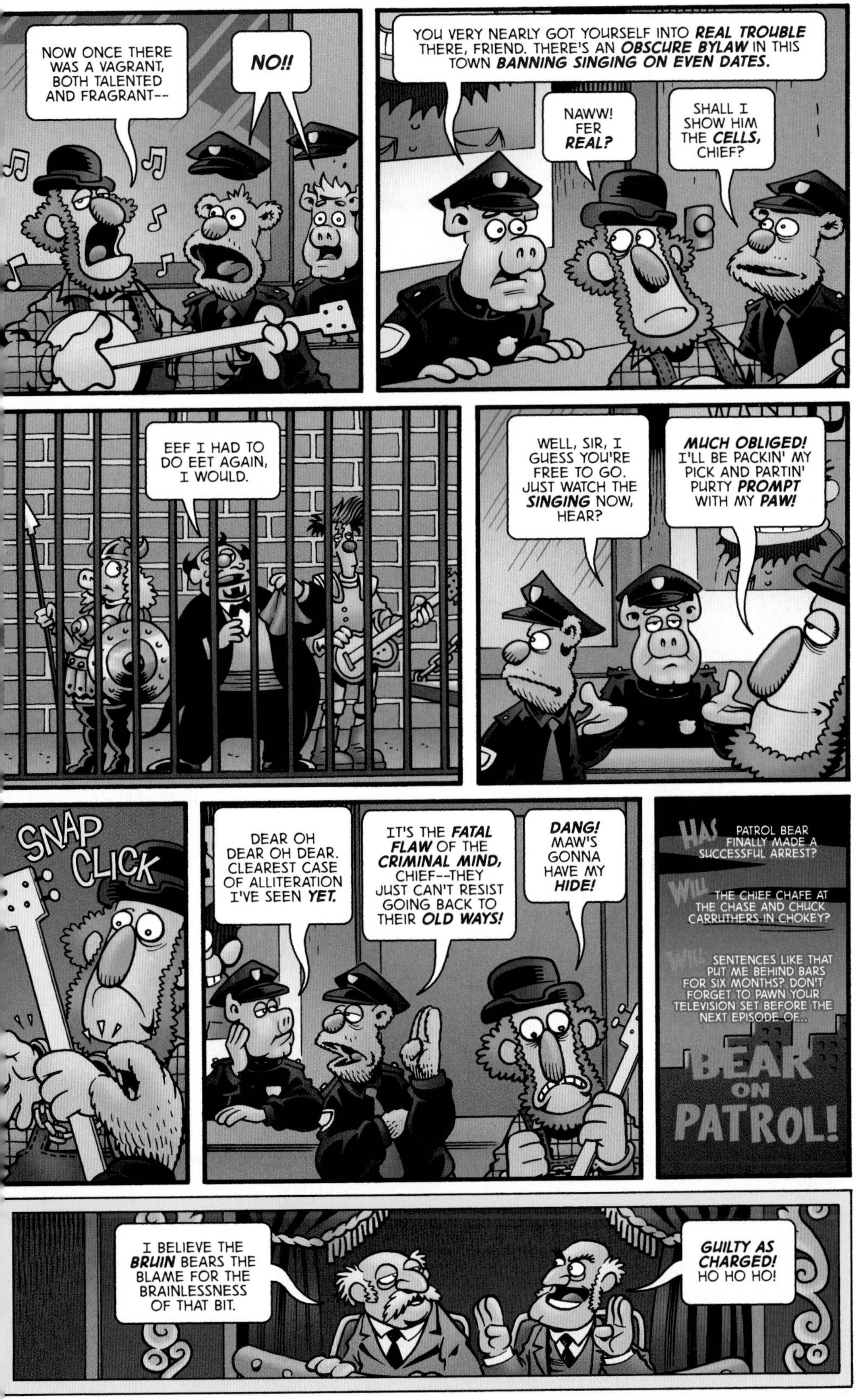
NOW ONCE THERE WAS A VAGRANT, BOTH TALENTED AND FRAGRANT--
NO!!
YOU VERY NEARLY GOT YOURSELF INTO REAL TROUBLE THERE, FRIEND. THERE'S AN OBSCURE BYLAW IN THIS TOWN BANNING SINGING ON EVEN DATES.
NAWW! FER REAL?
SHALL I SHOW HIM THE CELLS, CHIEF?
EEF I HAD TO DO EET AGAIN, I WOULD.
WELL, SIR, I GUESS YOU'RE FREE TO GO. JUST WATCH THE SINGING NOW, HEAR?
MUCH OBLIGED! I'LL BE PACKIN' MY PICK AND PARTIN' PURTY PROMPT WITH MY PAW!
SNAP
CLICK
DEAR OH DEAR OH DEAR. CLEAREST CASE OF ALLITERATION I'VE SEEN YET.
IT'S THE FATAL FLAW OF THE CRIMINAL MIND, CHIEF--THEY JUST CAN'T RESIST GOING BACK TO THEIR OLD WAYS!
DANG! MAW'S GONNA HAVE MY HIDE!
HAS PATROL BEAR FINALLY MADE A SUCCESSFUL ARREST?
WILL THE CHIEF CHAFE AT THE CHASE AND CHUCK CARRUTHERS IN CHOKEY?
WILL SENTENCES LIKE THAT PUT ME BEHIND BARS FOR SIX MONTHS? DON'T FORGET TO PAWN YOUR TELEVISION SET BEFORE THE NEXT EPISODE OF...
BEAR ON PATROL!
I BELIEVE THE BRUIN BEARS THE BLAME FOR THE BRAINLESSNESS OF THAT BIT.
GUILTY AS CHARGED! HO HO HO!

SHERMAN? SHEERRR-MAANNN...
GREAT WORK, GUYS! MISTER MCCOY, YOU'D BETTER GO AND GET READY FOR YOUR NEXT NUMBER!
Y'MEAN THAT WEREN'T FOR REAL? AND HERE I WAS GONNA GIT MAH COUSINS TO BREAK ME OUT!
THEY'D HAVE DONE IT, TOO... RIGHT AFTER WE BROKE THEM OUT.
HEY, BOSS GUY--YOU HAVEN'T SEEN SHERMAN ANYWHERE, HAVE YOU?
ER...WHO'S SHERMAN, EXACTLY?
YOU KNOW...SHERMAN! RAT. ABOUT MY SIZE. LOOKS A BIT LIKE A RAT.
OOO-KAYYY...
ALL WE CAN FIND IS THIS PIECE OF CLOTH NEXT TO HIS LOCKER!
HIS LOCKER? YOU RATS HAVE YOUR OWN LOCKERS?
LOCKER, SOUP CAN... IT'S A CLUE, AIN'T IT?
YOU KNOW...COME TO THINK OF IT, I DID SEE SOME THREADS SNAGGED ON A SHELF IN THE STOREROOM...
WHAT ARE WE WAITING FOR? TO THE STOREROOM, FLIPPER!
SHERMAN? SHEERRRMAANN...
MMPHH! MMMPPHH!
SHERMAN! YOU'RE OKAY!
POOR LITTLE GUY! THIS IS VERY, VERY STRANGE...
IT WAS THAT HAIRY FELLA! HE GRABBED ME AND TIED ME UP-- BROUGHT ME DOWN HERE AND... AND...
WHAT? WHAT??
H-HE...HE FORCED ME TO LISTEN TO THE DRUMS.
SHERM

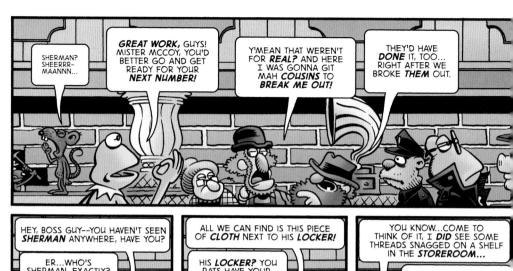

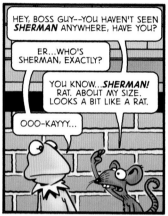

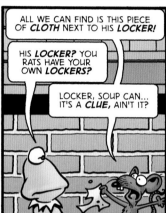

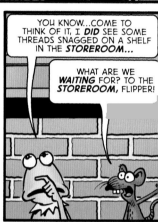

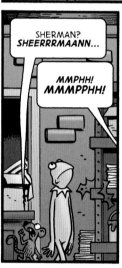

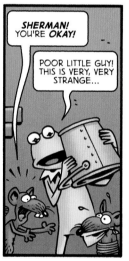

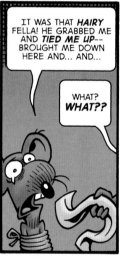

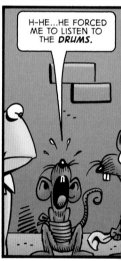

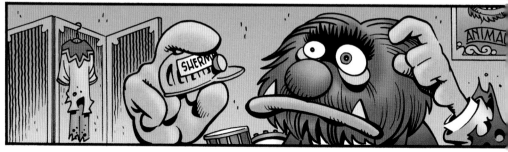

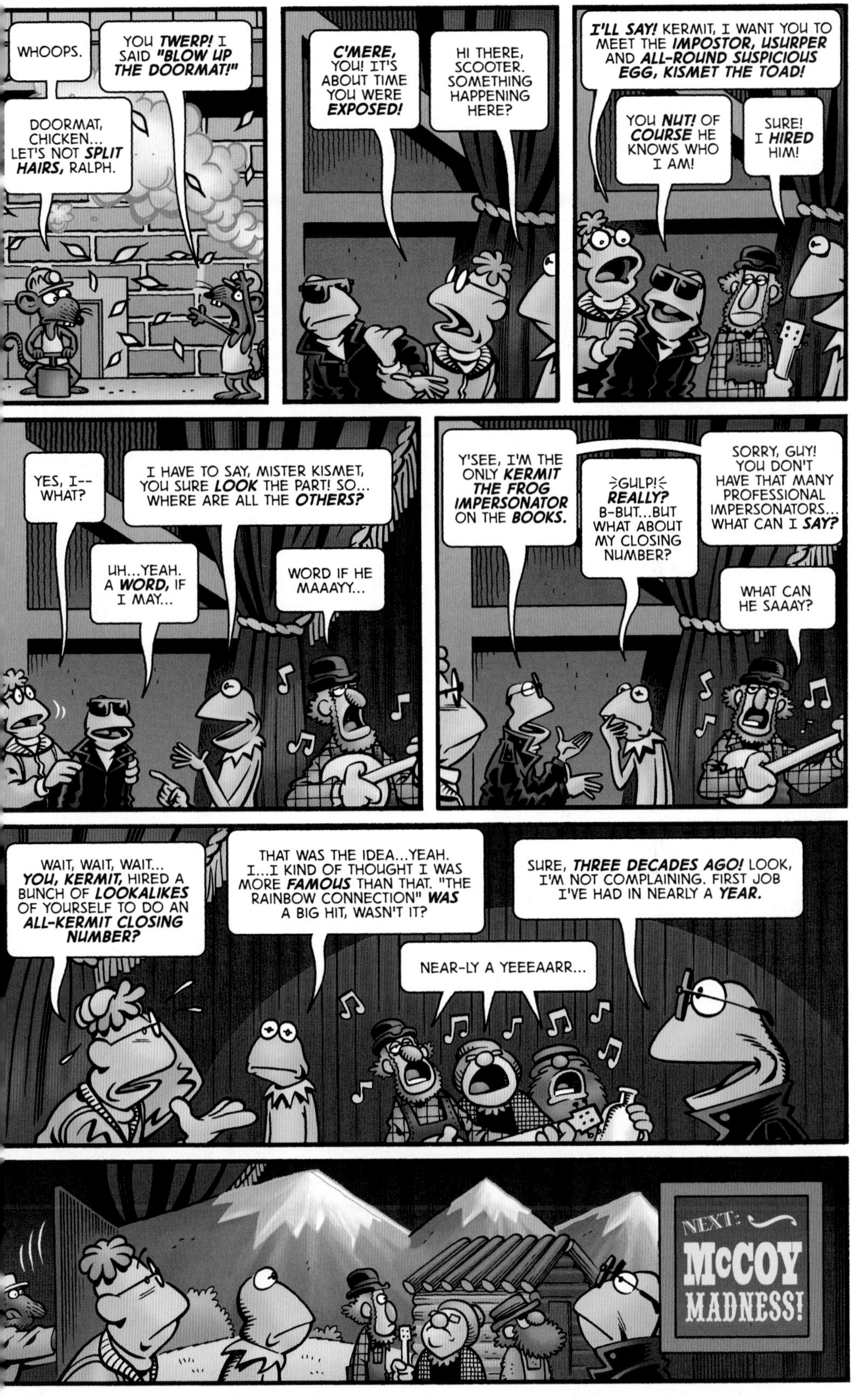

WHOOPS.
YOU TWERP! I SAID "BLOW UP THE DOORMAT!"
DOORMAT, CHICKEN... LET'S NOT SPLIT HAIRS, RALPH.
C'MERE, YOU! IT'S ABOUT TIME YOU WERE EXPOSED!
HI THERE, SCOOTER. SOMETHING HAPPENING HERE?
I'LL SAY! KERMIT, I WANT YOU TO MEET THE IMPOSTOR, USURPER AND ALL-ROUND SUSPICIOUS EGG, KISMET THE TOAD!
YOU NUT! OF COURSE HE KNOWS WHO I AM!
SURE! I HIRED HIM!
YES, I-- WHAT?
I HAVE TO SAY, MISTER KISMET, YOU SURE LOOK THE PART! SO... WHERE ARE ALL THE OTHERS?
UH...YEAH. A WORD, IF I MAY...
WORD IF HE MAAAYY...
Y'SEE, I'M THE ONLY KERMIT THE FROG IMPERSONATOR ON THE BOOKS.
GULP! REALLY? B-BUT...BUT WHAT ABOUT MY CLOSING NUMBER?
SORRY, GUY! YOU DON'T HAVE THAT MANY PROFESSIONAL IMPERSONATORS... WHAT CAN I SAY?
WHAT CAN HE SAAAY?
WAIT, WAIT, WAIT... YOU, KERMIT, HIRED A BUNCH OF LOOKALIKES OF YOURSELF TO DO AN ALL-KERMIT CLOSING NUMBER?
THAT WAS THE IDEA...YEAH. I...I KIND OF THOUGHT I WAS MORE FAMOUS THAN THAT. "THE RAINBOW CONNECTION" WAS A BIG HIT, WASN'T IT?
SURE, THREE DECADES AGO! LOOK, I'M NOT COMPLAINING. FIRST JOB I'VE HAD IN NEARLY A YEAR.
NEAR-LY A YEEEAARR...
NEXT: McCOY MADNESS!

THE MCMUPPETS AND THE MCCOY

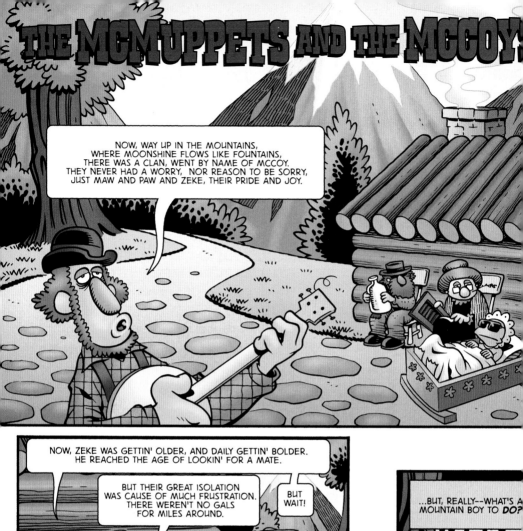

NOW, WAY UP IN THE MOUNTAINS,
WHERE MOONSHINE FLOWS LIKE FOUNTAINS,
THERE WAS A CLAN, WENT BY NAME OF MCCOY.
THEY NEVER HAD A WORRY, NOR REASON TO BE SORRY,
JUST MAW AND PAW AND ZEKE, THEIR PRIDE AND JOY.

NOW, ZEKE WAS GETTIN' OLDER, AND DAILY GETTIN' BOLDER.
HE REACHED THE AGE OF LOOKIN' FOR A MATE.

BUT THEIR GREAT ISOLATION
WAS CAUSE OF MUCH FRUSTRATION.
THERE WEREN'T NO GALS
FOR MILES AROUND.

BUT
WAIT!

...BUT, REALLY--WHAT'S A
MOUNTAIN BOY TO *DO?*

FOR WAY DOWN IN THE VALLEY
THERE LIVED A GAL NAMED SALLY,
THE OFFSPRING OF MCMUPPETS JEB AND SUE.
MCMUPPETS AND MCCOYS, SIR,
THEY FEUDED, MAN AND BOY, SIR...

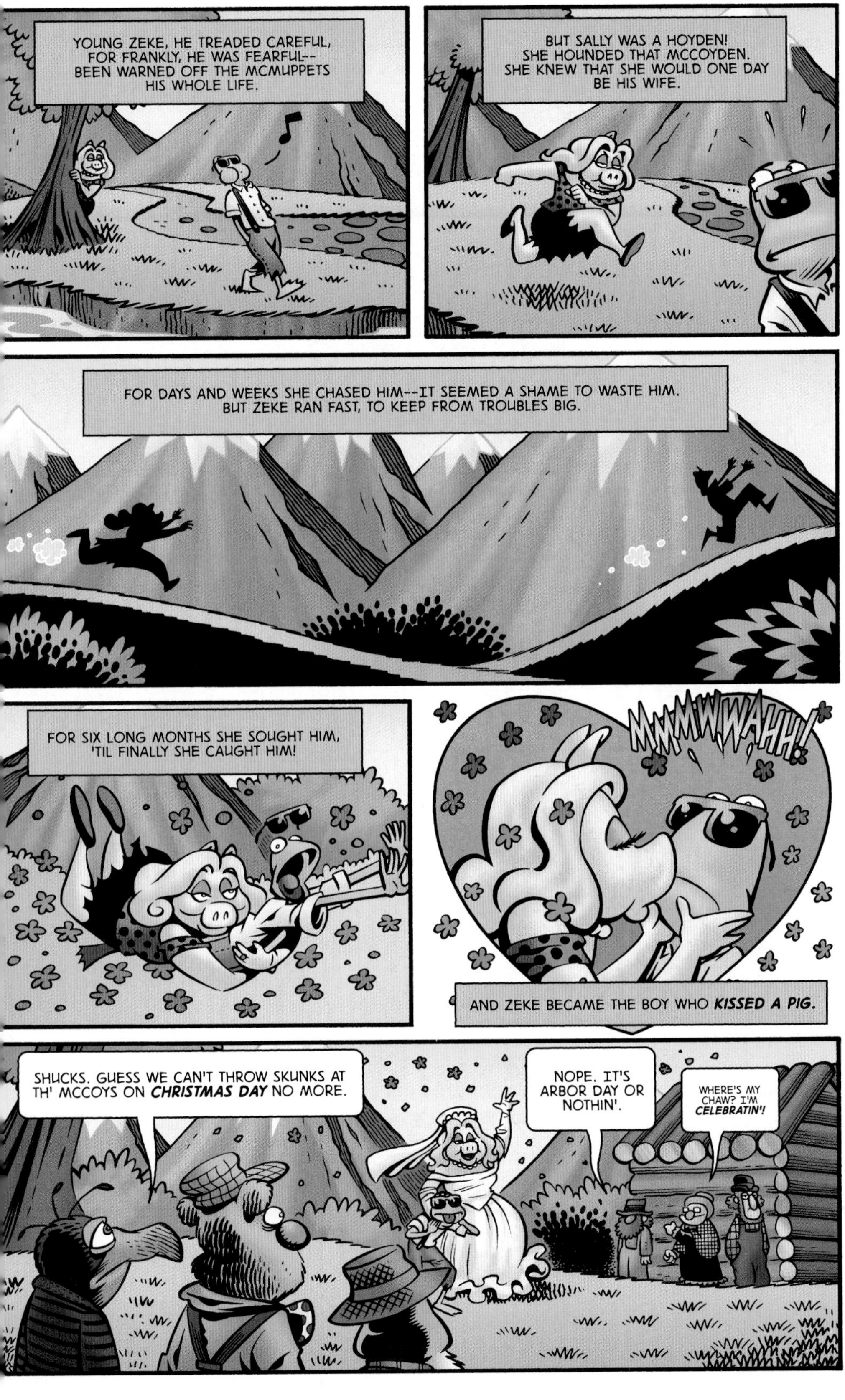
YOUNG ZEKE, HE TREADED CAREFUL, FOR FRANKLY, HE WAS FEARFUL-- BEEN WARNED OFF THE MCMUPPETS HIS WHOLE LIFE.
BUT SALLY WAS A HOYDEN! SHE HOUNDED THAT MCCOYDEN. SHE KNEW THAT SHE WOULD ONE DAY BE HIS WIFE.
FOR DAYS AND WEEKS SHE CHASED HIM--IT SEEMED A SHAME TO WASTE HIM. BUT ZEKE RAN FAST, TO KEEP FROM TROUBLES BIG.
FOR SIX LONG MONTHS SHE SOUGHT HIM, 'TIL FINALLY SHE CAUGHT HIM!
MMMWWAHH!
AND ZEKE BECAME THE BOY WHO *KISSED A PIG.*
SHUCKS. GUESS WE CAN'T THROW SKUNKS AT TH' MCCOYS ON *CHRISTMAS DAY* NO MORE.
NOPE. IT'S ARBOR DAY OR NOTHIN'.
WHERE'S MY CHAW? I'M *CELEBRATIN'!*

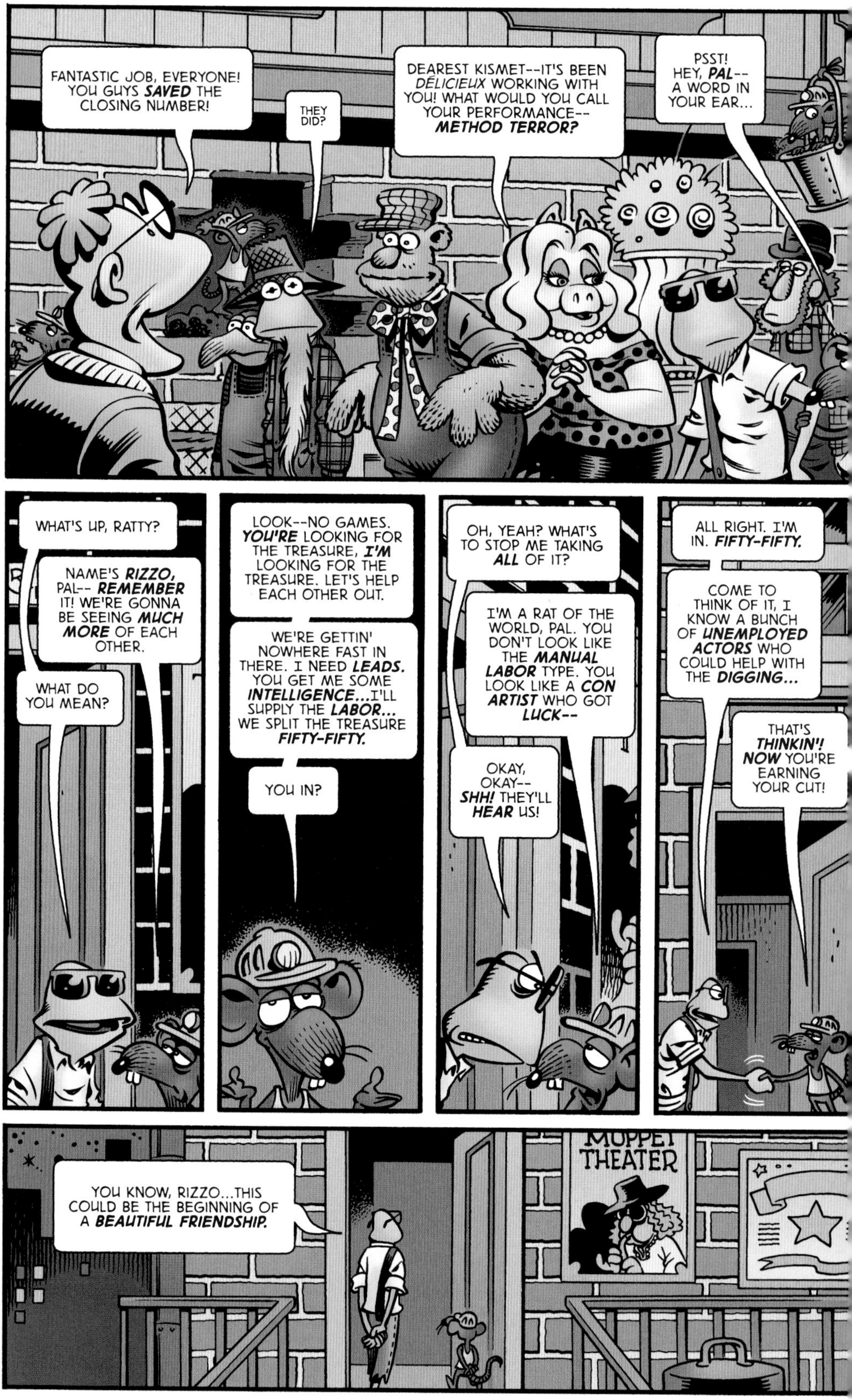
FANTASTIC JOB, EVERYONE! YOU GUYS **SAVED** THE CLOSING NUMBER!
THEY DID?
DEAREST KISMET--IT'S BEEN *DÉLICIEUX* WORKING WITH YOU! WHAT WOULD YOU CALL YOUR PERFORMANCE-- ***METHOD TERROR?***
PSST! HEY, **PAL**-- A WORD IN YOUR EAR...
WHAT'S UP, RATTY?
NAME'S ***RIZZO,*** PAL-- ***REMEMBER*** IT! WE'RE GONNA BE SEEING ***MUCH MORE*** OF EACH OTHER.
WHAT DO YOU MEAN?
LOOK--NO GAMES. ***YOU'RE*** LOOKING FOR THE TREASURE, ***I'M*** LOOKING FOR THE TREASURE. LET'S HELP EACH OTHER OUT.
WE'RE GETTIN' NOWHERE FAST IN THERE. I NEED ***LEADS.*** YOU GET ME SOME ***INTELLIGENCE...*** I'LL SUPPLY THE ***LABOR...*** WE SPLIT THE TREASURE ***FIFTY-FIFTY.***
YOU IN?
OH, YEAH? WHAT'S TO STOP ME TAKING ***ALL*** OF IT?
I'M A RAT OF THE WORLD, PAL. YOU DON'T LOOK LIKE THE ***MANUAL LABOR*** TYPE. YOU LOOK LIKE A ***CON ARTIST*** WHO GOT ***LUCK--***
OKAY, OKAY-- ***SHH!*** THEY'LL ***HEAR*** US!
ALL RIGHT. I'M IN. ***FIFTY-FIFTY.***
COME TO THINK OF IT, I KNOW A BUNCH OF ***UNEMPLOYED ACTORS*** WHO COULD HELP WITH THE ***DIGGING...***
THAT'S ***THINKIN'! NOW*** YOU'RE EARNING YOUR CUT!
MUPPET THEATER
YOU KNOW, RIZZO...THIS COULD BE THE BEGINNING OF A ***BEAUTIFUL FRIENDSHIP.***

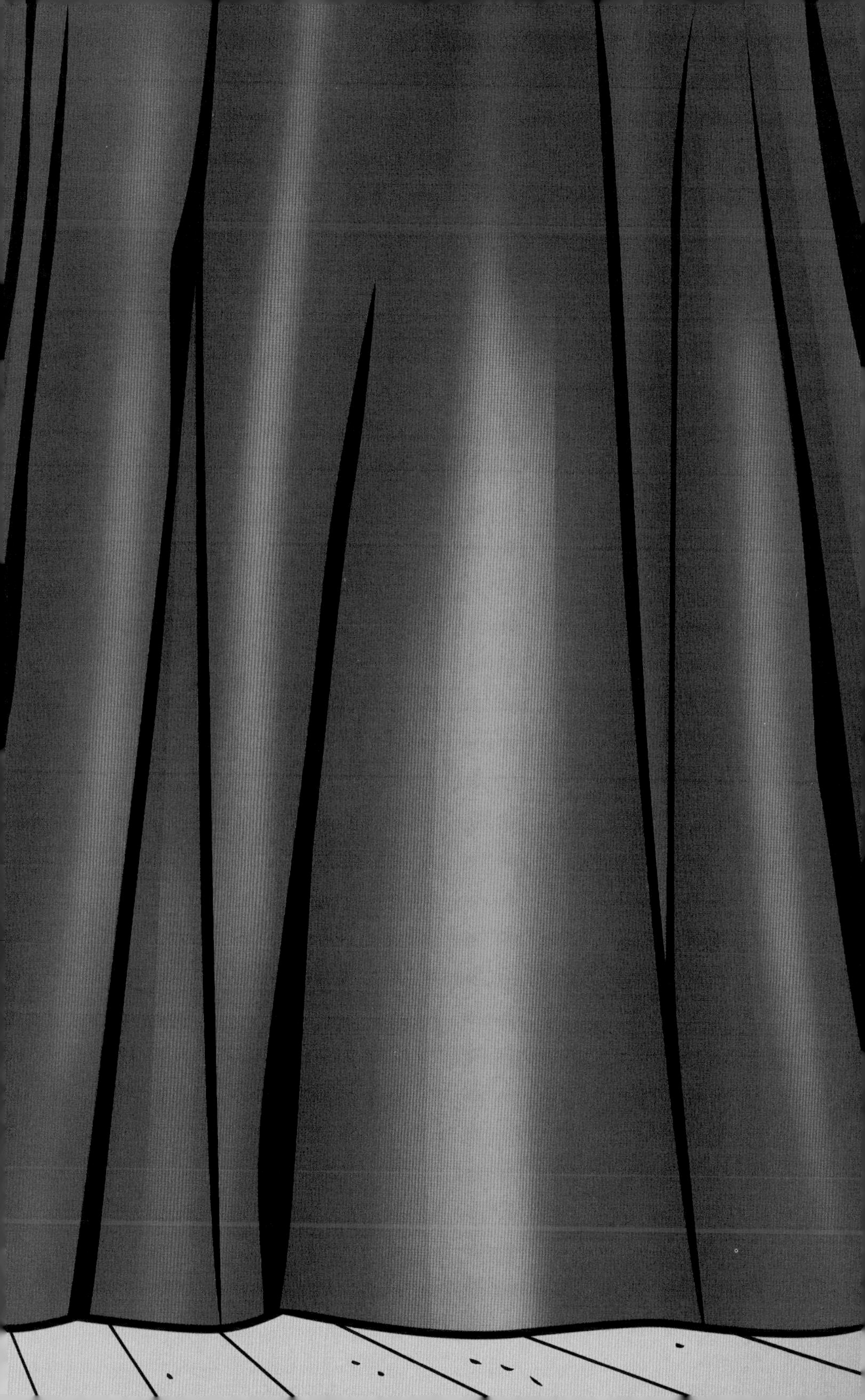

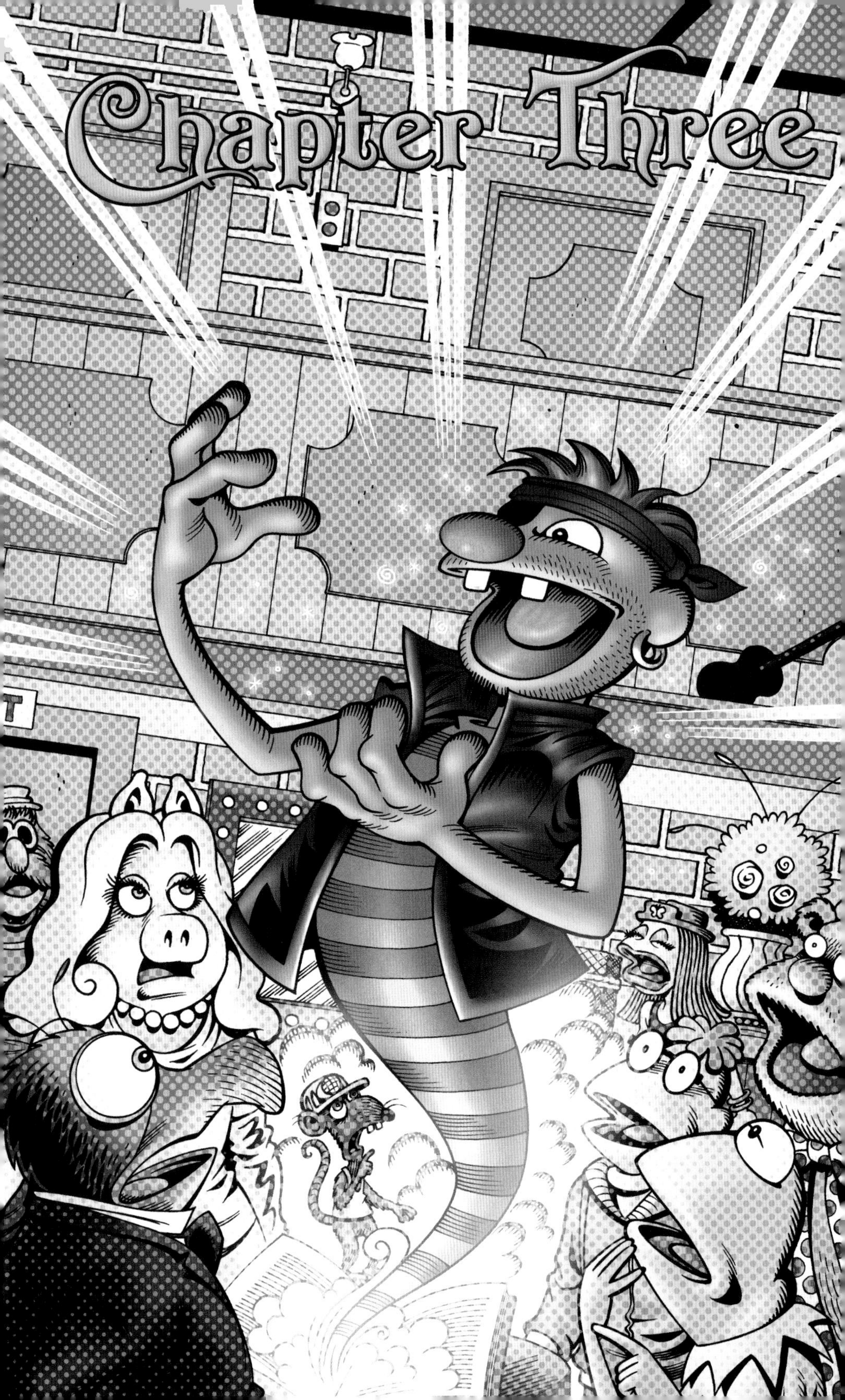
Chapter Three

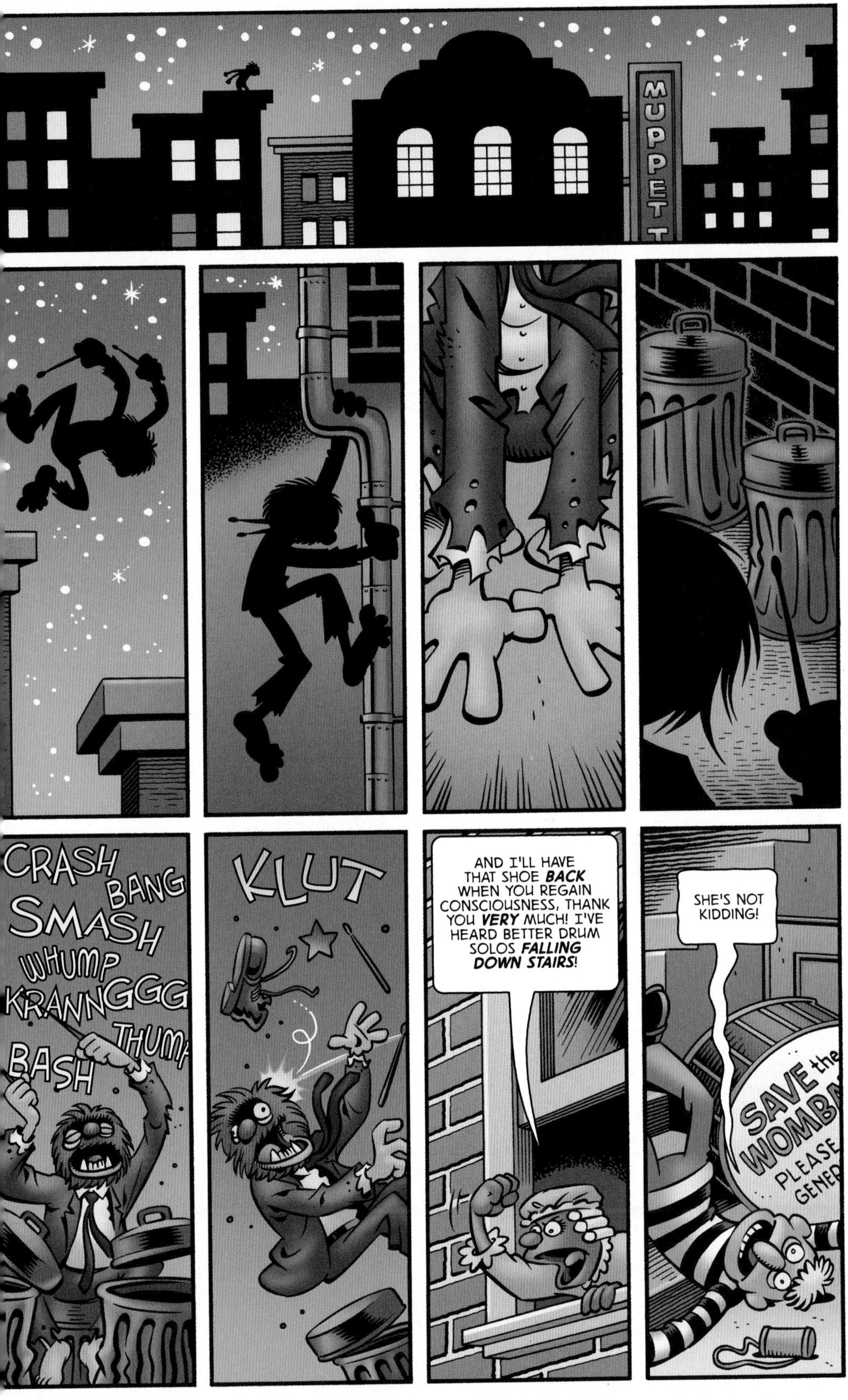

MUPPETT
CRASH
BANG
SMASH
WHUMP
KRANNGGG
THUM
BASH
KLUT
AND I'LL HAVE THAT SHOE BACK WHEN YOU REGAIN CONSCIOUSNESS, THANK YOU VERY MUCH! I'VE HEARD BETTER DRUM SOLOS FALLING DOWN STAIRS!
SHE'S NOT KIDDING!
SAVE the WOMB
PLEASE GENER

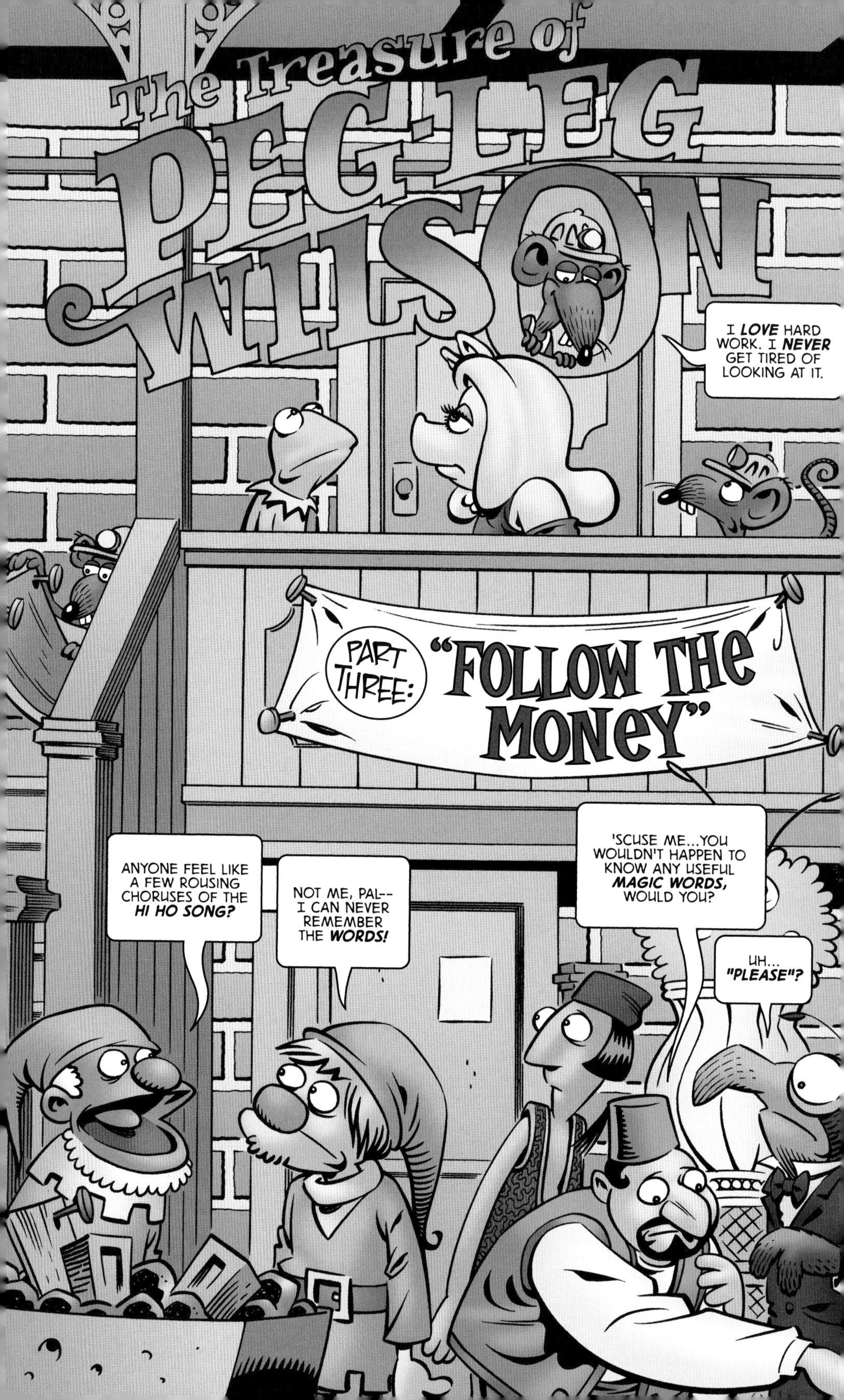
The Treasure of
PEG-LEG WILSON
I LOVE HARD WORK. I NEVER GET TIRED OF LOOKING AT IT.
PART THREE: "FOLLOW THE MONEY"
ANYONE FEEL LIKE A FEW ROUSING CHORUSES OF THE HI HO SONG?
NOT ME, PAL-- I CAN NEVER REMEMBER THE WORDS!
'SCUSE ME...YOU WOULDN'T HAPPEN TO KNOW ANY USEFUL MAGIC WORDS, WOULD YOU?
UH... "PLEASE"?

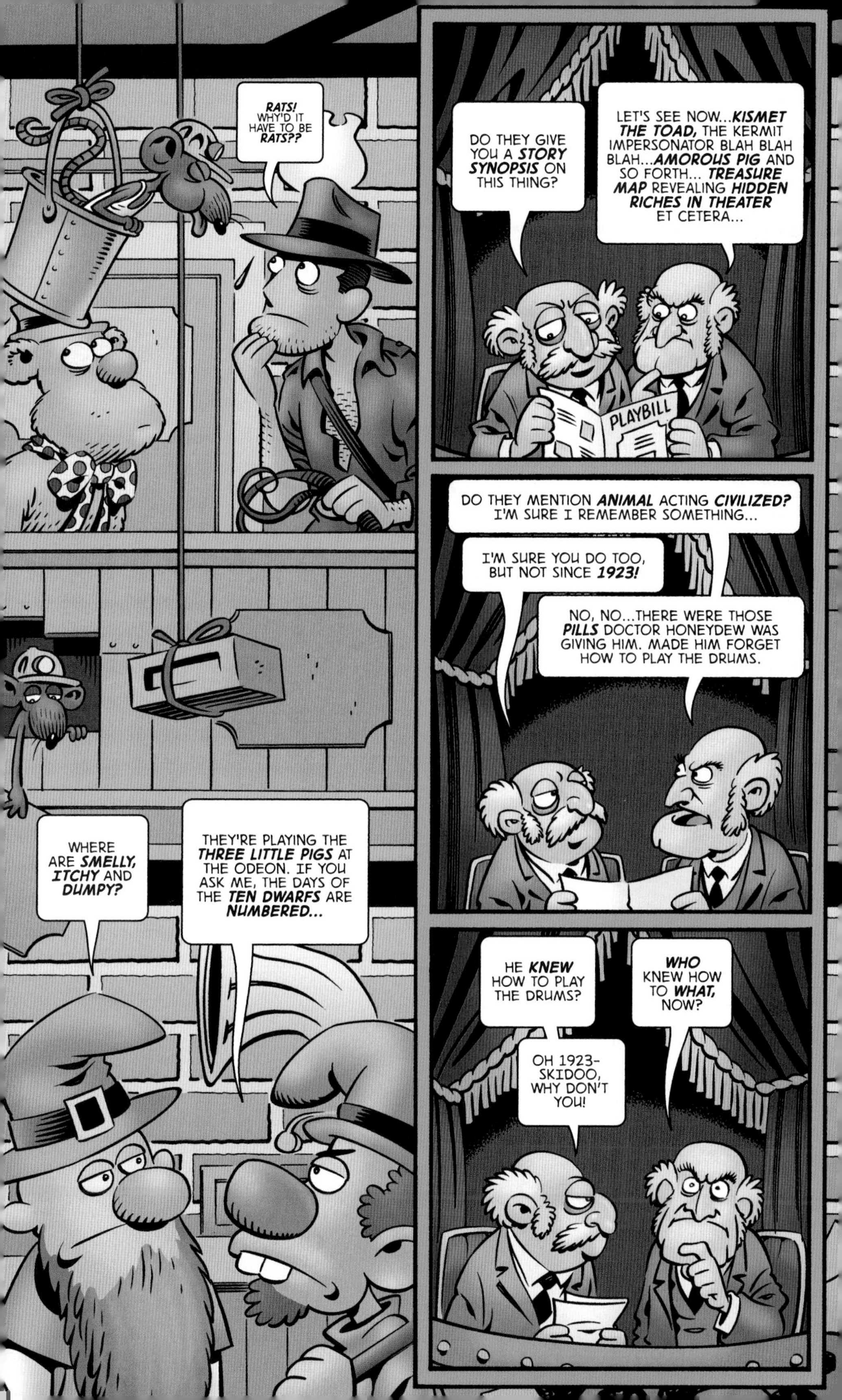
RATS! WHY'D IT HAVE TO BE RATS??
DO THEY GIVE YOU A STORY SYNOPSIS ON THIS THING?
LET'S SEE NOW...KISMET THE TOAD, THE KERMIT IMPERSONATOR BLAH BLAH BLAH...AMOROUS PIG AND SO FORTH... TREASURE MAP REVEALING HIDDEN RICHES IN THEATER ET CETERA...
PLAYBILL
DO THEY MENTION ANIMAL ACTING CIVILIZED? I'M SURE I REMEMBER SOMETHING...
I'M SURE YOU DO TOO, BUT NOT SINCE 1923!
NO, NO...THERE WERE THOSE PILLS DOCTOR HONEYDEW WAS GIVING HIM. MADE HIM FORGET HOW TO PLAY THE DRUMS.
WHERE ARE SMELLY, ITCHY AND DUMPY?
THEY'RE PLAYING THE THREE LITTLE PIGS AT THE ODEON. IF YOU ASK ME, THE DAYS OF THE TEN DWARFS ARE NUMBERED...
HE KNEW HOW TO PLAY THE DRUMS?
WHO KNEW HOW TO WHAT, NOW?
OH 1923-SKIDOO, WHY DON'T YOU!

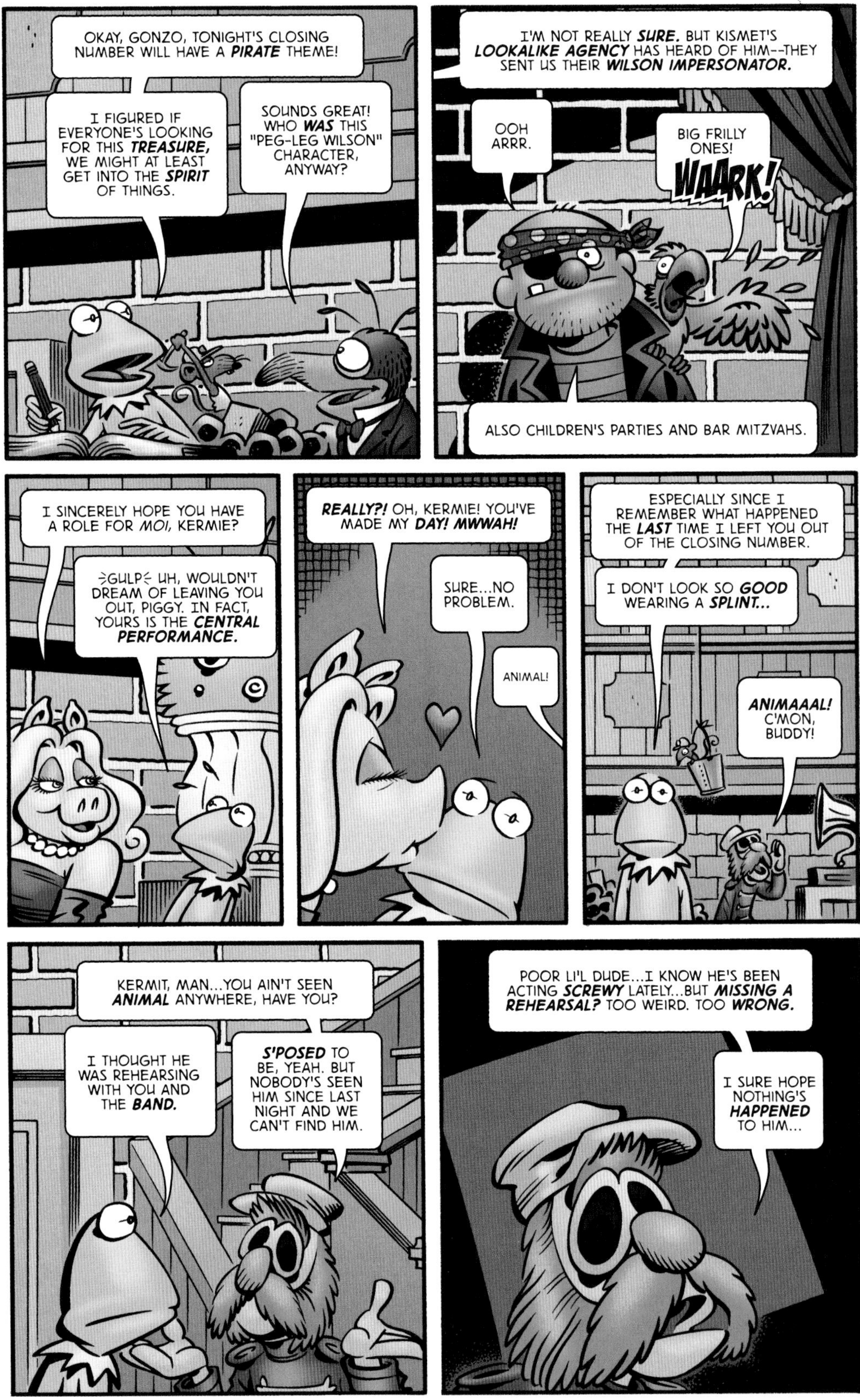

OKAY, GONZO, TONIGHT'S CLOSING NUMBER WILL HAVE A **PIRATE** THEME!
I FIGURED IF EVERYONE'S LOOKING FOR THIS **TREASURE,** WE MIGHT AT LEAST GET INTO THE **SPIRIT** OF THINGS.
SOUNDS GREAT! WHO **WAS** THIS "PEG-LEG WILSON" CHARACTER, ANYWAY?
I'M NOT REALLY **SURE.** BUT KISMET'S **LOOKALIKE AGENCY** HAS HEARD OF HIM--THEY SENT US THEIR **WILSON IMPERSONATOR.**
OOH ARRR.
BIG FRILLY ONES!
WAARK!
ALSO CHILDREN'S PARTIES AND BAR MITZVAHS.
I SINCERELY HOPE YOU HAVE A ROLE FOR *MOI,* KERMIE?
GULP UH, WOULDN'T DREAM OF LEAVING YOU OUT, PIGGY. IN FACT, YOURS IS THE **CENTRAL PERFORMANCE.**
REALLY?! OH, KERMIE! YOU'VE MADE MY **DAY! MWWAH!**
SURE...NO PROBLEM.
ANIMAL!
ESPECIALLY SINCE I REMEMBER WHAT HAPPENED THE **LAST** TIME I LEFT YOU OUT OF THE CLOSING NUMBER.
I DON'T LOOK SO **GOOD** WEARING A **SPLINT...**
ANIMAAAL! C'MON, BUDDY!
KERMIT, MAN...YOU AIN'T SEEN **ANIMAL** ANYWHERE, HAVE YOU?
I THOUGHT HE WAS REHEARSING WITH YOU AND THE **BAND.**
S'POSED TO BE, YEAH. BUT NOBODY'S SEEN HIM SINCE LAST NIGHT AND WE CAN'T FIND HIM.
POOR LI'L DUDE...I KNOW HE'S BEEN ACTING **SCREWY** LATELY...BUT **MISSING A REHEARSAL?** TOO WEIRD. TOO **WRONG.**
I SURE HOPE NOTHING'S **HAPPENED** TO HIM...

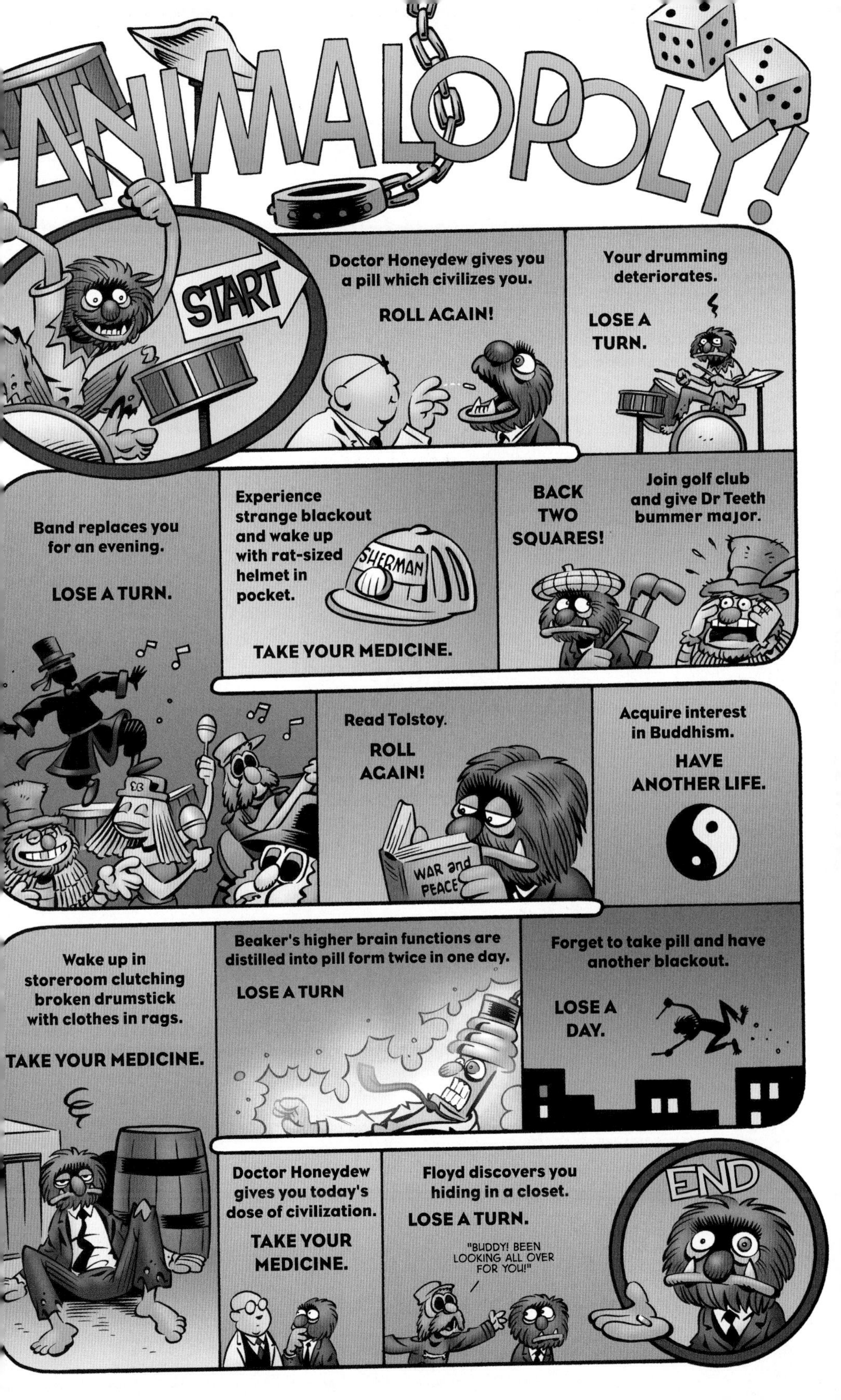
ANIMALOPOLY!
START
Doctor Honeydew gives you a pill which civilizes you.
ROLL AGAIN!
Your drumming deteriorates.
LOSE A TURN.
Band replaces you for an evening.
LOSE A TURN.
Experience strange blackout and wake up with rat-sized helmet in pocket.
SHERMAN
TAKE YOUR MEDICINE.
BACK TWO SQUARES!
Join golf club and give Dr Teeth bummer major.
Read Tolstoy.
ROLL AGAIN!
WAR and PEACE
Acquire interest in Buddhism.
HAVE ANOTHER LIFE.
Wake up in storeroom clutching broken drumstick with clothes in rags.
TAKE YOUR MEDICINE.
Beaker's higher brain functions are distilled into pill form twice in one day.
LOSE A TURN
Forget to take pill and have another blackout.
LOSE A DAY.
Doctor Honeydew gives you today's dose of civilization.
TAKE YOUR MEDICINE.
Floyd discovers you hiding in a closet.
LOSE A TURN.
"BUDDY! BEEN LOOKING ALL OVER FOR YOU!"
END

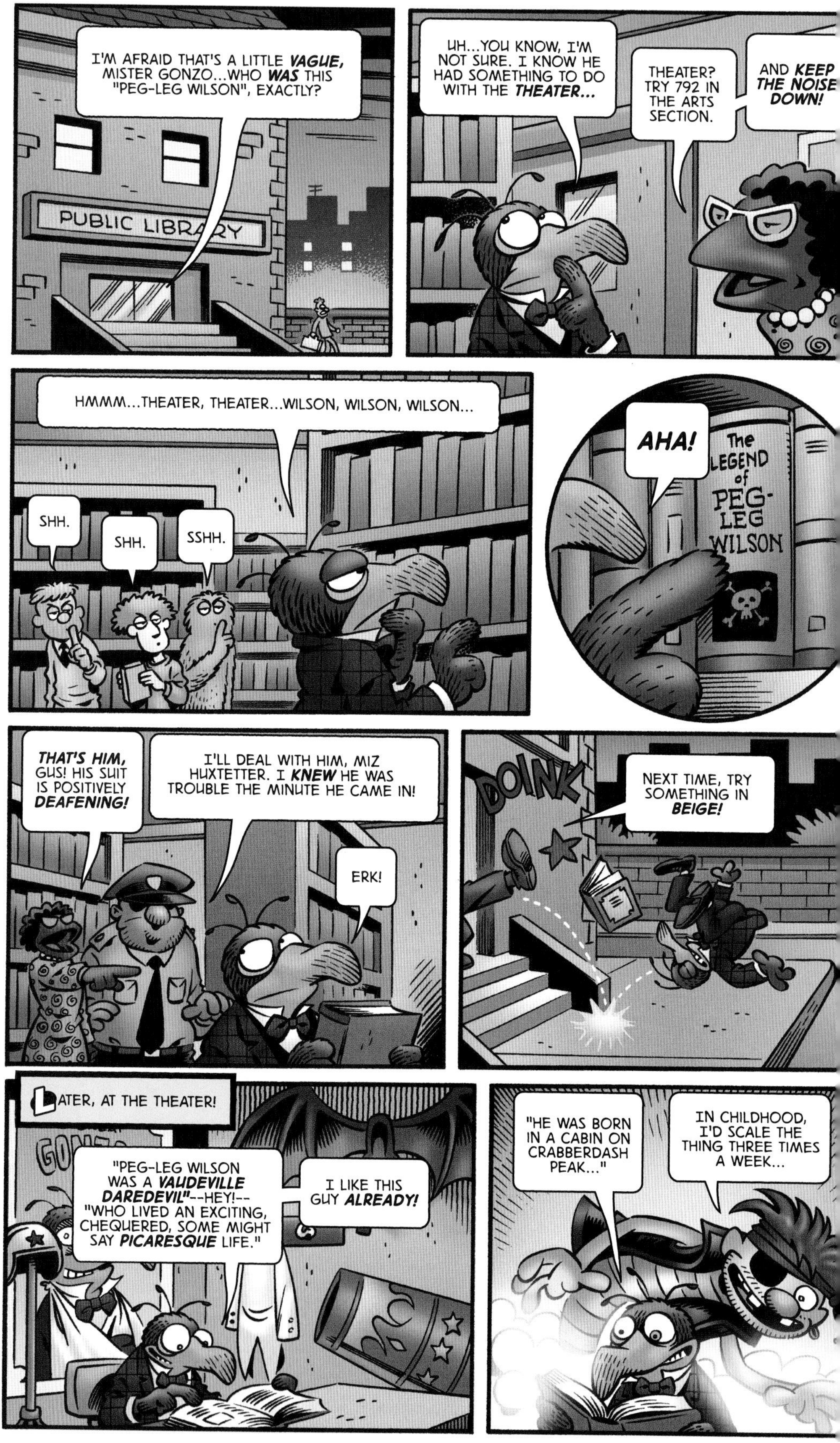
I'M AFRAID THAT'S A LITTLE VAGUE, MISTER GONZO...WHO WAS THIS "PEG-LEG WILSON", EXACTLY?
PUBLIC LIBRARY
UH...YOU KNOW, I'M NOT SURE. I KNOW HE HAD SOMETHING TO DO WITH THE THEATER...
THEATER? TRY 792 IN THE ARTS SECTION.
AND KEEP THE NOISE DOWN!
HMMM...THEATER, THEATER...WILSON, WILSON, WILSON...
SHH.
SHH.
SSHH.
AHA!
The LEGEND of PEG-LEG WILSON
THAT'S HIM, GUS! HIS SUIT IS POSITIVELY DEAFENING!
I'LL DEAL WITH HIM, MIZ HUXTETTER. I KNEW HE WAS TROUBLE THE MINUTE HE CAME IN!
ERK!
DOINK
NEXT TIME, TRY SOMETHING IN BEIGE!
LATER, AT THE THEATER!
"PEG-LEG WILSON WAS A VAUDEVILLE DAREDEVIL"--HEY!--"WHO LIVED AN EXCITING, CHEQUERED, SOME MIGHT SAY PICARESQUE LIFE."
I LIKE THIS GUY ALREADY!
"HE WAS BORN IN A CABIN ON CRABBERDASH PEAK..."
IN CHILDHOOD, I'D SCALE THE THING THREE TIMES A WEEK...

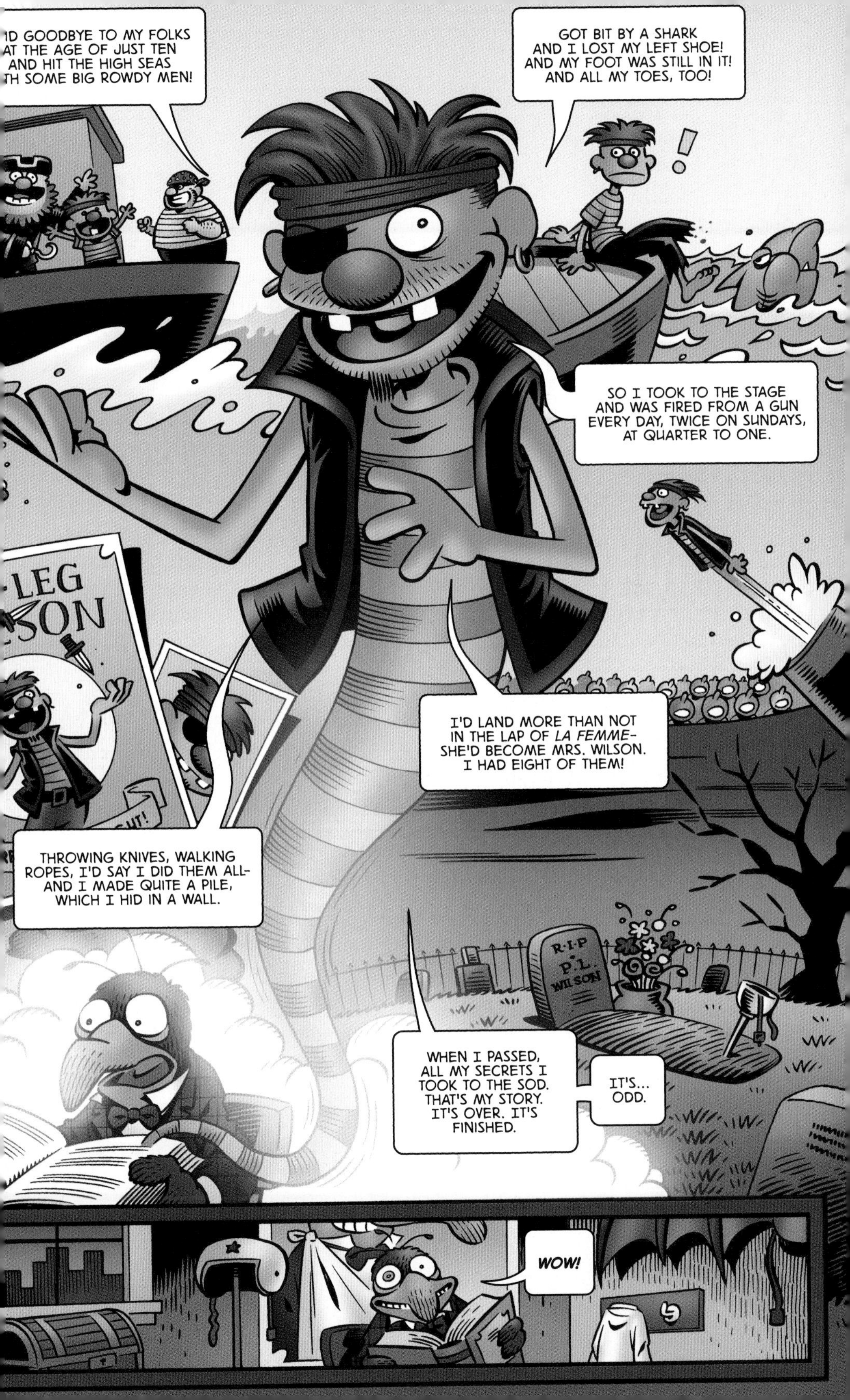
D GOODBYE TO MY FOLKS AT THE AGE OF JUST TEN AND HIT THE HIGH SEAS TH SOME BIG ROWDY MEN!
GOT BIT BY A SHARK AND I LOST MY LEFT SHOE! AND MY FOOT WAS STILL IN IT! AND ALL MY TOES, TOO!
SO I TOOK TO THE STAGE AND WAS FIRED FROM A GUN EVERY DAY, TWICE ON SUNDAYS, AT QUARTER TO ONE.
I'D LAND MORE THAN NOT IN THE LAP OF *LA FEMME*- SHE'D BECOME MRS. WILSON. I HAD EIGHT OF THEM!
THROWING KNIVES, WALKING ROPES, I'D SAY I DID THEM ALL- AND I MADE QUITE A PILE, WHICH I HID IN A WALL.
R·I·P P.L. WILSON
WHEN I PASSED, ALL MY SECRETS I TOOK TO THE SOD. THAT'S MY STORY. IT'S OVER. IT'S FINISHED.
IT'S... ODD.
WOW!

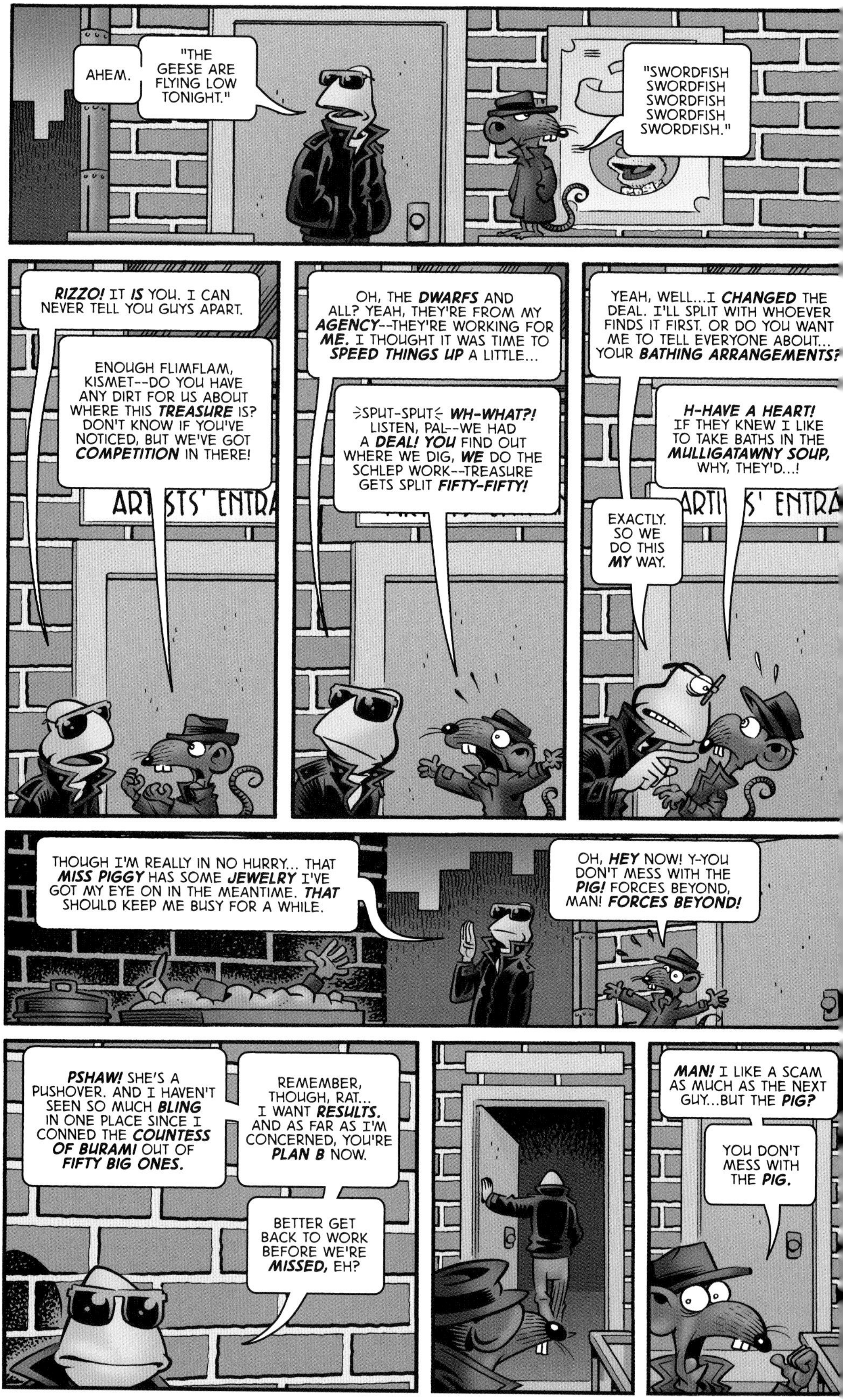

AHEM.
"THE GEESE ARE FLYING LOW TONIGHT."
"SWORDFISH SWORDFISH SWORDFISH SWORDFISH SWORDFISH."
RIZZO! IT IS YOU. I CAN NEVER TELL YOU GUYS APART.
ENOUGH FLIMFLAM, KISMET--DO YOU HAVE ANY DIRT FOR US ABOUT WHERE THIS TREASURE IS? DON'T KNOW IF YOU'VE NOTICED, BUT WE'VE GOT COMPETITION IN THERE!
ARTISTS' ENTRA
OH, THE DWARFS AND ALL? YEAH, THEY'RE FROM MY AGENCY--THEY'RE WORKING FOR ME. I THOUGHT IT WAS TIME TO SPEED THINGS UP A LITTLE...
SPUT-SPUT WH-WHAT?! LISTEN, PAL--WE HAD A DEAL! YOU FIND OUT WHERE WE DIG, WE DO THE SCHLEP WORK--TREASURE GETS SPLIT FIFTY-FIFTY!
YEAH, WELL...I CHANGED THE DEAL. I'LL SPLIT WITH WHOEVER FINDS IT FIRST. OR DO YOU WANT ME TO TELL EVERYONE ABOUT... YOUR BATHING ARRANGEMENTS?
H-HAVE A HEART! IF THEY KNEW I LIKE TO TAKE BATHS IN THE MULLIGATAWNY SOUP, WHY, THEY'D...!
EXACTLY. SO WE DO THIS MY WAY.
THOUGH I'M REALLY IN NO HURRY... THAT MISS PIGGY HAS SOME JEWELRY I'VE GOT MY EYE ON IN THE MEANTIME. THAT SHOULD KEEP ME BUSY FOR A WHILE.
OH, HEY NOW! Y-YOU DON'T MESS WITH THE PIG! FORCES BEYOND, MAN! FORCES BEYOND!
PSHAW! SHE'S A PUSHOVER. AND I HAVEN'T SEEN SO MUCH BLING IN ONE PLACE SINCE I CONNED THE COUNTESS OF BURAMI OUT OF FIFTY BIG ONES.
REMEMBER, THOUGH, RAT... I WANT RESULTS. AND AS FAR AS I'M CONCERNED, YOU'RE PLAN B NOW.
BETTER GET BACK TO WORK BEFORE WE'RE MISSED, EH?
MAN! I LIKE A SCAM AS MUCH AS THE NEXT GUY...BUT THE PIG?
YOU DON'T MESS WITH THE PIG.

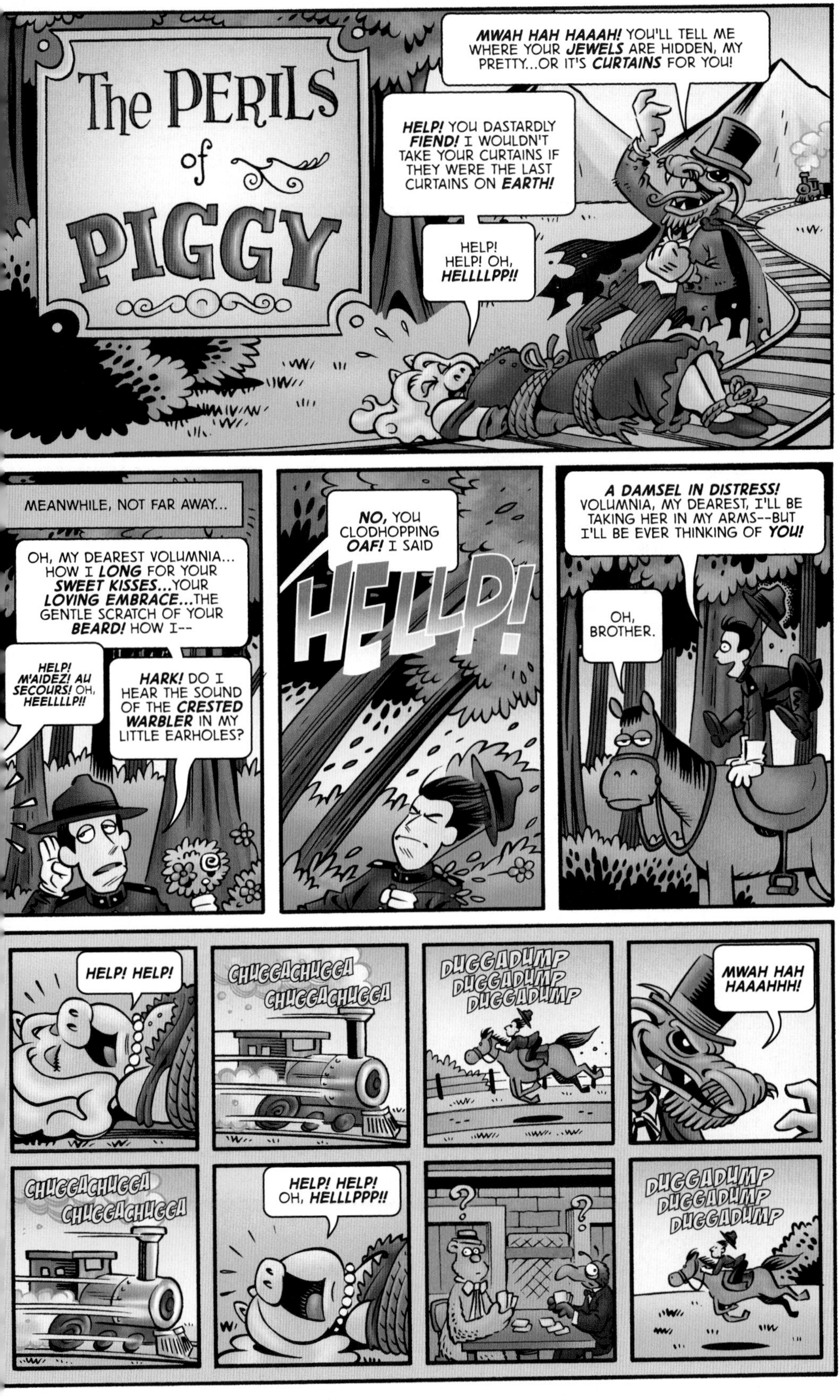
The PERILS of PIGGY
MWAH HAH HAAAH! YOU'LL TELL ME WHERE YOUR JEWELS ARE HIDDEN, MY PRETTY...OR IT'S CURTAINS FOR YOU!
HELP! YOU DASTARDLY FIEND! I WOULDN'T TAKE YOUR CURTAINS IF THEY WERE THE LAST CURTAINS ON EARTH!
HELP! HELP! OH, HELLLLPP!!
MEANWHILE, NOT FAR AWAY...
OH, MY DEAREST VOLUMNIA... HOW I LONG FOR YOUR SWEET KISSES...YOUR LOVING EMBRACE...THE GENTLE SCRATCH OF YOUR BEARD! HOW I--
HELP! M'AIDEZ! AU SECOURS! OH, HEELLLLP!!
HARK! DO I HEAR THE SOUND OF THE CRESTED WARBLER IN MY LITTLE EARHOLES?
NO, YOU CLODHOPPING OAF! I SAID
HELLP!
A DAMSEL IN DISTRESS! VOLUMNIA, MY DEAREST, I'LL BE TAKING HER IN MY ARMS--BUT I'LL BE EVER THINKING OF YOU!
OH, BROTHER.
HELP! HELP!
CHUGGACHUGGA CHUGGACHUGGA
DUGGADUMP DUGGADUMP DUGGADUMP
MWAH HAH HAAAHHH!
CHUGGACHUGGA CHUGGACHUGGA
HELP! HELP! OH, HELLLPPP!!
?
?
DUGGADUMP DUGGADUMP DUGGADUMP

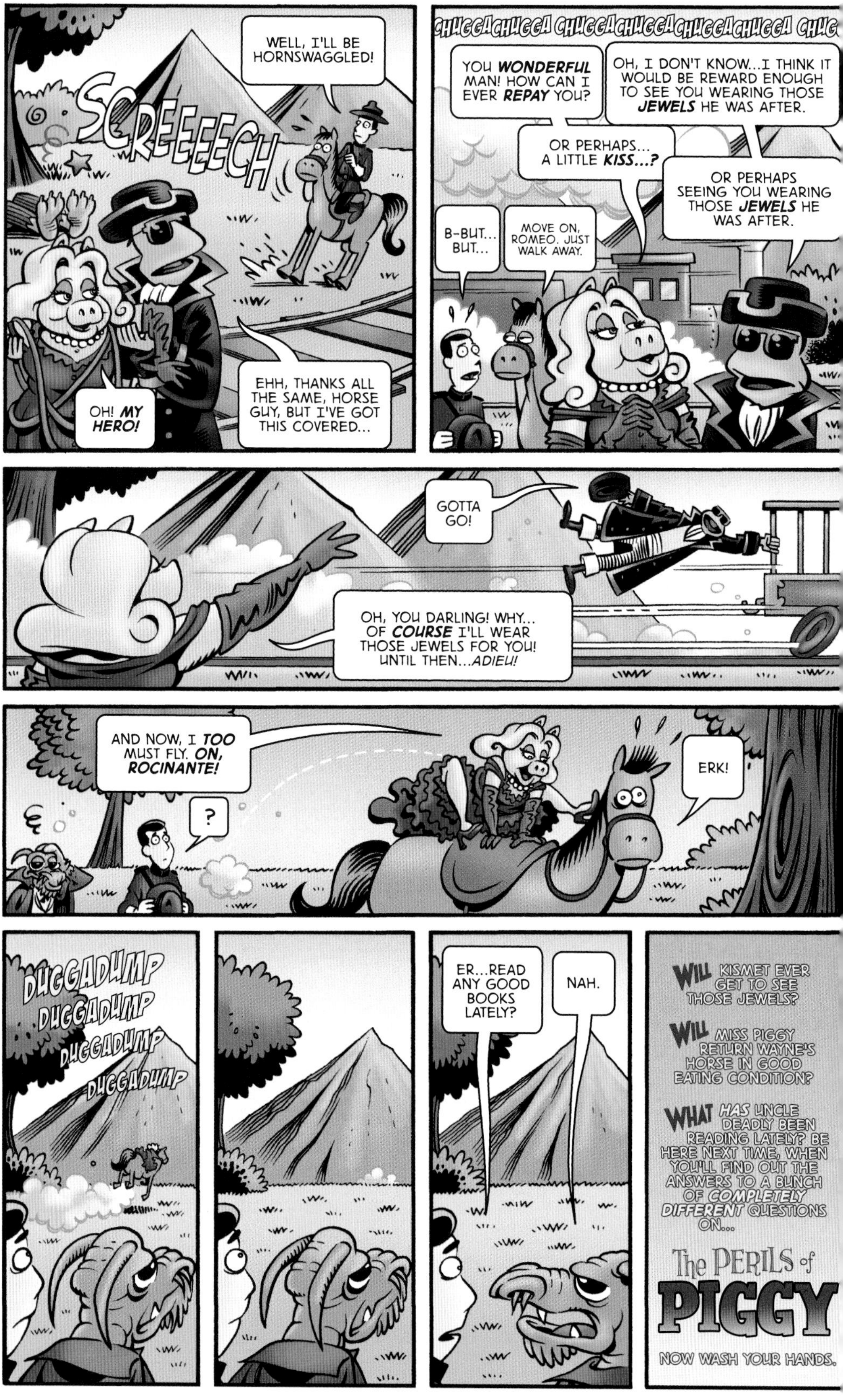
WELL, I'LL BE HORNSWAGGLED!
SCREEEEECH
OH! MY HERO!
EHH, THANKS ALL THE SAME, HORSE GUY, BUT I'VE GOT THIS COVERED...
CHUGGACHUGGA CHUGGACHUGGACHUGGACHUGGA CHUGG
YOU WONDERFUL MAN! HOW CAN I EVER REPAY YOU?
OH, I DON'T KNOW...I THINK IT WOULD BE REWARD ENOUGH TO SEE YOU WEARING THOSE JEWELS HE WAS AFTER.
OR PERHAPS... A LITTLE KISS...?
OR PERHAPS SEEING YOU WEARING THOSE JEWELS HE WAS AFTER.
B-BUT... BUT...
MOVE ON, ROMEO. JUST WALK AWAY.
GOTTA GO!
OH, YOU DARLING! WHY... OF COURSE I'LL WEAR THOSE JEWELS FOR YOU! UNTIL THEN...ADIEU!
AND NOW, I TOO MUST FLY. ON, ROCINANTE!
?
ERK!
DUGGADUMP
DUGGADUMP
DUGGADUMP
DUGGADUMP
ER...READ ANY GOOD BOOKS LATELY?
NAH.
WILL KISMET EVER GET TO SEE THOSE JEWELS?
WILL MISS PIGGY RETURN WAYNE'S HORSE IN GOOD EATING CONDITION?
WHAT HAS UNCLE DEADLY BEEN READING LATELY? BE HERE NEXT TIME, WHEN YOU'LL FIND OUT THE ANSWERS TO A BUNCH OF COMPLETELY DIFFERENT QUESTIONS ON...
The PERILS of PIGGY
NOW WASH YOUR HANDS.

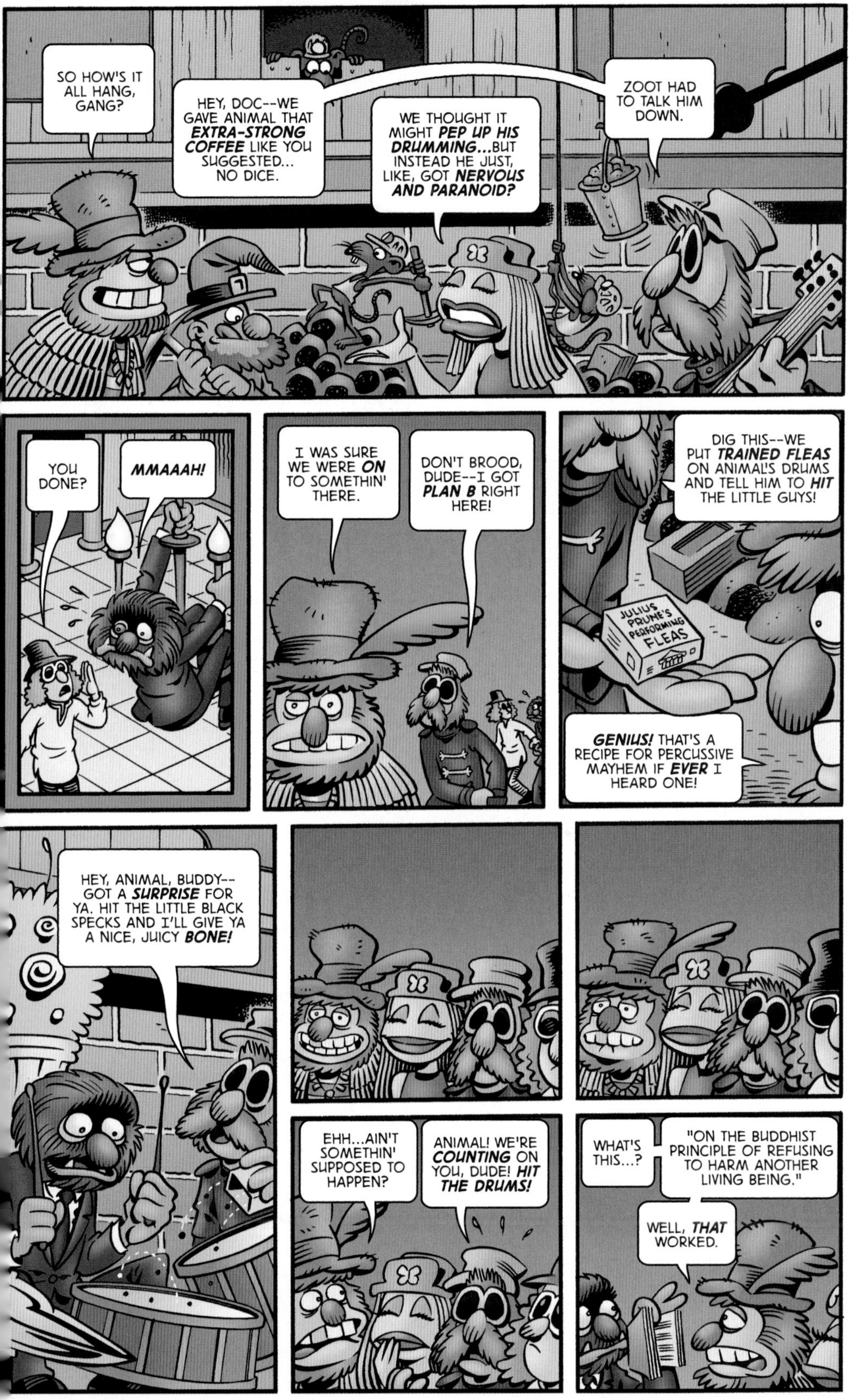
SO HOW'S IT ALL HANG, GANG?
HEY, DOC--WE GAVE ANIMAL THAT EXTRA-STRONG COFFEE LIKE YOU SUGGESTED... NO DICE.
WE THOUGHT IT MIGHT PEP UP HIS DRUMMING...BUT INSTEAD HE JUST, LIKE, GOT NERVOUS AND PARANOID?
ZOOT HAD TO TALK HIM DOWN.
YOU DONE?
MMAAAH!
I WAS SURE WE WERE ON TO SOMETHIN' THERE.
DON'T BROOD, DUDE--I GOT PLAN B RIGHT HERE!
DIG THIS--WE PUT TRAINED FLEAS ON ANIMAL'S DRUMS AND TELL HIM TO HIT THE LITTLE GUYS!
JULIUS PRUNE'S PERFORMING FLEAS
GENIUS! THAT'S A RECIPE FOR PERCUSSIVE MAYHEM IF EVER I HEARD ONE!
HEY, ANIMAL, BUDDY--GOT A SURPRISE FOR YA. HIT THE LITTLE BLACK SPECKS AND I'LL GIVE YA A NICE, JUICY BONE!
EHH...AIN'T SOMETHIN' SUPPOSED TO HAPPEN?
ANIMAL! WE'RE COUNTING ON YOU, DUDE! HIT THE DRUMS!
WHAT'S THIS...?
"ON THE BUDDHIST PRINCIPLE OF REFUSING TO HARM ANOTHER LIVING BEING."
WELL, THAT WORKED.

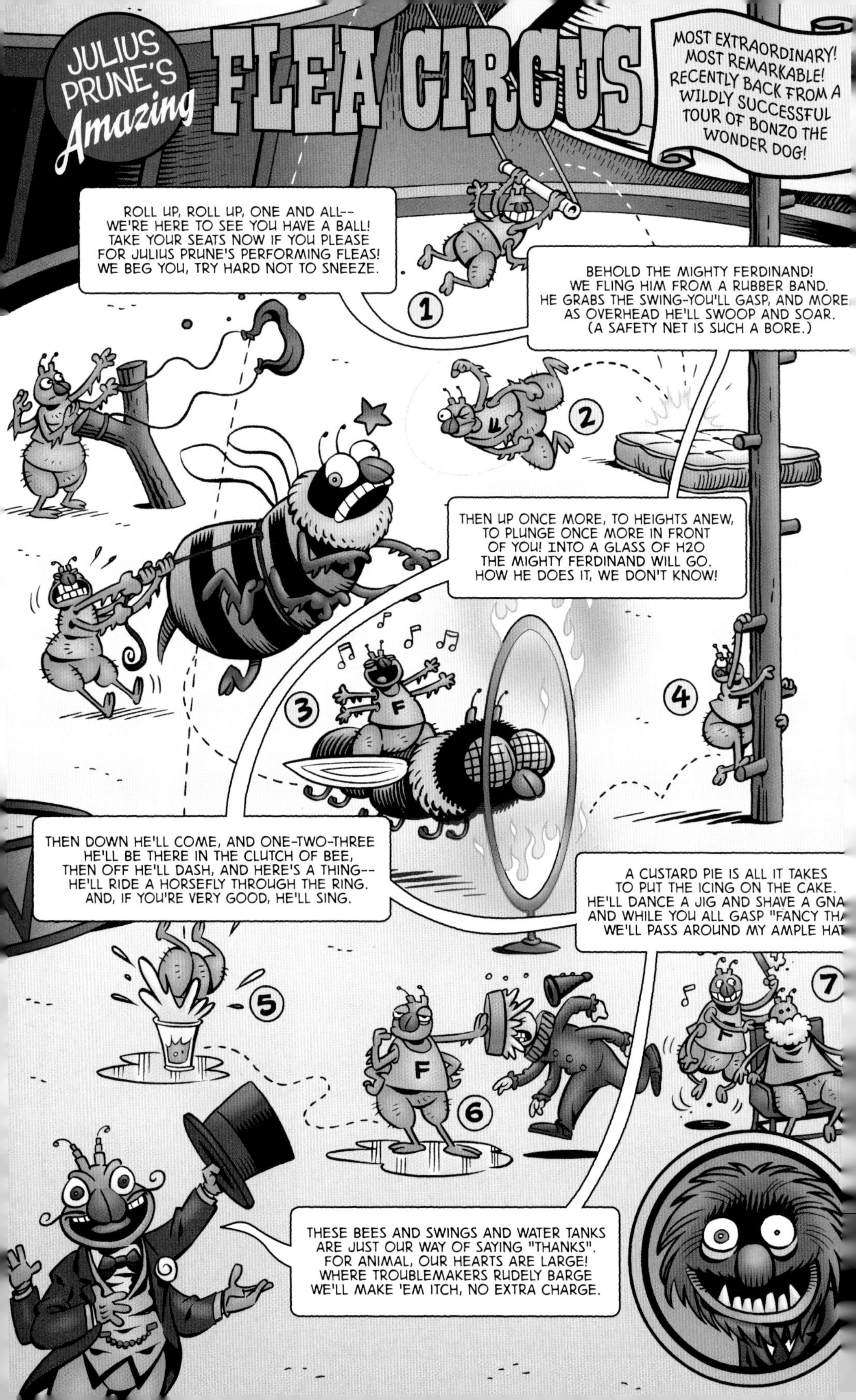
JULIUS PRUNE'S Amazing
FLEA CIRCUS
MOST EXTRAORDINARY! MOST REMARKABLE! RECENTLY BACK FROM A WILDLY SUCCESSFUL TOUR OF BONZO THE WONDER DOG!
ROLL UP, ROLL UP, ONE AND ALL-- WE'RE HERE TO SEE YOU HAVE A BALL! TAKE YOUR SEATS NOW IF YOU PLEASE FOR JULIUS PRUNE'S PERFORMING FLEAS! WE BEG YOU, TRY HARD NOT TO SNEEZE.
1
BEHOLD THE MIGHTY FERDINAND! WE FLING HIM FROM A RUBBER BAND. HE GRABS THE SWING-YOU'LL GASP, AND MORE AS OVERHEAD HE'LL SWOOP AND SOAR. (A SAFETY NET IS SUCH A BORE.)
2
THEN UP ONCE MORE, TO HEIGHTS ANEW, TO PLUNGE ONCE MORE IN FRONT OF YOU! INTO A GLASS OF H2O THE MIGHTY FERDINAND WILL GO. HOW HE DOES IT, WE DON'T KNOW!
3
4
THEN DOWN HE'LL COME, AND ONE-TWO-THREE HE'LL BE THERE IN THE CLUTCH OF BEE, THEN OFF HE'LL DASH, AND HERE'S A THING-- HE'LL RIDE A HORSEFLY THROUGH THE RING. AND, IF YOU'RE VERY GOOD, HE'LL SING.
A CUSTARD PIE IS ALL IT TAKES TO PUT THE ICING ON THE CAKE. HE'LL DANCE A JIG AND SHAVE A GNA AND WHILE YOU ALL GASP "FANCY THA WE'LL PASS AROUND MY AMPLE HAT
5
6
7
THESE BEES AND SWINGS AND WATER TANKS ARE JUST OUR WAY OF SAYING "THANKS". FOR ANIMAL, OUR HEARTS ARE LARGE! WHERE TROUBLEMAKERS RUDELY BARGE WE'LL MAKE 'EM ITCH, NO EXTRA CHARGE.

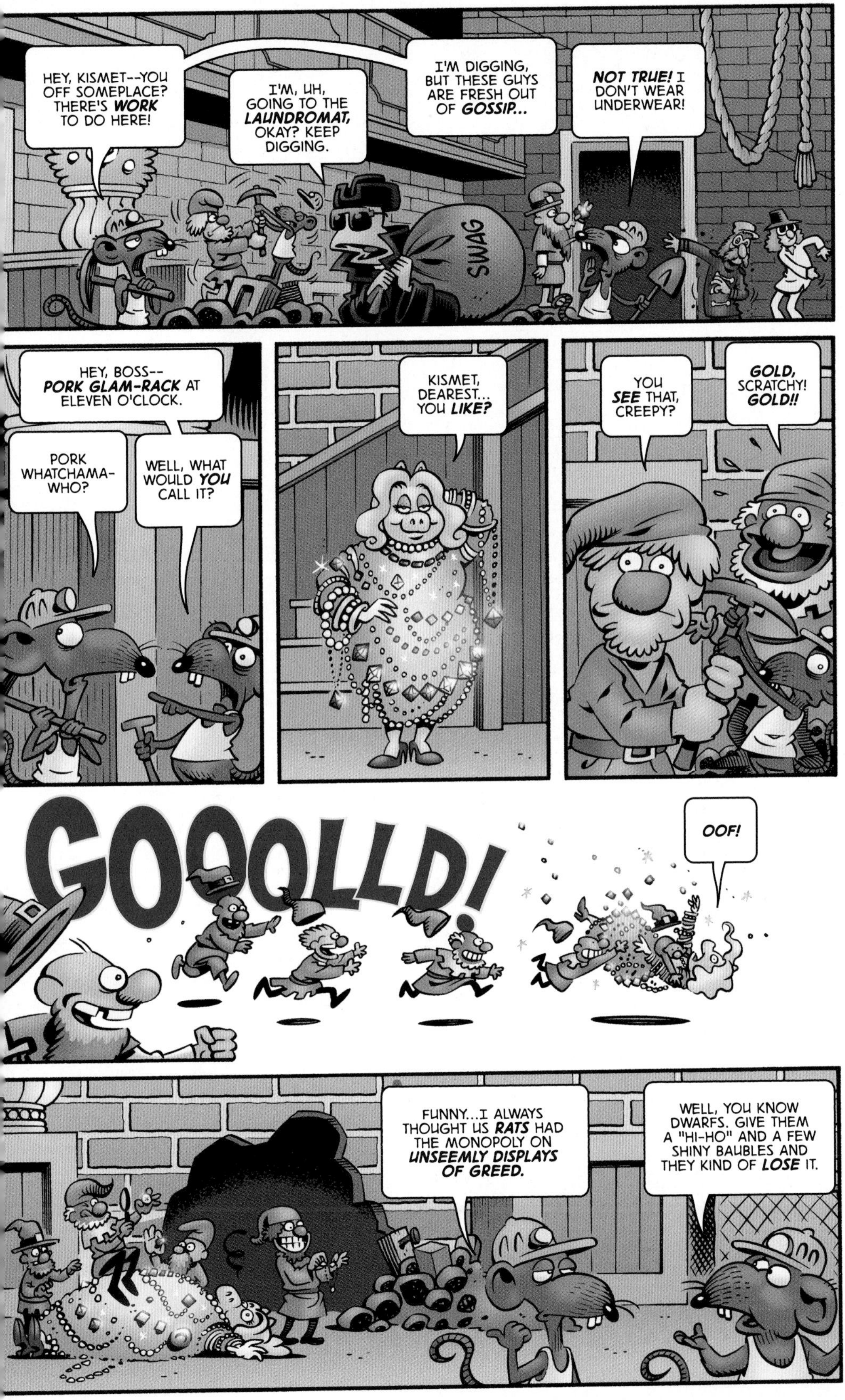
HEY, KISMET--YOU OFF SOMEPLACE? THERE'S WORK TO DO HERE!
I'M, UH, GOING TO THE LAUNDROMAT, OKAY? KEEP DIGGING.
I'M DIGGING, BUT THESE GUYS ARE FRESH OUT OF GOSSIP...
NOT TRUE! I DON'T WEAR UNDERWEAR!
SWAG
HEY, BOSS-- PORK GLAM-RACK AT ELEVEN O'CLOCK.
PORK WHATCHAMA-WHO?
WELL, WHAT WOULD YOU CALL IT?
KISMET, DEAREST... YOU LIKE?
YOU SEE THAT, CREEPY?
GOLD, SCRATCHY! GOLD!!
GOOOLLD!
OOF!
FUNNY...I ALWAYS THOUGHT US RATS HAD THE MONOPOLY ON UNSEEMLY DISPLAYS OF GREED.
WELL, YOU KNOW DWARFS. GIVE THEM A "HI-HO" AND A FEW SHINY BAUBLES AND THEY KIND OF LOSE IT.

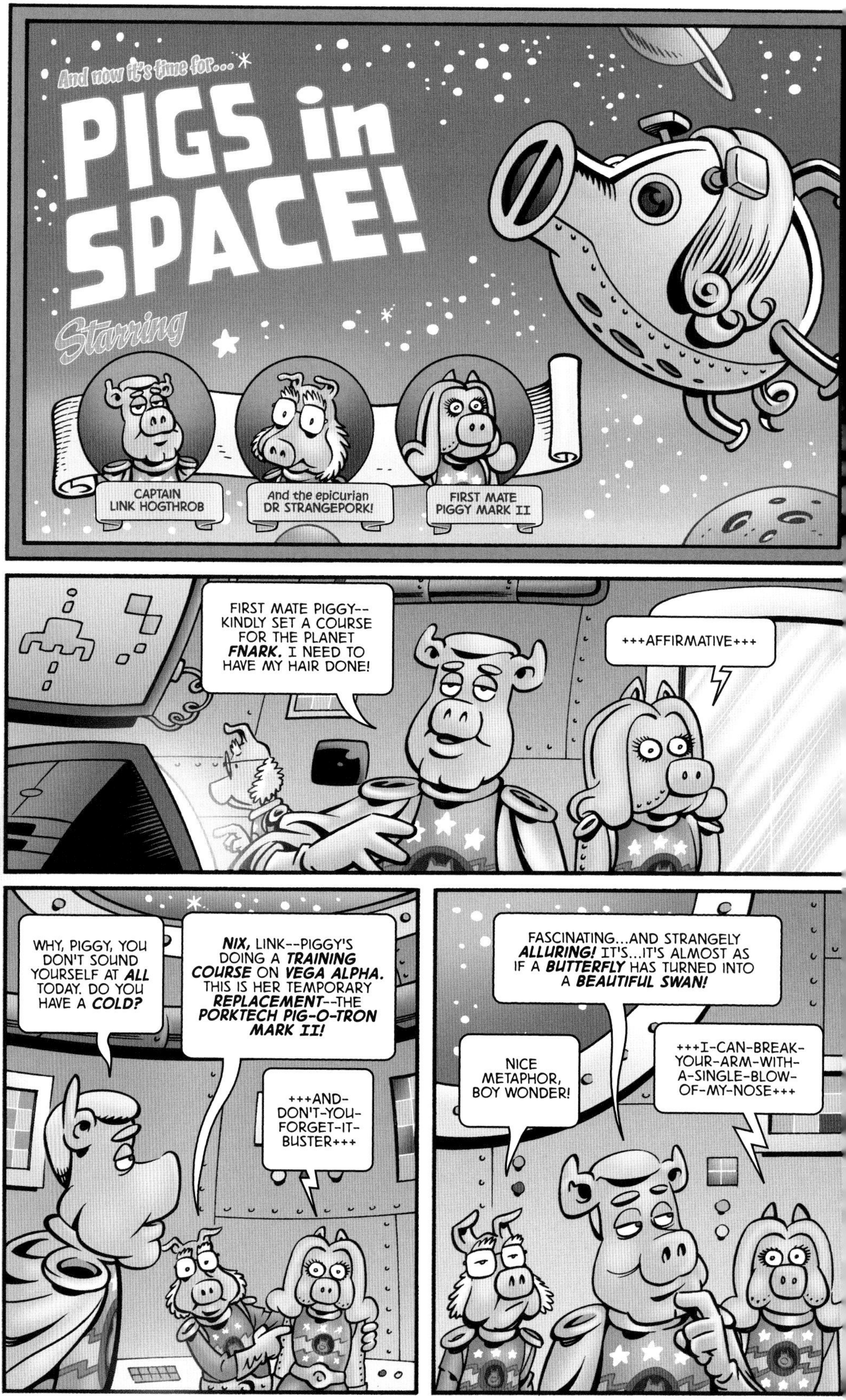

And now it's time for...
PIGS in SPACE!
Starring
CAPTAIN LINK HOGTHROB
And the epicurian DR STRANGEPORK!
FIRST MATE PIGGY MARK II
FIRST MATE PIGGY-- KINDLY SET A COURSE FOR THE PLANET FNARK. I NEED TO HAVE MY HAIR DONE!
+++AFFIRMATIVE+++
WHY, PIGGY, YOU DON'T SOUND YOURSELF AT ALL TODAY. DO YOU HAVE A COLD?
NIX, LINK--PIGGY'S DOING A TRAINING COURSE ON VEGA ALPHA. THIS IS HER TEMPORARY REPLACEMENT--THE PORKTECH PIG-O-TRON MARK II!
+++AND-DON'T-YOU-FORGET-IT-BUSTER+++
FASCINATING...AND STRANGELY ALLURING! IT'S...IT'S ALMOST AS IF A BUTTERFLY HAS TURNED INTO A BEAUTIFUL SWAN!
NICE METAPHOR, BOY WONDER!
+++I-CAN-BREAK-YOUR-ARM-WITH-A-SINGLE-BLOW-OF-MY-NOSE+++

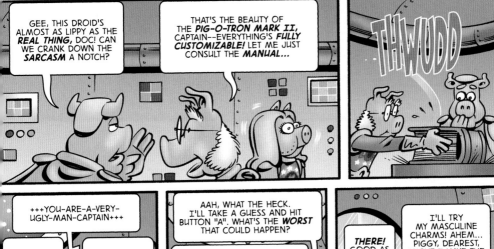

GEE, THIS DROID'S ALMOST AS LIPPY AS THE **REAL THING,** DOC! CAN WE CRANK DOWN THE **SARCASM** A NOTCH?

THAT'S THE BEAUTY OF THE **PIG-O-TRON MARK II,** CAPTAIN--EVERYTHING'S **FULLY CUSTOMIZABLE!** LET ME JUST CONSULT THE **MANUAL...**

THWUDD

+++YOU-ARE-A-VERY-UGLY-MAN-CAPTAIN+++

HURRY, DOC--SHE'S **TEASING** ME!

I'M LOOKING, I'M LOOKING! LOTTA PAGES HERE...

AAH, WHAT THE HECK. I'LL TAKE A GUESS AND HIT BUTTON "A". WHAT'S THE **WORST** THAT COULD HAPPEN?

ER...SHE COULD MOBILIZE AN ARMY OF ROBOTS TO TAKE OVER THE UNIVERSE?

YES, BUT APART FROM THAT.

THERE! GOOD AS NEW!

I'LL TRY MY MASCULINE CHARMS! AHEM... PIGGY, DEAREST, MIGHT I HAVE THE HONOR OF YOUR **COMPANY...?**

HIIIIIIII-HAAAAA!!!

OW.

OW.

OW.

OR POSSIBLY BUTTON "B".

WILL LINK TAKE THE PIGGY DROID TO THE OFFICERS' BALL?

WHICH BRAND OF CORNFLAKES DID DOCTOR STRANGEPORK GET HIS UNIVERSITY DEGREE FROM?

DOES OSTEOPATHY RELIEVE KARATE-RELATED INJURIES? ALL, SOME OR NONE OF THESE QUESTIONS WILL BE ANSWERED IN THE NEXT EXCITING EPISODE OF...

PIGS IN SPAAACE!

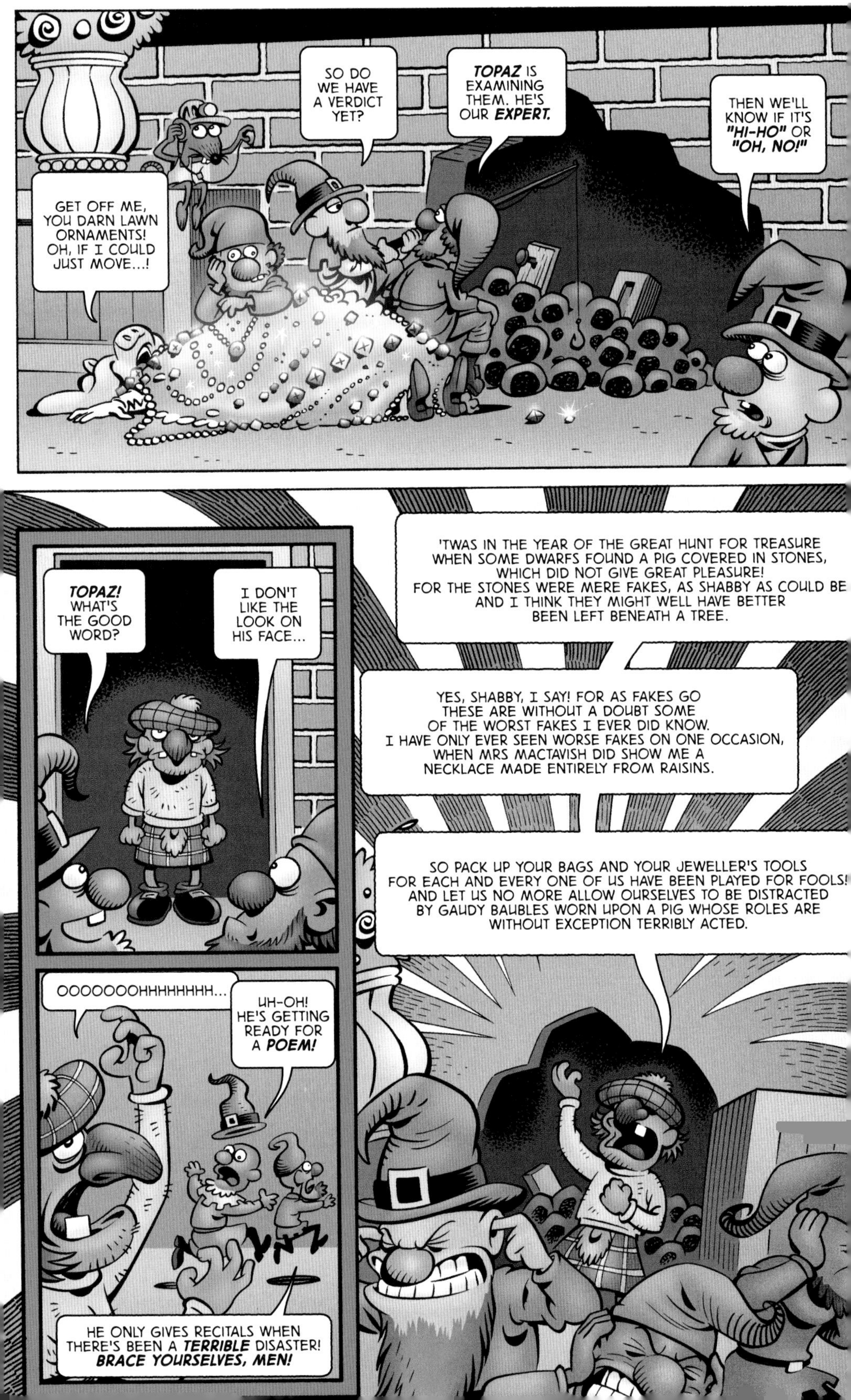

GET OFF ME, YOU DARN LAWN ORNAMENTS! OH, IF I COULD JUST MOVE...!
SO DO WE HAVE A VERDICT YET?
TOPAZ IS EXAMINING THEM. HE'S OUR *EXPERT.*
THEN WE'LL KNOW IF IT'S *"HI-HO"* OR *"OH, NO!"*
TOPAZ! WHAT'S THE GOOD WORD?
I DON'T LIKE THE LOOK ON HIS FACE...
OOOOOOOHHHHHHHH...
UH-OH! HE'S GETTING READY FOR A *POEM!*
HE ONLY GIVES RECITALS WHEN THERE'S BEEN A *TERRIBLE* DISASTER! *BRACE YOURSELVES, MEN!*
'TWAS IN THE YEAR OF THE GREAT HUNT FOR TREASURE WHEN SOME DWARFS FOUND A PIG COVERED IN STONES, WHICH DID NOT GIVE GREAT PLEASURE! FOR THE STONES WERE MERE FAKES, AS SHABBY AS COULD BE AND I THINK THEY MIGHT WELL HAVE BETTER BEEN LEFT BENEATH A TREE.
YES, SHABBY, I SAY! FOR AS FAKES GO THESE ARE WITHOUT A DOUBT SOME OF THE WORST FAKES I EVER DID KNOW. I HAVE ONLY EVER SEEN WORSE FAKES ON ONE OCCASION, WHEN MRS MACTAVISH DID SHOW ME A NECKLACE MADE ENTIRELY FROM RAISINS.
SO PACK UP YOUR BAGS AND YOUR JEWELLER'S TOOLS FOR EACH AND EVERY ONE OF US HAVE BEEN PLAYED FOR FOOLS! AND LET US NO MORE ALLOW OURSELVES TO BE DISTRACTED BY GAUDY BAUBLES WORN UPON A PIG WHOSE ROLES ARE WITHOUT EXCEPTION TERRIBLY ACTED.

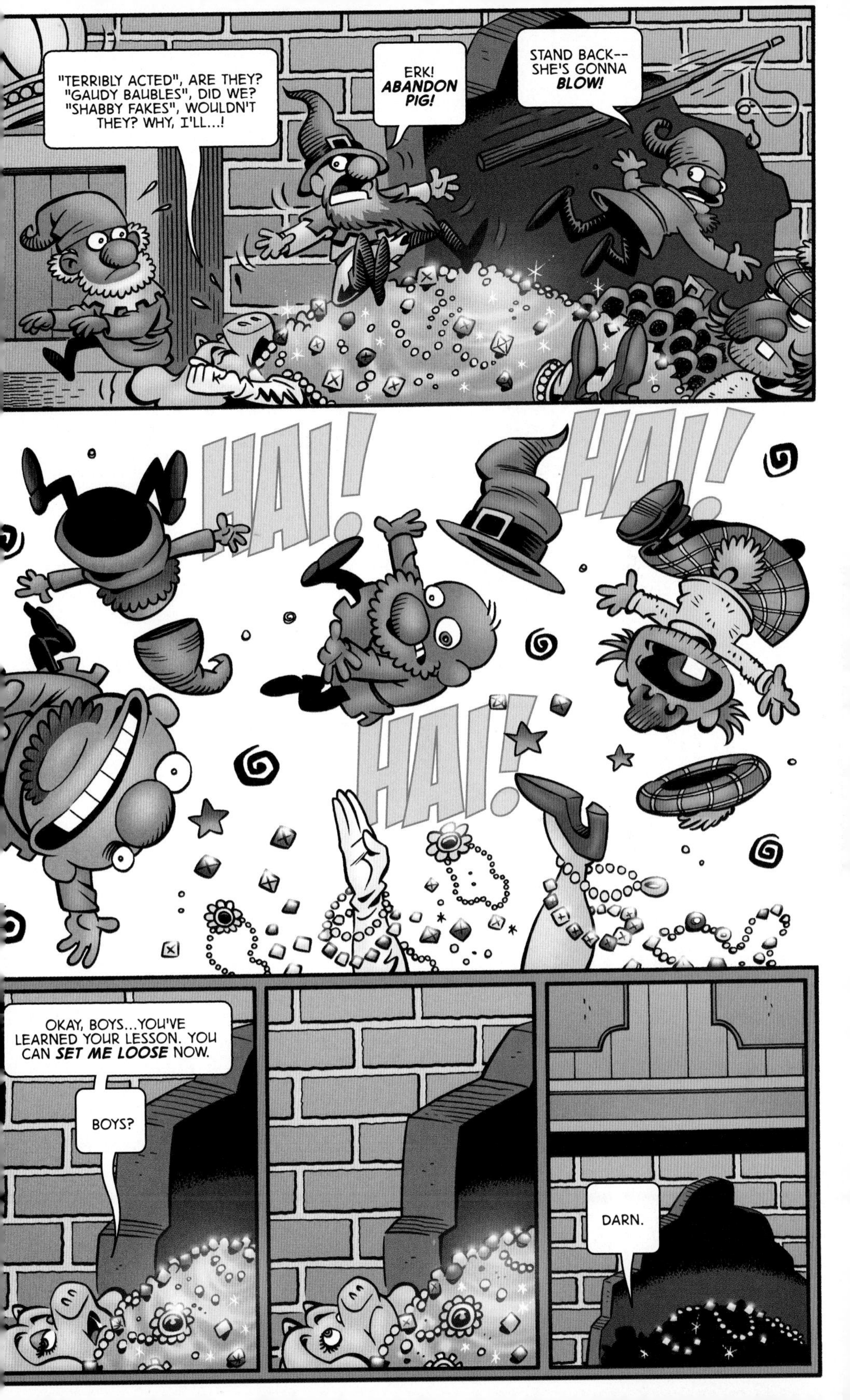
"TERRIBLY ACTED", ARE THEY? "GAUDY BAUBLES", DID WE? "SHABBY FAKES", WOULDN'T THEY? WHY, I'LL...!
ERK! *ABANDON PIG!*
STAND BACK-- SHE'S GONNA *BLOW!*
HAI! HAI! HAI!
OKAY, BOYS...YOU'VE LEARNED YOUR LESSON. YOU CAN *SET ME LOOSE* NOW.
BOYS?
DARN.

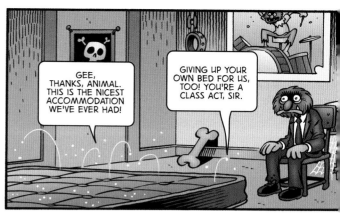

GEE, THANKS, ANIMAL. THIS IS THE NICEST ACCOMMODATION WE'VE EVER HAD!

GIVING UP YOUR OWN BED FOR US, TOO! YOU'RE A CLASS ACT, SIR.

HEY, MISTER ANIMAL?

GOT SOMETHING FOR YA.

IT'S NOT MUCH... BUT, WELL...WE WANT YOU TO HAVE THIS.

GO ON. TAKE IT.

TO ANIMAL
The Only Guy Who Was Ever Kind to Us

ANIMAL'S TREASURES

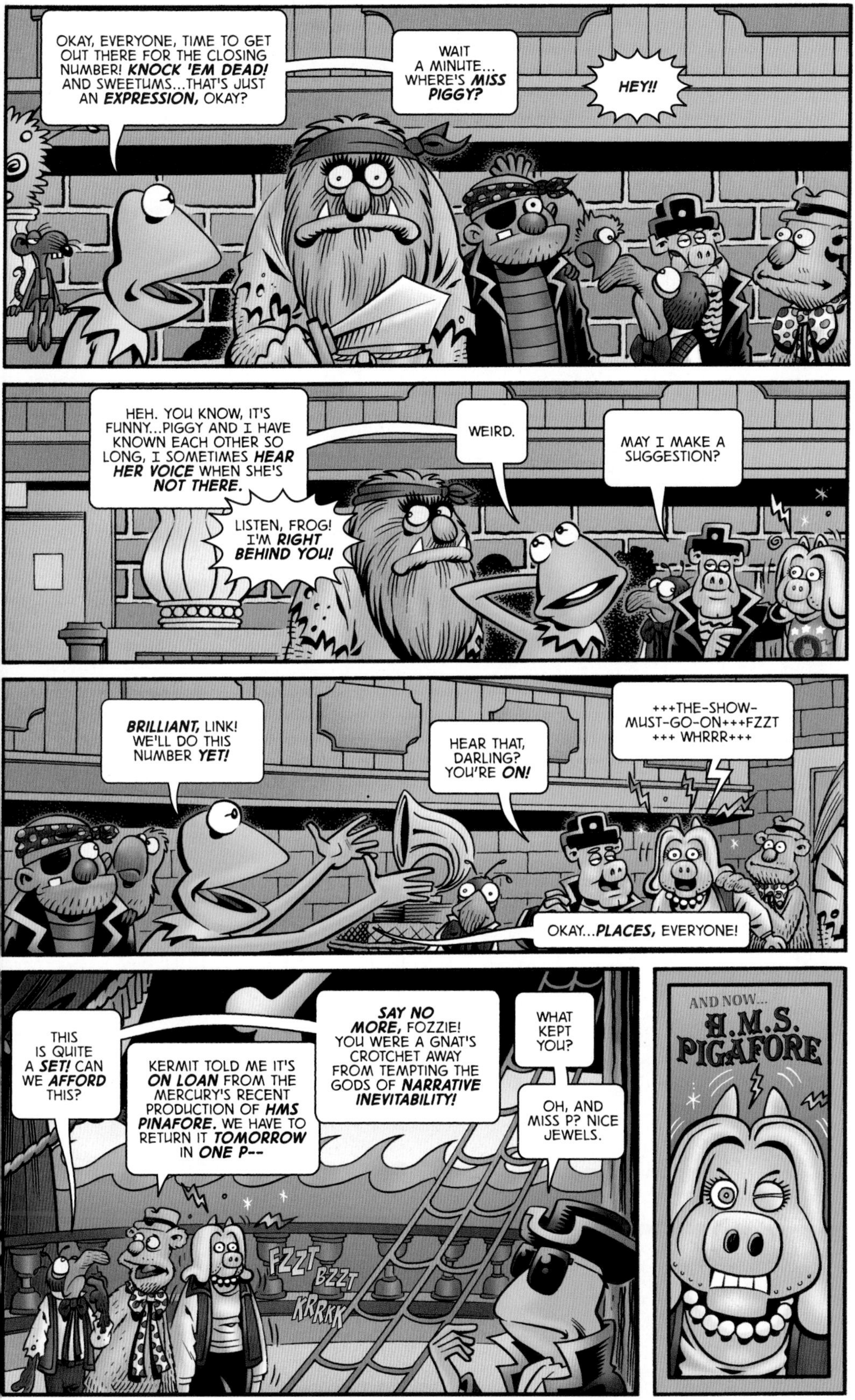
OKAY, EVERYONE, TIME TO GET OUT THERE FOR THE CLOSING NUMBER! KNOCK 'EM DEAD! AND SWEETUMS...THAT'S JUST AN EXPRESSION, OKAY?
WAIT A MINUTE... WHERE'S MISS PIGGY?
HEY!!
HEH. YOU KNOW, IT'S FUNNY...PIGGY AND I HAVE KNOWN EACH OTHER SO LONG, I SOMETIMES HEAR HER VOICE WHEN SHE'S NOT THERE.
WEIRD.
LISTEN, FROG! I'M RIGHT BEHIND YOU!
MAY I MAKE A SUGGESTION?
BRILLIANT, LINK! WE'LL DO THIS NUMBER YET!
HEAR THAT, DARLING? YOU'RE ON!
+++THE-SHOW-MUST-GO-ON+++FZZT +++ WHRRR+++
OKAY...PLACES, EVERYONE!
THIS IS QUITE A SET! CAN WE AFFORD THIS?
KERMIT TOLD ME IT'S ON LOAN FROM THE MERCURY'S RECENT PRODUCTION OF HMS PINAFORE. WE HAVE TO RETURN IT TOMORROW IN ONE P--
SAY NO MORE, FOZZIE! YOU WERE A GNAT'S CROTCHET AWAY FROM TEMPTING THE GODS OF NARRATIVE INEVITABILITY!
WHAT KEPT YOU?
OH, AND MISS P? NICE JEWELS.
FZZT
BZZT
KRRKK
AND NOW...
H.M.S. PIGAFORE

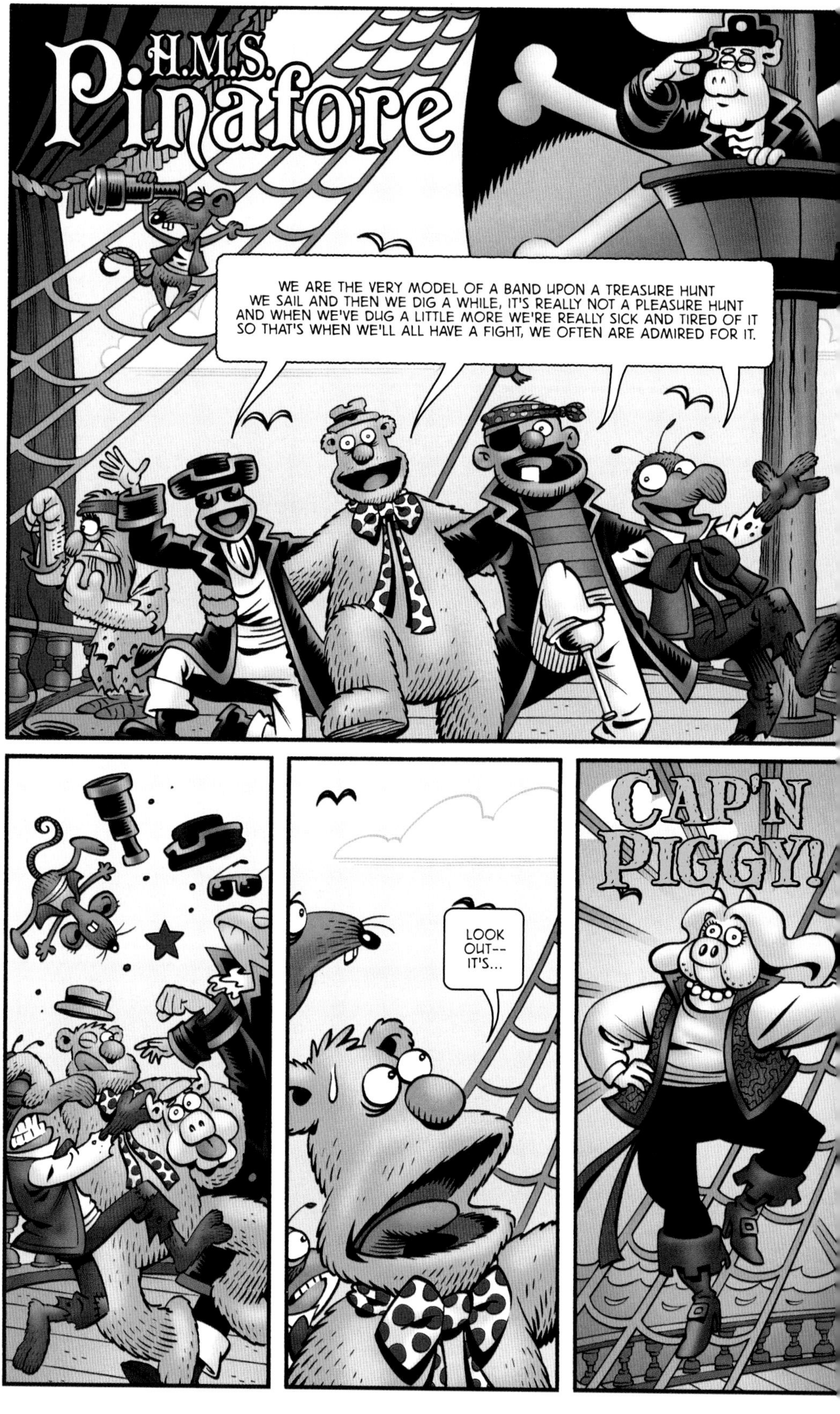
H.M.S. Pinafore
WE ARE THE VERY MODEL OF A BAND UPON A TREASURE HUNT WE SAIL AND THEN WE DIG A WHILE, IT'S REALLY NOT A PLEASURE HUNT AND WHEN WE'VE DUG A LITTLE MORE WE'RE REALLY SICK AND TIRED OF IT SO THAT'S WHEN WE'LL ALL HAVE A FIGHT, WE OFTEN ARE ADMIRED FOR IT.
LOOK OUT-- IT'S...
CAP'N PIGGY!

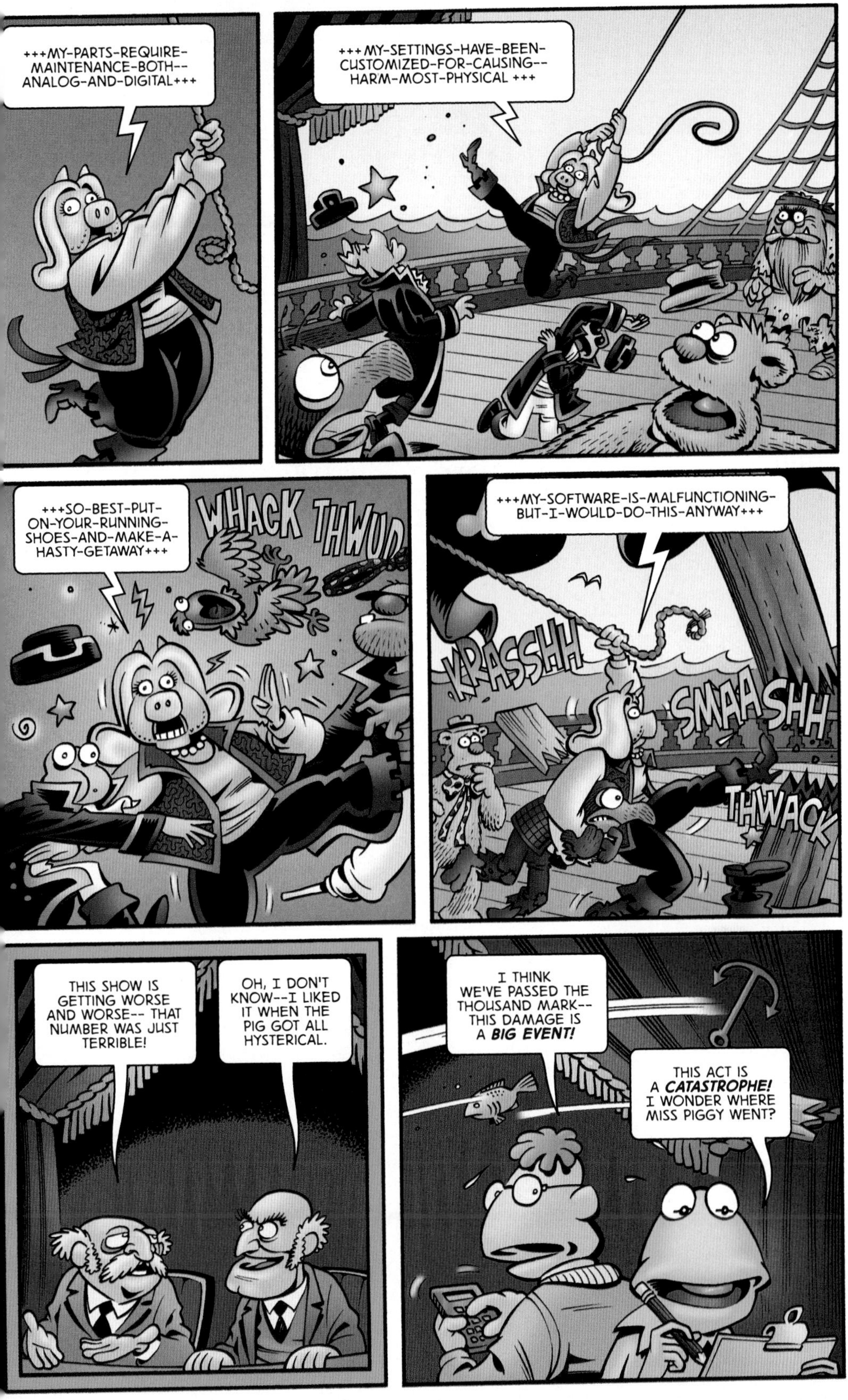

+++MY-PARTS-REQUIRE-MAINTENANCE-BOTH--ANALOG-AND-DIGITAL+++
+++MY-SETTINGS-HAVE-BEEN-CUSTOMIZED-FOR-CAUSING--HARM-MOST-PHYSICAL+++
+++SO-BEST-PUT-ON-YOUR-RUNNING-SHOES-AND-MAKE-A-HASTY-GETAWAY+++
WHACK
THWUD
+++MY-SOFTWARE-IS-MALFUNCTIONING-BUT-I-WOULD-DO-THIS-ANYWAY+++
KRASSHH
SMAASHH
THWACK
THIS SHOW IS GETTING WORSE AND WORSE-- THAT NUMBER WAS JUST TERRIBLE!
OH, I DON'T KNOW--I LIKED IT WHEN THE PIG GOT ALL HYSTERICAL.
I THINK WE'VE PASSED THE THOUSAND MARK-- THIS DAMAGE IS A *BIG EVENT!*
THIS ACT IS A *CATASTROPHE!* I WONDER WHERE MISS PIGGY WENT?

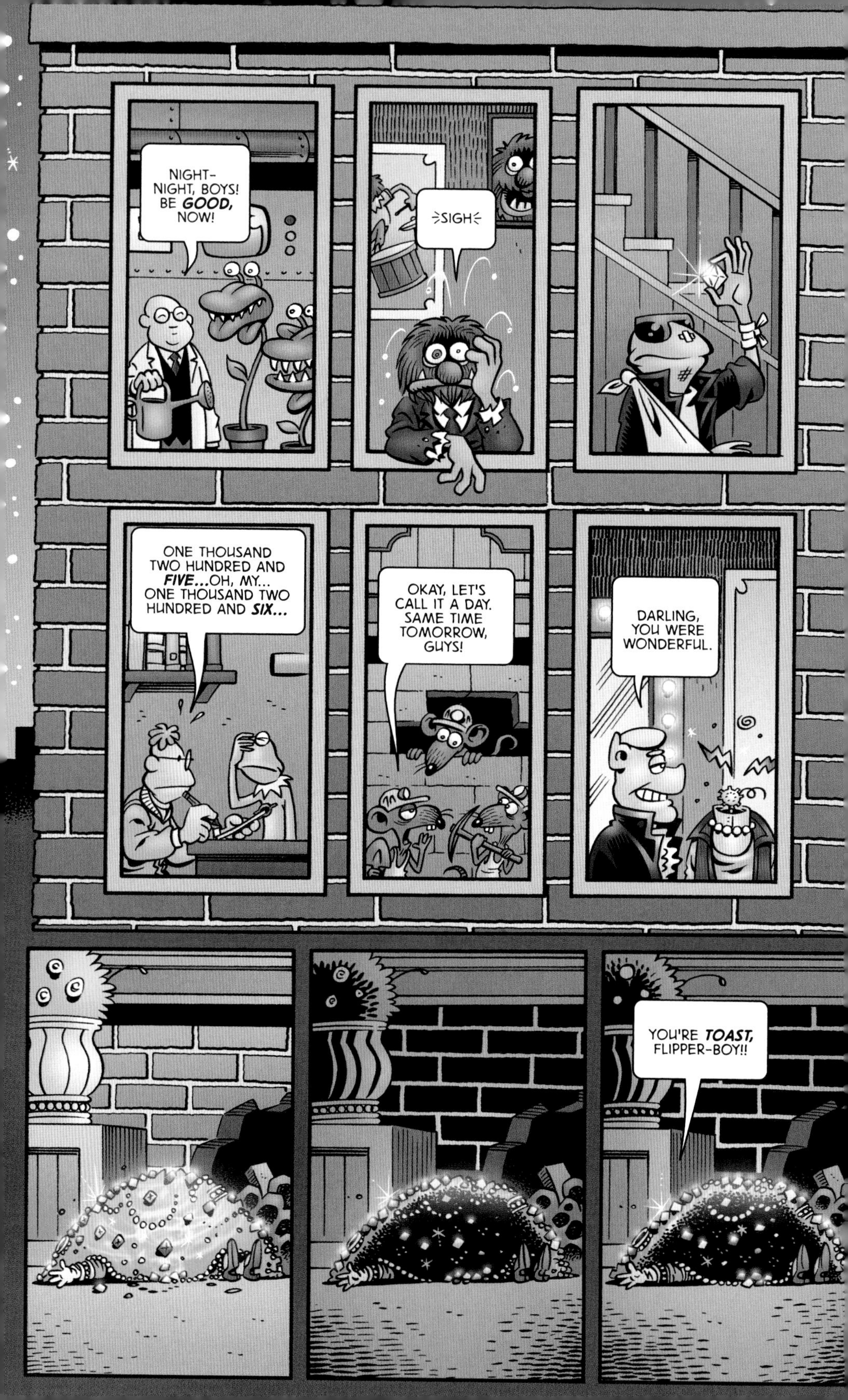
NIGHT-NIGHT, BOYS! BE **GOOD,** NOW!
⪢SIGH⪡
ONE THOUSAND TWO HUNDRED AND ***FIVE...***OH, MY... ONE THOUSAND TWO HUNDRED AND ***SIX...***
OKAY, LET'S CALL IT A DAY. SAME TIME TOMORROW, GUYS!
DARLING, YOU WERE WONDERFUL.
YOU'RE ***TOAST,*** FLIPPER-BOY!!

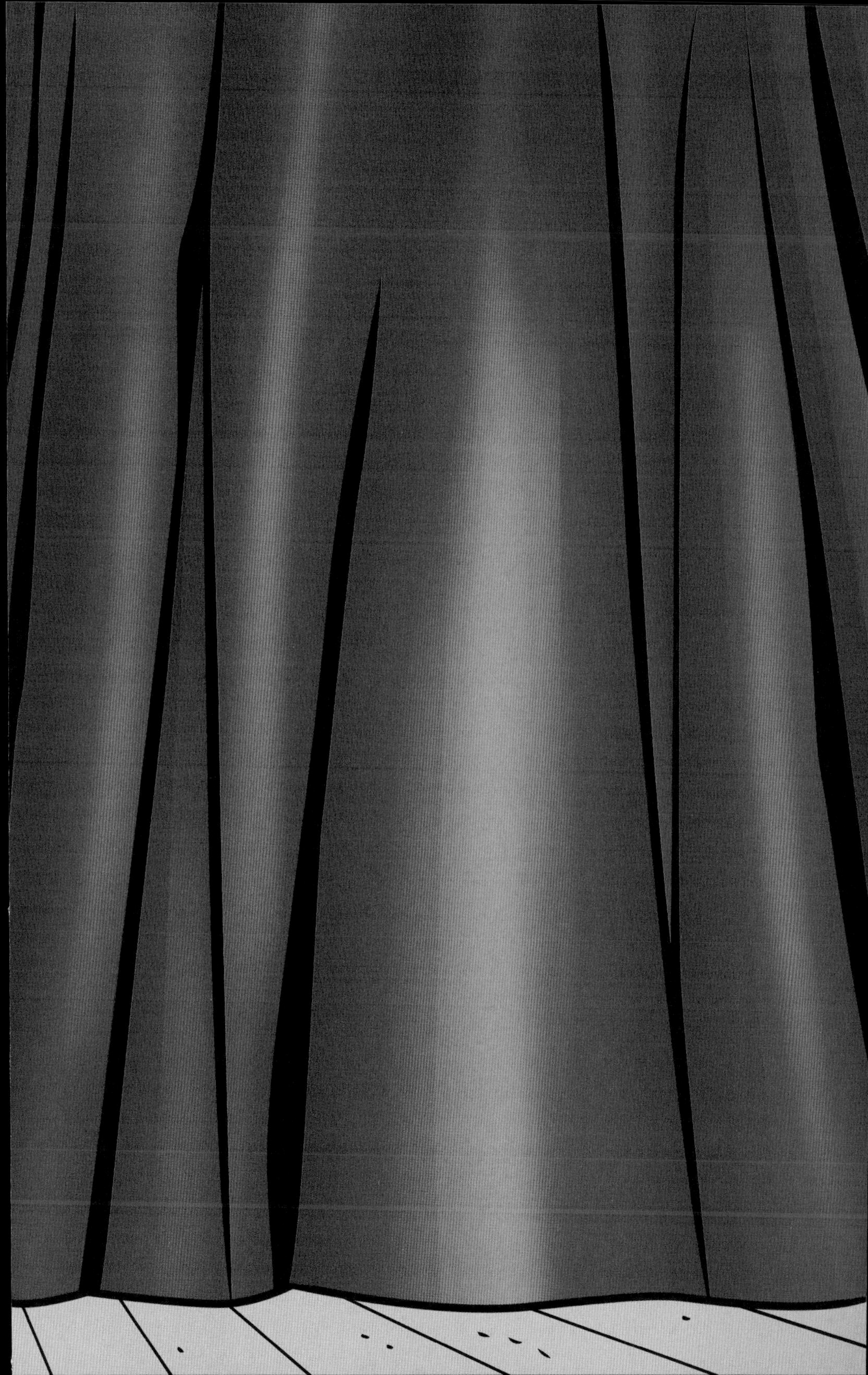

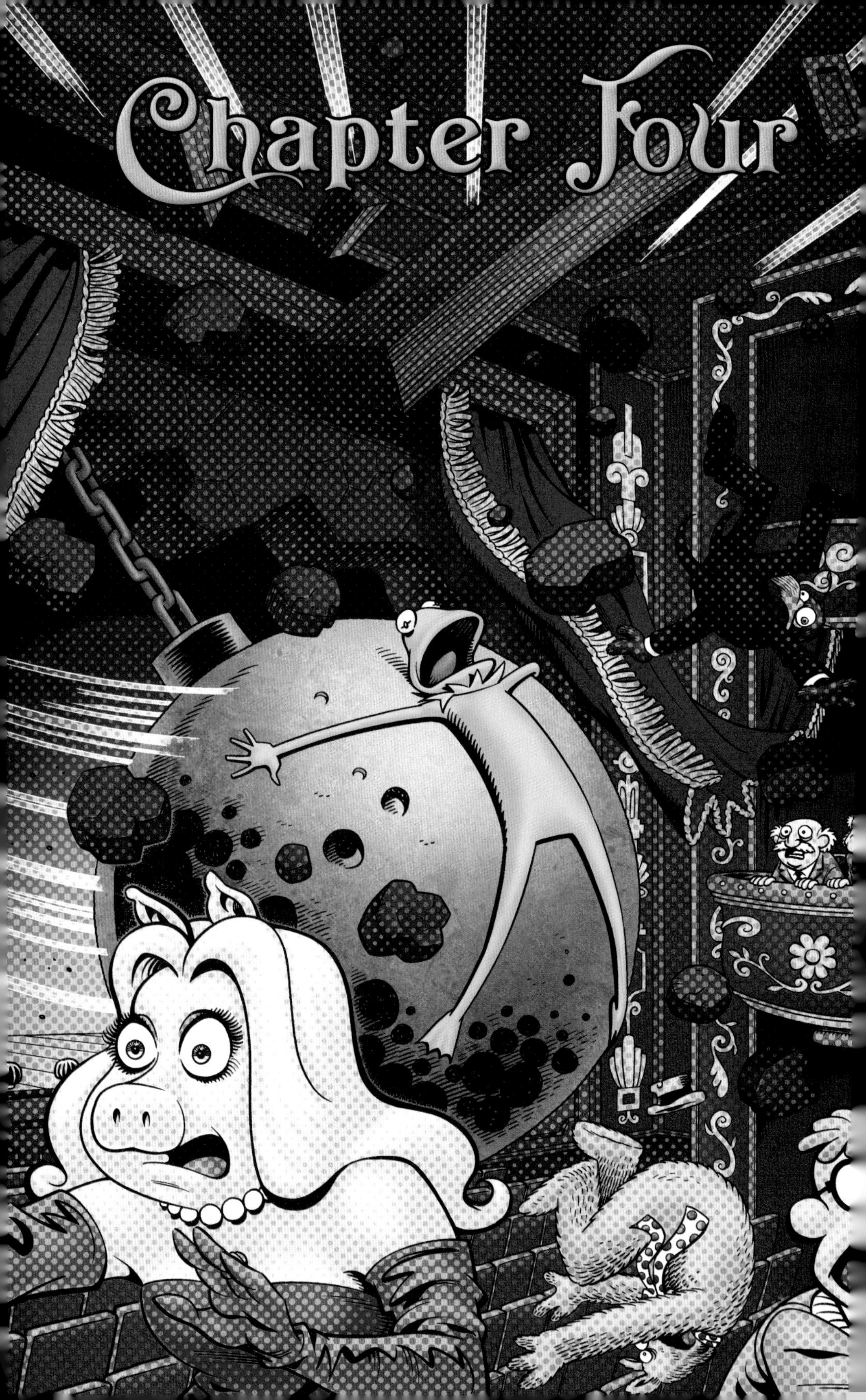
Chapter Four

ALL RIGHT, BROTHERS AND SISTERS--LET'S CALL THIS MEETING TO ORDER!

AS YOU KNOW, SCOOTER DISCOVERED A MAP TELLING US THAT TREASURE IS HIDDEN SOMEWHERE IN THIS BUILDING-- BUT, EHH, IT WAS A BIT VAGUE ABOUT THE DETAILS.

HEY, BROTHER RIZZO!

GET OFF!

DETAILS SHMETAILS!

SHH! HEAR ME OUT! HOWZABOUT, INSTEAD OF TRIPPIN' OVER EACH OTHER, WE COORDINATE OUR EFFORTS?

THEN, WHEN WE FIND THE LOOT, WE SPLIT YOUR CUT EVEN-STEVENS, SO EVERYONE GETS A PIECE!

SOUNDS -- HEY! "OUR CUT"?

SO WHAT'S YOUR CUT?

YEAH! THIS SOUNDS FISHY TO ME!

NAWWW, IT'S SIMPLE. I MERELY SPLIT THE DIFFERENTIAL OF THE SQUARE ON THE HYPOTENUSE, THEREBY ASSIGNING MYSELF A PROPORTIONAL AMOUNT IN DIRECT INVERSE RATIO TO MY CONTRIBUTIONS AS CHIEF POO-BAH, EVENTS CO-ORDINATOR. ANY QUESTIONS? GOOD.

$$\triangle \to \bigcirc \sqrt[3]{3}$$
$$\Rightarrow 5e\%$$
$$\pi \times \emptyset \uparrow \frac{32}{15} (2$$
$$= 485e < 32y$$

I TRUST RIZZO-- HE LOOKS OUT FOR US RATS. I'M SIGNIN' UP.

ME, TOO. HE WOULDN'T DO WRONG BY US.

NOT UNLESS HE COULD GET AWAY WITH IT.

MAYBE RIZZO WOULDN'T...BUT KISMET THE TOAD CERTAINLY WOULD! OH, TREASURE-- COME TO PAPA...!

ALL VERY INTERESTING... BUT ISN'T SOMEONE GOING TO MENTION ANIMAL'S JEKYLL AND HYDE PROBLEM, MISS PIGGY'S JEWELS TURNING OUT TO BE FAKES AND THOSE WEIRD GERANIUMS DOCTOR HONEYDEW IS GROWING?

WHAT, AND MAKE THIS COMIC COMPREHENSIBLE? YOU'RE NEW HERE, AREN'T YOU?

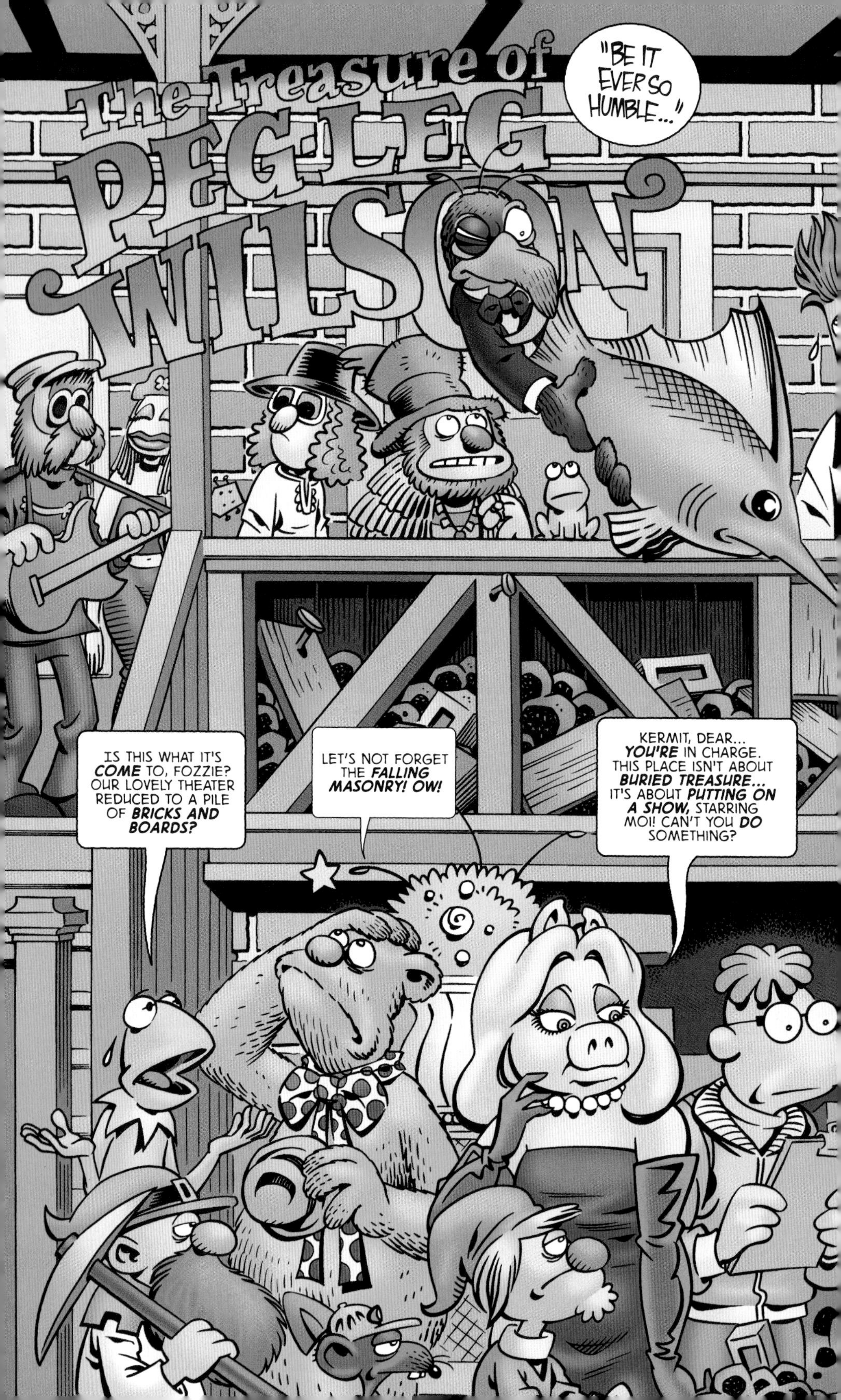
The Treasure of
PEGLEG WILSON
"BE IT EVER SO HUMBLE..."
IS THIS WHAT IT'S COME TO, FOZZIE? OUR LOVELY THEATER REDUCED TO A PILE OF BRICKS AND BOARDS?
LET'S NOT FORGET THE FALLING MASONRY! OW!
KERMIT, DEAR... YOU'RE IN CHARGE. THIS PLACE ISN'T ABOUT BURIED TREASURE... IT'S ABOUT PUTTING ON A SHOW, STARRING MOI! CAN'T YOU DO SOMETHING?

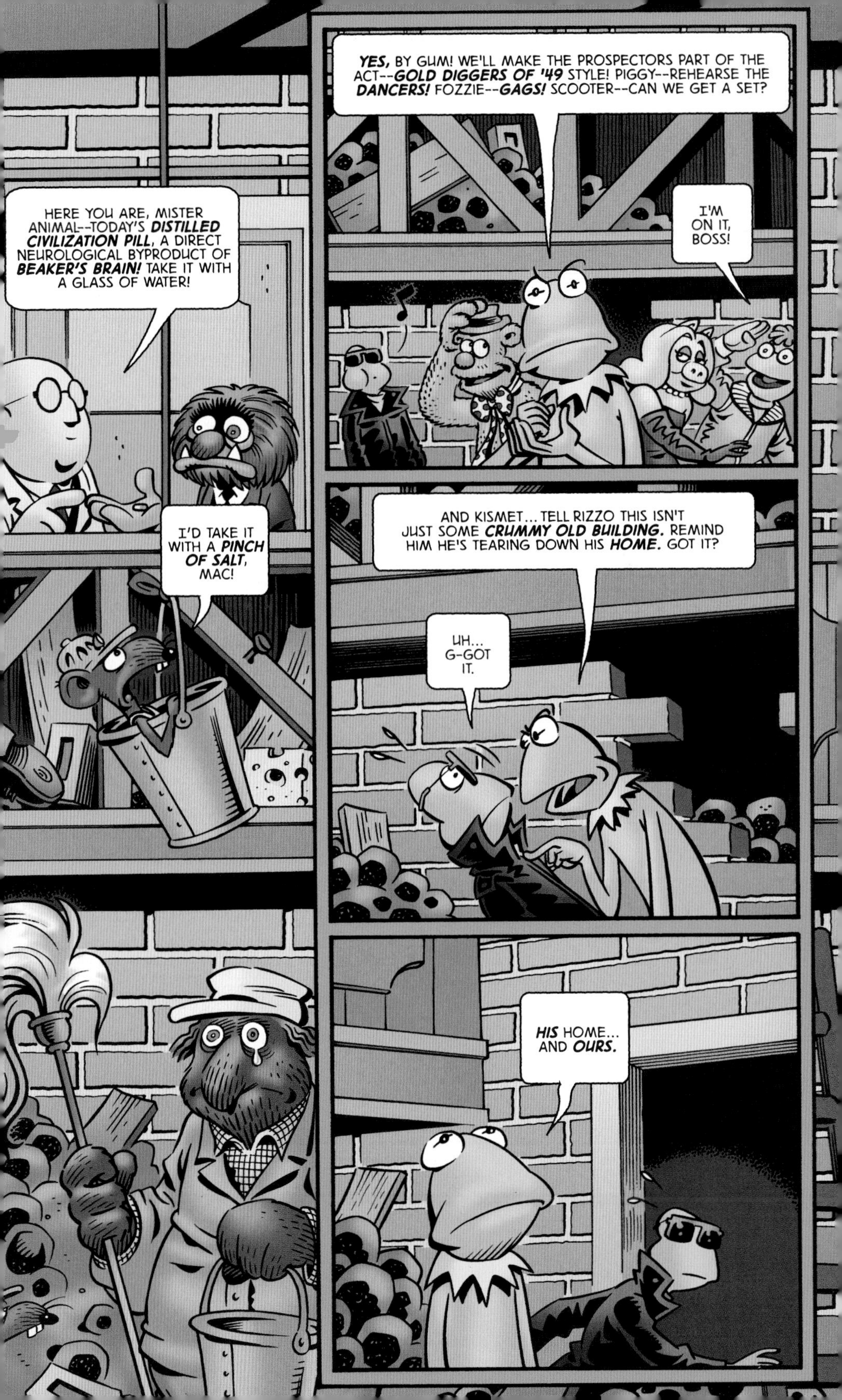

HERE YOU ARE, MISTER ANIMAL--TODAY'S **DISTILLED CIVILIZATION PILL**, A DIRECT NEUROLOGICAL BYPRODUCT OF **BEAKER'S BRAIN!** TAKE IT WITH A GLASS OF WATER!
I'D TAKE IT WITH A **PINCH OF SALT**, MAC!
YES, BY GUM! WE'LL MAKE THE PROSPECTORS PART OF THE ACT--**GOLD DIGGERS OF '49** STYLE! PIGGY--REHEARSE THE **DANCERS!** FOZZIE--**GAGS!** SCOOTER--CAN WE GET A SET?
I'M ON IT, BOSS!
AND KISMET... TELL RIZZO THIS ISN'T JUST SOME **CRUMMY OLD BUILDING.** REMIND HIM HE'S TEARING DOWN HIS **HOME.** GOT IT?
UH... G-GOT IT.
HIS HOME... AND **OURS.**

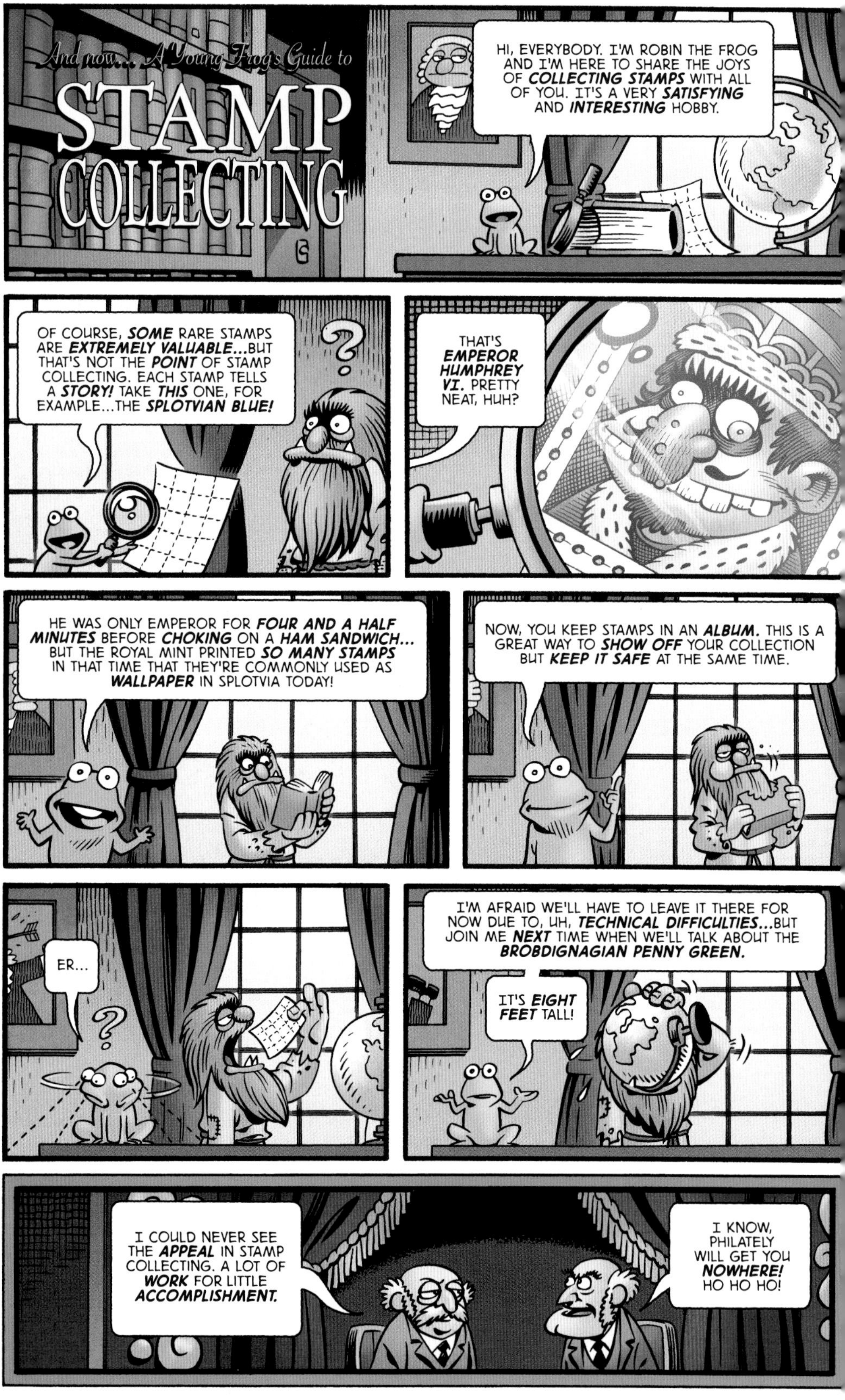
And now... A Young Frog's Guide to
STAMP COLLECTING
HI, EVERYBODY. I'M ROBIN THE FROG AND I'M HERE TO SHARE THE JOYS OF COLLECTING STAMPS WITH ALL OF YOU. IT'S A VERY SATISFYING AND INTERESTING HOBBY.
OF COURSE, SOME RARE STAMPS ARE EXTREMELY VALUABLE...BUT THAT'S NOT THE POINT OF STAMP COLLECTING. EACH STAMP TELLS A STORY! TAKE THIS ONE, FOR EXAMPLE...THE SPLOTVIAN BLUE!
?
THAT'S EMPEROR HUMPHREY VI. PRETTY NEAT, HUH?
HE WAS ONLY EMPEROR FOR FOUR AND A HALF MINUTES BEFORE CHOKING ON A HAM SANDWICH... BUT THE ROYAL MINT PRINTED SO MANY STAMPS IN THAT TIME THAT THEY'RE COMMONLY USED AS WALLPAPER IN SPLOTVIA TODAY!
NOW, YOU KEEP STAMPS IN AN ALBUM. THIS IS A GREAT WAY TO SHOW OFF YOUR COLLECTION BUT KEEP IT SAFE AT THE SAME TIME.
ER...
?
I'M AFRAID WE'LL HAVE TO LEAVE IT THERE FOR NOW DUE TO, UH, TECHNICAL DIFFICULTIES...BUT JOIN ME NEXT TIME WHEN WE'LL TALK ABOUT THE BROBDIGNAGIAN PENNY GREEN.
IT'S EIGHT FEET TALL!
I COULD NEVER SEE THE APPEAL IN STAMP COLLECTING. A LOT OF WORK FOR LITTLE ACCOMPLISHMENT.
I KNOW, PHILATELY WILL GET YOU NOWHERE! HO HO HO!

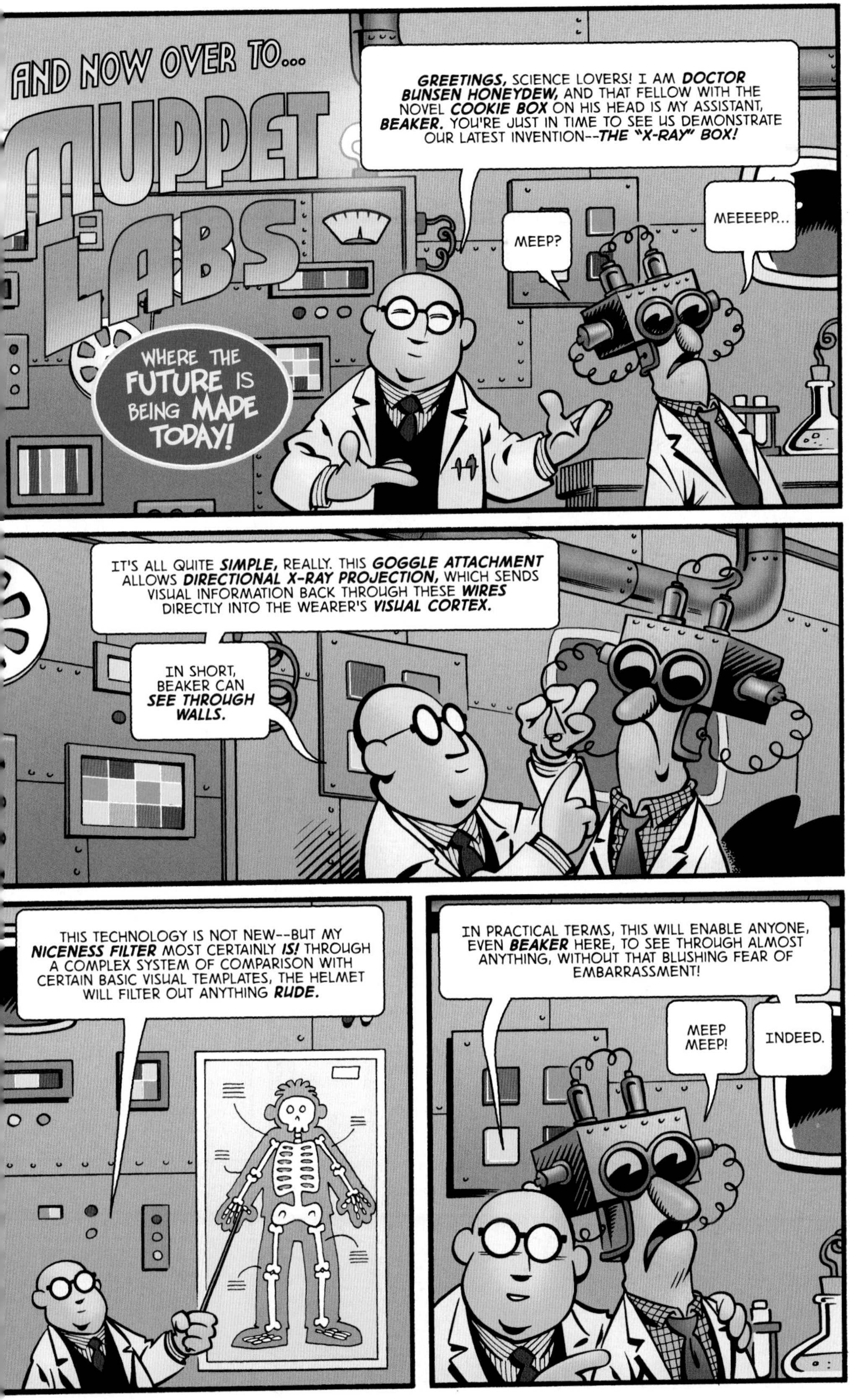
AND NOW OVER TO...
MUPPET LABS
WHERE THE FUTURE IS BEING MADE TODAY!
GREETINGS, SCIENCE LOVERS! I AM DOCTOR BUNSEN HONEYDEW, AND THAT FELLOW WITH THE NOVEL COOKIE BOX ON HIS HEAD IS MY ASSISTANT, BEAKER. YOU'RE JUST IN TIME TO SEE US DEMONSTRATE OUR LATEST INVENTION--THE "X-RAY" BOX!
MEEP?
MEEEEPP...
IT'S ALL QUITE SIMPLE, REALLY. THIS GOGGLE ATTACHMENT ALLOWS DIRECTIONAL X-RAY PROJECTION, WHICH SENDS VISUAL INFORMATION BACK THROUGH THESE WIRES DIRECTLY INTO THE WEARER'S VISUAL CORTEX.
IN SHORT, BEAKER CAN SEE THROUGH WALLS.
THIS TECHNOLOGY IS NOT NEW--BUT MY NICENESS FILTER MOST CERTAINLY IS! THROUGH A COMPLEX SYSTEM OF COMPARISON WITH CERTAIN BASIC VISUAL TEMPLATES, THE HELMET WILL FILTER OUT ANYTHING RUDE.
IN PRACTICAL TERMS, THIS WILL ENABLE ANYONE, EVEN BEAKER HERE, TO SEE THROUGH ALMOST ANYTHING, WITHOUT THAT BLUSHING FEAR OF EMBARRASSMENT!
MEEP MEEP!
INDEED.

NOW, I FEEL A **DEMONSTRATION** IS IN ORDER. BEAKER-- FETCH OUR **MASONRY EXPERT!**

MEEP!

THIS IS **VINCE SHABBY,** A BRICKLAYER, WHO HAS KINDLY OFFERED TO BUILD A **WALL** AROUND BEAKER.

SURE THING, DOC. HEY, IT'S A REAL **MESS** OUT THERE!

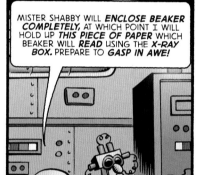

MISTER SHABBY WILL **ENCLOSE BEAKER COMPLETELY,** AT WHICH POINT I WILL HOLD UP **THIS PIECE OF PAPER** WHICH BEAKER WILL **READ** USING THE **X-RAY BOX.** PREPARE TO **GASP IN AWE!**

BETTER LIVING THROUGH SCIENCE!

AND IT LOOKS LIKE WE'RE DONE! **THANK YOU,** MISTER SHABBY--NOW, **LET SCIENCE COMMENCE!**

BEAKER, MY BOY... CAN YOU READ THIS PIECE OF PAPER?

MMM... MEEP MEEP MEEPMEEP MEEP **MEEEEP?**

SPLENDID! NOT A COMMA OUT OF PLACE! BEAKER, **WE'VE DONE IT!** COME OUT AND **TAKE A BOW!**

BEAKER?

MEEP?

OH DEAR.

MEEP MEEP MEEEEP...

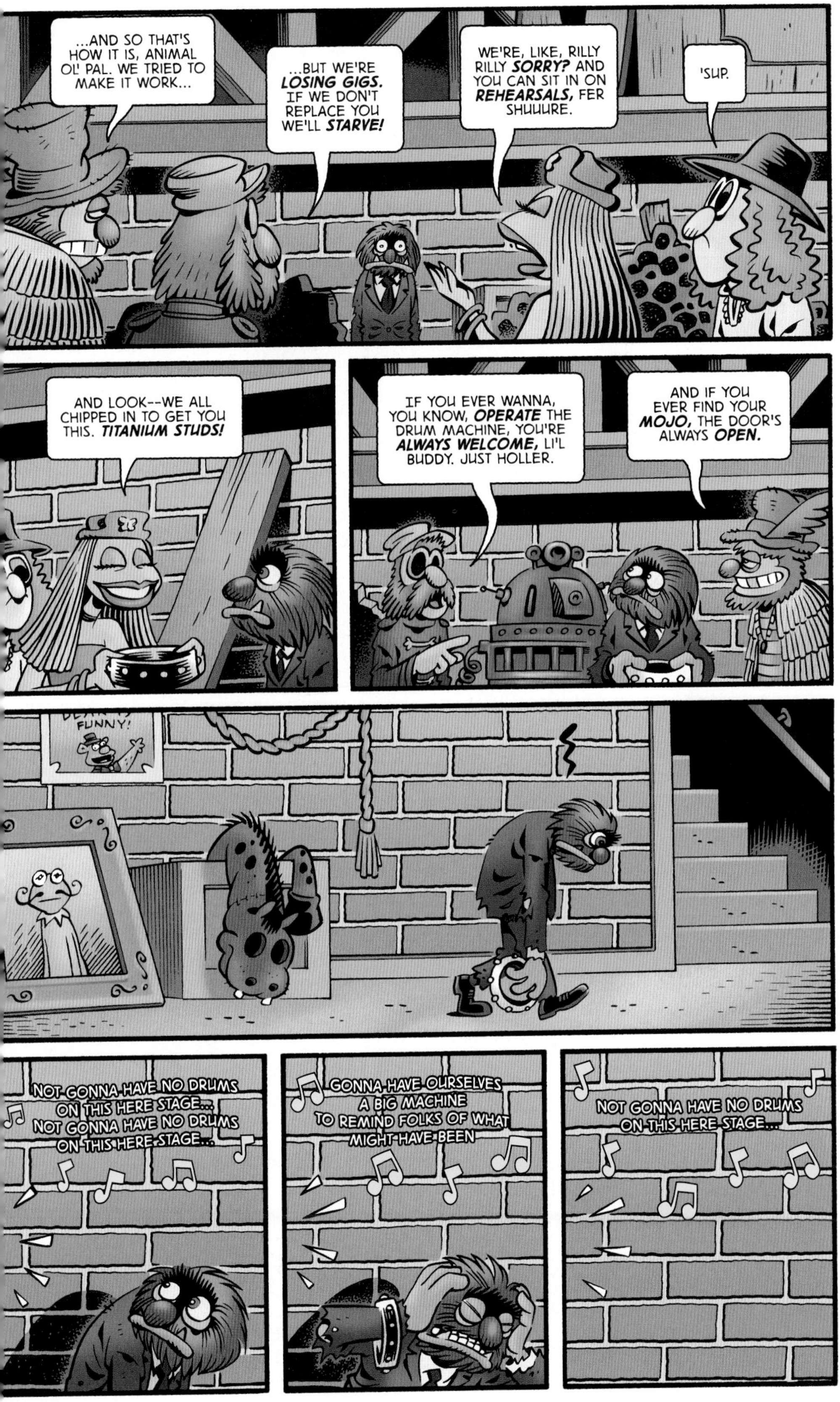
...AND SO THAT'S HOW IT IS, ANIMAL OL' PAL. WE TRIED TO MAKE IT WORK...
...BUT WE'RE LOSING GIGS. IF WE DON'T REPLACE YOU WE'LL STARVE!
WE'RE, LIKE, RILLY RILLY SORRY? AND YOU CAN SIT IN ON REHEARSALS, FER SHUUURE.
'SUP.
AND LOOK--WE ALL CHIPPED IN TO GET YOU THIS. TITANIUM STUDS!
IF YOU EVER WANNA, YOU KNOW, OPERATE THE DRUM MACHINE, YOU'RE ALWAYS WELCOME, LI'L BUDDY. JUST HOLLER.
AND IF YOU EVER FIND YOUR MOJO, THE DOOR'S ALWAYS OPEN.
FUNNY!
NOT GONNA HAVE NO DRUMS ON THIS HERE STAGE... NOT GONNA HAVE NO DRUMS ON THIS HERE STAGE...
GONNA HAVE OURSELVES A BIG MACHINE TO REMIND FOLKS OF WHAT MIGHT HAVE BEEN
NOT GONNA HAVE NO DRUMS ON THIS HERE STAGE...

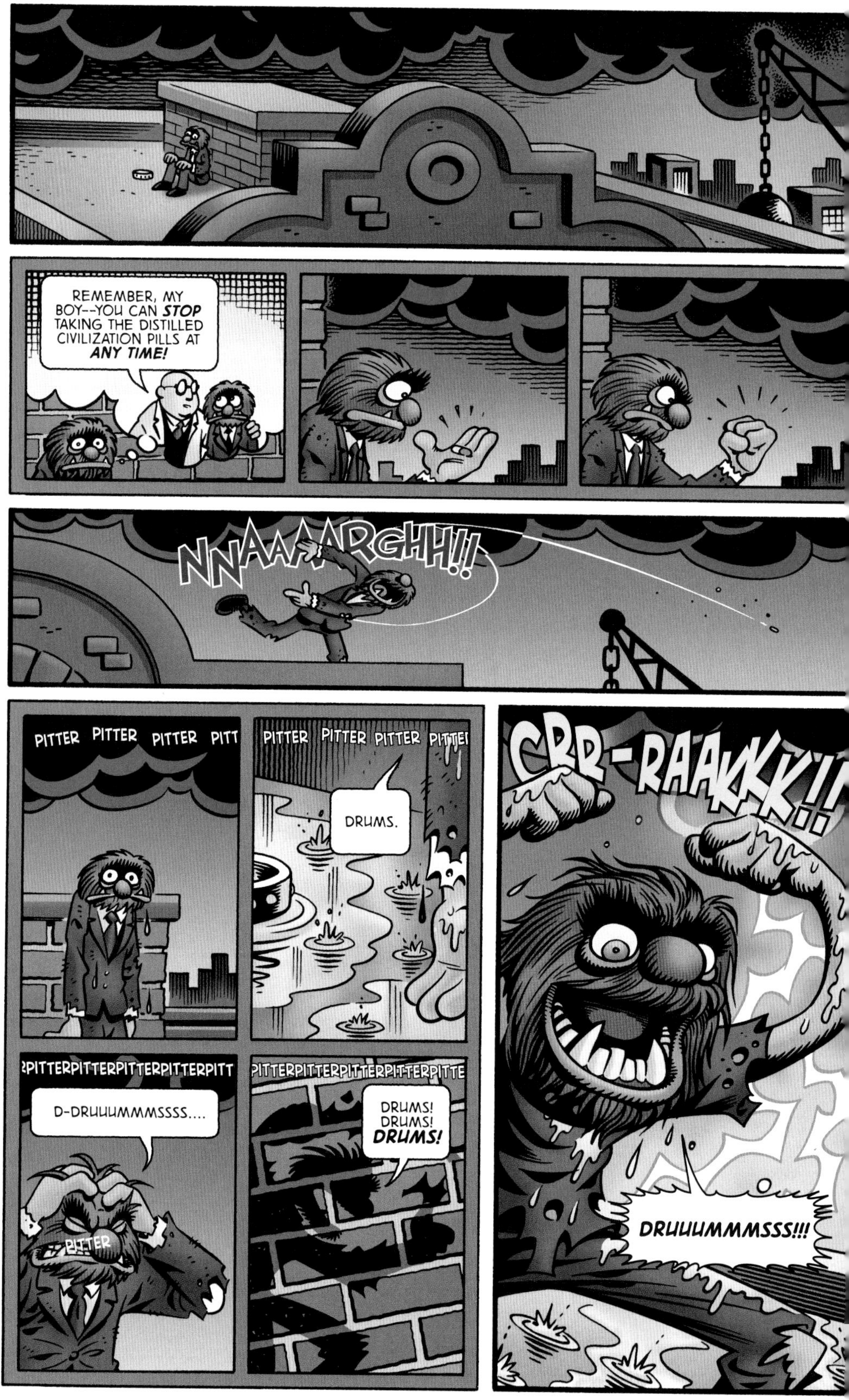

REMEMBER, MY BOY--YOU CAN STOP TAKING THE DISTILLED CIVILIZATION PILLS AT ANY TIME!
NNAAAARGHH!!
PITTER PITTER PITTER PITT
PITTER PITTER PITTER PITTER
DRUMS.
PITTERPITTERPITTERPITTERPITT
D-DRUUUMMMSSSS....
PITTER
PITTERPITTERPITTERPITTERPITTE
DRUMS! DRUMS! DRUMS!
CRR-RAAKKK!!
DRUUUMMMSSS!!!

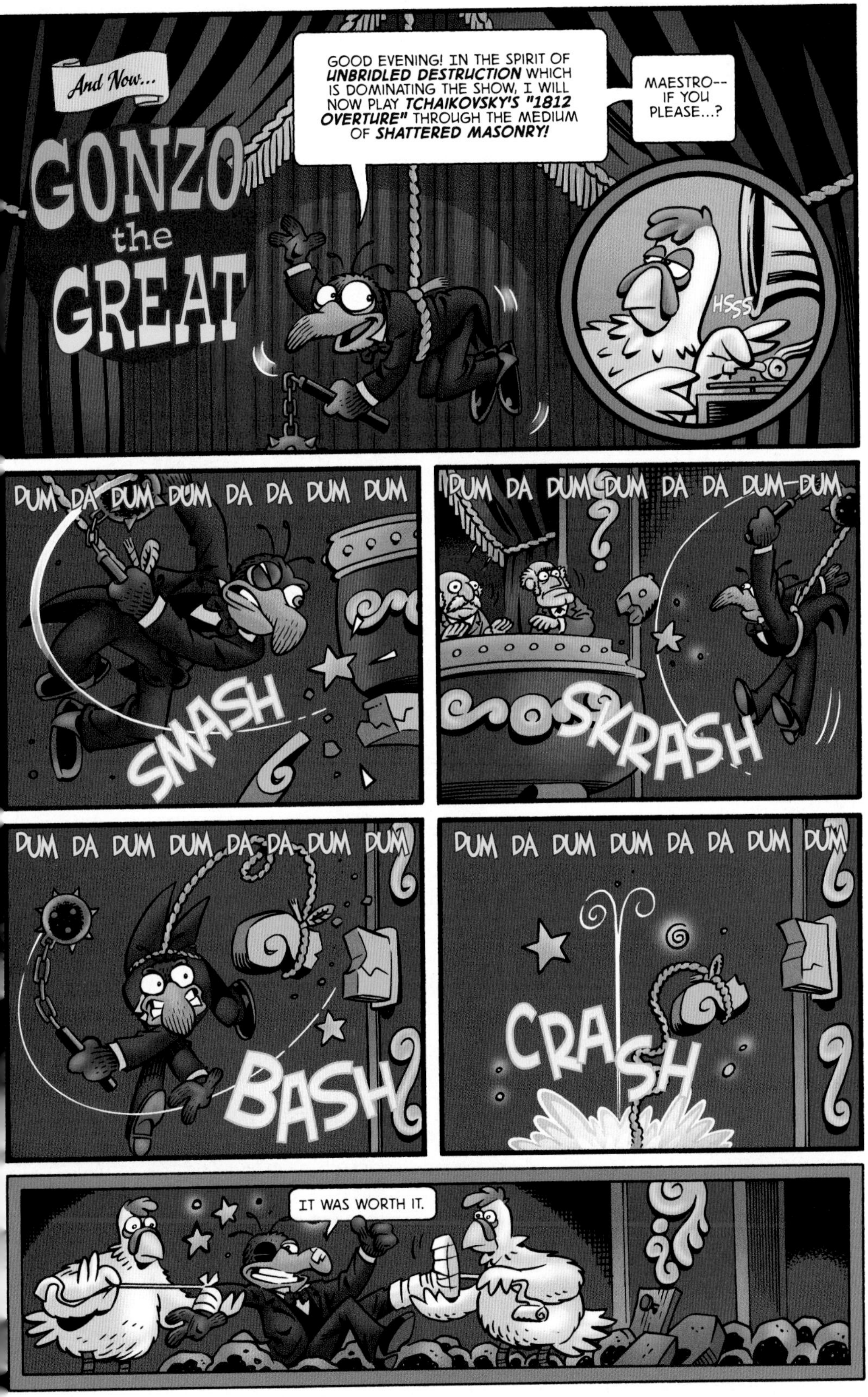

And Now...
GONZO the GREAT
GOOD EVENING! IN THE SPIRIT OF UNBRIDLED DESTRUCTION WHICH IS DOMINATING THE SHOW, I WILL NOW PLAY TCHAIKOVSKY'S "1812 OVERTURE" THROUGH THE MEDIUM OF SHATTERED MASONRY!
MAESTRO-- IF YOU PLEASE...?
HSSS
DUM DA DUM DUM DA DA DUM DUM
SMASH
DUM DA DUM DUM DA DA DUM-DUM
SKRASH
DUM DA DUM DUM DA DA DUM DUM
BASH
DUM DA DUM DUM DA DA DUM DUM
CRASH
IT WAS WORTH IT.

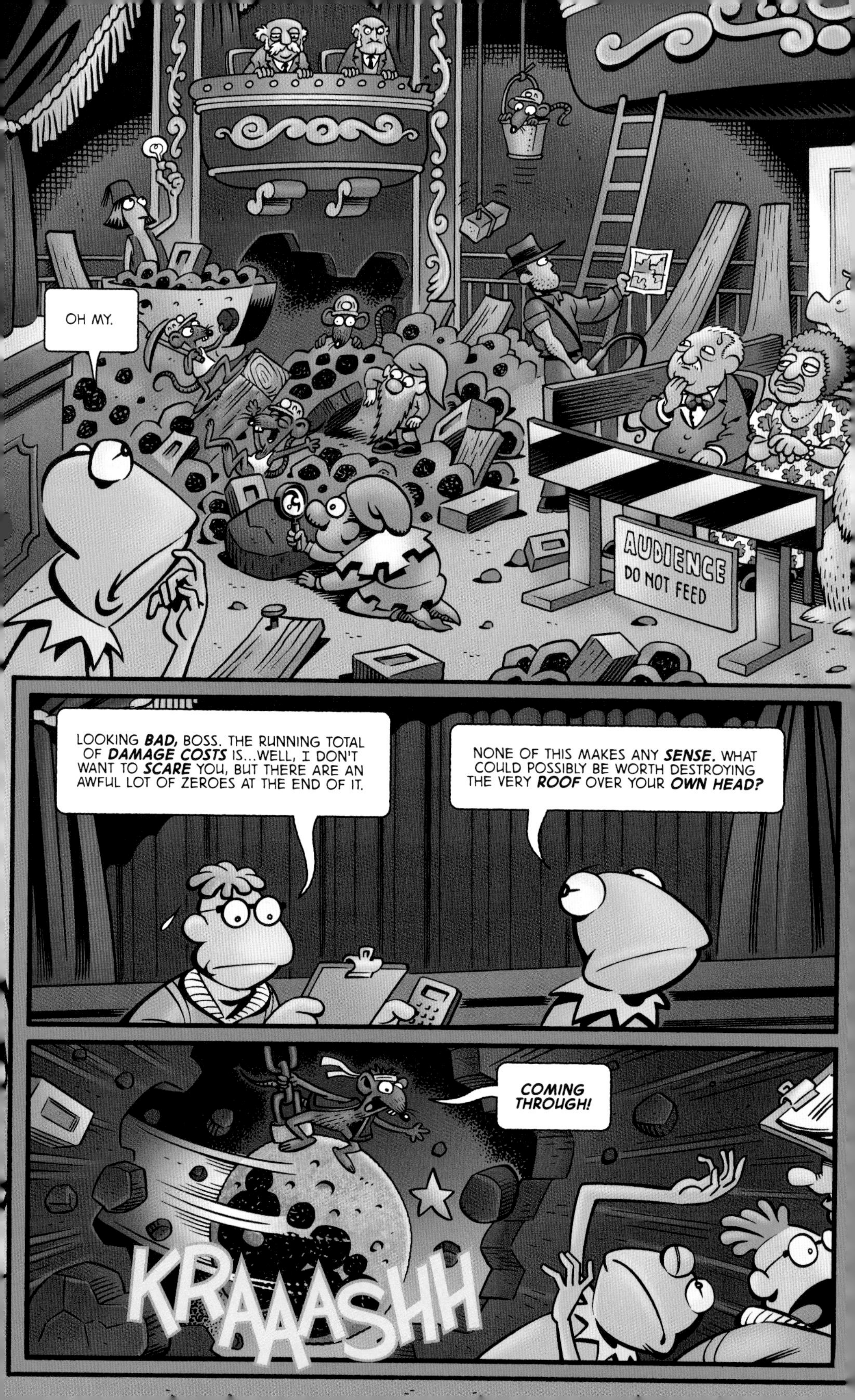
OH MY.
AUDIENCE
DO NOT FEED
LOOKING BAD, BOSS. THE RUNNING TOTAL OF DAMAGE COSTS IS...WELL, I DON'T WANT TO SCARE YOU, BUT THERE ARE AN AWFUL LOT OF ZEROES AT THE END OF IT.
NONE OF THIS MAKES ANY SENSE. WHAT COULD POSSIBLY BE WORTH DESTROYING THE VERY ROOF OVER YOUR OWN HEAD?
COMING THROUGH!
KRAAASHH

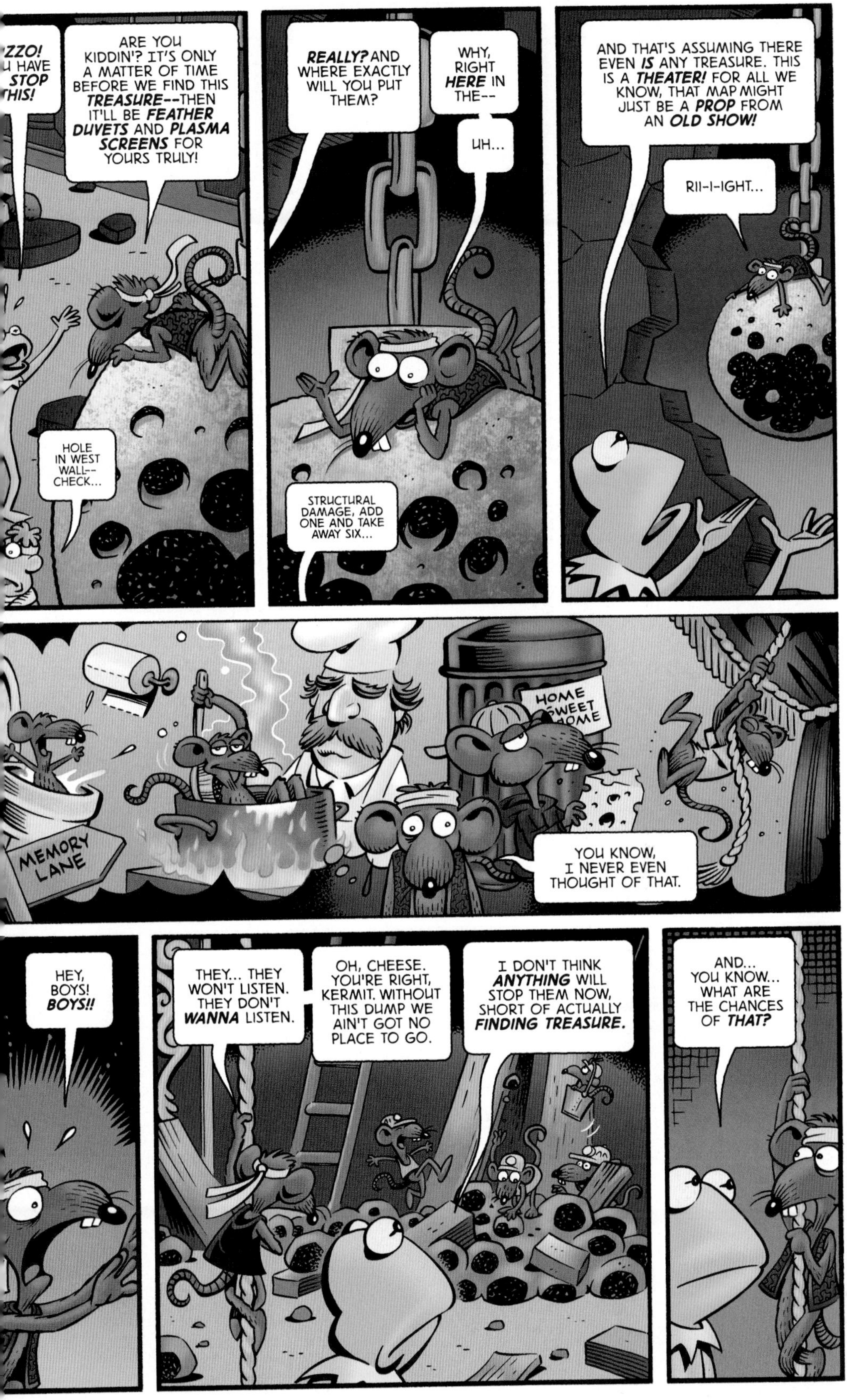
ZZO! U HAVE STOP HIS!
ARE YOU KIDDIN'? IT'S ONLY A MATTER OF TIME BEFORE WE FIND THIS TREASURE--THEN IT'LL BE FEATHER DUVETS AND PLASMA SCREENS FOR YOURS TRULY!
HOLE IN WEST WALL-- CHECK...
REALLY? AND WHERE EXACTLY WILL YOU PUT THEM?
WHY, RIGHT HERE IN THE--
UH...
STRUCTURAL DAMAGE, ADD ONE AND TAKE AWAY SIX...
AND THAT'S ASSUMING THERE EVEN IS ANY TREASURE. THIS IS A THEATER! FOR ALL WE KNOW, THAT MAP MIGHT JUST BE A PROP FROM AN OLD SHOW!
RII-I-IGHT...
MEMORY LANE
HOME SWEET HOME
YOU KNOW, I NEVER EVEN THOUGHT OF THAT.
HEY, BOYS! BOYS!!
THEY... THEY WON'T LISTEN. THEY DON'T WANNA LISTEN.
OH, CHEESE. YOU'RE RIGHT, KERMIT. WITHOUT THIS DUMP WE AIN'T GOT NO PLACE TO GO.
I DON'T THINK ANYTHING WILL STOP THEM NOW, SHORT OF ACTUALLY FINDING TREASURE.
AND... YOU KNOW... WHAT ARE THE CHANCES OF THAT?

HMM.

MUPPET LABS

THERE, NOW, BEAKER. DIDN'T HURT A *BIT.*

M- MEEP...

DOC! HEY, *DOC!* YOU *HAVE TO SEE* THIS!

BUT BEAKER AND I ARE IN THE MIDST OF A VERY DELICATE, NOT TO MENTION PAINFUL, PROCEDURE.

DOC, I GUARANTEE YOU'LL *FLIP* WHEN YOU SEE WHAT'S IN THE *BASEMENT!* IT'S, UH...

GERANIUMS! BIGGEST ONES I EVER SAW! AND THE *COLOR...* WHY, I WOULDN'T BE SURPRISED IF IT'S A *NEW SPECIES!*

GERANIUMS?!

MY BOY, WHY DIDN'T YOU *SAY* SO? *BEAKER!* FETCH *PROFESSOR SNOOD* OF THE *HORTICULTURAL SOCIETY* WITHOUT DELAY!

MEEP! *MEEP!*

NOW, THE *TREASURE!* TREASURE, TREASURE, IN THE...

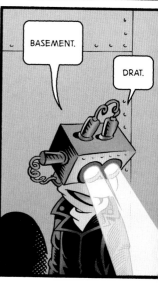

BASEMENT.

DRAT.

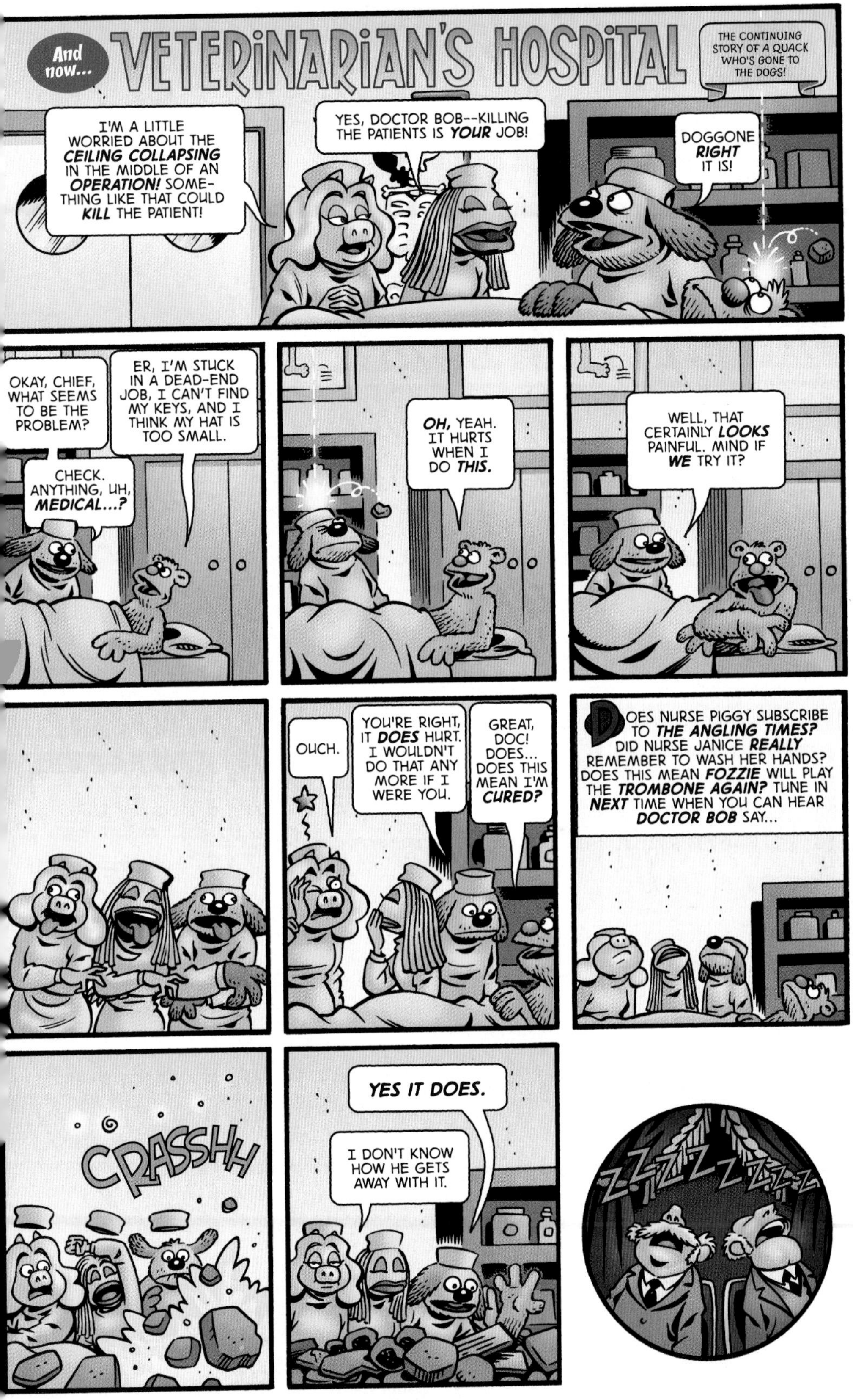

And now...
VETERINARIAN'S HOSPITAL
THE CONTINUING STORY OF A QUACK WHO'S GONE TO THE DOGS!
I'M A LITTLE WORRIED ABOUT THE CEILING COLLAPSING IN THE MIDDLE OF AN OPERATION! SOMETHING LIKE THAT COULD KILL THE PATIENT!
YES, DOCTOR BOB--KILLING THE PATIENTS IS YOUR JOB!
DOGGONE RIGHT IT IS!
OKAY, CHIEF, WHAT SEEMS TO BE THE PROBLEM?
ER, I'M STUCK IN A DEAD-END JOB, I CAN'T FIND MY KEYS, AND I THINK MY HAT IS TOO SMALL.
CHECK. ANYTHING, UH, MEDICAL...?
OH, YEAH. IT HURTS WHEN I DO THIS.
WELL, THAT CERTAINLY LOOKS PAINFUL. MIND IF WE TRY IT?
OUCH.
YOU'RE RIGHT, IT DOES HURT. I WOULDN'T DO THAT ANY MORE IF I WERE YOU.
GREAT, DOC! DOES... DOES THIS MEAN I'M CURED?
DOES NURSE PIGGY SUBSCRIBE TO THE ANGLING TIMES? DID NURSE JANICE REALLY REMEMBER TO WASH HER HANDS? DOES THIS MEAN FOZZIE WILL PLAY THE TROMBONE AGAIN? TUNE IN NEXT TIME WHEN YOU CAN HEAR DOCTOR BOB SAY...
CRASSHH
YES IT DOES.
I DON'T KNOW HOW HE GETS AWAY WITH IT.
ZZZZZZZZZ

DEAR ME. WHAT SORT OF GERANIUM COULD POSSIBLY THRIVE IN *PITCH BLACKNESS?* PERHAPS THERE'S BEEN A *MISTAKE...*

CLICK

THERE WE GO!

GOODNESS--THIS *CAN'T* BE RIGHT. I SMELL A *RAT.*

THWAK

RATS HAD NOTHING TO DO WITH IT.

TREASURE, ON THE OTHER HAND ﹥NNNGGHH!﹤ HAS EVERYTHING TO DO WITH *EVERYTHING!*

OOOH, BABY! *THE TREASURE OF PEG-LEG WILSON--AT LAST!* AND IT'S MINE, *AAALLLL* MINE! *MWAHAHAHAHAAA!*

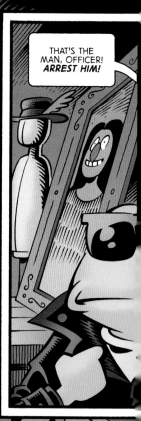

THAT'S THE MAN, OFFICER! *ARREST HIM!*

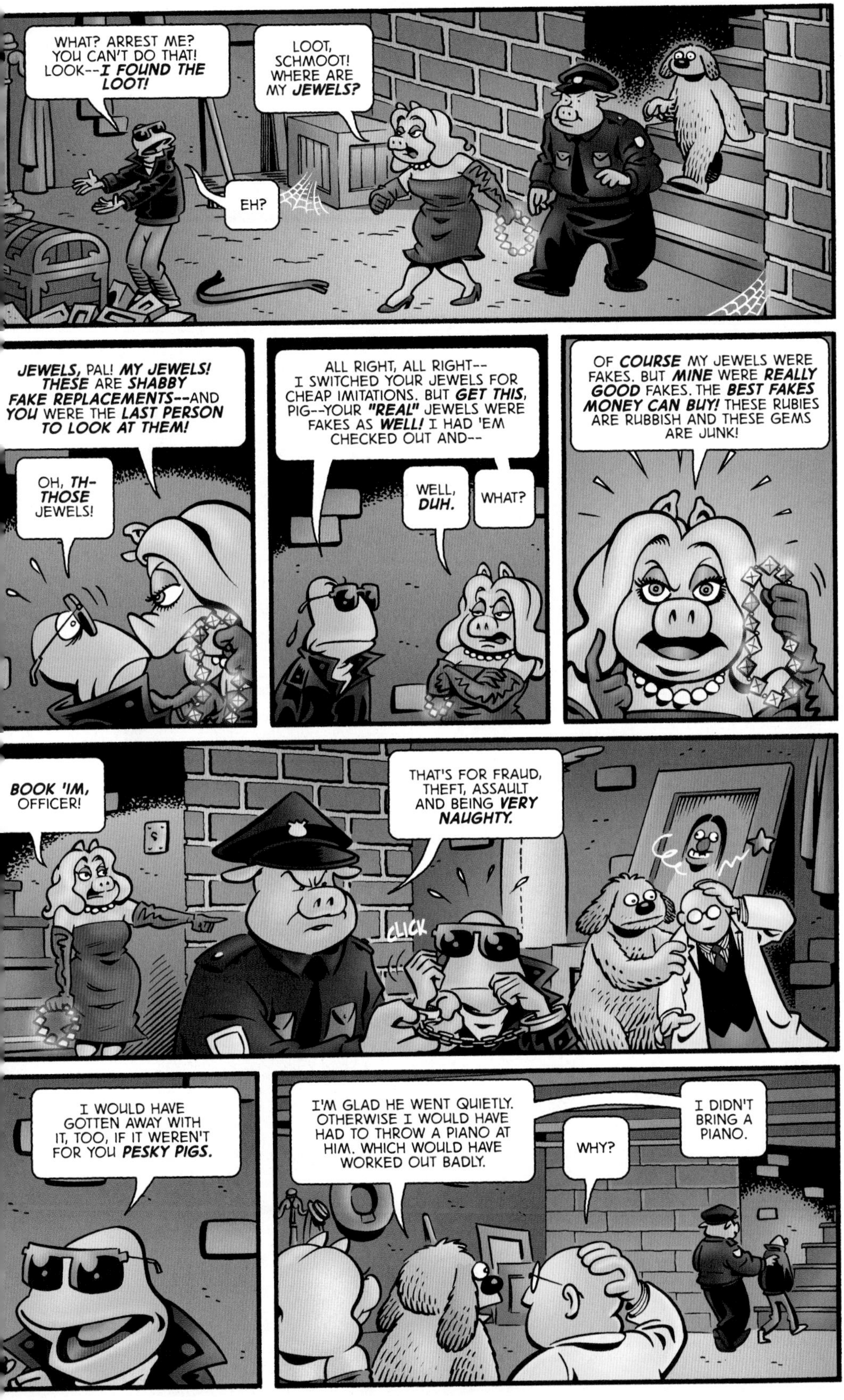
WHAT? ARREST ME? YOU CAN'T DO THAT! LOOK--I FOUND THE LOOT!
LOOT, SCHMOOT! WHERE ARE MY JEWELS?
EH?
JEWELS, PAL! MY JEWELS! THESE ARE SHABBY FAKE REPLACEMENTS--AND YOU WERE THE LAST PERSON TO LOOK AT THEM!
OH, TH-THOSE JEWELS!
ALL RIGHT, ALL RIGHT-- I SWITCHED YOUR JEWELS FOR CHEAP IMITATIONS. BUT GET THIS, PIG--YOUR "REAL" JEWELS WERE FAKES AS WELL! I HAD 'EM CHECKED OUT AND--
WELL, DUH.
WHAT?
OF COURSE MY JEWELS WERE FAKES. BUT MINE WERE REALLY GOOD FAKES. THE BEST FAKES MONEY CAN BUY! THESE RUBIES ARE RUBBISH AND THESE GEMS ARE JUNK!
BOOK 'IM, OFFICER!
THAT'S FOR FRAUD, THEFT, ASSAULT AND BEING VERY NAUGHTY.
CLICK
I WOULD HAVE GOTTEN AWAY WITH IT, TOO, IF IT WEREN'T FOR YOU PESKY PIGS.
I'M GLAD HE WENT QUIETLY. OTHERWISE I WOULD HAVE HAD TO THROW A PIANO AT HIM. WHICH WOULD HAVE WORKED OUT BADLY.
WHY?
I DIDN'T BRING A PIANO.

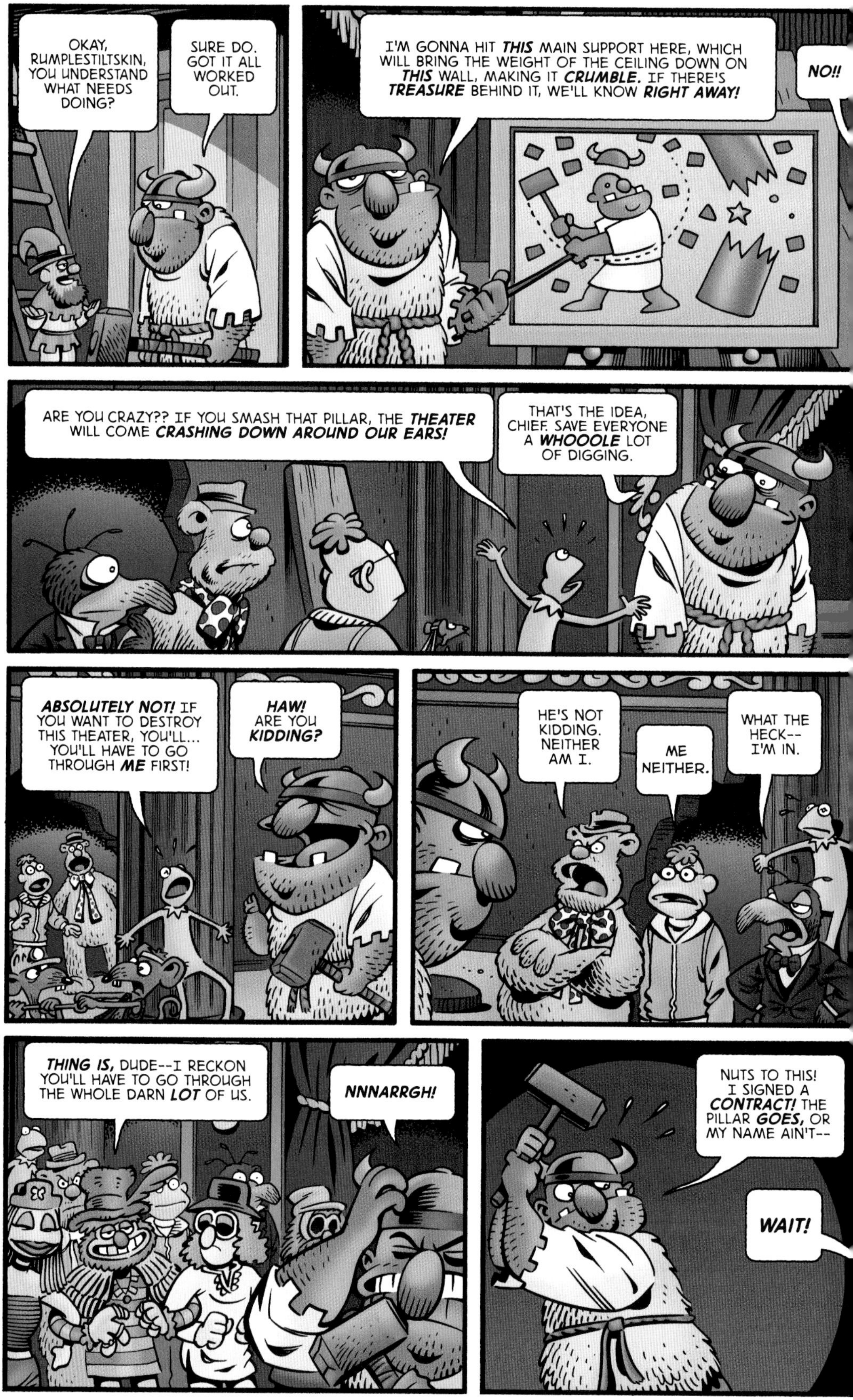
OKAY, RUMPLESTILTSKIN, YOU UNDERSTAND WHAT NEEDS DOING?
SURE DO. GOT IT ALL WORKED OUT.
I'M GONNA HIT THIS MAIN SUPPORT HERE, WHICH WILL BRING THE WEIGHT OF THE CEILING DOWN ON THIS WALL, MAKING IT CRUMBLE. IF THERE'S TREASURE BEHIND IT, WE'LL KNOW RIGHT AWAY!
NO!!
ARE YOU CRAZY?? IF YOU SMASH THAT PILLAR, THE THEATER WILL COME CRASHING DOWN AROUND OUR EARS!
THAT'S THE IDEA, CHIEF. SAVE EVERYONE A WHOOOLE LOT OF DIGGING.
ABSOLUTELY NOT! IF YOU WANT TO DESTROY THIS THEATER, YOU'LL... YOU'LL HAVE TO GO THROUGH ME FIRST!
HAW! ARE YOU KIDDING?
HE'S NOT KIDDING. NEITHER AM I.
ME NEITHER.
WHAT THE HECK-- I'M IN.
THING IS, DUDE--I RECKON YOU'LL HAVE TO GO THROUGH THE WHOLE DARN LOT OF US.
NNNARRGH!
NUTS TO THIS! I SIGNED A CONTRACT! THE PILLAR GOES, OR MY NAME AIN'T--
WAIT!

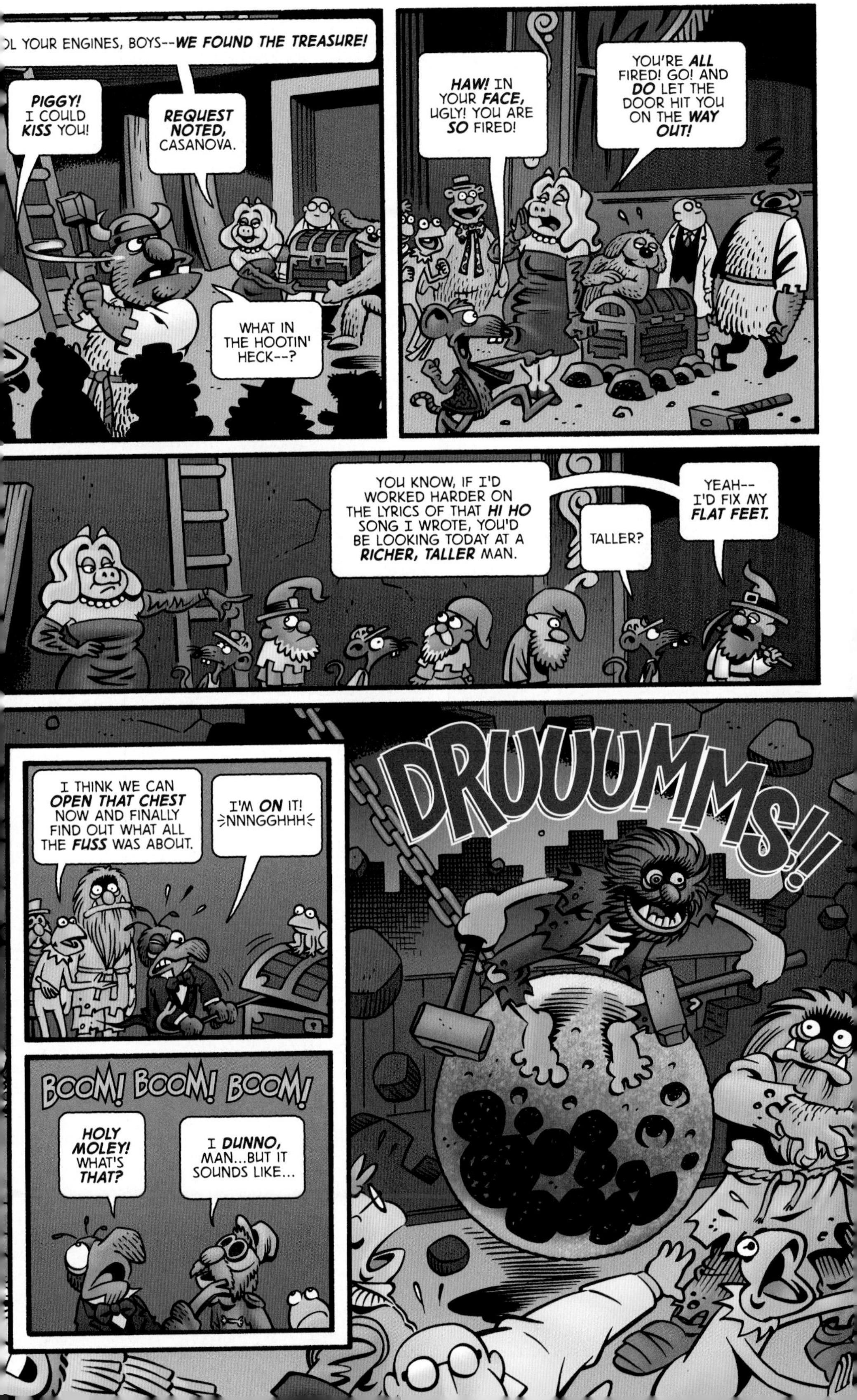

...OL YOUR ENGINES, BOYS--WE FOUND THE TREASURE!
PIGGY! I COULD KISS YOU!
REQUEST NOTED, CASANOVA.
WHAT IN THE HOOTIN' HECK--?
HAW! IN YOUR FACE, UGLY! YOU ARE SO FIRED!
YOU'RE ALL FIRED! GO! AND DO LET THE DOOR HIT YOU ON THE WAY OUT!
YOU KNOW, IF I'D WORKED HARDER ON THE LYRICS OF THAT HI HO SONG I WROTE, YOU'D BE LOOKING TODAY AT A RICHER, TALLER MAN.
TALLER?
YEAH-- I'D FIX MY FLAT FEET.
I THINK WE CAN OPEN THAT CHEST NOW AND FINALLY FIND OUT WHAT ALL THE FUSS WAS ABOUT.
I'M ON IT! NNNGGHHH
BOOM! BOOM! BOOM!
HOLY MOLEY! WHAT'S THAT?
I DUNNO, MAN...BUT IT SOUNDS LIKE...
DRUUUMMS!!

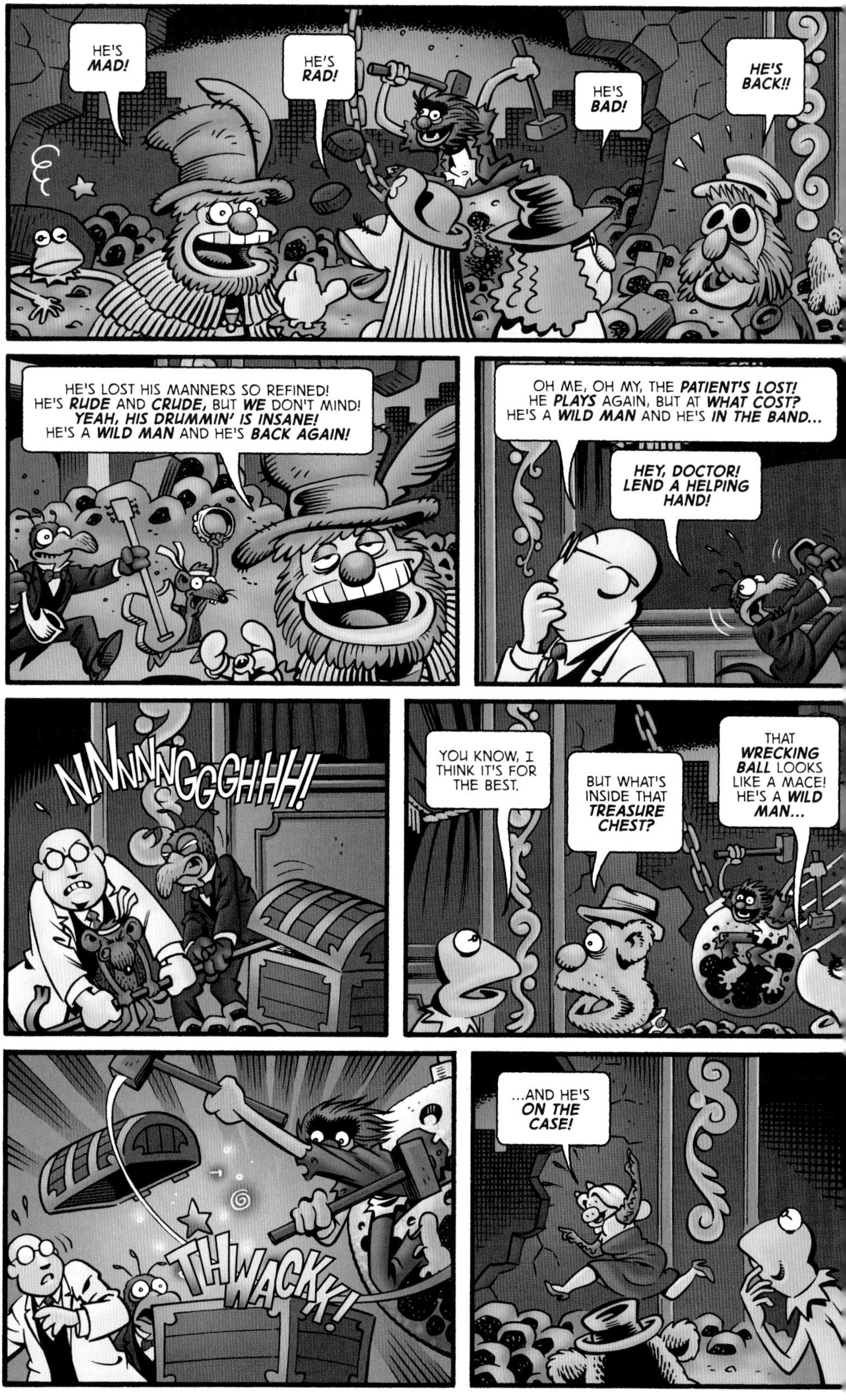

HE'S *MAD!*
HE'S *RAD!*
HE'S *BAD!*
HE'S BACK!!
HE'S LOST HIS MANNERS SO REFINED! HE'S *RUDE* AND *CRUDE,* BUT *WE* DON'T MIND! *YEAH, HIS DRUMMIN' IS INSANE!* HE'S A *WILD MAN* AND HE'S *BACK AGAIN!*
OH ME, OH MY, THE *PATIENT'S LOST!* HE *PLAYS* AGAIN, BUT AT *WHAT COST?* HE'S A *WILD MAN* AND HE'S *IN THE BAND...*
HEY, DOCTOR! LEND A HELPING HAND!
NNNNNGGGHHH!
YOU KNOW, I THINK IT'S FOR THE BEST.
BUT WHAT'S INSIDE THAT *TREASURE CHEST?*
THAT *WRECKING BALL* LOOKS LIKE A MACE! HE'S A *WILD MAN...*
THWACKK!
...AND HE'S *ON THE CASE!*

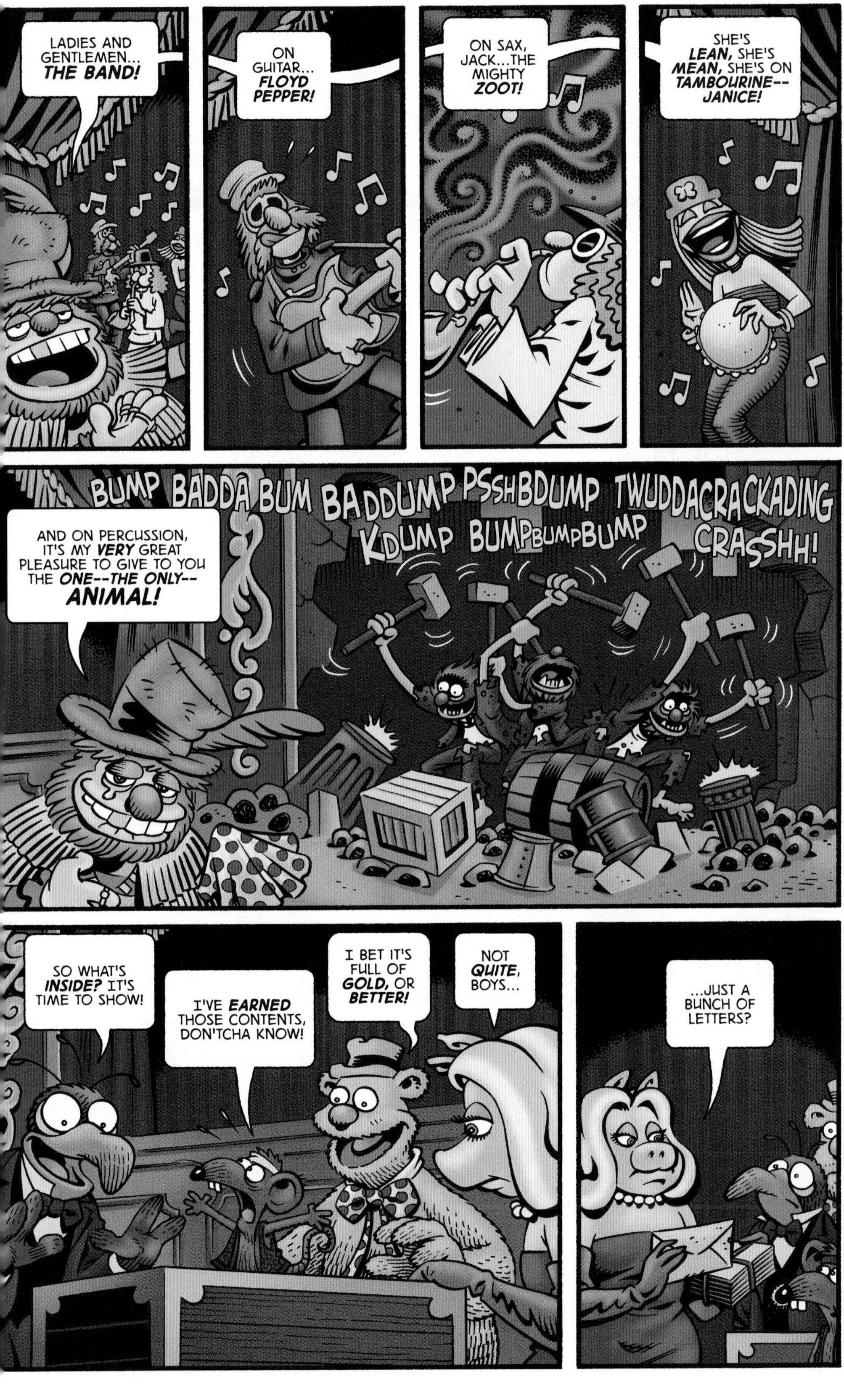
LADIES AND GENTLEMEN... THE BAND!
ON GUITAR... FLOYD PEPPER!
ON SAX, JACK...THE MIGHTY ZOOT!
SHE'S LEAN, SHE'S MEAN, SHE'S ON TAMBOURINE-- JANICE!
BUMP BADDA BUM BADDUMP PSSHBDUMP TWUDDACRACKADING
KDUMP BUMPBUMPBUMP CRASSHH!
AND ON PERCUSSION, IT'S MY VERY GREAT PLEASURE TO GIVE TO YOU THE ONE--THE ONLY-- ANIMAL!
SO WHAT'S INSIDE? IT'S TIME TO SHOW!
I'VE EARNED THOSE CONTENTS, DON'TCHA KNOW!
I BET IT'S FULL OF GOLD, OR BETTER!
NOT QUITE, BOYS...
...JUST A BUNCH OF LETTERS?

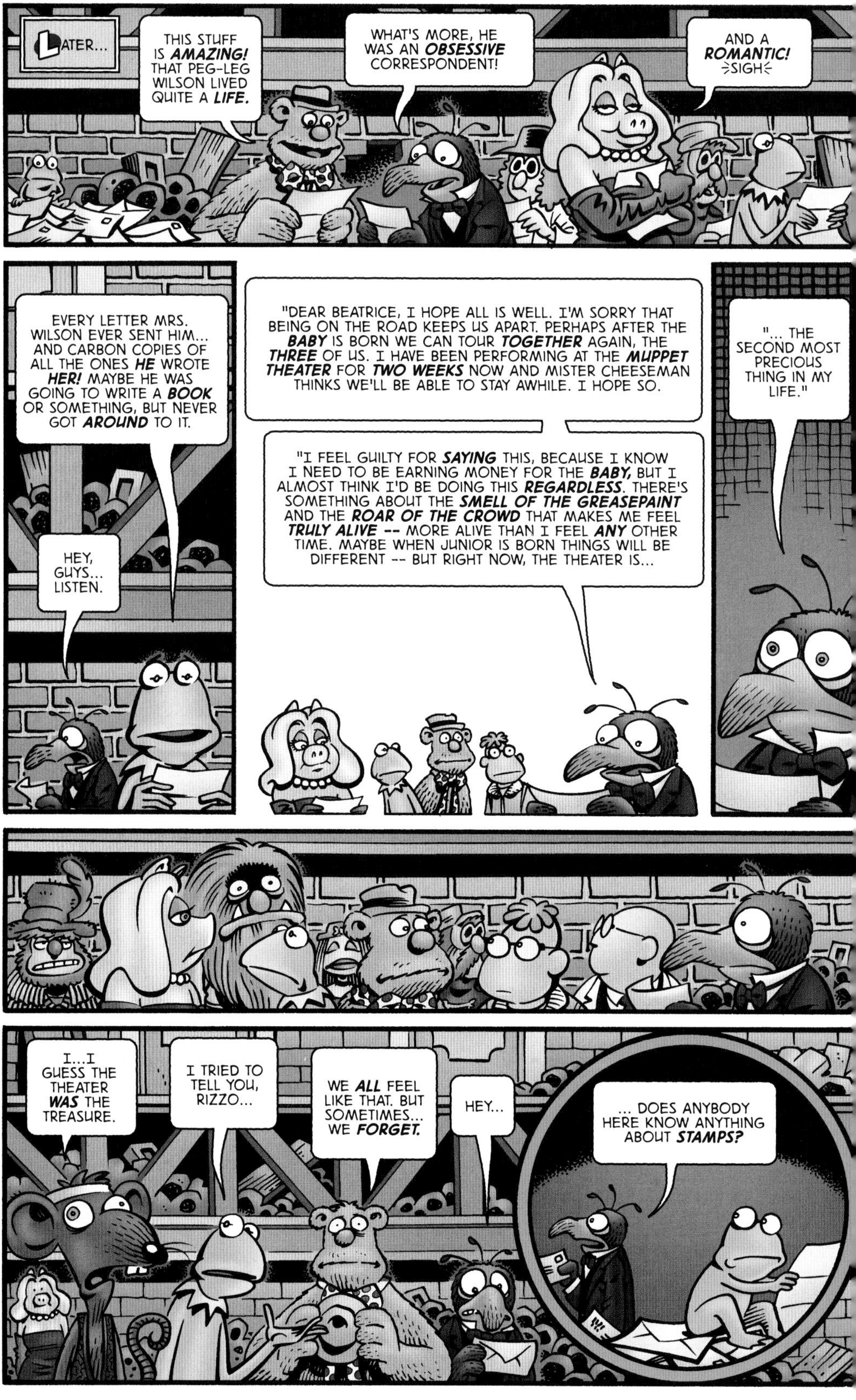
LATER...
THIS STUFF IS AMAZING! THAT PEG-LEG WILSON LIVED QUITE A LIFE.
WHAT'S MORE, HE WAS AN OBSESSIVE CORRESPONDENT!
AND A ROMANTIC! SIGH
EVERY LETTER MRS. WILSON EVER SENT HIM... AND CARBON COPIES OF ALL THE ONES HE WROTE HER! MAYBE HE WAS GOING TO WRITE A BOOK OR SOMETHING, BUT NEVER GOT AROUND TO IT.
HEY, GUYS... LISTEN.
"DEAR BEATRICE, I HOPE ALL IS WELL. I'M SORRY THAT BEING ON THE ROAD KEEPS US APART. PERHAPS AFTER THE BABY IS BORN WE CAN TOUR TOGETHER AGAIN, THE THREE OF US. I HAVE BEEN PERFORMING AT THE MUPPET THEATER FOR TWO WEEKS NOW AND MISTER CHEESEMAN THINKS WE'LL BE ABLE TO STAY AWHILE. I HOPE SO.
"I FEEL GUILTY FOR SAYING THIS, BECAUSE I KNOW I NEED TO BE EARNING MONEY FOR THE BABY, BUT I ALMOST THINK I'D BE DOING THIS REGARDLESS. THERE'S SOMETHING ABOUT THE SMELL OF THE GREASEPAINT AND THE ROAR OF THE CROWD THAT MAKES ME FEEL TRULY ALIVE -- MORE ALIVE THAN I FEEL ANY OTHER TIME. MAYBE WHEN JUNIOR IS BORN THINGS WILL BE DIFFERENT -- BUT RIGHT NOW, THE THEATER IS...
"... THE SECOND MOST PRECIOUS THING IN MY LIFE."
I...I GUESS THE THEATER WAS THE TREASURE.
I TRIED TO TELL YOU, RIZZO...
WE ALL FEEL LIKE THAT. BUT SOMETIMES... WE FORGET.
HEY...
... DOES ANYBODY HERE KNOW ANYTHING ABOUT STAMPS?

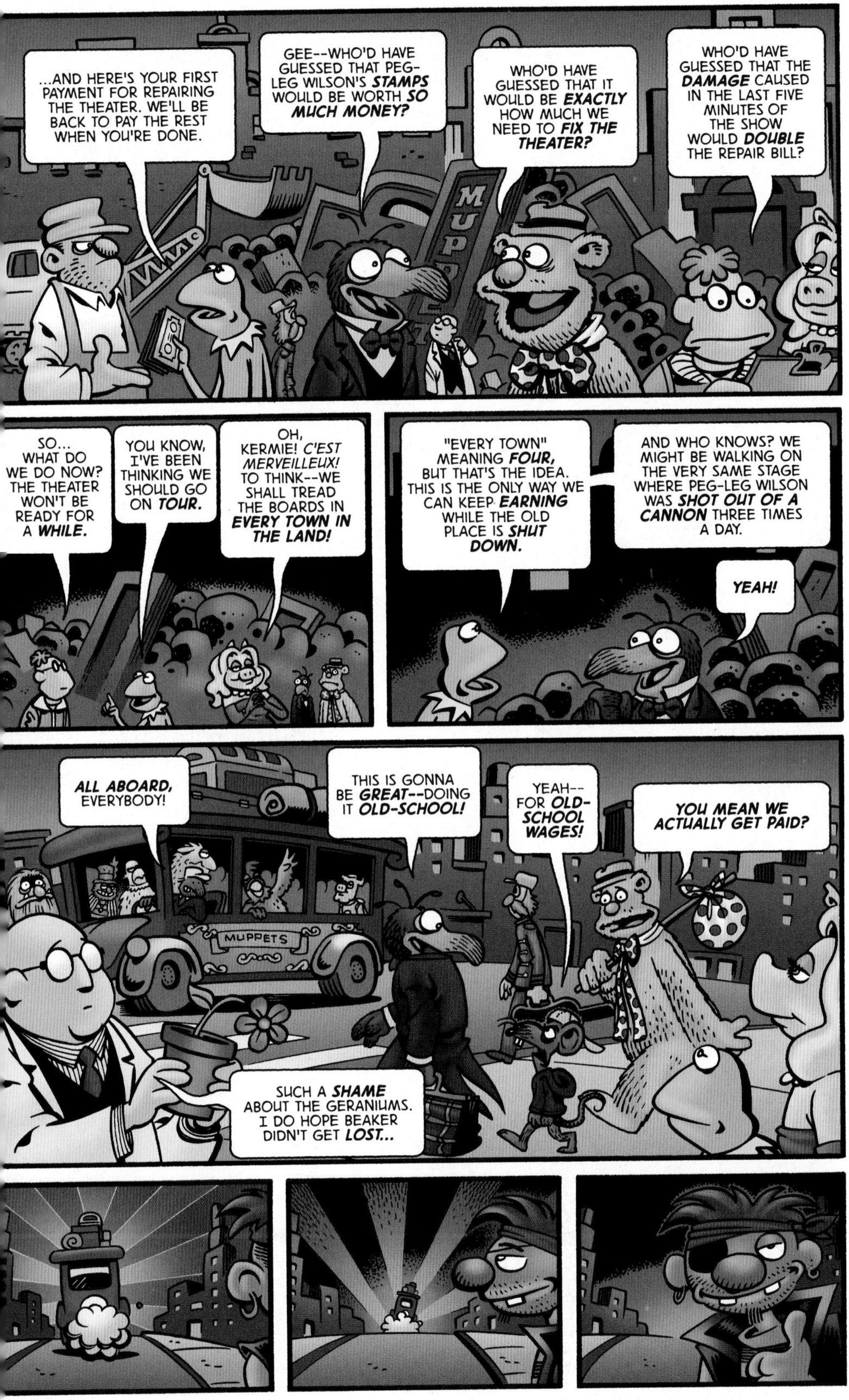
...AND HERE'S YOUR FIRST PAYMENT FOR REPAIRING THE THEATER. WE'LL BE BACK TO PAY THE REST WHEN YOU'RE DONE.
GEE--WHO'D HAVE GUESSED THAT PEG-LEG WILSON'S STAMPS WOULD BE WORTH SO MUCH MONEY?
WHO'D HAVE GUESSED THAT IT WOULD BE EXACTLY HOW MUCH WE NEED TO FIX THE THEATER?
WHO'D HAVE GUESSED THAT THE DAMAGE CAUSED IN THE LAST FIVE MINUTES OF THE SHOW WOULD DOUBLE THE REPAIR BILL?
MUPPETS
SO... WHAT DO WE DO NOW? THE THEATER WON'T BE READY FOR A WHILE.
YOU KNOW, I'VE BEEN THINKING WE SHOULD GO ON TOUR.
OH, KERMIE! C'EST MERVEILLEUX! TO THINK--WE SHALL TREAD THE BOARDS IN EVERY TOWN IN THE LAND!
"EVERY TOWN" MEANING FOUR, BUT THAT'S THE IDEA. THIS IS THE ONLY WAY WE CAN KEEP EARNING WHILE THE OLD PLACE IS SHUT DOWN.
AND WHO KNOWS? WE MIGHT BE WALKING ON THE VERY SAME STAGE WHERE PEG-LEG WILSON WAS SHOT OUT OF A CANNON THREE TIMES A DAY.
YEAH!
ALL ABOARD, EVERYBODY!
THIS IS GONNA BE GREAT--DOING IT OLD-SCHOOL!
YEAH--FOR OLD-SCHOOL WAGES!
YOU MEAN WE ACTUALLY GET PAID?
MUPPETS
SUCH A SHAME ABOUT THE GERANIUMS. I DO HOPE BEAKER DIDN'T GET LOST...

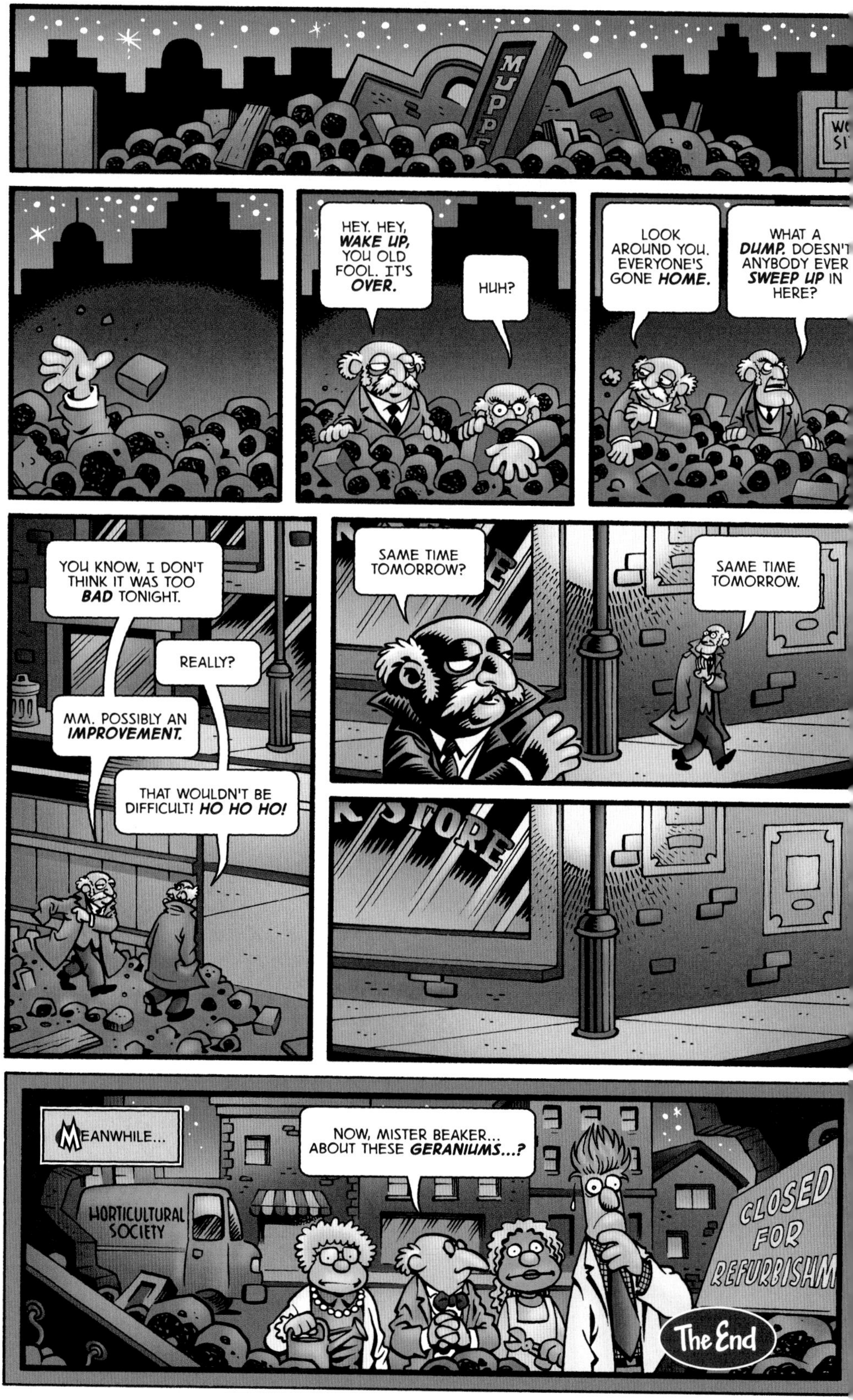
MUPP
HEY. HEY, *WAKE UP,* YOU OLD FOOL. IT'S *OVER.*
HUH?
LOOK AROUND YOU. EVERYONE'S GONE *HOME.*
WHAT A *DUMP.* DOESN'T ANYBODY EVER *SWEEP UP* IN HERE?
YOU KNOW, I DON'T THINK IT WAS TOO *BAD* TONIGHT.
REALLY?
MM. POSSIBLY AN *IMPROVEMENT.*
THAT WOULDN'T BE DIFFICULT! *HO HO HO!*
SAME TIME TOMORROW?
SAME TIME TOMORROW.
STORE
MEANWHILE...
NOW, MISTER BEAKER... ABOUT THESE *GERANIUMS...?*
HORTICULTURAL SOCIETY
CLOSED FOR REFURBISHM
The End

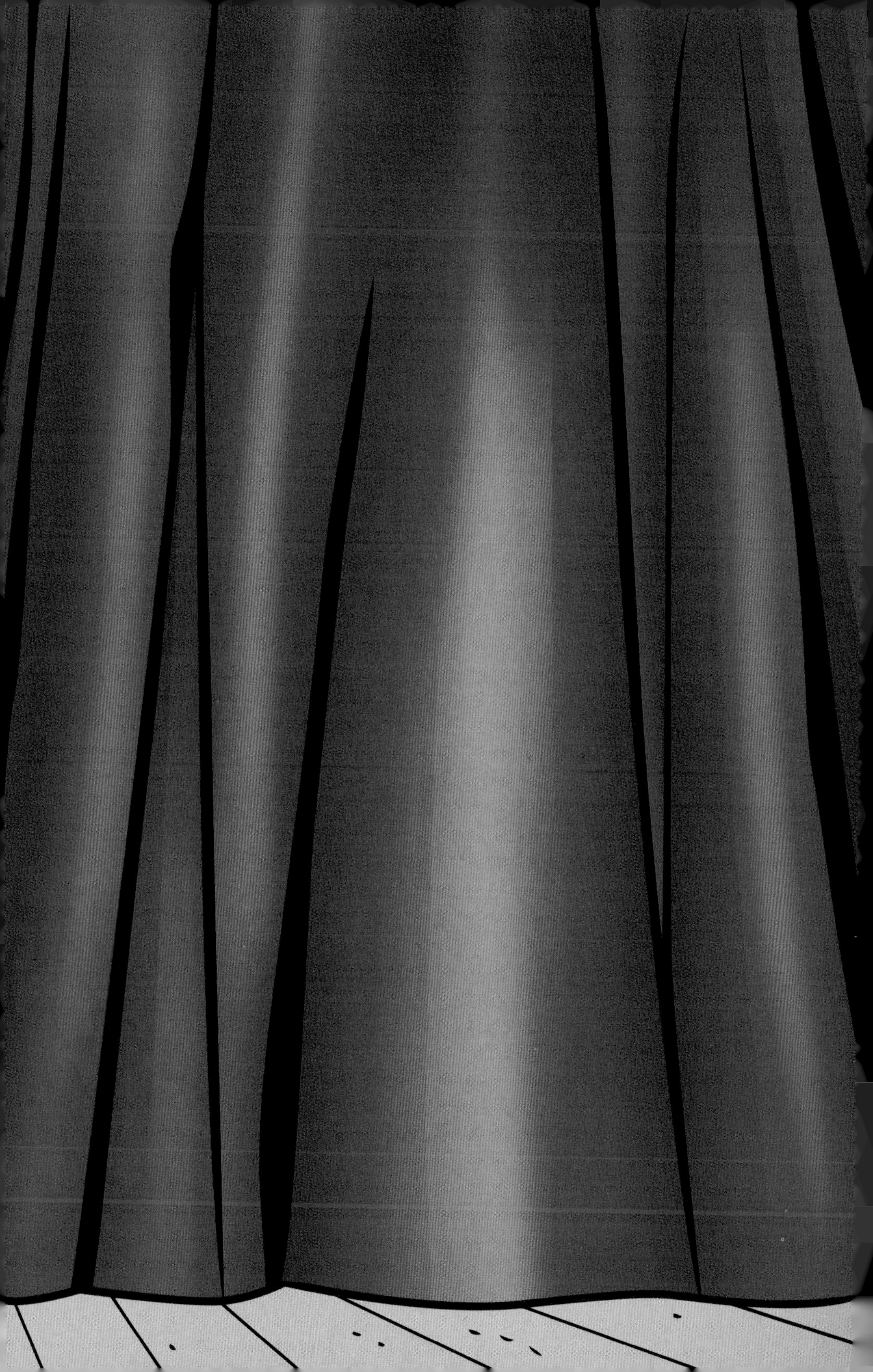

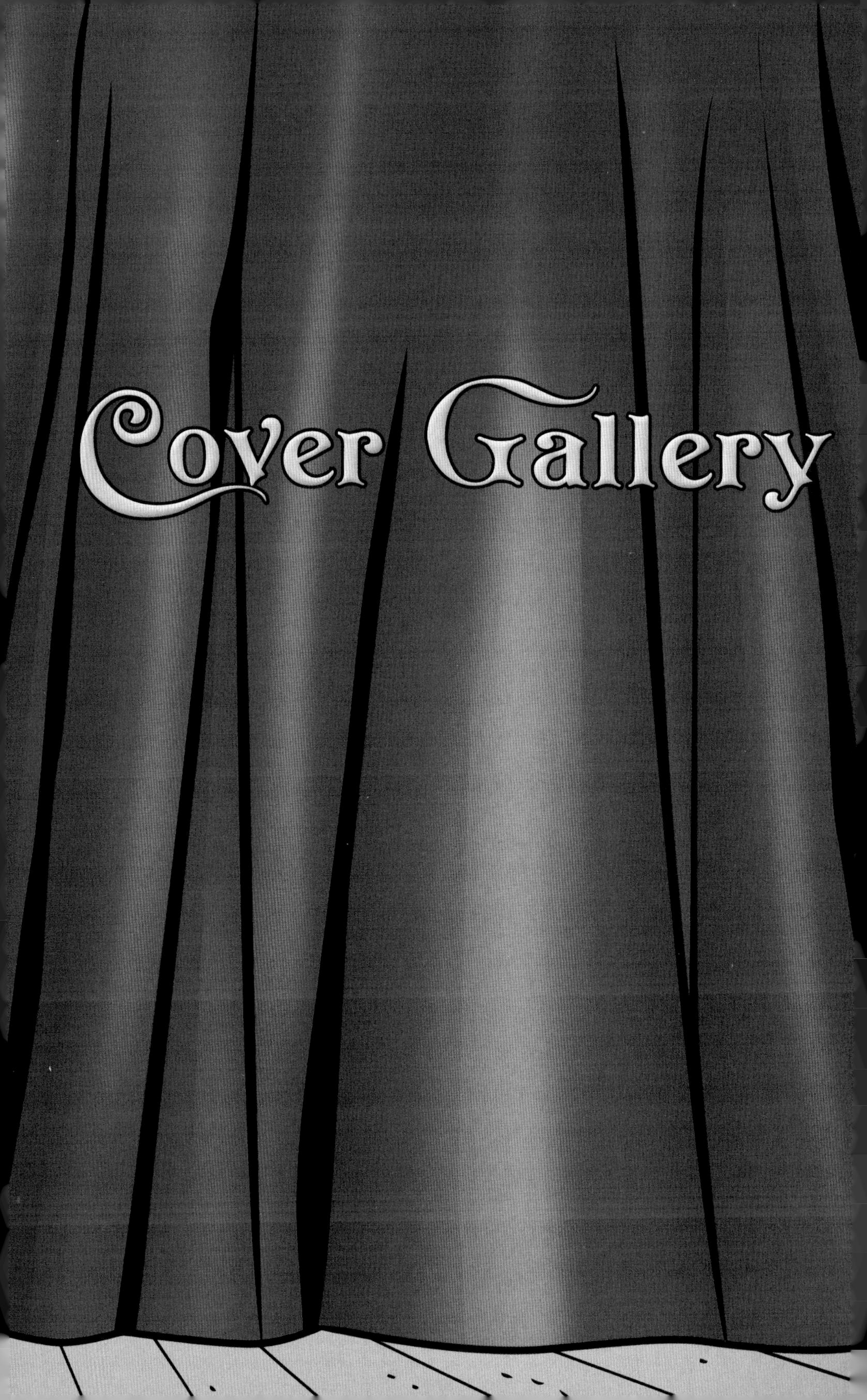
Cover Gallery

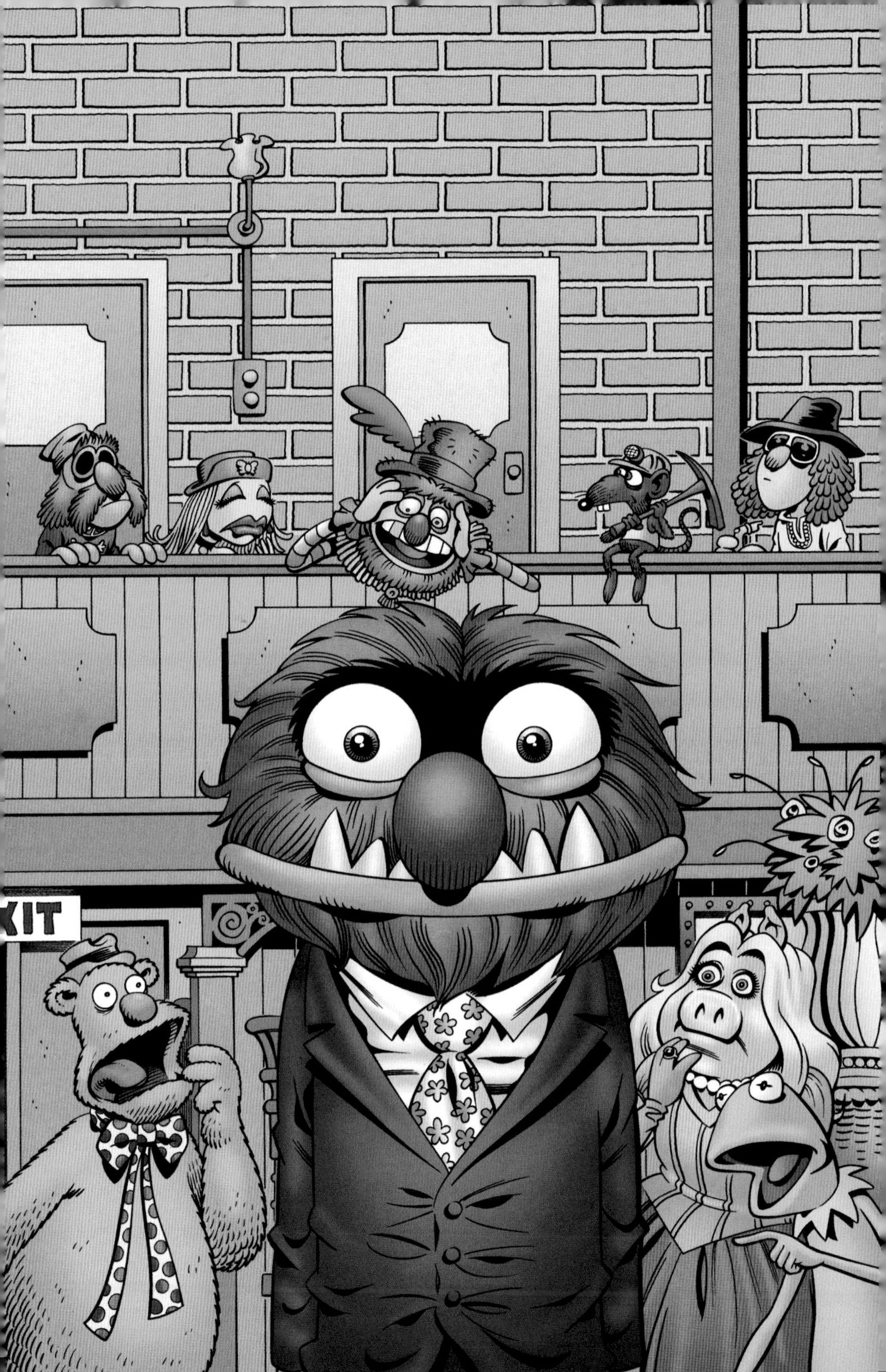
XIT

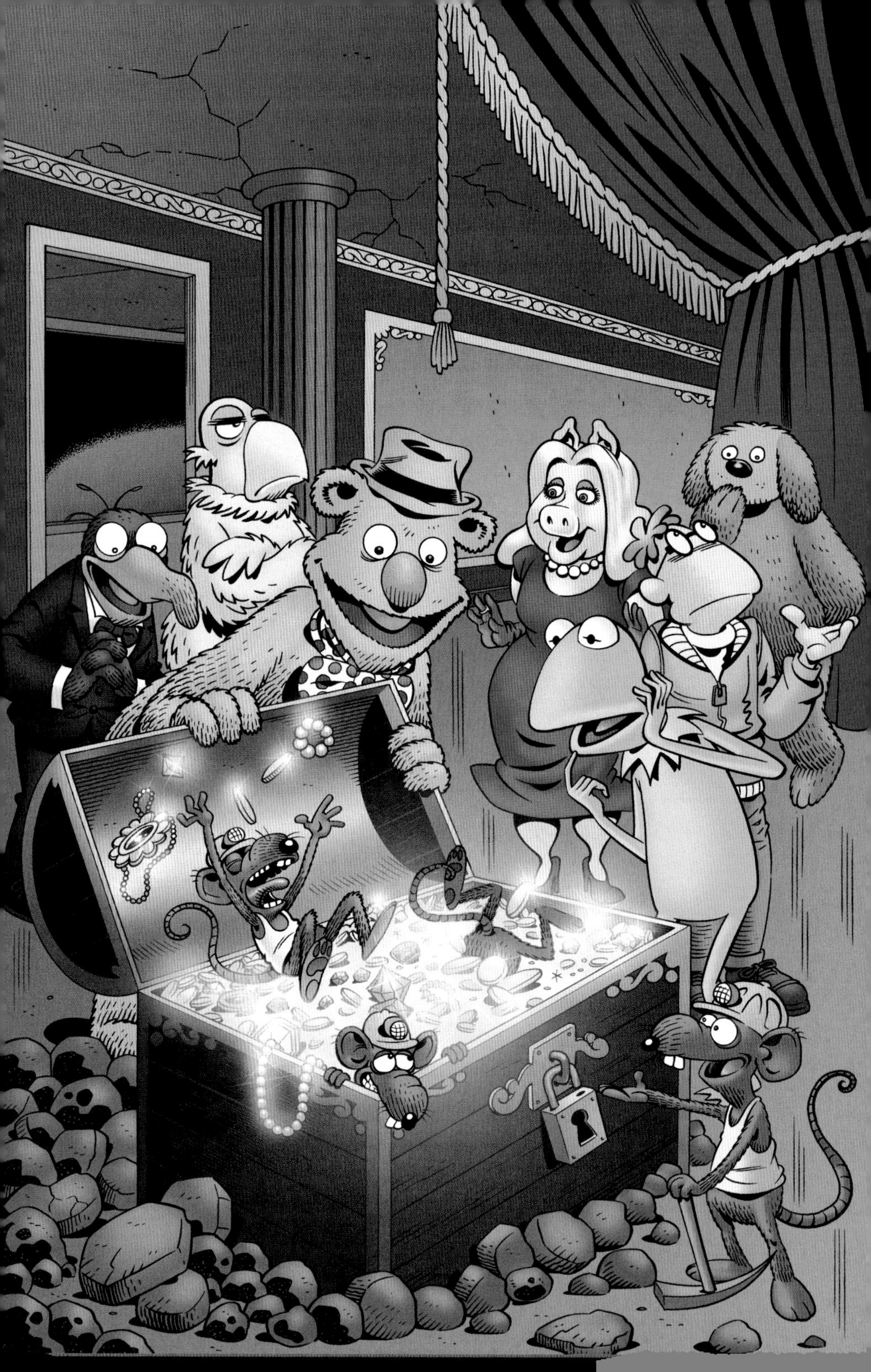

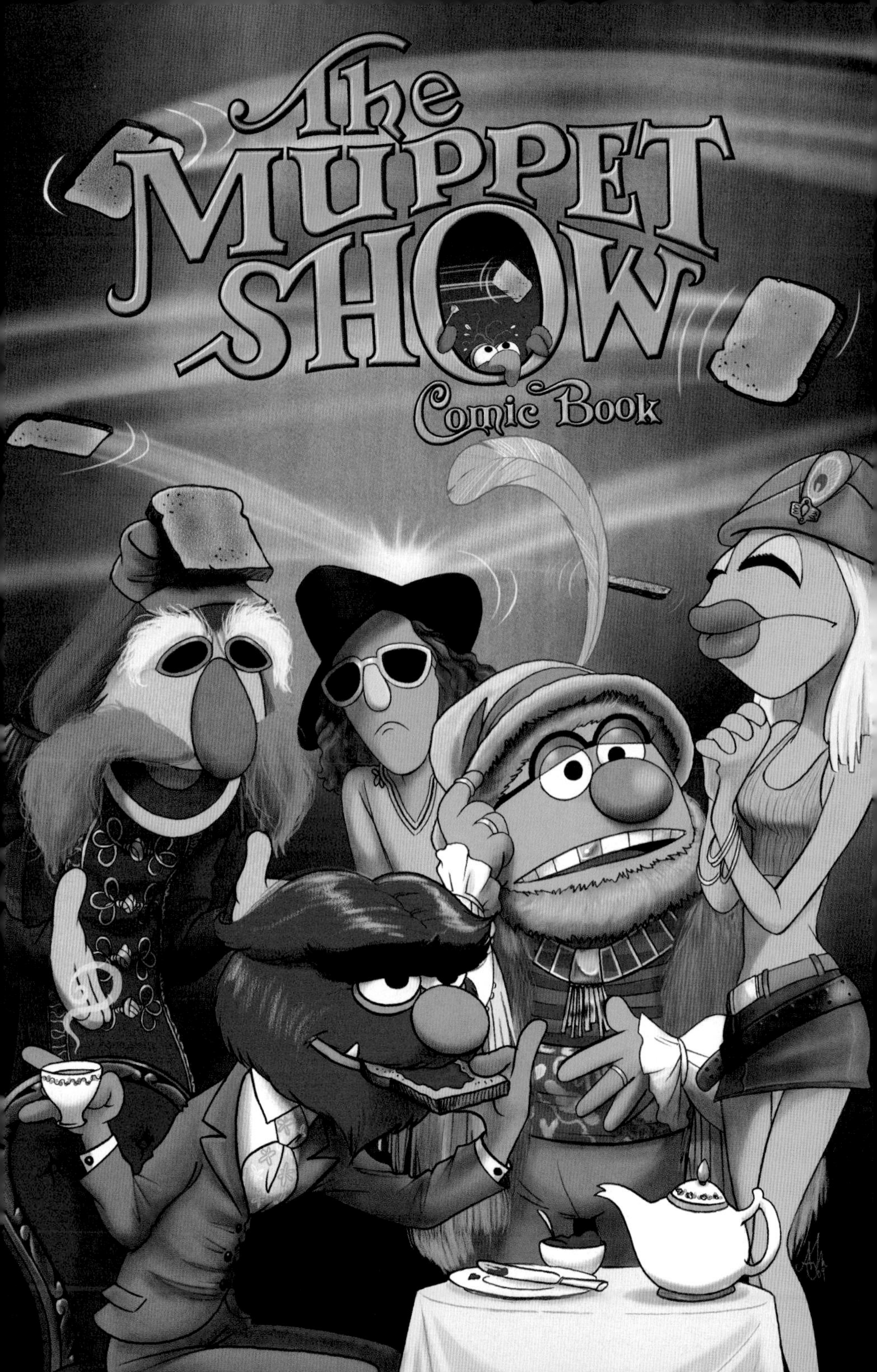
The
MUPPET
SHOW
Comic Book

ULTIMATE COMICS EXCLUSIVE: AMY MEBBERSON

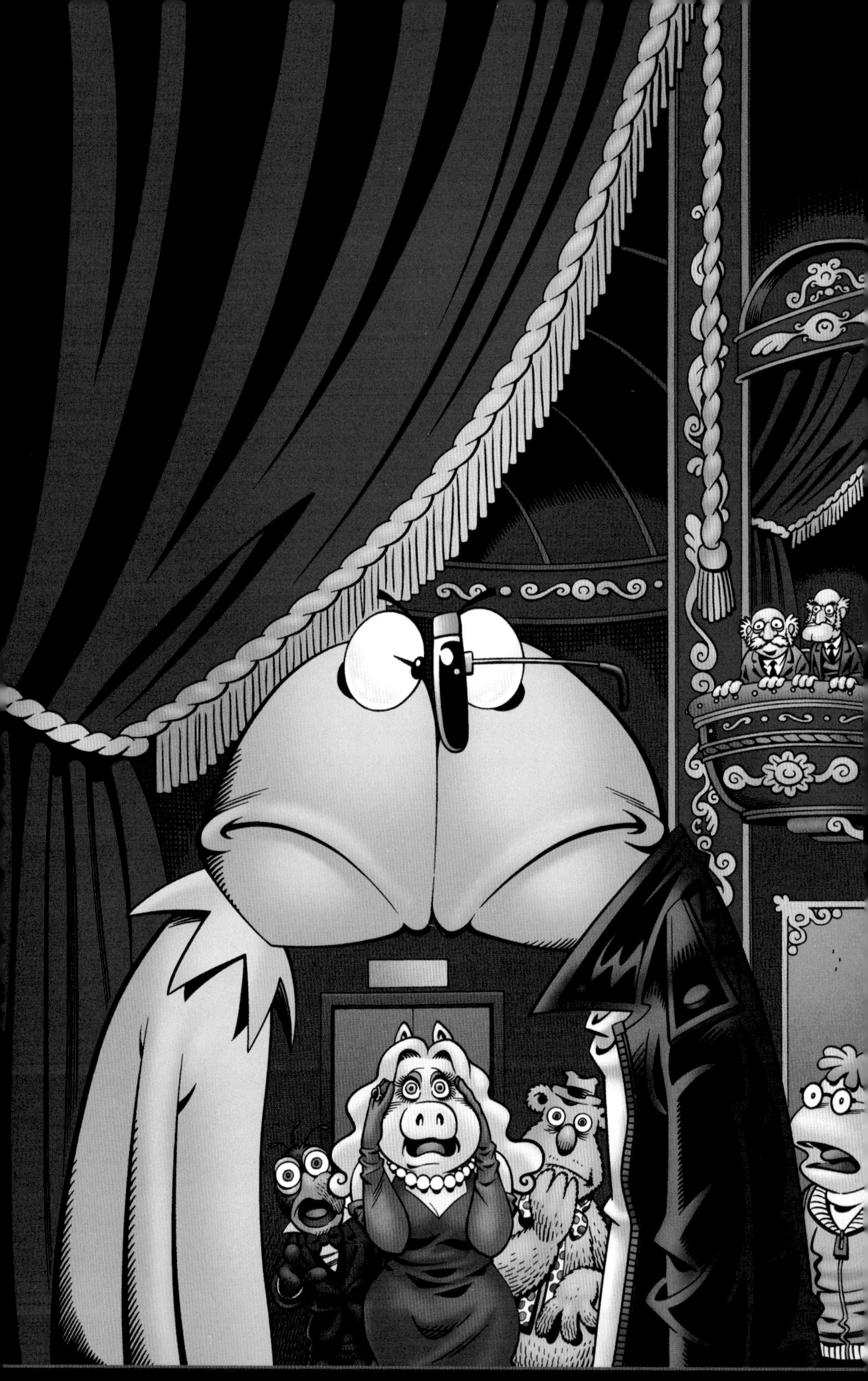

COVER 24: ROGER LANGRIDGE

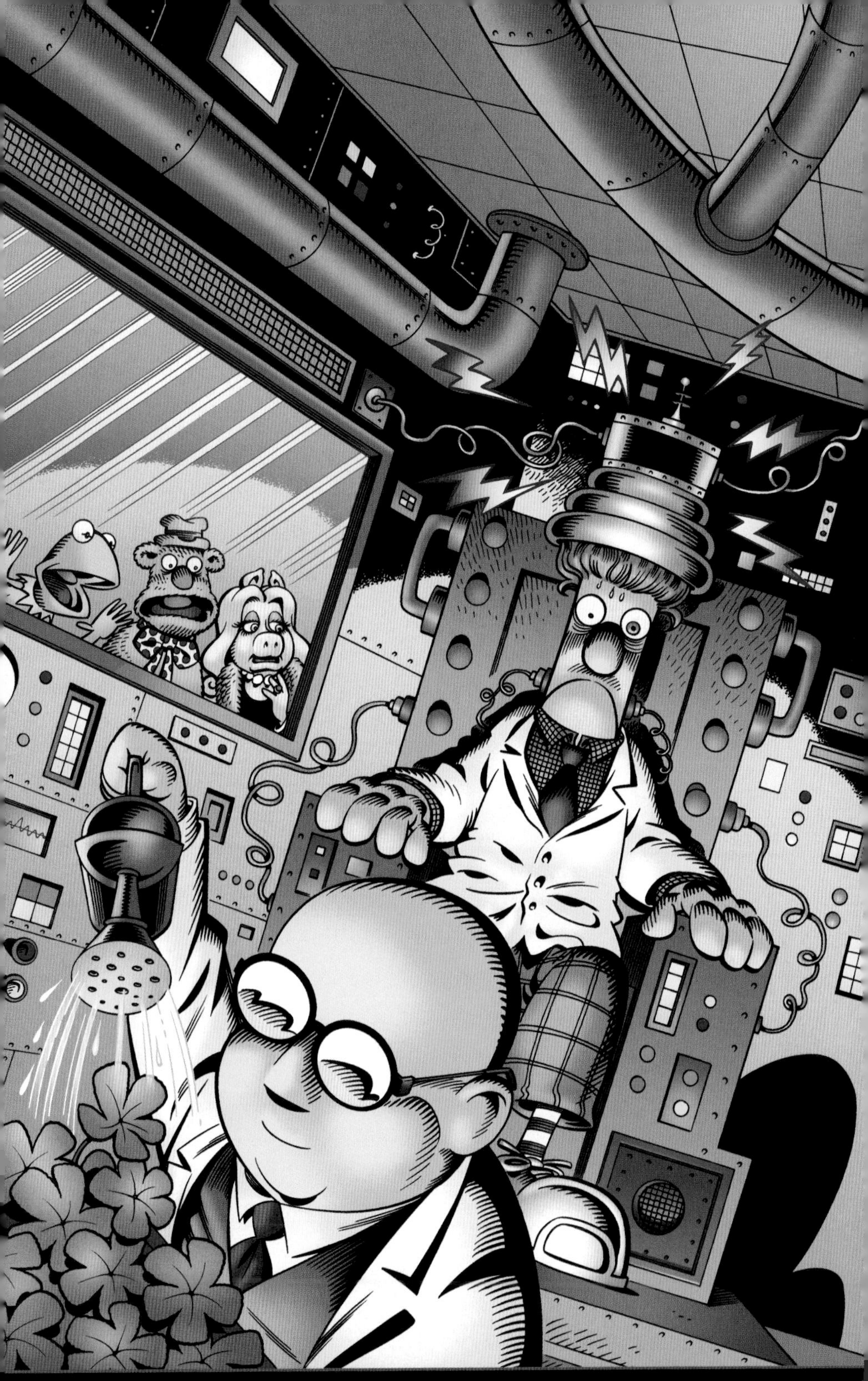

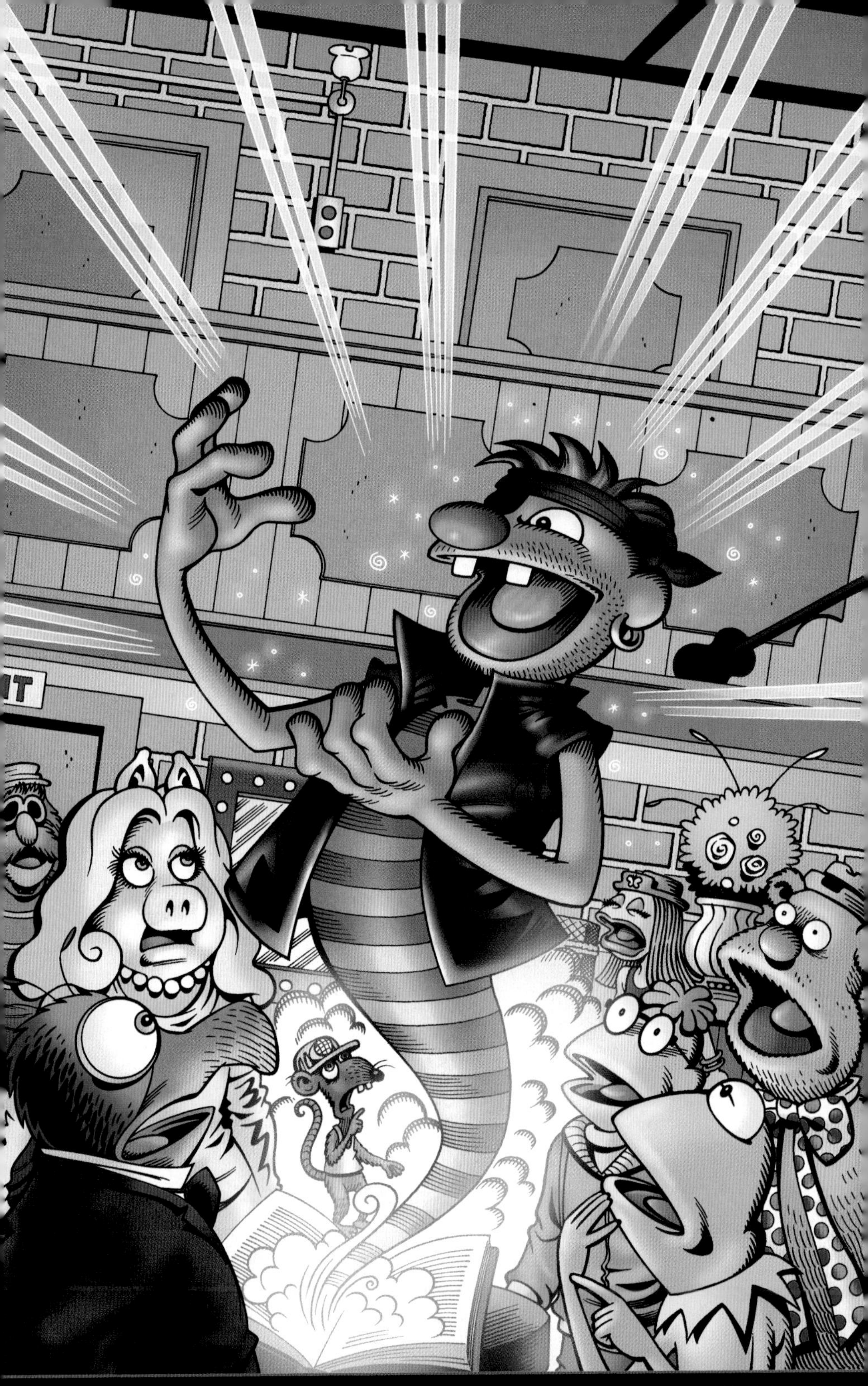

COVER 4B: ROGER LANGRIDGE

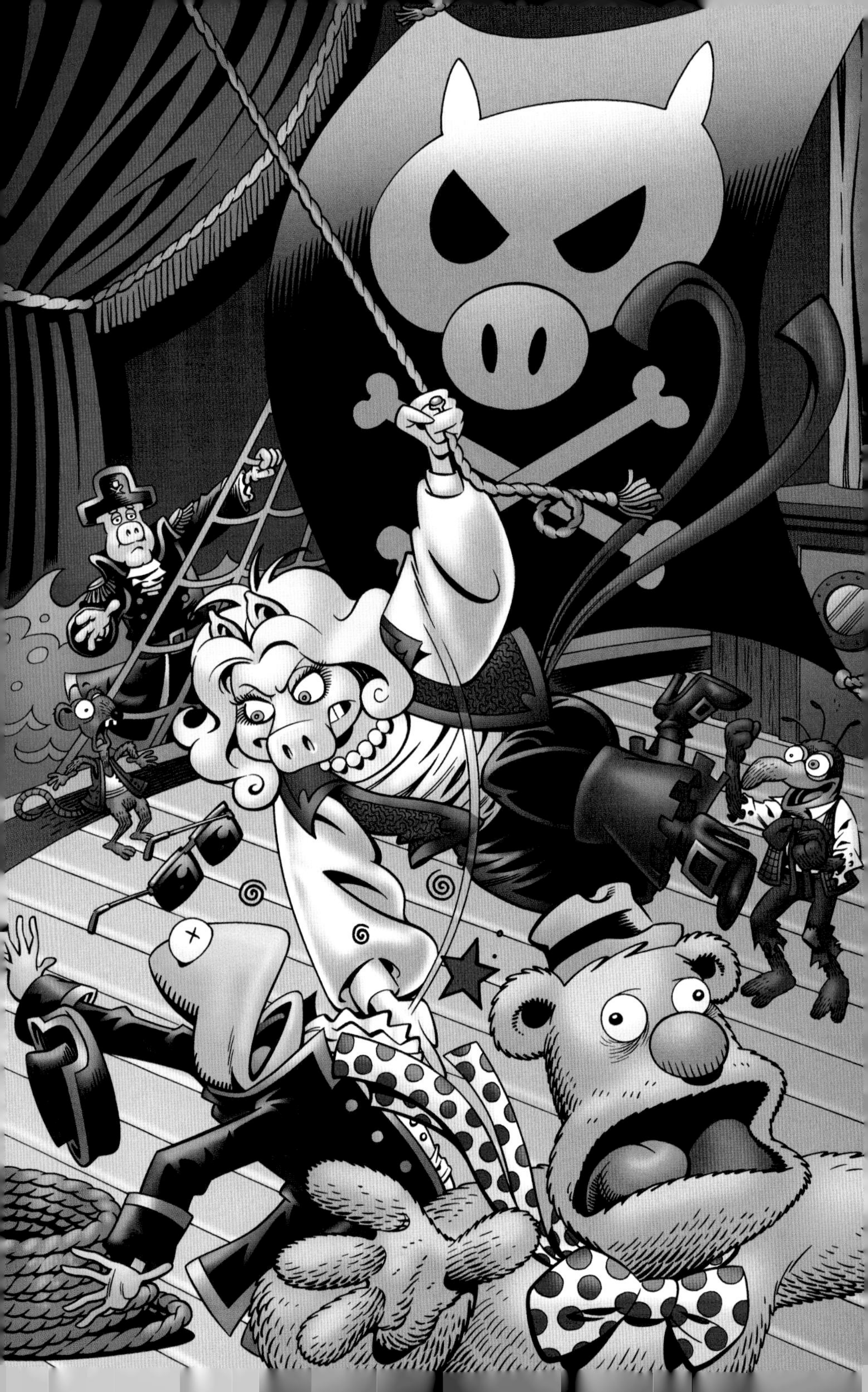

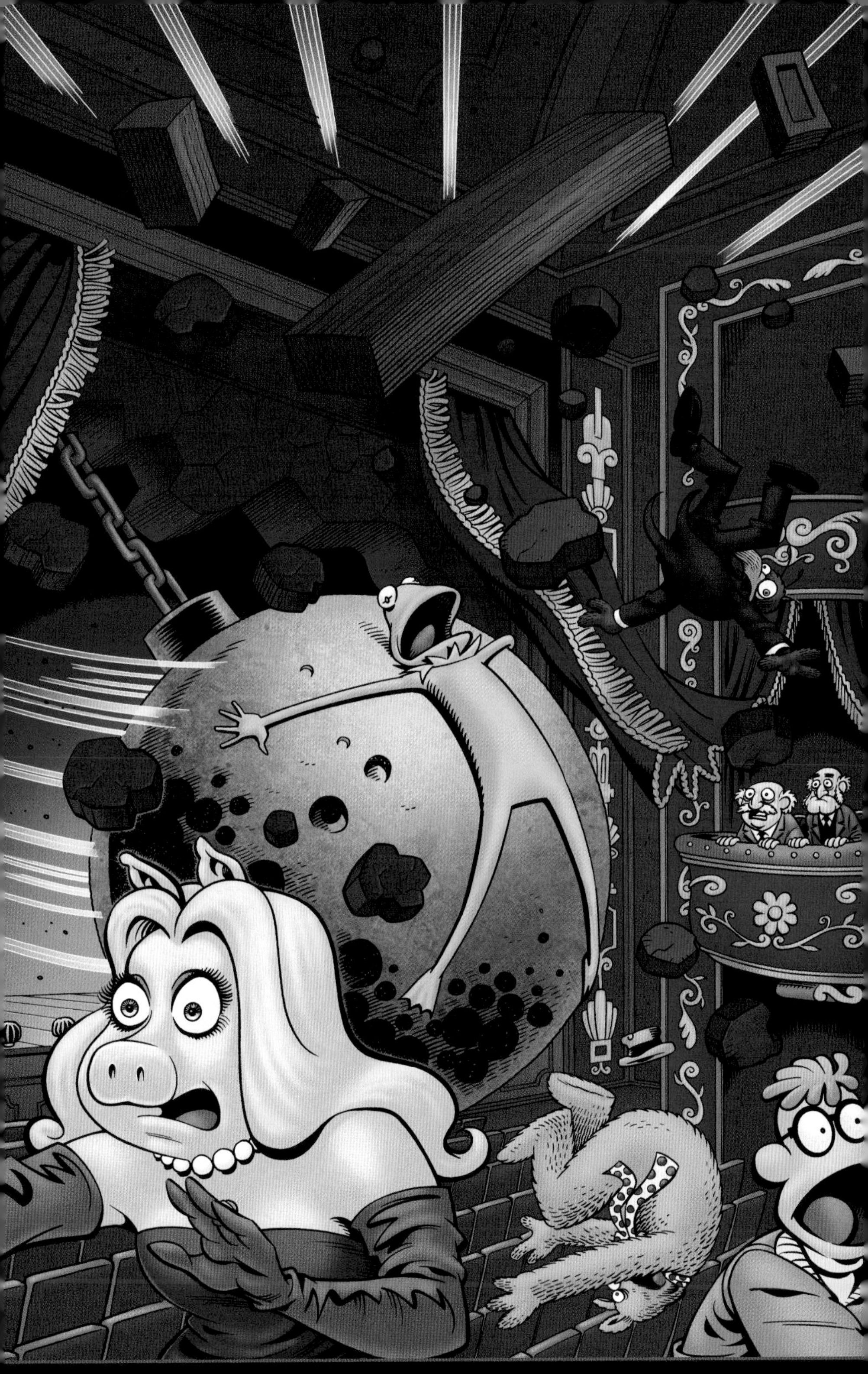

COVER 4A: ROGER LANGRIDGE

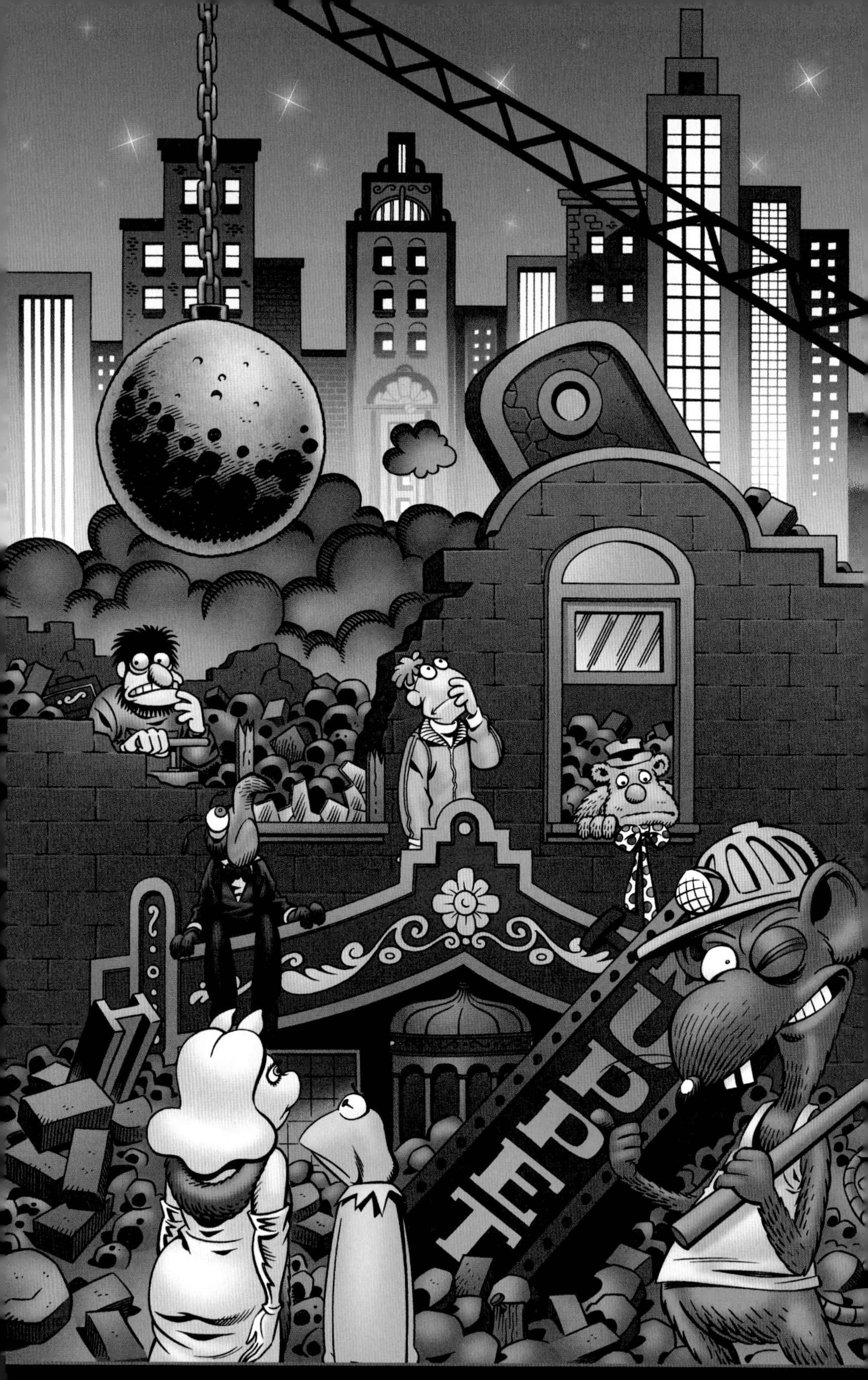

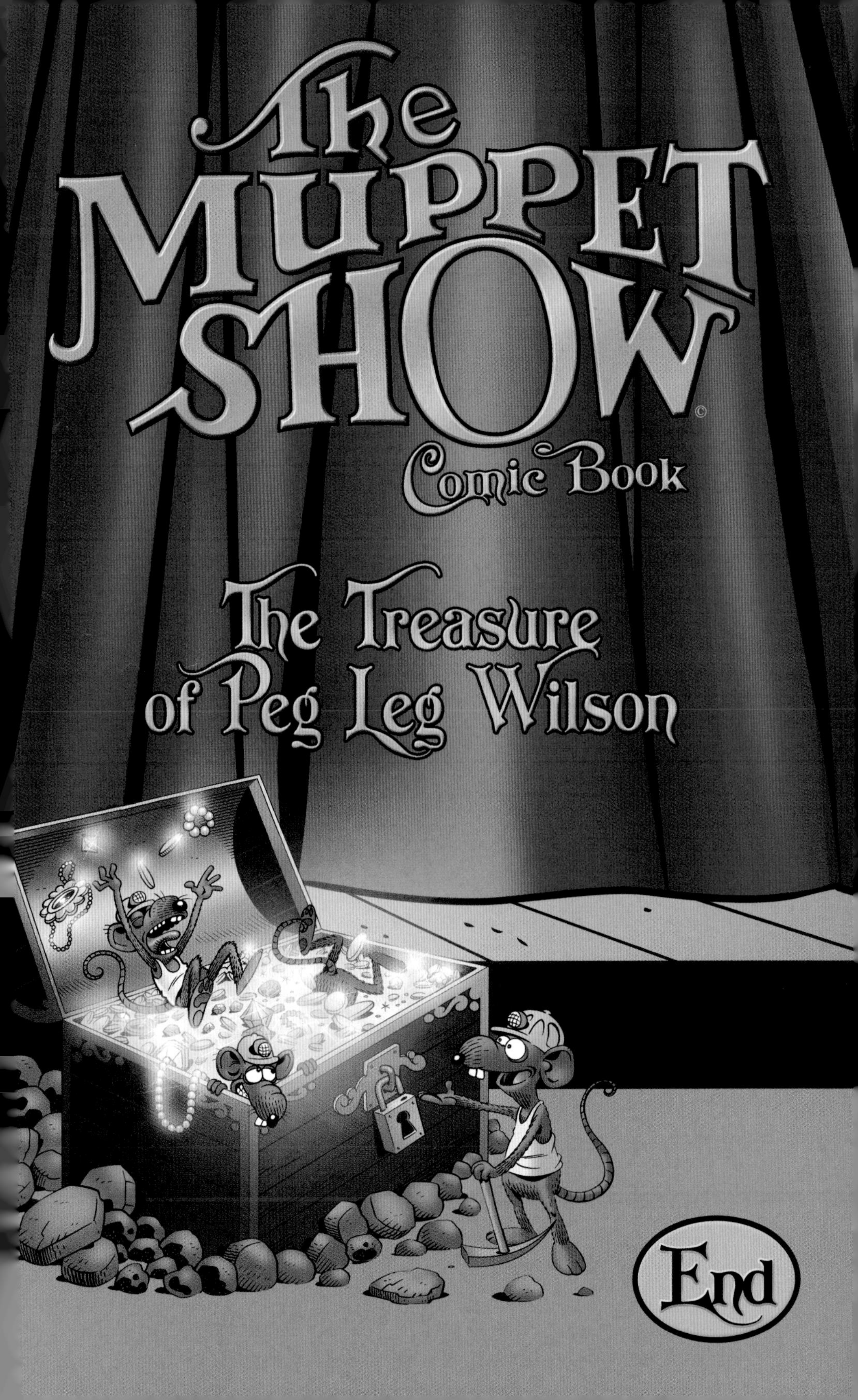
The
MUPPET
SHOW©
Comic Book
The Treasure
of Peg Leg Wilson
End

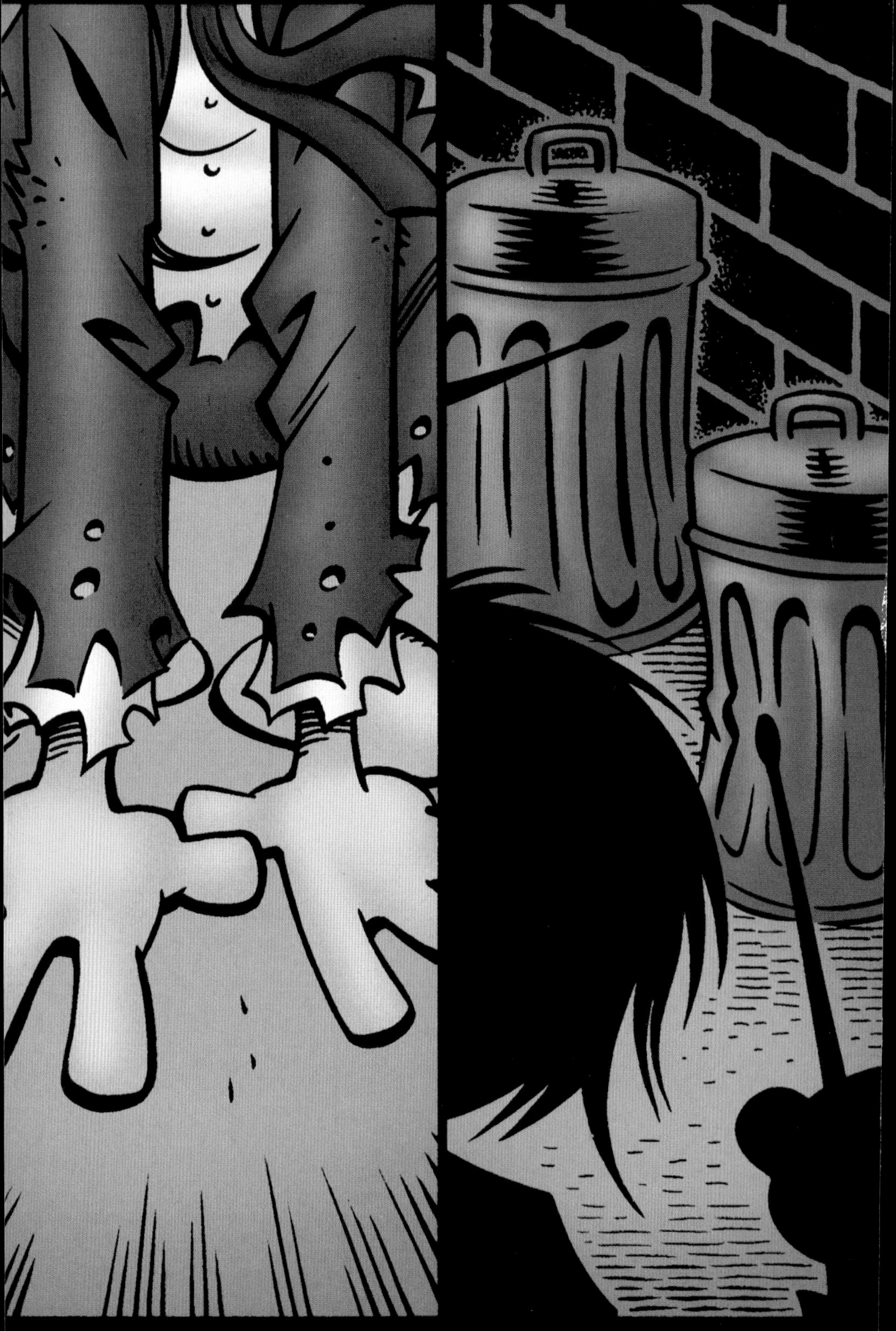